Exposé

Paul Ilett

Copyright © 2015 Paul Ilett
All rights reserved.

ISBN: 1507870965
ISBN 13: 9781507870969

For
Barbara Peach
and Gerry Murnane

1

COLIN MERRONEY'S ENTIRE adult life had been consumed by other people's secrets. He had spent more than thirty years exposing the private lives of the rich and famous, and wore his title of the 'Kiss-and-Tell King' like a badge of honour. He knew his track record was second to none and that dozens of other journalists had tried and failed to steal his crown, but no one could touch him. Over the years he had targeted everyone from actors and sports stars to politicians and royalty. It was Colin who broke the exclusive story about the young England player with a weakness for transsexual hookers, and the married 'Songs of Praise' presenter who had a secret posse of lesbian lovers. He had exposed the dogging obsession of the nation's favourite TV chef, and dramatically ended dozens of ministerial careers by catching a never-ending procession of MPs with their pants down.

Everyone in the public eye knew that, one day, they might get the phone call of doom from Colin Merroney. It was a reputation he cherished, a reputation that had won him countless press awards and paid for his expensive London house. And throughout his career no one had ever challenged his right to probe the private lives of celebrities or expose their secrets for the world to see. But more recently times had changed. The previous couple of years had not been kind to Colin's newspaper, the *Daily Ear*, or the rest of the tabloid press. He and his colleagues had found themselves more and more in the spotlight, with their working practices under increasing levels of scrutiny and criticism. They were now subject to a government inquiry, police investigations and numerous court cases with the smallest details of their work picked to pieces by thousands of pedants across the likes of Twitter. After decades of doing what it pleased, the media was suddenly being held to account. And Colin hated it.

Over the past year, one way or another, he had become the public face of the *Daily Ear*. In countless media training sessions, he had been the only member of staff who'd been able to offer plausible arguments, shrewdly rebut accusations and maintain a humorous demeanour throughout. His editor Leonard Twigg flatly refused to speak to other parts of the media (particularly the BBC) and the newspaper's owner, Howard Harvey, simply couldn't control his temper long enough to get through an entire interview. They had tried out *Daily Ear* columnist Valerie Pierce a few times, but it was felt she lacked Colin's warmth and credibility. And they only ever wheeled out the company's chief executive as an absolute last resort. Gayesh Perera was considered a weak link but, coming from India, had proven a useful figurehead whenever the paper had been accused of being racist. Which it often was.

And so partly through his own skill, and partly through the failure of his colleagues, Colin was considered a safe pair of hands. As a result he'd appeared on the BBC, ITN, *Sky News* and *This Morning*, to name just a few. That evening, he'd even been roped into doing *Newsnight*. He begrudged the amount of time he had spent in radio and television interviews in defence of himself and his newspaper, but he knew there simply wasn't anyone else who could do it.

Colin also suspected it helped that, despite pushing 50, he had kept his looks. His hair had remained full with no whispers of grey, and he had held off his middle-age spread. His suits were from one of the new bespoke tailors on Savile Row, ensuring he never dressed like an old man. And although, at five foot five inches, he'd spent most of his life wishing he was taller he now accepted he'd kept a boyish quality that belied his actual age. He also knew there were entire threads on gay forums dedicated to screen grabs of his crotch. The size of his bulge was legendary in the newspaper industry and his young wife assured him it was important to keep the gays happy, which is why he always wore tight trousers for TV interviews.

But there was a strange atmosphere in the *Newsnight* studio that evening. He had felt it the moment he arrived. The presenter had been unusually frosty with him. She seemed to have a look of pity in her eyes, like she could smell blood, and Colin didn't trust BBC journalists at the best of times. It was never a fair fight. They always had people helping them, whispering in their ear. Up beyond the bright lights of the *Newsnight* studio was a whole gallery of overpaid producers, and Colin imagined they had spent their entire day lolling around in a pampered brainstorming session, sprawled out across luxurious leather sofas and drinking expensive lattes. They would have pored over all the articles on newspaper standards where he had been quoted and then dissected every comment he had made. They would have reduced his every sentence to a base level until they could find something, some tiny hole, in his argument which they could fixate on during a TV debate. Others had tried and failed, of course, but for some unknown reason tonight felt different.

Newspaper standards was hardly new territory for Colin or the *Newsnight* team. In fact, this was Colin's second appearance on *Newsnight* on the same topic. The only new element was the second studio guest, Adam Jaymes. He was a 28-year-old performer who held a lifetime of grudges against the *Daily Ear*. He had started his career as a child actor in a soap and later gone on to be a popular Doctor Who companion. He had then been a surprise hit on the West End stage before becoming a Tony-nominated Broadway performer too. Of late, he was breaking into US TV with a regular role on *True*

Blood and a guest spot on *Glee*. It was like the phrase 'rising star' had been created just for him.

But Colin had a personal vendetta against Adam. The actor was the only person who had managed to maintain his privacy and successfully evade all of Colin's attempts to infiltrate his personal life. For years, Colin had suspected the actor was gay and had dedicated an enormous amount of his own time and the *Daily Ear*'s resources to publicly out him. But somehow Adam had remained impossibly elusive and then had selfishly beaten Colin to the punch by releasing a statement through the Press Association. Adam Jaymes had come out with dignity and on his own terms, and Colin had never forgiven him for it.

Despite his public statement, Adam had remained as private and mysterious as ever. Colin had licked his wounds and then redoubled his efforts to get some dirt on the star. If he couldn't out him, he would sure as hell get the exclusive story about Adam's first gay relationship. But even that didn't work out in Colin's favour. He had sent the *Ear*'s chief photographer Jason Spade to Los Cabos in Mexico where he finally came up trumps and captured Adam canoodling with a gay American billionaire. Unfortunately Jason couldn't claim it was the result of an inside tip from Colin because no one had even known Adam Jaymes was in the area. Jason had actually been sent to Los Cabos to pap William and Kate and had simply followed the wrong yacht.

But accident or not, it was still the first time anyone had managed to take such intimate photographs of the actor and the pictures caused an international sensation: the handsome and muscular British star and the dashing American entrepreneur 10 years his senior, wearing nothing but swimming trunks and snogging on the deck of a private boat. The *Ear*'s website crashed the moment the pictures were uploaded, and Jason made a small fortune on re-sales.

However, Colin's victory was short-lived when the couple released a statement to announce they had been secretly dating for more than a year. To make matters worse, the Los Cabos cruise wasn't just a holiday, it was their honeymoon. The world's media, Colin included, had missed the whole thing. There were suggestions online that Colin had lost his touch, and there were mutterings within the *Daily Ear*'s own newsroom along the same lines. As far as Colin was concerned, Adam Jaymes had a lot to answer for.

There was a flutter of activity on the other side of the studio, and through a small group of excited technicians and assistants Adam Jaymes appeared as he was quietly escorted to his seat. Despite their long history, Colin and Adam had never actually met face to face and it was slightly disconcerting for Colin to finally see his opponent in the flesh looking so self-assured and handsome. He was wearing a smart, three-piece grey suit and a blue tie. His dark hair was swept back from his face, and his dusky brown eyes seemed to note that Colin was present without actually making contact.

The *Newsnight* studio seemed busier than last time and Colin suspected not all the technicians, assistants and producers "on duty" that night were really on duty at all. They were there to catch a glimpse of Adam. Perhaps, he wondered, that was the cause of the strange atmosphere in the studio: the BBC's 'gay mafia' out in force to support one of their own. But whatever additional support Adam might have in the studio, Colin remained confident he would easily hold his own throughout the discussion.

The presenter was engrossed in a two-way with a BBC reporter who was giving a rundown of another day at the inquiry from outside Parliament. Colin hated two-ways; "Reporters interviewing other reporters? Narcissists! You won't catch me doing that," he thought to himself. But he had learnt it was best to start each interview by being as civil as possible and so as Adam took the seat opposite, Colin smiled at him and then silently mouthed the word 'hello'.

But Adam didn't reply. He offered Colin little more than a cold, hard stare and swiftly turned his back to watch the rest of the presenter's two-way. "Well," Colin thought, "that was fucking rude."

Fiona McCoy hadn't intended to stay in London forever. She was going to finish her degree and then move back home to Edinburgh, get a job near her parents and marry a local lad. Her three-year stay in London was simply meant to be a big adventure, one she would be able to tell her future children and grandchildren about. And everything had been going according to plan. She'd rented a flat with a couple of fellow students, had a part-time job waiting tables in an upmarket restaurant and thrown herself into the city's nightlife with great enthusiasm. Life had been good.

But then Colin Merroney had entered her life, a funny and charming older man who had dined at her restaurant eight months earlier. Despite the age difference (almost thirty years, she eventually discovered) there had been an instant chemistry. He had a killer smile, all dimples and white teeth, and through a number of good humoured exchanges quickly proved himself to be both clever and funny. He had complimented the prettiness of her eyes and talked with genuine fondness of the many business trips he'd made over the years to her home city.

After two courses and many bottles of wine, he excused himself from the table and followed her into the 'staff only' area. Throwing caution to the wind, she had taken him by the hand and led him into the linen closet, expecting a few minutes of drunken fumbling and groping. But instead he had surprised her with an astonishing session of intense, passionate love-making. And as they had stumbled from the closet, laughing and a little embarrassed, Colin had passed Fiona his business card and they had made a casual plan to meet up again at some point.

But those casual plans proved fortuitous as, within a couple of weeks, Fiona realised she was pregnant. She had seen a lot of men over the years. Her sense of humour, curvy figure and flame-red hair meant she was rarely without a date. But she had genuinely felt there was something different about Colin, this short older man with amazing hair and confident voice. They really seemed to have a connection, despite the age difference.

Colin was a life-long bachelor who'd never been in a long term relationship or had kids. His job simply hadn't allowed for it. But whisked along by the excitement of the linen closet encounter and the romantic notion that they had simply 'clicked', he asked Fiona to marry him and she said yes. Within weeks of telling Colin she was pregnant, Fiona became Mrs Merroney and moved into his home in Wapping. She finished her degree and then watched from the sidelines as her university friends all left London. The life she had mapped out for herself no longer existed. She was 400 miles from home, married and pregnant and spent most of her days alone because her husband was always chasing some story in another part of the country. She filled her time trying new recipes in an expensive kitchen which, prior to her moving in, had never been used. And it was during those lonely months that she could sense a change in herself, as though she was becoming a quieter person. She could feel her quick wit and her ability to colour any conversation with humour and sharp observations gradually drain away. Hardest of all was the change in her own body. She had hoped to be like one of those celebrity mums, sailing through pregnancy without gaining an ounce of fat and just wearing her pregnancy bump like a fashion accessory. But her body had other ideas and the extra three stone left her constantly tired and with back pain.

That night she had guests: Colin's parents and his best mate Terry and his wife Laura, both friends from Colin's school days. They had congregated at the house to watch Colin's latest TV appearance. Fiona's lower back was hurting, she felt over-heated and the smell of the canapés she had prepared were making her feel nauseous, but she was determined to be the perfect host. Her pretty freckled face was shiny and flushed, and her long red hair was tied back in a ponytail to keep it out of the way. "Now, has everyone got a drink?" she asked, trying to hide the fact that she was already out of breath.

"Yes darling," Mrs Merroney responded. She patted the empty space next to her. "Now come and sit down, you'll wear yourself out."

Colin's mum and dad were on the couch, both comfortably decked out in cardigans and slippers. Terry and Laura were sitting on the two-seater, the Thames framed in the bay window behind them. Terry looked every bit his age, with grey receding hair and a pot belly from too many beers. Laura was a businesswoman and always looked well turned out, even for informal gatherings such as this. She made an effort with her appearance in a way her husband had clearly given up many years earlier.

Terry grabbed the remote control from the coffee table and turned the volume up. "He's on" he said with excitement, swirling a glass of brandy in his other hand. "He'll rip the shit out of the pair of them, no problem. Go on my son!"

"Why does he always sit like that?" wondered Mrs Merroney. "He needs to sit up straight with his knees together. He looks like he's lounging around, not taking it seriously."

Terry and Laura smirked at each other.

"You must tell him, Fiona, when he gets home, that his mother wants him to sit properly when he's on television in the future."

Mr Merroney had fallen asleep and started to snore, and so Fiona took the glass of bitter from his hand before it spilt on the carpet and placed it on the coffee table. She then picked up a plate of canapés and offered them around. "Does anyone fancy a samosa or bhaji?" she asked. She failed to get any response and so finally lowered herself down onto the seat next to her mother-in-law.

"Fiona, how come it's always Colin that ends up doing these interviews?" asked Laura. "I mean, he's very good but it does seem a bit unfair that he has to take the heat for the whole newspaper. "

"Oh, I don't think the editor likes to do interviews," Fiona replied. "Besides, I don't think any of them would be able to handle it as well as he does."

"Well I hope they're giving him a bonus." Laura sat back in her armchair and continued to sip from her glass of red wine, gently stroking the arm of the two-seater. "And he does look great on TV."

"As a newspaper, our glass is definitely half-full. If we can find something good to say about a celebrity, we say it. We're proud to say it. We're the *positive* paper." Colin was pleased to have been able to start the discussion. It gave him the chance to make a few generic sound bites rather than having to respond to anything Adam had to say.

"Are you surprised to hear that, Adam Jaymes? The *Daily Ear* is known for positive, pro-celebrity reporting?" the presenter probed, with an incredulous tone to her voice.

Adam ran his fingers through his dark hair, his brown eyes sparkling in the studio lights in the way only a celebrity's ever did. "I think it just underlines how detached from reality Colin and his colleagues at the *Daily Ear* have become," he said, his tone calm and measured.

Colin got an unexpected buzz from Adam using his name. A famous person, using his name! On telly! But he quickly regained his composure and as Adam continued with his response, Colin tried to remember each of the five points he needed to make during the interview, one point for each finger on his right hand. The first (his thumb) he had already used - promoting positive stories when they had the chance. Point two (index finger) was about the hypocrisy of celebrities who whored their private lives for publicity one minute and then complained about invasion of privacy the next.

Colin had very little time for celebrity privacy arguments. You want privacy? Then don't become a household name. They'd all asked for it, he thought, one way or another – Grant, Miller, Partridge, all the others. And what was the angle on Adam Jaymes? Oh, that's right. Point three (middle finger): Adam Jaymes had appeared in a movie that was partly funded by Harvey Media International which owns Harvey News Group which owns the *Daily Ear*. So he's a hypocrite.

Taking money from the Harvey family and then moaning about them behind their backs.

The presenter suddenly swung around and looked at Colin. "That's an interesting point, Colin. What do you say to that?" she asked.

Oh shit! "Sorry?"

"What do you say to Adam's accusation that in the current climate your paper has become increasingly driven by sales rather than journalism?"

"Oh bollocks!" he replied which, in that moment, seemed a perfectly good answer.

"Ah-ha! Brilliant!" roared Terry. "Brilliant."

"Oh, and please tell him his mother doesn't want him swearing on television as well."

The presenter raised her hand and gestured for Colin to be quiet. She stared straight into the camera, which Colin thought presenters weren't supposed to do. Or is that actors? "Can I just apologise to the viewers at home for that," she said. "This is a live programme, and sometimes when we're discussing controversial issues our guests can forget where they are." She looked at Colin again. "If I could ask you to articulate your point of view in a more appropriate manner?"

Over her shoulder, Colin could see that Adam Jaymes was staring him down, his brown eyes strangely lifeless, as though hiding a great dark secret. What was it, what was going on in that famous head of his? "Yes, of course," Colin replied, smiling and apologetic. "I'm sorry for my language but I've heard all this before and I frankly I find it offensive."

Point four, wedding ring finger. "If you are in the public eye, your behaviour will be scrutinised. It's right that your behaviour is scrutinised. With all due respect, if the Government brings in measures to control the press then that power of scrutiny will be lost. Our ability to expose corruption and hypocrisy will be lost. As an example, the

MPs' expenses scandal would never have been exposed. That's the harsh reality of the sort of press controls Adam Jaymes is endorsing."

"That's complete nonsense," Adam Jaymes replied, his tone remaining even-tempered and polite. "And besides, your newspaper barely covered the MPs' expenses story. Throughout that entire episode, you continued to concentrate on the private lives of the rich and famous. One of the biggest political scandals of the century and the *Daily Ear* felt it more important that its readers hear about the sexual indiscretions of the latest Big Brother housemates."

His voice sounded far more English than when he'd been a guest judge on *America's Got Talent* the week before, Colin thought. "We need to have the freedom and the protection, in law, to expose hypocrisy," Colin replied, trying to create a neat segue into his big reveal about Adam's HMI funded film role, but Adam talked over him.

"You don't expose hypocrisy. You expose private matters that are no one else's concern," the actor replied. "You pursue celebrities regardless of the impact you have on their health, their lives or their loved ones. And you do this to sell papers and to *make money*, not because there are any genuine, honourable, editorial justifications for your actions."

"Well, talking about making money -" Colin started, but his second attempt at a segue was interrupted again, this time by the presenter.

"Colin, if I can move on to today's inquiry which reviewed your paper's controversial coverage of the vicious street attack on premiership footballer Steve Yorke. He was beaten unconscious outside a night club by a group of fans from a rival club. Your photographer had been waiting outside the club and took photographs during the attack, but did not intervene."

"Now, be fair, there were a lot of them. There was nothing he could do," Colin said. He knew this story well and felt he was on solid ground. "And those photographs helped catch the men who carried out the attack. They're in prison now because of our photographs."

The presenter nodded. "However, it was confirmed at today's hearing that your photographer was so busy taking pictures, he didn't call the police or even for an ambulance. What he did do, however, was collect a blood sample from the scene of the attack which you then had tested for HIV."

"And the test came back positive!" Colin exclaimed proudly, as though the test result somehow justified the action.

"And you put that on the front page of your paper," Adam interrupted. "That poor man had been viciously assaulted and when he *eventually* woke up in hospital he discovered he was HIV positive from the front page of your newspaper. Are you seriously going to argue that was in any way ethical?"

Colin was nodding, hard. "Yes, I can. Premiership footballers sleep around. Steve Yorke could have been having unprotected sex with dozens of women. We likely saved a lot of innocent girls from the risk of infection. It was a tough call, but we made it and we stand by it."

"And what about the *Daily Ear*'s controversial 'Celebrity DNA' project. Your paper secretly acquired DNA samples from four male celebrities and their children, and then you had those samples tested to see if those men genuinely were the fathers of those children."

"That's a little bit out of context," Colin said, knowing that in truth the *Newsnight* presenter had hit the nail on the head.

"That's already been widely condemned by – among others - MPs and children's charities. Even the Press Complaints Commission stated it was 'not entirely happy' with the practice, which is one of the strongest criticisms the PCC has ever made. And at today's hearing, the editors of two rival tabloids both said they were appalled by it. When your own peers are criticising your conduct, it must suggest you are on very shaky ground."

Colin glared at Adam who appeared to be sailing happily through the interview with little challenge, and he was left with the unsettling feeling there was more going on than a simple TV debate. The actor's cool confidence wasn't just bravado. It ran deeper than that.

Colin suspected Adam Jaymes was holding back, as though the actor didn't feel the need to participate completely in the discussion. And Colin's unease was made all the more intense when he noticed the tiniest hint of a smile on the actor's handsome face.

"How do you think he's doing?" Fiona asked.

"She does seem to be picking on him, doesn't she?" Mrs Merroney said. "Why isn't she having a go at that dark-haired boy instead?"

"She's probably not allowed to," Terry said, looking less than impressed with the way the interview was going. "You know all those stupid equality policies the BBC has. She'd probably break some law if she had a go at a gay bloke."

"Oh, I don't think he's gay," Mrs Merroney said, shaking her head. "I remember him in *Eastenders*. He got Sharon pregnant."

"Now, we have to talk about the soap actress Pearl Martin," the presenter continued. "Adam, of course, you were her co-star for many years and are on record for blaming the *Daily Ear* for her suicide. And at the inquiry this week, her sister Patricia claimed Pearl took her own life because she couldn't cope with the *Daily Ear*'s highly critical coverage of her battle with depression. In particular, your columnist Valerie Pierce was singled out."

Colin threw up his hands. How was this simple discussion running away from him? "The Press Complaints Commission rejected almost all of the complaints that were made against Valerie," he retorted. "And I think it important to remember that Pearl Martin was a drug addict *and* an alcoholic – "

"She was neither a drug addict *nor* an alcoholic," Adam immediately retorted and for the briefest of moments there was a hint of genuine passion in his voice. Pearl had been his friend. She had played his older sister on *EastEnders* and by all accounts they'd had an equally close relationship off-screen. If anything was ever going to liven up this discussion, it was *always* going to be a mention of Pearl.

"She was not a drug addict. She had prescription drugs to help manage her depression. And she was not an alcoholic, but she was accused of such by Valerie Pierce if she was photographed with as much as a single glass of wine in her hand. She struggled every day just to get out of bed, and every day her friends and family tried to hide the latest edition of your disgusting rag from her so she wouldn't see the latest fabricated story. She lost her career because of you. Her child was taken into care because of you. And in the end she took her own life because of you. To be honest, Colin, you may as well have driven her to Beachy Head yourself."

Colin noted a familiar image of Pearl had appeared on the screen behind the presenter. It was the picture most the papers had published on their front pages, the morning after her body had been found at the foot of Beachy Head. Her ghostly pale features and grey eyes had always made Colin feel she was never meant to have a long or happy life. But it wasn't that picture that the *Daily Ear* had used on its front page that day. Leonard Twigg had insisted on a photograph that appeared to show Pearl staggering from a nightclub draped over Adam Jaymes' shoulders and waving a half-empty pint glass in her hand.

"She was a bad mother," Colin retorted abruptly, "and that had nothing to do with depression. One minute she was claiming to be a *supermum*, juggling her responsibilities at home with her acting career. The next she's off at a showbiz party and her kid is home alone."

"That never happened," Adam said. "Valerie Pierce wrote that with absolutely no evidence."

"It was hypocrisy, and it is absolutely right to expose hypocrisy. And that is what the *Daily Ear* is proud to do." Colin didn't waste airtime expressing sympathy for Pearl's family anymore. He had done that in the past but the *Ear*'s PR director, Derek Toulson, had told him not to do it again. He felt an expression of sympathy suggested the paper was in some way culpable. Instead Colin was told to defend the *Ear*'s coverage as strongly as if Pearl were still alive. "If you place yourself in the public eye, the way you behave will be scrutinised. If you publicly state that people should live their lives against a certain set of values, then you have obliged yourself to live by those same values. And the *Daily Ear* will use all means that are not illegal to expose lies, hypocrisy or fraud."

There was a moment of pause. The presenter was about to ask Adam for a final response, but before she could utter any words he fixed Colin with his sparkling eyes and posed a question of his own. "But surely, that can be applied to you?" he said, that tiny smile looking more pronounced.

"I'm a reporter. My job is to investigate – "

"No, no," Adam interrupted. "You have placed yourself in the public eye. And you have spent the past year promoting a set of values. Your newspaper, the *Daily Ear*, has a very pronounced set of values. And you use those values - quite aggressively - to justify your exploitation of the private lives of celebrities."

The presenter raised her hand, ready to interrupt, but the voice in her ear told her not to. "Let this one play out," it said.

"The *Daily Ear* stands for traditional British family values, there is no secret about that," Colin said. And he suddenly realised he had nothing else to say. His mind had gone blank. Adam had him completely flummoxed. That stare. That hint of a smile. Where the hell was this line of questioning going? Colin couldn't even remember what point he was supposed to be making with his little finger.

"Your paper and, indeed, you yourself have exposed the private lives of hundreds - if not thousands - of celebrities over the past 30 years. And a staple part of your work has been catching married celebrities who are having an affair."

Colin nodded.

"But is it not an hypocrisy for someone in the public eye, as you are, to expose adultery through your newspaper when you are, in fact, committing adultery yourself?"

The living room was silent. Fiona stared at the telly, her face glowing bright red. She was humiliated at the mere suggestion that her husband was being unfaithful, never mind that the accusation had been made on national TV. Her own parents were watching. Her friends. Her ex-colleagues from the restaurant. She'd tweeted and told them all to watch. And she had never doubted Colin, not once. Throughout all of his assignments and all of those conferences, she had never questioned him or asked to go with him, or checked up on him. She had never once looked at his emails, or gone through the messages on his phone. She'd never checked his credit card bill or called a hotel to check he was actually there. It's what made their marriage work, Colin had said. She was different to all the other reporters' wives, he had said. And that was why he loved her so much.

Out of the corner of her eye she could see Terry leaning forward in his seat, looking at her with his mouth open. "Where the hell did that come from?" he asked, sounding completely perplexed. Fiona found his confusion strangely reassuring. Surely if Colin was having an affair, his best mate would know it? She turned to him and shrugged.

And then she noticed his wife, Laura. Funny, loud, outspoken, lovely Laura. Busty, brassy, forty-something Laura. Best friends with Terry and Colin since school. Colin had even been best man at their wedding. But now, in the sitting room, she wasn't loud or outspoken. She was silent. Frozen, in fact, her eyes fixed on the TV screen, her face completely white. "Are you OK, Laura?" Fiona asked. And when Laura didn't respond, Fiona's world fell apart.

The presenter had intended to intervene but the voice in her ear kept telling her not to, and Adam wasn't about to stop. He leant forward and suddenly, in a smooth, sweeping motion, pulled a leather satchel from under his chair.

"I think, sadly, that's all we have time for ... ", the presenter started. But no one was listening anymore. Adam was centre stage. He pulled a number of large white cards from the satchel and sat with them on his lap, smiling. And then he turned the first card around, and there – on the other side – was a photograph of Colin in some bar, kissing Laura. "Now, I know that isn't your wife, Colin. Because your wife is a red-head, not blonde. And she's also much younger. And pregnant."

The presenter looked at the picture. She then looked to the gallery, and then at Colin, and then back to the gallery. And then back to the picture. 'That's certainly not his wife,' she thought.

Colin's head was about to explode. Blood and fear and guilt and panic were pumping through his veins at a rate of knots. He broke out in a cold sweat, and could feel the perspiration breaking through his shirt and trickling over his raised brow. He had no more words, just a huge, dry lump in his throat and a look of absolute sweaty horror on his face.

"And what about this one?" Adam asked, and flipped over the next card. There were Colin and Laura again, still kissing. But this time in the street, outside a hotel. Laura's hair was much shorter in that one. Clearly a different occasion.

"And this one?" Not kissing this time, but both in bath robes, standing on a hotel balcony, enjoying the view and a morning fag together.

Laura left without a word. She simply put down her glass of wine, collected her coat from the hall cupboard and let herself out.

Terry, filled with hate and rage, didn't stop her. He didn't even acknowledge her. But the moment he heard the front door bang, he burst into tears and sat with his head in his hands sobbing. Mrs Merroney went over and held him. "I never liked her," she said. "I always thought she was a dirty girl. That's why I didn't let Colin go out with her at school."

Fiona didn't say a word. She sat quietly stroking her pregnancy bump and wondering what she should do with the leftover canapés. But as Terry's sobbing grew louder she could feel a panic beginning to rise up inside of her. She was alone and pregnant, living in a city where she barely knew anyone and where her husband had just been publicly outed as an adulterer. The unpleasant reality of the situation was about to take hold and she couldn't bear the thought of crying in front of Colin's parents or Colin's equally shell-shocked friend. She heaved herself up from the settee and collected as many glasses and plates as she could and then quietly walked through to the kitchen where she busied herself with the washing up.

"These photographs have been taken over the past few months in about a dozen different locations," Adam said. "Now bearing in mind your traditional British family values, how do you justify cheating on your young, pregnant wife?"

The presenter looked to Colin, whose mouth was moving as though he was trying to form some words, but nothing was coming out. "This is the most extraordinary outburst we have ever had on *Newsnight*," she said. "Colin, if I could just ask you – "

"Fuck you!" he shouted suddenly and jumped to his feet. "This is a fucking BBC trick. Is this what the fucking licence fee pays for these days?"

"Can I just apologise *again* for the language - "

"Fuck you! Fuck *Newsnight*! Fuck the BBC!" With that, Colin walked off the set trying to rip his microphone from his jacket as he went. And as he stormed from the studio, the presenter looked to the camera again. "Can I just apologise once more for the language used by our guest. I hope you appreciate this is an unprecedented incident on *Newsnight*." She turned to Adam who was neatly tucking his cards back into his satchel. "Adam, for someone who has spoken so strongly in the past about invasion of privacy – surely, you can't get a greater invasion of privacy than this. And you perpetrated it."

Surprisingly, Adam agreed. "This was a very difficult course of action to take," he said, a note of genuine sorrow in his voice. But then, as the presenter recalled, he was an award-winning actor. "For years, many of us have campaigned for stronger control of the press in the UK, or – at the very least – greater protection from press intrusion. But nothing has happened. Indeed, things have gotten worse. Careers have been ruined, families destroyed and in some cases, lives have been lost. It seemed to me the only way to bring this home to the media in this country and, in particular, the staff at the *Daily Ear* was to give them first-hand experience of what this sort of reporting does to the lives of real people."

"And so you chose to humiliate Colin Merroney on live television, and potentially destroy his marriage?"

Adam relaxed into his seat and turned to the camera. "Colin is just the first of a number of employees at the *Daily Ear* who are about to get a taste of their own medicine." Clearly, he was no longer talking to the presenter but directly to those people watching at home. "My team is uploading the full details about Colin Merroney's adultery to my website as we speak, where you can see plenty more pictures and read the full, exclusive story."

"There are more exposés to come?"

Adam nodded at the presenter and then turned back to the camera, maintaining a look of sadness. "Regretfully, yes. Every three days, for the next couple of weeks, I'll be uploading a new exposé to my website regarding someone who works at the *Daily Ear* or its parent company Harvey News Group. The stories won't be nice, and I'm sure the consequences will be severe. But I genuinely feel this course of action is necessary, because the repercussions of allowing the media in this country to continue spiralling out of control would be disastrous." He turned to the presenter. "So to quote Colin, it was a tough call but I made it and I'll stand by it."

"But who are the other people on your 'hit list'?"

Adam smiled. "Suffice to say that, on the day of publication, each exposé will be uploaded to my website at 9pm."

"And whoever the story is about – they'll find out by logging onto your website along with everyone else?"

"No, no," Adam responded, as though the presenter had suggested something completely unreasonable. "Just before the story goes live I will personally phone the man or woman whose private life is about to be exposed to let them know that it's their turn. All in all, I think I'm being very fair."

Fiona sat alone in the kitchen sipping mineral water from a wine glass, the room dimly illuminated by the light above the stove. She had spoken to her parents and they had booked her train journey home for the next day. The house already felt strange again. It was someone else's home. Fiona's home was 400 miles north. Mr and Mrs Merroney had offered to stay but she wanted to be by herself, so they had poured Terry into their car and driven him back to their house for the night.

At 11.30pm, Colin arrived. She heard him rattling at the front door, trying to get in, calling to her, begging her to let him explain. It went on for about 20 minutes. Then he started shouting angrily, but not at Fiona. There was someone else outside. She heard a man say, "Come on Colin, you know the routine, we're only doing our job," and then sarcastic laughter before Colin started shouting angrily again. Finally, she heard a car pull up, a taxi. She heard the boot slam, which would have been the taxi driver taking the suitcase of neatly folded clothes she had left for Colin on the door step. Just as she had whenever he went away on one of his assignments. And then a car door slammed, and the taxi drove away.

Fiona hadn't had the opportunity to mourn her marriage in secret, or to take a few days to privately deal with her husband's adultery before choosing who, if anyone, she would confide in. Everyone had found out the same moment she did. She now knew Colin was not the man she was going to spend the rest of her life with. She would get up early the next day, pack her things and catch a train to Edinburgh. Her bizarre, unexpected London life had been a horrible mistake. It was time Fiona McCoy returned home.

2

Best. #Newsnight. Ever.

cannot be allowed to abuse his position and use his super-rich American 'husband' to bully the British media and get his revenge for the suicide of

I hope @RealAdamJaymes will do the same for local papers too. The wankers at my local rag deserve a good kicking!

"must not let reporters be frightened away from exposing hypocrisy"

PLEASE tell me the staff at @TheEar aren't REALLY expecting public sympathy #getreal #WellDoneAdamjaymes

"**BUT MANY WILL** say to you, as the former chairman of the Press Complaints Commission, that Adam Jaymes would not have chosen this course of action if your organisation had done its job properly and"

Hopefully that spiteful hag #ValeriePierce is next #WellDoneAdamjaymes

I met Colin Merroney once. He was a complete cock. That is all. #WellDoneAdamjaymes

"but can I just ask what legal protection the reporters at the *Daily Ear* actually have? Because it *could* be seen as the worst kind of hypocrisy if they seek injunctions against Adam Jaymes' website when the tabloids have spent so much time attacking celebrities for trying to use the law"

If you missed it, you can see @RealAdamJaymes SLAUGHTER Daily Ear reporter Colin Merroney on @BBCNewsnight on the BBC iPlayer

"got exactly what he deserved, and that's a taste of his own medicine"

Colin Merroney was a total shag monster when he was young. He may not be tall, but is (famously) big where it counts #shortmansyndrome

I may well be on Jaymes' hit list, after all there is clearly no love lost between the two of us, especially after

Gay men are so funny. Unless you piss them off. In which case they drag you onto @BBCNewsnight to publicly ruin your life

While everyone's slapping @RealAdamJaymes on the back, remember he destroyed two innocent families just to prove a point

without a doubt, what is unpalatable to many in the media is the thought that Jaymes may be right. If a reporter sits as judge and jury on the private lives of the rich and famous

I can't believe I have to wait three days for @RealAdamJaymes to do his next exposé #WellDoneAdamjaymes

Does anyone know what key I need to press to get a little accent above the second 'e' in expose? #WellDoneAdamjaymes

"The BBC has denied any prior knowledge that Adam Jaymes was going to use his appearance on last night's Newsnight *to"*

Is @RealAdamJaymes trying to bankrupt Harvey Media International? I hear his 'husband' wants to buy a cheap media company #beingcynical #WhoWillBeNext?

3

"*I'VE ALWAYS CONSIDERED Adam Jaymes to be a fraud and a liar,*" typed Valerie Pierce, fag ash spilling onto her keyboard. "*Now it seems I can add the words 'bully' and 'hypocrite' to the list.*" She drew on her cigarette and surveyed the scene of complete carnage that was playing out on the other side of her glass office wall. The *Daily Ear* newsroom appeared to be in meltdown.

"I am telling you now, Felicity, that if anyone comes in here today to tell me I'm not allowed to smoke, I will stub out my cigarette on their face. I swear it. Right. On. Their. Face!" she spat, clearly spoiling for a fight. Valerie loathed Adam Jaymes at the best of times but his *Newsnight* victory had sent him straight to the top of her 'most hated' list for the day.

"Oh, I don't think you need worry about that," Felicity replied. "Everyone's too busy. You could probably start a small camp fire in here and no one would notice."

Valerie had taken a liking to Felicity which was unusual because, as a rule, she tended not to like the young. Felicity was an intern, an attractive black girl who always seemed to underplay her prettiness as though she didn't want it noticed. She was smart and well-spoken and had been endlessly helpful with all sorts of tasks that Valerie couldn't be bothered to do herself. She had just brought Valerie a morning coffee from Starbucks, and been invited to stay to keep her out of the way until things calmed down. They watched as lawyers, PR advisors and even a few rarely seen executives rushed in and out, while senior reporters argued in groups around the newsroom where the phones hadn't stopped ringing since *Newsnight*.

"They're trying to form a company view on how we should cover this story," Valerie said. "How the hell do you cover a story when you *are* the fucking story?"

"Are you worried?" Felicity asked.

"Should I be?" Valerie elegantly sat round and leaned across the back of her chair, blowing smoke as she spoke.

Felicity nodded. "Well, it's just that someone set up a poll on Facebook."

Valerie gave a 'so what?' shrug. She had a casual knowledge of social media and certainly had no interest in what it had to say about her.

"And you are favourite to be next."

Valerie narrowed her eyes. "Do I owe you for the coffee?" she asked.

"No, you've already given me the money."

"Of course, of course," she said. "My memory's shot to pieces these days." She tapped the side of her forehead. "Too much going on in this old noggin. But nothing a good stroke wouldn't sort out."

Felicity wasn't quite sure how to respond but smiled and let out a little chuckle, assuming that's what Valerie had wanted to hear. Valerie stood and walked slowly to the glass wall which overlooked the newsroom. She had recently turned 53, the age her mother had been when she had died. Valerie had written endlessly about this fact, and the traumatic journey she had travelled before, during and after her own 53rd birthday. A major part of this journey had been a decision to finally cut her long brown hair into a power bob. And whilst Valerie had concentrated on the emotionally charged narrative leading to that life-changing haircut, most other people had commented, more simply, on how it framed her sharp features in a far more severe and unflattering way.

She was wearing her favourite trouser suit which was purple, her signature colour. She'd bought it in the mid-eighties and was proud it still fitted all these years later without any alterations. Not only did she think it looked good, but it had been useful ammunition whenever she wrote a disparaging article about any fat women who dared to appear on television.

"You got 47% of the vote," Felicity revealed. There was silence and Felicity shuffled from foot to foot, waiting to see if she had crossed a line. She'd heard a story that two men once tried to mug Valerie on the underground, but ran off when she turned round and glared at them. Right now, she thought that story was probably true.

"Only 47%?" Valerie said, with half a smile. "I'm disappointed." She returned to her laptop, trying to ignore the blur of action in the newsroom and re-focus on her column. "Quite exciting for you though, eh Felicity?", she said. "Being here, today, the morning after Adam Jaymes declared war on the *Daily Ear*. You'll be able to eat out on this story for decades. Believe me, *decades*."

"Oh, no, no," Felicity said. "I'm not going to gossip, honestly. That's not what I'm like at all."

"Oh, it's not gossip, dear. It's a story. A great story that's only just begun. And all caused by that man." Valerie gestured with her cigarette hand to her computer screen, and the opinion piece she had started to write about Adam. "That man stands in judgement of all of us, but built *his* career on a big fat lie. He got legions of teenage girls to fall in love with him. He even had millions of mums tuning into Doctor Who each week on the promise he'd get his shirt off in every episode. And so he got to be rich and famous and adored, but the whole time he knew his public image was a complete falsehood. Until one day he moves into *musical* theatre where, let's face it, pretty much every man is gay. And finally he admits it. 'Hi girls, guess what? I'm a homosexual.' That was unforgiveable."

"But some gay people do struggle for years to come to terms with – "

"Stop!" Valerie snapped and turned to face Felicity again. "I won't have a word said in defence of that man this morning. Not. One. Word."

Felicity pursed her lips and gently nodded.

Valerie knew Adam Jaymes was popular, but for the life of her could not see the appeal. Mums loved him, sci-fi geeks worshipped him and teenage girls fancied him. He'd even been voted most popular 'bromance' by the readers of FHM pushing David Beckham into second place and Johnny Depp into third. But it was the *Daily Ear*'s own readers who Valerie had found most exasperating, after voting Adam Jaymes the 'world's most beautiful man' in a poll for the *Ear*'s Saturday magazine. Hadn't they *read* their own newspaper? Didn't they know they were supposed to *despise* Adam Jaymes, not fancy him?

"You know the most disappointing thing about Adam Jaymes," Valerie said, "is that he has never once spoken to me directly. He's never asked for a meeting, or tried to call me, or even just sent me a letter or an email. The few conversations we've had have always been played out in public. I write something in my column; he responds in an interview with another newspaper. What sort of person behaves like that? And he always, *always* accuses me of 'gutter journalism'." She drew again on her cigarette. "Gutter journalism," she hissed, "and this from a man whose idea of auditioning for a part is having his face jammed up against the wall of a public lavatory."

"Oh!" Felicity hadn't meant to make a noise, but the poison spilling from Valerie's mouth had caught her by surprise. She didn't know how to respond to what had just been said.

Valerie smiled. "Have I finally managed to shock you, Felicity? How else do you think a man with such a mediocre talent could get so far so quickly?"

"I ... I ... well, no, but, it's just that I don't think there's ever been any suggestion that he got any of his roles by doing that. Most people consider him extremely talented."

Valerie raised her shoulders. "But you never know, do you?" she said.

Felicity quickly moved the conversation on by offering to help source some pictures for that week's column, and Valerie gave her a list of images to research. "Now, I have to attend the morning meeting," she announced. "Assuming there is still going to be a morning meeting."

Her heart pounding, Felicity left the office and closed the door behind her. Valerie began to look through some of the angry comments she had scribbled into her notebook the night before, after watching Colin Merroney's life ripped to shreds on live TV. She had sent him a few texts, but not had a reply. She doubted she would hear from him for a while. "Adam Jaymes," she said again, her lips curled with disgust.

Secretly, Valerie was rather pleased to have a legitimate reason to write about Adam Jaymes again. She considered him a nemesis and had several old scores to settle. For Valerie, he personified everything that was wrong with modern Britain's increasingly liberal attitudes towards non-traditional lifestyles. Even the *Daily Ear*'s own readers appeared less angry and more open-minded which had made Valerie feel increasingly out of step with them. But she considered that to be Adam Jaymes' fault too.

Several years earlier when he had issued his famous public statement confirming he was gay, Valerie had leapt gleefully onto the story and dedicated her entire column to it. With great fury she had demanded he hand back his numerous TV awards because, she claimed, *'Tens of thousands of heartbroken female fans would not have paid good money to phone-vote for him if they'd known he was a closet homosexual'.*

She had fully expected her angry words to strike a chord with Middle England, but there followed an unexpected outpouring of love and support for Adam that resulted in the column getting a record number of complaints. Her attack on the actor was even debated in parliament. Leonard Twigg publicly supported Valerie but quickly dispatched her to Spain to "write a number of in-depth features about expats". Worse still, he temporarily replaced her with an infuriatingly earnest, hand-wringing TV agony aunt who used Valerie's own column to rip to pieces everything she had written about Adam Jaymes the week before. A month later, once the fuss had died down, Valerie returned to work and found she had been moved to a much smaller office, just off the main newsroom. It was Twigg's silent way of letting her know his support only stretched so far.

Valerie blamed Adam Jaymes for the whole affair, and one thing she certainly knew how to do was hold a grudge. And so when Adam was caught on a yacht with an American billionaire, she patiently watched events unfold and waited for her 'in'. When it was confirmed the two had secretly married, Twigg instructed her to make it the focus of that week's column. "Appear neutral, but give people a few negative points to think about," he had said. "You know – make sure words like 'marriage', 'wedding' and 'husband' are all in apostrophes. I don't care if it's legal over there. It's not legal over here. Yet."

But Valerie ignored the 'be neutral' directive and wrote a scathing article about Adam's move to the States. *"What better way for an unexceptional individual like Adam Jaymes to promote his career in America than to marry one of its most famous and richest citizens? And does anyone really think he will give a moment's thought to the fans he is abandoning? Yes, the British fans that were responsible for making him the success he is today? The words 'drop', 'brick' and 'hot' spring to mind!"* Surprisingly Twigg waved the column through and it was published with only a relatively small ripple of complaints. Valerie had been almost disappointed.

She noticed Twigg standing in the newsroom, glaring at the scene of madness around him. He was a small man with a large head, always impeccably dressed. There was never a hair out of place, a stain on his collar or a crease in his shirt. And for a newspaper man he had a surprising dislike of the noise, rush and heat of a newsroom. He liked order, and quiet, and punctuality. He liked news to be researched, and measured, and considered, and precise.

"Poor Leonard," murmured Valerie. "This must be like hell".

He looked over to her and then nodded towards his office. The morning meeting was about to begin.

"Colin was one of our own. What happened to him hurt the whole business," said Gayesh Perera, the short and portly chief executive of the Harvey News Group. None of the editorial staff knew him particularly well, as he was rarely seen around the office. But on this momentous day he had graciously cancelled all of his appointments and decided to take control of the morning meeting. "We need to think like the police do when one of them is shot. We have an officer down, and the threat is still out there." He looked around the room, expecting his stolen words to have somehow rallied the assembled senior staff into action.

But no one flinched. Everyone was looking at Twigg. Only Twigg's opinion mattered. Their editor was seated at the end of the table, scribbling notes into his leather-bound pad. He was clearly not happy that Gayesh was at his morning meeting. He was even less happy that Gayesh was trying to position himself as chair. "Mmm, mmm," was the only noise Twigg made, as though agreeing. Valerie was on his left and there was an empty chair to his right where Colin usually sat. The rest of the seats were taken by a mix of senior staff from different teams and departments. Felicity was at the back, taking the minutes.

The morning meeting was always tense. Twigg had an alarming ability to look as though he wasn't paying attention, but everyone in the room had learnt the hard way that this was rarely the case.

His mind processed information with astonishing clarity, and he was able to articulate with devastating severity just how wrong you were, or how badly you had failed. It was an irony that every single member of staff wanted an invitation to Twigg's morning meeting. If they were at his meeting, they had finally arrived. But the meeting was so stressful that everyone who was invited soon wished they hadn't been. "Right," Twigg exclaimed suddenly, and looked up from his pad. "Thank you for your stirring words, Gayesh. I'm sure everyone found them motivating," he said, sounding completely indifferent. "So now that's out of the way we can start."

Gayesh knew he had been dismissed, but wasn't about to relinquish control of the meeting so easily.

"Has anyone heard from Colin?" Valerie chipped in.

"Yes!" Gayesh interjected. "Has anyone - "

"I spoke to him this morning, Valerie," said Twigg. "He's tough. He'll be fine. We've put him up in a hotel and are keeping everyone away from him."

"This company will always protect - "

"And what about Jaymes?" asked Twigg, talking over Gayesh as though he wasn't even there. "Where's Adam Jaymes now? What's he doing?" He looked around the room, his gaze moving from nervous face to another nervous face until he reached the serene, pale, rounded features of Oonagh Boyle, editor of the paper's website.

They had a prickly relationship, Twigg and Oonagh. He'd been editor for more than 30 years and made the *Ear* the bestselling daily in the UK. But Oonagh had breezed into the company 18 months earlier and with maddening aplomb soon made *dailyear.com* the biggest news website in the world. And as the ratio of profit continued to swing from print to online Twigg had felt, for the first time, that he truly had a rival at the company.

The tone of their relationship had been sealed the night the London Olympics opened. Furious at what he considered to be a reprehensible plug for the NHS and multiculturalism during the opening ceremony, Twigg self-published a pounding critique of the whole affair, calling it *"little more than a shameful, lefties-pleasing pile of hokum that left the rest of the world spinning with confusion and contempt"*. It instantly did the rounds on Twitter which quickly brought it to Oonagh's attention who decided it was not the right moment for the *Ear* to be drawing a line in the sand. And so within an hour she had deleted the article itself and then permanently blocked Twigg's access to the website.

She remained the only person in the morning meetings that he was never rude to. He wouldn't even disagree with her in front of the rest of the team. Often Twigg would make it clear how he wanted a story to be handled, and Oonagh would casually dismiss his instructions as being completely wrong for her 'online readers'. But Twigg would say nothing. He didn't understand the internet or social media nearly well enough to wade in for a fight. And so he tried his best to stay blissfully unaware of Oonagh, her team and her website. But he hoped that, one day, she would call it wrong and quickly be dispatched from the company.

"I can answer that," she said coolly, accentuating her smooth Irish accent simply to annoy Twigg further. She pushed her long, thick black hair behind her shoulders and swiped her fingers across her iPad. "He flew to LA last night, pretty much as soon as *Newsnight* finished. He's doing some promotional work for his *Glee* episodes. The first one airs in the US next week."

Twigg shook his head with disbelief. "So he's dropped us into the middle of this almighty shit-storm, and then pisses off back home?"

"It's also worth noting that he recently opened a Twitter account," Oonagh continued. "Which, bearing in mind how obsessively private he is, did seem a little strange at the time."

"He's a fucking hypocrite," Valerie spurted, unable to control herself. Twigg gently patted her hand, a signal for her to be quiet. Few others would receive such kind treatment from Twigg, and it was a subtle gesture that immediately made almost everyone else in the room jealous.

Oonagh continued as though she hadn't been interrupted. "He tweeted for the first time this morning. Just four words. '*Project Ear is underway*'." She put down her iPad and knitted her fingers together. "Project Ear was *hash-tagged.*"

A few people in the room gasped, but Valerie had no idea what any of that meant and so simply spluttered and pulled a face to reinforce her on-going disapproval of both Adam Jaymes and the internet. But she wasn't about to admit she didn't know what Twitter was because that would hand the fat Irish whore (her nickname for Oonagh) the chance to patronise her with an answer, and so she simply sneered at her instead.

Oonagh continued. "His second tweet was a link to BBC iPlayer so people can watch last night's *Newsnight*. Now typically *Newsnight* isn't watched by many people. On a really good day, it might get almost a million viewers. But a contact of mine at the BBC tells me the episode on iPlayer has already been viewed more than four million times."

"And how many followers does Jaymes have on Twitter?" asked Twigg.

"As of this morning, 5,276,002. This time yesterday he had just over four million. That's a 25% increase in, well, a matter of hours."

Valerie made more scoffing noises and her face was curled up with hatred. "So here is a man who's spent most of his career moaning about privacy and press intrusion, and now he's going to be happily 'tweeting' about how rich and famous and handsome he thinks he is?" She looked around the room, expecting everyone else to look equally appalled. But everyone else had realised what Oonagh was actually saying.

"I think you've missed the point, Valerie," she said, sweetly. "He's set up his Twitter account solely to promote his campaign against this newspaper and drive traffic to his website."

"And I would think everyone in this room has looked at the website?" Twigg supposed, and everyone nodded. "So who wants to tell me about it?" Silence. No one wanted to contribute in case they said the wrong thing in front of Twigg.

"Oh for pity's sake," Twigg muttered, and then pointed at the intern. "Felicity, please tell this bunch of silent idiots about Adam Jaymes' website."

Felicity looked up from her shorthand notes, and realised everyone was looking at her. Valerie was at the other end of the table, smiling. Felicity could not work out if it was a kind and supportive smile, or the smile of someone expecting her to royally mess up.

"Well," she said, a nervous lump rising in her throat. "It's actually a microsite that you access via Adam Jaymes' main website. It's been designed to look like a news website. Or, more precisely, to look like the *Daily Ear*'s website."

The room was silent, but Twigg was nodding, which seemed a good sign.

"The article about Colin, likewise, has been written as though it were a *Daily Ear* exposé. It's clearly intended to parody the *Daily Ear*, probably as a way of reinforcing what Adam Jaymes said on Newsnight about using our own methods against us. The headline 'Kiss-and-Tell King Caught in Sex Tryst' reflects a number of headlines the *Daily Ear* has run over the years. And there's also a digital countdown clock on the front page ... which ... ," her voice cracked slightly, so she swallowed hard and then continued, "which appears to be counting down to 9pm on Friday."

"9pm Friday," Oonagh repeated, "which is the date and time of his threatened second exposé."

"Thank you, Felicity," Twigg said. "Most succinct."

"Well," Valerie said, her voice cutting through the air like a shard of glass. "I still think he's a hypocrite and I shall be saying exactly that in my column this week."

Oonagh sighed, wearily. "Valerie, I think the purpose of this meeting is for us to discuss and agree how we are going to cover this story." She then smiled at Twigg. "Over to you," she said.

Twigg had been in the office since 3am and didn't need a discussion about how they were going to cover the story. He'd already spoken to Howard, the company lawyers, Derek Toulson and Colin. He *knew* how they were going to cover the story. "Here's what we are going to do," he said. "We'll give the story minimal coverage and nothing on the front page. We will not be presenting it as any kind of *war* between the *Daily Ear* and Adam Jaymes. Instead, we will treat it as Adam's personal vendetta against Colin. I will write a few words about press freedom for the editor's column, and suggest that the *Newsnight* team had been in cahoots with Jaymes all along." He grinned. "There's nothing like a bit of BBC bashing to deflect attention."

Everyone in the room wanted to show how strongly they agreed with Twigg, so they all made approving noises and nodded their heads. Someone even clapped. "Our public line is that it's business as usual," he said. But then he frowned, and pointed his finger. For everyone in the room, it felt like he was pointing directly at them. "And I'm telling you all now," he said, firmly, "that if anyone in this building speaks to another paper, radio station or TV journalist about this issue, I will sack them on the spot. Is. That. Clear?"

Everyone nodded again.

"Couple of things PR-wise, Leonard", Derek interjected. PR wasn't a profession Twigg respected but Derek had been surprisingly useful in the past and Twigg returned his loyalty by pretending to value his input. "I had a call first thing from Lizzie at the BBC's *Question Time*. Following *Newsnight*, they want you for tomorrow night's panel. They said they'll take Valerie again if you're not available, but would rather have you."

Twigg shook his head. "No. And that's a no for Valerie too. Next?"

"I've had a couple of sponsors contact me about this year's *Amazing People Awards*. They're wobbling a bit. I've calmed them down, but I think a call from you would help."

Twigg agreed. "Email me their details and I'll call them later today. Anything else?"

"No, that's it for now."

"Good. Meeting over. Back to work everyone." Twigg closed his notepad and returned to his desk. He opened his laptop and started to type and everyone apart from Gayesh left his office. Gayesh stood and closed the door and then walked up to Twigg and leaned over the desk, staring straight into his face. "You are very lucky that I didn't sack *you* on the spot," he said. "How dare you dismiss me like that."

Twigg was uninterested in Gayesh but was aware that he had an entire newsroom as his audience, watching furtively from the other side of his glass wall. This was Twigg's office, his team, his world. He kept it all in order and a big part of that was the discipline he imposed through intimidating his staff. No one was about to undermine him in front of his people. "Go away," he said.

"I'm chief executive. Your boss," Gayesh said.

Twigg continued to type.

"I'm the person you report to," Gayesh continued, but Twigg was reading an email, and would only respond with his usual "Mmmm, mmmm".

"As of now, I want an hourly update from you."

"Mmmm."

"And until this is over, *I'll* be chairing the morning meetings."

"Mmmm, mmmm."

"I will be speaking to Howard this afternoon and then you and I will have another conversation."

"Mmmm."

"In my office. On the top floor."

Twigg closed the lid on his laptop. "Oh, about your office. I forgot to mention. You need to vacate it immediately."

Gayesh stood up straight and stared at Twigg. "What?" he bellowed. "Are you really trying to piss me off even more than you have already?"

"Sam Harvey is flying into London this afternoon," Twigg said with a soft, cold tone that was markedly different to the voice he used for his more day-to-day rants. He reserved this voice for special occasions, and no one who heard it ever continued their career at the Daily Ear. "He's going to be working with me over the next couple of weeks to manage the situation. And he needs an office. I've given him yours."

Gayesh curled up his lips, and for a moment seemed ready to grab Twigg round the throat. "You are in no position to give my office to anyone," he growled, spraying spit halfway across Twigg's desk. "I will be returning to *my* office now and I will give Howard a call."

"Oh, one more thing," Twigg said. "Howard has decided his son has spent too much time running their TV company in Los Angeles. He thinks this is a good opportunity for him to get stuck into the newspaper industry."

Gayesh just stared at Twigg. He knew what was coming. He had known it was on the cards for some time. But he had hoped that, if he was seen to take control of the current scandal, he would be able to wing it for another year or so.

"More specifically," Twigg concluded, "as chief executive of Harvey News Group." He gestured to the door behind Gayesh. "These gentlemen will see you from the building."

When Gayesh turned he came face to face with two security guards. "The Harvey family thanks you for your hard work." Twigg looked down, opened his laptop and started typing again.

Humiliated, bewildered and lost for words Gayesh left the office and, followed by the security guards, walked through the newsroom which had fallen strangely silent. The last thing he would remember seeing as he was escorted out was Valerie Pierce, standing in her office, smoking a cigarette with a huge smile on her face.

4

AFTER A STRESSFUL 10-hour flight from LA, Sam Harvey arrived at Heathrow feeling extremely ill-prepared. He had a one paragraph brief on Project Ear, which had left him with the impression it was little more than a silly TV spat between an actor and a reporter. He couldn't understand why his father had dispatched him so suddenly, and so completely, to London.

The phone call between the two had been abrupt. "Gayesh is out. I'm making you chief executive. You're moving to London today. You can live at the house. Twigg will email you a brief. It's about time you got your hands dirty."

And after that brief phone call and a couple of short emails, here he was stepping off a plane in London as Harvey News Group's new boss. His clean, sunny life was gone and with it his entire support network. His PA and team of researchers, lawyers, policy advisors, creatives and accountants had stayed behind in the States. Together they had made the Harvey Network the second highest-rated broadcast network in the 18–49 demographic in America. In reality, though, Sam knew he'd had very little to do with that success. On paper, of course, it certainly looked like he had led the company to new heights. Ten years ago, at the tender age of 21, his father had prised him from his mother's bosom and sent him to America to run THN, and within just three years the company was nipping at the heels of the likes of Fox and CBS.

But Sam knew how heavily he had relied on his team - utterly and completely. They were the people who had seen him through his twenties, a brilliant and reliable team who had told him what was going on, where to be, what to think, what to say, what decisions to make and what to sign. Because in his heart, Sam knew he was a lightweight. He hid behind a carefully crafted image, one that was the polar opposite of his high-profile, blustering and impulsive father. He was considered to be the quiet man of the family, the rarely-seen, thoughtful and analytical businessman. He was a man who listened rather than spoke, who considered his options slowly rather than making quick decisions on gut instinct.

But the image was a falsehood. Sam was rarely seen because he didn't want a public profile. Out of sight, out of mind - that could have been his catch-phrase. He didn't speak very often because he didn't have anything credible to say. Every day, he knew he was always on the verge of expressing an opinion that was catastrophically stupid and that knowledge kept him in a near constant state of panic. And the reason he took so long to make a decision was because he needed endless meetings and reassuring advice from his top team before agreeing a course of action.

"*It's about time you got your hands dirty.*" His father's words were still ringing in his ears. And *dirty* was the right word, he thought. The *Daily Ear was* dirty, always had been. It had a nasty news agenda, was run by slick, untrustworthy executives, was staffed by unpleasant journalists and all working from grotty offices where it seemed to be perpetual twilight outside. For his entire adult life, Sam had done everything to keep the *Ear* at arm's length, hoping to avoid ever having to involve himself with it. Clearly, that was another battle with his father that he had lost.

As he paced quickly through the terminal, briefcase in hand, he spotted a BBC camera team some distance away and realised they were looking for him. Clearly, his arrival had sparked some interest with the British media. But Sam was confident he would make it to his car without being stopped. He knew there was nothing exceptional about the way he looked. He wasn't tall or muscular or handsome. He was average and bespectacled and thin and ever so slightly beige. His ordinariness was a camouflage that usually made him invisible to unwelcome eyes. And as he stepped freely from the airport to his awaiting car, he smiled at the knowledge that a BBC reporter was going home empty-handed.

"The office, please," he said to the driver as he took his seat.

"Actually sir, I've been instructed to take you straight to the house," replied the chauffeur. "Father's orders."

Sam sighed. "OK, the house it is then." He had expected his father to have organised a late night introduction with the company's great and good, all of them ordered to stay until the early hours to meet their new boss. But this was going to be a quiet conversation at the family home, and that made Sam worry there was more to this Project Ear business than he'd been led to believe. His father seemed rattled, and that was a rarity. The drive to Holland Park gave Sam just over an hour to catch up on his reading. He switched on his iPad and started scanning across all the websites his PA had saved to his favourites just before he left Los Angeles. It included a number of British newspapers as well as the *Huffington Post* and a couple of influential media blogs.

To his surprise, he found the *Newsnight* incident was the top story pretty much everywhere (apart from at the *Daily Ear*). Gayesh's dismissal led one *Telegraph* columnist to reflect that *"it would seem the Daily Ear's statement that it's 'business as usual' is far from true"*. "But it was only a silly TV spat," Sam whispered to himself. The car arrived at Campden Hill Square, and Sam was pleased to find there weren't any reporters or photographers waiting at the front gates. This was the four-storey, Georgian house he'd lived in for most of his childhood and it remained, by far, his favourite of all the properties the family owned.

Audrey, his mother, had kept it as part of the divorce settlement and lovingly maintained Sam's bedroom as though he still lived there. For the most part she and his father, Howard, had stayed on good terms. They had taken a pragmatic approach to *life-after-divorce* which meant Audrey often let him use the house for important family meetings, particularly those where they didn't want 'other people' involved. And that's why Sam worried. It was being treated as a family issue. He found his parents sitting at the breakfast table in the kitchen on the lower ground floor. His mother was sipping a hot chocolate and his father was eating from a wooden bowl filled with pistachios.

"Sam, dear," his mother said with delight, and immediately stood to give him a big hug. Oh, how he loved his mother. He loved her clear voice and bright smiling face. He loved that, without a hint of vanity, she had let her hair go completely grey and the conventional, unfussy way she dressed. But most of all, he loved the unflappable way she handled even the most demanding situation. Her embrace lasted moments, and when she stepped away his giant father was looming over him, his hand outstretched. "I completely understand if you're pissed off with me, but I wouldn't have brought you home if it wasn't important."

"Twigg's note wasn't much good," Sam said. "So I assume there's more to this than meets the eye." He shook his father's hand and could feel grease and salt from the nuts being pressed into his palm. The handshake suddenly turned into an unexpected hug ending with the inevitable back-pat. Sam knew his father only did that when he felt the need to compete with Audrey's more naturally tactile manner. "Good to see you back home, son."

Howard was a big man, six foot five inches tall and several stones overweight. He had a cumbersome physique which somehow managed to make even the most exquisitely tailored suit look cheap and ill-fitting. And his tight mop of thick curly hair was dyed dark brown, a failed attempt to look younger. At times, Sam could barely believe the two had ever been married – his petite, flawless, elegant mother and his lumbering, coarse, poorly-dressed father. But then, growing up, he'd not seen them spend much time together so their dynamic as a married couple had remained something of a mystery to him.

"I'm going to make supper," Audrey said. "Toasted cheese and ham sandwich?"

"Yes please," Sam replied, knowing his mother always bought the best cheese and finest ham. He sat at the table with his father as his mother busied herself at the counter.

"So, Adam Jaymes," Howard said. "Took us all by surprise, I can tell you."

"Bit of an understatement," Audrey remarked, and then chuckled and continued preparing Sam's supper.

Howard sighed and then nodded in agreement. "We've kept this *Newsnight* incident nailed down as best we can, and as a one-off we can easily limit the damage. But Adam Jaymes said we have two weeks of this. If that's true, we could be in serious shit."

Sam frowned. None of this was adding up, he thought. "Dad, the discussion about media ethics isn't new. It's been rumbling on for more than a year. The *Daily Ear* was already slap-bang in the middle of that discussion. All Jaymes' doing is getting some cheap laughs at the expense of the sordid private life of Colin Merroney. So what?"

Howard piled another handful of nuts into his mouth, and chewed while he spoke. "We will not survive two weeks of this shit," he replied. "I've had Derek Toulson run through our reputation management system. There are at least a dozen significant corporate actions that we would not be able to defend publicly. If Jaymes' got wind of even one of those, the *Ear* will go the same way as the *News of the World*."

Sam was astonished. "You would close the *Daily Ear*?" he asked.

"I wouldn't, no," Howard replied. "But *you* might have to."

Sam realised his father had positioned him as the hatchet man. If things went against them, Sam Harvey would be remembered, first and foremost, as the man who closed the UK's most popular daily paper. The idea turned him on a little. "How did things get so bad?" he asked.

Howard continued chewing. "Gayesh took his eye off the ball, big time," he said. "It turns out he was too busy swanning around with politicians and celebrities. I should have sacked him after that disaster with the footballer and the HIV test. My fault, but now it's your problem."

Audrey turned around, onion in hand. "Sam, dear, my awards are in a couple of weeks' time," she said. "I can't have this hanging over them."

"Oh Audrey!" Howard boomed, frustrated at his ex-wife's lack of focus. "For fuck's sake. Your *Amazing People Awards* are not the priority here." He regretted saying it as soon as the words had left his mouth. He knew they were a priority. Perhaps not corporately, but certainly in terms of the status quo of the Harvey family. And so he quickly back peddled. "I'm sorry. Audrey, I'm sorry."

The ceremony was usually broadcast live on primetime ITV, and Howard knew how disappointed Audrey had been when ITV dropped out of that year's event. She'd had no option but to go with an offer from Channel 5, a TV channel with less gravitas and a much smaller potential audience. And now Howard felt just awful for rubbing her nose in it with his own thoughtless criticism. "Of course the awards are a priority," he said. "Sam, look after your mother's awards too."

Sam smiled reassuringly at his mother. "I'll meet the event team tomorrow," he said. "I'll make sure we distance the awards completely from what's going on at the *Ear*."

"And how will you do that?" Howard asked, putting him completely on the spot. But Sam was lucky on that occasion, because he had an answer ready. There had been a similar issue involving sponsors for the teen awards in LA a few years previously and Sam remembered how his team had quickly sorted it out.

"If need be, we'll just drop the *Daily Ear*'s branding and bump up one of the other sponsors to be the main partner, " Sam replied "I know it's last minute but it can be done. Maybe we'll offer it to Channel 5 since they're showing it."

Howard looked ready to bite his son's head off, but Sam knew this was not the time to be barked at. What was it that dreadful Valerie Pierce had said to him once? "Announce your opinion with confidence and people will think you're an academic. It's all in the delivery."

"I know what you're going to say, Dad," Sam said, quickly intercepting his father's response. "And I know the history of the awards and the *Daily Ear*. But this isn't the time for pussying around. And I'm telling you now, Dad, that I won't be pussying around."

Sam waited for his father's response but could see his mother smiling proudly at him from the other side of the kitchen. Oh, how lovely that he had made her proud.

"Whatever you need to do, son," Howard eventually replied, although he clearly wasn't happy. "And one more thing. Adam Jaymes aside, you might want to have a good look at the company accounts. And not the official ones either."

Sam had the impression that Harvey News Group was buoyant, that it had somehow kept itself profitable when everyone else in the marketplace was going to the wall. "I don't know what you mean. Not the official ones?"

Howard groaned. "I want you to get a realistic idea of the company's financial situation. I know that Gayesh only ever gave me half the story. I've grown very suspicious of the top floor. Too many of the senior accountants have an *understanding* with members of the executive team. I think they've used all the tricks in the book to make me think things are going well."

"That's easy enough," Sam said, dismissively. "I'll have lunch with Uncle Tony. He'll give me the run down." Tony Runwell had been a friend and colleague of the Harveys since before Sam was born, and had been Director of Finance at Harvey News Group for more than two decades. Sam had many fond memories of Uncle Tony, most of them involving him falling over drunk at Christmas parties.

"No you will not," Howard replied, angrily. "*Uncle Tony* is the last person you will go to. And this is a piece of work *Uncle Tony* will know nothing about."

"Dad!" Sam said, shocked at the venom in Howard's voice as he said the man's name. "What the hell's Uncle Tony done?"

"That is for you to find out," Howard replied grimly. "You'll need someone good but new, a young accountant who hasn't bought into this 'easy money' mindset. Oonagh Boyle's got a good lad in her back pocket. Use him. But do not let anyone know what you're up to."

The front door slammed and Howard's wife clunked her way through the passageway and down the small flight of stairs to the kitchen. Sam noticed his mother's usually placid demeanour change ever so slightly as Estelle entered the kitchen. The smile on her face became larger, the pretence of a welcome, and she stood taller as though trying to compete with Estelle's six-inch heels.

"Hello Sam," Estelle said brightly and kissed him on the head, ruffling his hair like a schoolboy's. She was only a few years older than he, but her role as step-mother defined their relationship in such a way as to make their ages irrelevant. He was the little boy, and she was his father's wife.

"I'm making supper, Estelle," Audrey said, still smiling.

Estelle dropped her pink Birkin bag on the kitchen table, kissed Howard on the lips and sat down next to him, linking her arm through his. "Oh, no thank you, Audrey sweetheart," she said. "I ended up eating quite late. But I wouldn't say no to an espresso, if one's going."

Sam had expected Estelle to do what she always did after an evening out and drop a few names. Perhaps the restaurant, or the chef, or the people she'd eaten dinner with, or the designer who'd provided her little black dress for the evening. But, to his surprise, she just smiled at everyone and waited for her coffee. He also noticed her voice was slightly smoother and deeper than before, the inflections only occasionally hinting at her Essex roots. Clearly, Sam thought, Estelle's efforts to be more 'classy' were finally beginning to show.

"You look nice this evening," she said to Audrey. "What's that you're wearing?"

Audrey turned from the coffee maker and automatically stood with her elbows out, looking down at her clothes as if seeing them for the first time. "Oh, this? It's M&S," she said.

Estelle tried to look impressed. "Well," she said, "it's lovely. It looks like it could be a label."

"It has a label," Audrey replied, as though mystified. "It says Marks and Spencer."

Estelle laughed, and snuggled back against Howard's chest. "Oh, you're still the funny one!" she said, flapping her wedding-ring hand in Audrey's direction.

There followed several minutes of awkward chatter, as Audrey dished up supper and Estelle lectured everyone on how rude Londoners were compared with people from Essex. Sam noted that the family business stopped being discussed the moment Estelle entered the room.

He had tried his best to like his step-mother, because he knew in his heart she wasn't a bad person. She was always polite to his mother and genuinely seemed to love his father, and not just for his money (although she obviously did love money). And he also knew she wasn't responsible for his parents' divorce. In fact, she didn't meet Howard until months after their separation. But the media had still labelled her a home wrecker and gold digger and, shamefully, his father had never publicly denied those accusations. Howard's damning silence was something, Sam suspected, which had hurt Estelle deeply but she had never complained.

So he just took her for what she was: an ageing Essex girl who'd failed to marry a footballer and so landed one of the UK's richest businessmen instead. As she happily chatted away, Sam's mind began to wander to the early days of Estelle and Howard's relationship. In particular, he recalled the events which followed that infamous night when they had appeared in public together for the first time. They had eaten dinner at The Ivy and Howard had given into pressure from his Head of PR and agreed for a number of photographers to be there as they arrived. Estelle had been keen to make an impression and do Essex proud. But she'd worn a bit too much make-up, and her tan was a bit too dark, and her hair had been set a bit too solidly making it look like a large wig. Her heels had made her seem almost as tall as his colossus of a father, and she had waved her hand too close to the cameras making it seem out of proportion with the rest of her body. A few unflattering press photos later, and the rumours that Estelle was a transsexual had followed her ever since. Her failure to deliver another heir to the Harvey fortune had, in the eyes of a disapproving public, added more fuel to the fire. And as Sam sat and listened to whatever it was Estelle was saying, his gaze became fixated on her neck. He thought he could see something moving up and down, a lump in her throat. And he began to worry that his father's unease about Project Ear was not entirely related to the newspaper.

5

VALERIE PIERCE ALWAYS enjoyed tea at the Ritz. It wasn't because of the grand opulence of the tea room, or the attentive, well-mannered waiters. It wasn't even for the fine china or the quality of the sandwiches and cakes. She simply enjoyed looking down her nose at the other guests. And, oh, how she hated them. She hated the foreign tourists (particularly the Americans) who wanted to try something typically English, but then wasted their sitting by stealthily taking pictures on their phones when the waiters weren't looking.

Then there were the working class families who couldn't really afford the Ritz but who, she assumed, had flogged all their DVD boxsets to pay for a special day out. She hated how they would sit quietly in their best clothes, unable to glean any enjoyment from the experience because they found it all so intimidating. And then, of course, there were the theatre-goers. Valerie loathed them the most. She hated how they would swan in like they owned the place, with the sort of bravado that came from too many coach trips to London. But once at their table the veil would quickly drop and they would spend the rest of their sitting looking surprised and impressed with everything, even the cutlery.

Four women at a nearby table (on their way to *Les Mis*, Valerie suspected) reacted with such awe when the waiter delivered their tiered sandwich stand that she couldn't hold her tongue. "Oh for goodness sake," she muttered, only partially under her breath, "You'd think they'd never seen a bloody sandwich before".

Audrey was sitting opposite with a small pair of reading specs balanced on the end of her nose, looking through Valerie's media plan for the *Amazing People Awards*. "Play nicely, dear," she chirped. "The tourists keep this place open."

Valerie sipped her tea. Audrey was one of the few people – the *very* few people – that she could never bring herself to criticise. They'd known each other for the better part of 25 years, and although they couldn't exactly class themselves as friends, they certainly were more than just acquaintances. Her allegiance to Audrey was one of the reasons she had never accepted any of the lunch invitations from Estelle. And from time to time, Audrey's insights into the rich and famous had proven incredibly useful. Through her charity work and social scene she was always bumping into celebrities, politicians and royalty and would happily share her views on how people looked or behaved. Usually, those stories would give Valerie some valuable ideas for her column.

"I've bumped it up a gear," Valerie said, talking business again. "We need to work a little harder, what with it being on Channel 5."

"Yes, this is good." Audrey put the paperwork back into her bag and slipped her glasses away too. "It's going to be tricky this year," she admitted. "Sam was even talking about dropping the *Ear*'s brand for the event."

Valerie shrugged. "It is what it is," she said. "We've been knocked back before, and we always come back stronger than ever. This little farce won't last long."

"Farce?"

"Oh, of course," Valerie purred. "Adam Jaymes, taking on the *Daily Ear* for the good of the British people? Oh please! We're an easy target at the moment because of this bloody inquiry. He's just jumping on the bandwagon, trying to score some cheap publicity for himself.

You mark my words, the public will wise up to what he's doing and once all this is over his career will be dead in the water. The *Daily Ear* will still be here."

Audrey wished she could be as confident. But the previous night's conversation had left her feeling uneasy. And that morning, perhaps foolishly, she had visited the Project Ear website hoping it would put her mind at ease. She was searching for reassurance, for something to suggest that Sam was right and it was little more than a childish quarrel. Instead, she had come face to face with the reality of what Adam Jaymes had done to Colin. She had seen the detail with which his affair had been picked apart, the clarity of the secretly taken photographs. But worst of all was the unbridled delight that seeped through every word of the exposé. Whatever Adam's real motivations, he was clearly enjoying doing it.

"Tell me about the office," she said. "How are the staff?"

Valerie sipped her tea and thought for a moment before responding. In her head she had already started to create a narrative on the Project Ear saga, for a book she would write at some point in the future. She liked the idea of it being a war, or at least a great battle. It sounded more dramatic than the reality, which was a lot of people it suits running around like headless chickens and shouting at each other.

"We certainly feel under fire," she said. "There's very much an 'in the trenches' mentality at the moment. But it's been strangely unifying too. It brought all us old soldiers back together. I spoke to people in the company yesterday that I haven't spoken to in years. Years!"

"My enemy's enemy?"

Yes, that. I'll use it. "Something like that," Valerie said.

Audrey ordered a fresh pot of tea and the sandwiches were replaced with cakes. "There's a countdown, you know, on his website."

"Ticking quietly away like a landmine, just waiting for some poor soul to step on it," Valerie replied, and then decided her 'war' analogy had run its course for that conversation. "Yes. It all hits the fan again tomorrow night at 9pm. You know I'm favourite, don't you, to be next on Adam Jaymes' hit list?"

Audrey grinned. "Don't take this the wrong way, dear, but I hope you are. If anyone could brazen this out, it's you."

Valerie laughed out loud and immediately all the other guests turned to look at her, a wall of alarmed faces. 'Was laughter a faux pas in the Ritz?' they all seemed to be thinking. 'Was this woman in the purple suit about to be escorted from the premises?'

Valerie laughed again, just to make a point. "He can print anything he likes," she said to Audrey. "I've lived my life by my own standards. If he wants to criticise those standards, let him. But I've nothing to be ashamed of."

Audrey didn't reply. "You've got nothing to be worried about either, Audrey," Valerie said. "Of course you haven't. Let's face it, the most controversial thing you ever did was marry Howard. And I still suspect you only did that to annoy your father."

With that comment, the mood lifted and they both smiled. "Oh no, my father liked Howard," Audrey said, but then clarified her comment. "Well, he *grew* to like him."

"I wish I'd been a fly on the wall the first time you took him home," Valerie said. "The lanky, working class boy from Ilford visiting the Grosvenor family's historic Norfolk estate. Be honest, your parents were horrified weren't they?"

"To be fair I think they were perplexed more than horrified," Audrey said. "Howard was so handsome back then, in the seventies. I think that's the first thing my mother saw when we walked in. A very handsome young man, trying his hardest to fit in. She could see why I liked him."

"But your father?"

"Daddy took him shooting. I thought for a moment I'd never see poor Howard again. He was useless with a gun, of course. But he knew how to talk business, had a real passion for it even then. By the time they came home that evening, I think my father was a little enamoured with him too."

Valerie had interviewed Audrey's father once, years ago, for a series of features about fox hunting. She remembered him being very old and very polite. Helpfully, he had also been willing to say anything Valerie wanted so long as the article backed the campaign against the Hunting Act. "Your father was a very fair man," Valerie said.

Audrey was silent. She had never been one to over-share, and was certainly not prone to melodrama. But as her expression changed ever so slightly, hinting at a sadness that she was far too proud to admit, Valerie realised that she still mourned her old life as Mrs Howard Harvey. "It's a blessing they're not here, Mummy and Daddy," Audrey said, pouring from the tea pot that had just been delivered to the table. "I think it would have broken their hearts to know that we're not together anymore."

Suddenly, their quiet moment of reflection was shattered. A fierce young woman had spotted them from the corridor, marched over to their table and started yelling at Valerie. A stream of insults was fired so rapidly from the woman's mouth that, at first, it was difficult to gauge precisely what offence Valerie had caused.

Audrey sipped her tea, as though nothing was happening, and then started to pick at a French fancy. Valerie stared at the young woman, trying to place her. But she had the generic look of many minor female celebrities – long blonde hair, dark tan, big boobs and tight clothes. She could be from *TOWIE*, Valerie thought. But then she might also be a WAG or someone from *Hollyoaks* or the *X-Factor*. It was so hard to tell these days.

Valerie listened hard to what the woman was shouting and just managed to distinguish the words 'bitch', 'lies' and 'bitch' (again). The waiters didn't quite know what to do, and Valerie noticed one slip away to find the manager. "I'm sorry," Valerie said, loudly, interjecting during one brief moment when the woman had paused for breath, "but who are you again?"

"Who am I? You absolute monster!" the woman screeched. "You write an entire page attacking my husband and me, ridiculing our wedding, the most important and ... and *wonderful* day of my life ... and then you don't even have the decency to remember my name. How many people's lives have you tried to ruin that you can't even remember what your victims look like?"

Valerie tried to recall the last time she had written about someone's wedding. Was this one of those *dreadful* little trollops from *Big Brother*? "I'm sure whatever I wrote was meant in good faith," she said, and then waved her hand as if to send the woman away.

But that gesture was the final straw. The woman saw a sparkling glass of champagne nearby, the theatre-goers at that table enjoying the show. She picked it up and tossed the contents directly into Valerie's face. "Have a drink on me, you evil witch!" she screeched and stormed out, tweeting as she went. The tea room erupted into conversation as the manager appeared and apologised for what had just happened. A waiter brought napkins for Valerie to dry herself, and the group at the nearby table were given a complimentary bottle of champagne.

"It would be nice, dear," Audrey said "if we could get through at least one meal without a complete stranger throwing a drink in your face."

Valerie mopped her cheeks. "Hmmm," she said, "I think this champagne is burned."

Sam looked around his new office and was already missing the space, sunshine and technology of the one he'd left behind in Los Angeles. He knew it was likely to be the largest office in the building but it was half the size of his old one. And although the heavily textured glass walls afforded him some privacy, they still left him feeling exposed.

His introductions with the executive team had been mostly routine, but he was surprised at how reassured they all were by having a *Harvey* in the building again. Even Twigg, who Sam had never liked, had met him with a smile and been thoroughly supportive during his morning of back-to-back meetings. He had escorted Sam around the building, and covered all the tricky questions before it became obvious that Sam didn't know the answers.

One of the senior team had even suggested Sam's presence had given back to the company some "much needed gravitas". But Sam didn't like the word gravitas. He worried it raised expectations around him undeservedly. He stood at his large window and stared at the view. The view was OK, he decided, overlooking the Thames and with Canary Wharf in the distance. He hadn't realised how striking London's skyline had become over the past 10 years.

A knock at the door brought his attention back inside the room. "Come in," he said. A young woman entered, carrying some files. He had met her earlier when she had made him a coffee. "These are all the cuttings we have on Adam Jaymes and the more recent cuttings on Project Ear," she said, and placed them on his desk.

"Thank you," he said and then cautiously added, "... Miss Snow?"

She smiled. "That's it. Well done, Mr Harvey! But you can call me Felicity."

He returned her smile. "There is one thing I am a bit confused by," he admitted. He sat at his laptop and clicked opened his calendar. "I seem to have lots of appointments in my diary already. I'm pretty much solidly booked for the next two months."

Felicity nodded. "Because Mr Perera left so suddenly, I transferred all his appointments to you. I thought we could go through them together and I can cancel those which you don't think are necessary."

Sam was still perplexed. "But none of them are anything to do with the business," he said. "They're all seminars and conferences, and restaurant bookings or gallery openings, or theatre trips. He's got all sorts of meetings with all sorts of people, but I can't work out how any of them are related to his role as chief executive."

During her internship, Felicity spent a month in the chief executive's office and had quickly come to the same conclusion about Gayesh. But she also knew, as an intern, it wasn't her place to talk down a member of staff. "He did get invited to an awful lot of events," she said, "and so that was his diary for the coming few months."

Sam dropped his face into his open palms and released a disapproving groan. "Oh dear lord. No wonder things got into such a mess. How on earth did he run a company of this size when he was never bloody here?" he asked. He flopped back into his chair and stared at the ceiling. The company had needed leadership, but all the evidence suggested Gayesh had done little else during his five years as chief executive but schmooze people he thought could get him a seat in the Lords. He sat up and looked at Felicity, who had taken the chair opposite him and was waiting with a notebook and pen in hand. "I'm sorry," he said. "But this is so frustrating."

Felicity could tell he was reaching out to her, trying to engage her in a conversation. Intern or not, she realised he was looking for an early ally to give him the truth about the way his predecessor had run things. "I think Mr Perera saw himself as the public face of Harvey News Group," she said, softly. "I think he saw his role as being very outward-facing, and he left the day-to-day business to the rest of the executive team."

Sam looked at Felicity, "And no one ever complained that he wasn't doing any work?"

Felicity shrugged and shook her head. "If you want me to be very honest, Mr Harvey, I think the executive team liked having him out of the way. It meant they could get on with running things. Whenever he was here, I think they felt he was very much under their feet."

Secretly, Sam felt a little relieved. Perhaps stepping into Gayesh's shoes wasn't going to be so difficult. All he needed to do was provide a degree of leadership, draw up some clear red lines for the organisation and offer Twigg his help with the fallout from Project Ear. But overall, he just needed to keep a respectful distance from the executive team so they could continue running the show. Sam knew his head still wasn't in the right place, and so asked Felicity for a cup of coffee so he could have a few moments to himself. He then sat quietly in his new office, wondering how long it had taken the facilities team to strip away any remnants of his predecessor. Not long, he guessed. He doubted Gayesh had ever really committed to it as a work space. For Gayesh it seemed the city of London and all of its facilities had been his work space.

Sam had always admired his father's judgement, that amazing ability to walk into a room of a hundred graduates and spot a future business leader. Howard rarely ever poached from other companies because he liked to find raw talent, and then invest his time and money to produce a new star. They weren't always young or clever or well educated. They were often just people who had talent and were still looking for that lucky break. Sam knew the list. It had started with Twigg, Howard's first major find; hired straight from Cambridge and put in charge of a group of local papers that formed the original parts of the Harvey News Group. Twigg quickly showed an astonishing aptitude for understanding his readers and driving up sales, and was moved into the major league the moment Howard bought the *Daily Ear* in 1983. The paper was the company's first major purchase, and at the time was a failing national daily that was considered little more than a pale imitation of the *Sun* and the *Mail*. Howard sacked pretty much everyone at the top and handed Twigg the editorship. Twigg and the *Daily Ear* turned out to be a match made in heaven.

Colin had been one of Howard's discoveries too, in the early days of the *Daily Ear*. He had been a young trainee reporter who no one would take seriously, until he exchanged a few pleasantries with Howard during a brief journey in a lift and (according to Howard) that was all it took. Colin was fast-tracked through the system and within a couple of years had been transformed into one of Fleet Street's most sought-after newshounds. And as the years went by, Howard found dozens of other unknowns and turned them into industry stars, including the likes of Valerie Pierce and Jason Spade.

His latest find had been Oonagh Boyle. He came across her during a weekend break with Estelle in Dublin. Howard had been queuing in a coffee shop and heard Oonagh chatting to a friend about a web strategy she was writing for a children's charity. He followed her out of the shop and, after a 10-minute conversation in the middle of the street, offered her a job with a six-figure salary and relocation expenses. It was a great story that both Howard and Oonagh had repeated in various trade press interviews, and so Sam had always assumed it was at least mostly true.

But Gayesh hadn't been one of Howard's. He'd been hired during one of Harvey Media International's more turbulent periods when Howard had been abroad, juggling too many balls. He had allowed himself to be pressured into a quick appointment and so agreed for an outside firm to run the selection process. Sam knew that, in retrospect, the process had been too long and complicated and had relied heavily on generic point scoring and automated responses. Howard had not been able to play a meaningful role and just waved it all through, giving his long-distance approval. Perhaps, Sam wondered, his father was simply too proud to admit his mistake and so had allowed Gayesh to coast for all these years.

Felicity returned with his coffee and sat back down, notebook in hand again.

"You look poised to do some work," Sam said and smiled. "Are you my PA?"

"Actually, I'm just an intern" she replied. "But Mr Perera's PA resigned yesterday, when she heard Mr Perera had left. And so Mr Twigg asked me to work with you until a replacement is appointed."

"How long have you been here?"

"Six months."

"And you've worked across the company?"

"Yes, I've had placements in quite a few of the departments."

An intern? Brilliant! Smart, work ethic, keen, and months of experience of how all the departments at the *Daily Ear* operate. That was exactly what Sam wanted to hear. "Felicity, I'll be relying on you quite a bit in the coming weeks," he said. "Just until I've settled in of course."

Felicity didn't know it, but she had just been enlisted into Sam's *London* team.

There was a knock, and another member of the executive floor's support staff poked his head around the door. "Sorry to bother you," he said, "but there's a barber here for Mr Perera."

Sam glanced at Felicity. "Barber?"

"It's a traditional Turkish barber," she replied. "Wet shave, hot towels, head massage. Mr Perera said it helped him think."

Sam's mouth was slightly open, and for a moment he thought he might just laugh at the ridiculous extent of Gayesh's self-indulgence. But then Felicity added, "It's booked and paid for, Mr Harvey. It seems a shame to waste the appointment."

And so Sam spent the next hour using the time to think.

6

"GAYESH WAS A lazy, status-driven freeloader." Sam poured himself another glass of wine and glared at his father across the table. Howard could tell his son was trying to instigate a row and, he suspected, had wanted to do so since being ordered back to the UK. And although he liked these occasional flashes of passion from his usually composed boy, he wasn't enjoying being chastised in his own home within earshot of his wife.

Estelle had nipped out to the roof terrace for a cigarette. She had always thought Gayesh was a waste of space, and Howard knew she would be thrilled that someone was finally agreeing with her. "He did the job," Howard said. "And when he stopped doing the job, I fired him. End of."

With more than a hint of exasperation is his voice, Sam replied. "And at what point did he do the job, Dad? Seriously, have you seen his diary? It's like we gave him a five-year paid holiday."

"I know, I know," Howard said, his hand raised to signal the conversation was definitely drawing to an end. "I've seen his diary. His PA emailed it to me last week by accident. It's one of the reasons he left without a fight." He stood up and started to clear away the dinner plates. He'd cooked his famous pork belly roast as a welcome home for Sam and was a little deflated after Estelle and Sam had eaten it without much comment. It usually provoked great enthusiasm from dinner guests. Clearly, he thought, his wife and son had been spoiled by too much fine dining in expensive restaurants.

"Dad, I'm not going to labour the point," Sam said, "but I'm going to review all the senior staff over the coming week. Any under-performers, and they'll go the same way as Gayesh." He was pleased to have the chance to talk about sacking people. It presented an image he knew his father would appreciate, a toughness he doubted Howard – or, indeed, anyone else – would think he owned. It also pleased Sam to highlight Gayesh's shortcomings, and deflect the conversation away from his own performance.

The layout of Howard and Estelle's modern, open plan apartment meant the conversation could continue uninterrupted as Howard cleared away the main course and brought in the dessert and coffee. "You do whatever you need to do," Howard said. "You know who my untouchables are but everyone else is fair game. It might do the company some good to give everyone a shake up." And then, with a mischievousness tone in his voice, Howard added, "Oh, and that's a nasty nick you've got behind your ear, son. Shaving cut?"

Sam automatically raised his hand to cover the red mark where the barber had caught him earlier that day. "Just a little gash. It was a Turkish," he said, defensively.

"Really? And when did you find time to get out of the office for that, then?"

Sam knew he'd been rumbled and just shook his head and sighed. "It was a one-off," he said, "just a one-off."

Estelle finished her cigarette break and tottered back in from the roof terrace. "Aw, lovely view of Hyde Park this evening," she said. "You know, sometimes I think it's almost worth being addicted to cigarettes just for that view."

"Disgusting habit," Howard muttered, and grimaced.

Estelle ignored him. "So have you boys finished talking business?" she trilled. "Because I wasn't ear-wigging, but I'm sure I heard someone mention Gayesh's name in the same sentence as the word 'lazy'."

Sam chuckled at his step-mother's helplessly unsubtle approach to gossip. "I was just telling Dad that I agree with everything you ever said about Gayesh."

"I never took to him," she declared, "and it wasn't because he was Indian. But I'm out and about a lot during the day, all my charities and events. And you can only bump into a man so many times before you start to wonder why he's never at work." She sipped her coffee and then smiled at them both. "Anyway, more to the point: who's Adam Jaymes going to do next?" She put down her cup and leaned forward as though they were all girls together about to have a big gossip.

"Oh for God's sake, Estelle!" exclaimed Howard, appalled at his wife's gossipy nature.

"It's a reasonable question," she responded, still smiling. "That story about Colin caused a lot of problems. I received so many text messages I had to switch my phone off. And I've never had to do that before."

"Actually Dad, Estelle is making a valid point," Sam said, prompting Estelle to pull her 'I told you so' face at Howard. "I had to spend an hour with our HR director this afternoon. There's been a massive increase in calls to the company's counselling line, and thirteen people have quit since *Newsnight*. Everyone's terrified."

"Sounds like Colin's not the only person at the *Daily Ear* with a secret to hide," Estelle said, and spooned a large chunk of New York cheesecake into her mouth.

"I need to work on our lines with Derek Toulson," Sam continued. "I've agreed that we're going to have individual reputation management plans in place for as many potential stories as we can. But I can't do that unless I know what the specific risks are."

"Well, I can tell you that Valerie Pierce is top of the list to be next. I saw that on the *Holy Moly* email," Estelle said, proud to share her knowledge with the table. "And she looks the sort to have a few skeletons in her closet."

"Estelle!" Howard yelled, frustrated that his wife didn't appear to take the situation seriously.

"Well, she does," Estelle replied. "She does. Just look at her."

Howard went quiet, and started pushing his dessert around his plate. Sam and Estelle exchanged glances, as both realised he was keeping something to himself.

"Dad, I find it hard to believe there is any part of Valerie's life that she hasn't written about already," Sam said. "I mean, the woman's shared the intimate details of her father's alcoholism and her husband's death and her estranged daughter and the mother-in-law who hated her. If there's anything she hasn't shared with her readers, it's got to be pretty damning. And I've only got 24 hours to prepare for it."

"I need to know too," snapped Estelle.

"No you don't," Howard replied. But then he sighed, and nodded. "Estelle, you keep your gob shut about this. Not a word to *anyone* about what I'm about to tell you."

Estelle smiled and then ran her fingers across her lips, as though zipping her mouth closed.

"It was a few years ago - " Howard started.

Felicity could feel a tension in the air the moment she set foot through the door of the Cock and Bull. It was dark and grimy and, all these years after the smoking ban, it somehow still stank of stale cigarettes. She could imagine that at one time the pub would have been beautiful with its etched glass, crystal chandeliers, art deco lamps and hand-carved mahogany details.

But at some point in its history, possibly in the eighties when all the papers had started to leave Fleet Street, it had gone downhill. It reeked of decades of neglect and despair. There was a general rumble of conversation from the customers, a small group of men in their forties or fifties. Most of them looked as though the spent far too much time at the bar, and none seemed pleased to see Felicity in their pub.

A younger man behind the bar gestured towards her with his hand and then pointed to the creaky wooden door on the other side of the pub leading to the snug. She realised he was the one who had called the news desk, to warn them of the potential problem. She nodded at him, a slight gesture of thanks, and then gripped the strap to her shoulder bag and walked through the crowd of customers towards the door. As she caught sight of their confused, angry and surprised expressions she wondered whether it was her age, gender or skin colour that was causing offence. Or perhaps all three.

Once through the door she found Colin sitting alone at a tall table, an array of empty pint glasses in front of him. He was half collapsed, his chin only just propped up by one hand. In his day, seven pints of ale would have been a breeze. But after a few years of more sensible drinking, seven pints had wiped him out. A massive flat screen television was on the wall next to the bar, looking ridiculously out of place against the historic furnishings of the room. It was tuned to *Sky News* and the volume was muted, but she could see the presenters were discussing Project Ear with Hugh Grant.

Felicity quietly pulled herself up onto the stool next to Colin and gently prodded him to see if he was asleep. Almost immediately he sat up and, bleary eyed, looked at her. "Mr Merroney, it's me. Felicity. Remember? I'm the intern."

He stared at her for a moment, his brow raised, and then he belched. For a second, Felicity thought he was going to follow up with some sick. But then his expression settled down and he looked as though he knew what was going on. "I thought Valerie was coming," he said, carefully pronouncing each syllable so as not to sound too drunk.

"Mrs Pierce is in a meeting, but is going to meet us back at your hotel. But she asked me to come and collect you. I have a car waiting outside."

Colin screwed up his face, like a child who was on the verge of a sulk. Even though his evening had dissolved into a weepy, intoxicated haze he had still expected Valerie to show up. "She doesn't want to be seen with me in public?" he asked, one syllable at a time again.

Felicity didn't like being around people who were seriously drunk. She knew how unpredictable they could be. And this one, this drunken man who was almost old enough to be her grandfather, looked ready to either vomit over her or grab at her boobs. "No, she's going to meet us at your hotel," she repeated, reassuringly. For a moment, it looked as though Colin was going to stagger to his feet and leave with her. But instead he put his head back to the table and passed out, a line of dribble rolling down his chin. Felicity looked around the empty snug and was relieved no one else was there.

"Valerie was driving home from some party with her two little granddaughters in the back seat. She misjudged a corner and hit the kerb. Nothing major, but she was spotted by a couple of policemen in a patrol car. They pulled her over and she was breathalysed. Turns out she'd had a few too many glasses of wine and was twice the legal limit. Let's be fair, it's easily done."

"Yes, but that's not the point, Dad," Sam replied. "Valerie's job is all about waving her middle class morality in everyone's face, and alcohol abuse is a major bugbear for her. Look what she did to Pearl Martin."

"The point," Howard continued, "is that if there's going to be a story about Valerie, that's going to be it."

Estelle had, in truth, been hoping for something a little more salacious. But she understood why it could be so damaging. "I've never heard this story," she said. "How come it was never in the papers?"

"Twigg pulled a few strings with the police," Howard said, a slight hint of pride in his tone. "He managed to get the case moved to a little magistrates' court in the middle of nowhere. There was only one local newspaper, a little weekly advertiser. We owned it. So Toulson called the editor and told him that if he valued his job, he wouldn't send any reporters to court that day."

"But what happened to Valerie?" Estelle asked, wondering if the three-times winner of *Female Columnist of the Year* had secretly done time.

"It was a first offence," Howard replied. "The prosecution went on and on about her having her granddaughters in the car, but Valerie said all the right things to the magistrates and avoided anything serious. She was fined, banned for a couple of years. Nothing major."

Sam sighed a loud, depressed sigh. "So in that one story, we have Valerie drink-driving with two children in the car, a senior police officer *presumably* taking a bung to move the case out of the city, and our own PR director threatening to sack a local newspaper editor to stop the case from being reported."

Howard nodded, getting a little irritated by his son's critical tone. "Yes, that just about sums it up. But that police officer is now Assistant Commissioner with the Met Police. He's done very well over the years because of us. And that newspaper editor is now one of your chief sports reporters on the *Ear*. It was win-win for everyone."

"From our point of view, yes," Sam said. "But Toulson knows all about this already. He was involved."

"It's one of the corporate actions he's aware of, yes. And before you ask, Valerie knows it's probably one of the stories that Adam Jaymes has lined up. Toulson's with her now. They're working on her statement together."

"But Dad, I should know this," Sam said. He could feel his temper beginning to build again. It wasn't a sensation he was used to, but something about Toulson always brought out the worst in him. "He should have told me this today when we met. I can't protect the company, or its staff, if he keeps me in the dark on major reputational risks like this." He was suddenly aware that his voice was getting high pitched and was worried he was sounding too much like a whiney little boy. He decided to take it down a notch or two and quickly returned to a more appropriate tone. "I will have another word with him tomorrow," he said. "I will make it perfectly clear that I am the *only* Harvey he will be dealing with from now on. But *you* need to respect that as well, Dad. I haven't moved five thousand miles to sit there like a child with all the adults in the room talking over my head. I'm chief executive. Toulson reports to me."

"It's up to you to make them all believe that, Sam," Howard replied, and a cold expression crossed his face. "If they still ring me, ask for my advice or help, that's because you're not stepping up. This is about you proving you have influence, and showing that it makes a difference to *them* that you're at the top table."

"I proved myself already," Sam retorted. "Ten years in LA, and I - "

"The Harvey Network proved itself," Howard interrupted. "And it's true that no one phoned me to complain about you. But no one picked up the phone to tell me you were doing a good job either. All I had was a chart showing our figures going up. That doesn't mean a thing."

Sam didn't respond, as a horrible truth began to dawn on him. Everything he had brought back from America with him, the modicum of success he felt he could call his own, it was all for nothing.

"You *didn't* prove yourself in LA because I will tell you when you are proving yourself," Howard continued, his booming voice now echoing around the apartment. "And this is it. Now, here in London. *This* is where you prove yourself."

Sam's heart was pounding. He couldn't believe what his father was saying. All the things Sam had secretly thought about himself, all the things he had tried to keep hidden, Howard was saying it all out loud. He had seen through Sam's accomplishments and realised the truth: his son was not a great leader but had simply been in charge when great things had happened.

"*This* is where you prove yourself," Howard said again, but more quietly. Estelle was giving him the evils from the other end of the table, not impressed that he was so brutally scolding the step-son she adored.

"Oh, you Harvey boys and your testosterone," she declared, trying to lighten the mood. "You'll be out on the terrace next, having a sword fight."

But Sam knew the conversation needed to be closed properly. "I don't agree with what you're saying, Dad," he said. "But you will have your proof."

And Howard allowed a small hint of a smile to nudge the side of his mouth, a little gesture to let his son know he was still in the game. "Estelle and I are heading to New York tomorrow," he said. "We're not due back in London until your mother's awards evening. I don't expect to have to cut our trip short and come back early."

The awards were only a couple of weeks away. Surely, Sam thought, he could hold the fort for two weeks.

"So, now you two have had your little squabble and let off a bit of heat, can we get back to the story?" Estelle asked. "What exactly is going to be Valerie's excuse for driving drunk?"

Sam waved his hand towards his dad, offering him the floor again.

"The day of the party, her husband has been diagnosed with cancer," Howard said. "And she was so frightened by the news she simply miscounted how much wine she'd drunk."

"Oh, the poor thing," Estelle said.

"So if Adam Jaymes does pick on Valerie, we'll have a statement ready and a feature. It's going to be our own exclusive. You know the sort of thing. 'How the support of my family brought me through some very dark days'. Cancer victims are always sympathetic."

"And is that true?" Sam asked. "That was the day her husband found out he had cancer?"

Howard winked at him. "It was around about that time," he said, and then popped a big chunk of cheesecake into his mouth.

Felicity and her driver helped Colin to his room. The staff at the budget hotel had seen far worse things than a man so drunk he could barely walk, and little attention was paid to him. Valerie had arrived a few moments earlier and sat quietly in the lobby. She followed them to his room, waited until Colin was on his bed, and then sent the others away with a softly whispered 'thank you'. She used the little plastic kettle to boil some water and made a couple of strong coffees, before gently piling all the available pillows behind Colin so he could sit up and sip his drink.

"I thought you'd stood me up," he said, only half awake.

"Of course I didn't, darling," Valerie replied, perched on the edge of the bed. She gently pushed the hair from his sweaty forehead. "We're all in the same boat, aren't we? The old guard, under attack. We have to stick together."

Colin just wanted to sleep. Unconsciousness was a far more appealing place to be. He could feel his body shutting down, his mind winding to a close for the day and his dark little hotel room was drawing in around him. But he was reassured by Valerie's presence. She was the first familiar face he'd seen since *Newsnight*, the first sign that he may still have friends willing to be seen with him. So he sipped his coffee and endeavoured to stay in the room with his friend. She had made an effort to come and see him and was perhaps even risking her reputation, being alone in a hotel with a known adulterer. But she didn't seem to care, as she sat holding her cup in both hands and looking at him with a warm smile that few people ever saw.

"You being here, it means a lot," Colin said and smiled back at her, accidentally allowing a trickle of coffee to dribble down his chin. Valerie placed both their cups on the side and then pulled a packet of tissues from her handbag and wiped his face. She had come to the hotel ready to give him a bit of a ticking off, for exposing himself to further risk by getting drunk in the Cock and Bull. It would only have taken one stray reporter from another newspaper to wander in through the door, she thought, and what an exclusive that would have been. Thank goodness the bar manager had the sense to give the *Ear*'s news desk a call. But her drunken friend, vulnerable and alone, was in no fit state for anything and so she watched as he quickly fell asleep.

She had always been fond of him, the little boy with the man's voice. They had joined the *Ear* at about the same time and had both been keen to make their mark. But whereas Valerie had always been able to swan into a room and demand respect, even in the sexist newsrooms of the eighties, Colin had put up with years of ridicule and mean-spirited pranks from the older reporters. Valerie remembered him as a very young man rushing up to his news editor, all bright-eyed and bushy-tailed, with his first genuine exclusive kiss-and-tell. "And I can prove it," he had announced proudly, "it's true!" The news editor had just returned from a match and had a football rattle on his desk, which he immediately starting whirling around his head, shouting "True story alert! True story alert!", creating a roar of laughter across the newsroom. But Colin never allowed the other staff to get him down and so just laughed along with them all. He even adopted the rattle as his own and started to whirl it around his head shouting "True story alert!" whenever he had a story he thought he could actually substantiate. And Valerie knew that same rattle still sat on the news desk next to him as a constant reminder of the obstacles he had to overcome. Only now when Colin used it there was no longer laughter but good humoured cheering from across the newsroom.

And that was the quality Valerie had first seen in Colin, his amazing capacity to bounce back. She had liked his drive and his positive energy, and the fact that his poor background had given him a desire to do better than his parents. Week after week she had watched from the sidelines as he had put his ridiculers to shame. He got people to talk who wouldn't talk to anyone else. He pulled information out of the air that no one else had been able to get. He somehow managed to manoeuvre around any obstructions, closed doors or deceptions and get to the heart of a story, whether the subject of that story wanted him to or not. His work ethic had been second to none and he had been willing to do almost anything to get ahead of the field. And despite the best attempts of countless news editors and senior reporters to take credit for his work, Howard noticed Colin and he soon joined Valerie in the Harvey family's inner circle. By his 21st birthday, Colin had been promoted above his own managers and became one of the paper's highest paid members of staff. But money didn't seem to matter to Colin. Yes, he bought himself a nice house but only because he felt it was the grown-up thing to do (and it certainly pleased his parents). In reality, though, his job was all that really counted.

Colin had married his career many years earlier. As far as Valerie had been concerned, Fiona was as much Colin's mistress as the middle-aged trollop he'd be banging in every Premier Inn across the UK. Colin had never been interested in anything beyond good dinner conversation and casual sex. But then, completely out of the blue, along had come Fiona. Valerie had been surprised by their sudden marriage and had secretly wondered if Colin's proposal had been driven by some sort of midlife crisis as much as his desire to do the right thing. Either way, she had always suspected he was going to struggle with fidelity. And within weeks of his marriage she had noticed he was already finding it difficult to balance his work life with his unexpected home life. He hadn't tried to reduce his long hours, or modify his ever-changing shifts, or say no to the last minute instructions to jet off to some god-awful, back-of-beyond to find a celebrity who was misbehaving. And Valerie had suspected there were other parts of Colin's 'old life' he might not have completely surrendered either. Adam Jaymes' exposé, whilst terrible, hadn't been a surprise to her.

She didn't think badly of Colin for having sex outside of his marriage. In fact, she had always told her female readers never to pursue their suspicions if a husband appeared to be playing away from home. *"Isn't it a dark secret we all have to face at some point in our lives,"* she had written, *"that a successful marriage might last because of a husband's infidelity, and not in spite of it?"* But she had been disappointed with the circumstances of Colin's affair, and found it an unnecessary complication to have cheated with his best friend's wife. "Silly boy," she said to him, as he lay asleep next to her. "You have an expense account. That's what hookers are for." She looked around the plain, economy offering of the London hotel and saw a digital alarm clock on the other side of the bed. Its large red counter was at four minutes past midnight. It was Friday. Adam Jaymes' second victim had less than 24 hours left. "Come and get me, you bastard," she whispered. "I'm ready for you."

7

"EXPLAIN IT TO me," Twigg demanded, and stared at Oonagh who was sitting on the other side of his desk. Annoyingly, for Twigg, she didn't flinch or stumble for words. She simply stared back at him with that contented expression that always hinted at pity. Twigg was in no mood for Oonagh's composed and thoughtful approach to conversations. He wanted a rise out of her, a bit of passion and fight. He wasn't going to get anywhere if she just sat there, smiling at him. Earlier that morning, he had summoned Felicity into his office and asked her to show him how *dailyear.com* was handling the whole Project Ear story. He was not happy with what he saw. It would appear that life on the *Ear*'s website had continued as normal, to the point where there were a number of articles publicising Adam's upcoming Glee episodes. "Well?" he asked again.

"Leonard, I don't believe it's necessary for me to explain myself to you," Oonagh replied, coolly.

Twigg knew she was daring him, trying to draw him into a conversation he wasn't prepared to have. Not on that day, at least. But he felt it was time for a shot across the bows, to let Oonagh know he was watching her. He knew, however, that she was clever. She was certainly no Gayesh Perera. She wasn't going anywhere, and would not roll over for him. "Right, well let me re-frame that. I do not think it is good for the *Daily Ear*'s website to deviate so completely from our editorial lines. Adam Jaymes is about to publish his second exposé. And yet to look at our website, you'd think we were his PR manager."

Oonagh smiled at him with an expression that made him feel like he was a grandfather who was about to have a video recorder explained to him for the first time. "Leonard, I understand you have trouble grasping even the simplest aspects of the internet and social media. But I would expect you to appreciate the size of the American market. *dailyear.com* now has. I have more readers in the US than the *New York Times* website. I have more than 40 million unique visitors each month, and more and more of those are in the States."

"So?" Twigg responded indifferently as though Oonagh was waffling, avoiding the point.

"Leonard, I'm well aware of this paper's history with Adam Jaymes. But he is incredibly popular both in this country and in the States. His *True Blood* storyline was a huge success, and they're expecting his *Glee* episodes to deliver one of the biggest audience shares they've seen in a long time."

Twigg knew all about Adam's role in *True Blood*. Disgusting! The *Daily Ear* had been quick to criticise his decision to take the role, and the explicit nature of his "gay sex scenes" with Eric the vampire. Valerie had used her column to round on him for betraying "his young British fans, who had followed him each week as Doctor Who's plucky side-kick", and for "leaping gaily into a sordid adult world of explicit sex, violence, foul language and Godless values".

"More than that, his husband also has a very high personal rating with the American public," Oonagh continued. "His companies are considered to be ethical and clean, with some of the best health care benefits in the country. Imagine a young, gay, American version of Richard Branson. Only richer. And good looking. And no weird beard. That's who Adam's married to."

Twigg narrowed his eyes and stared at Oonagh, unhappy at her use of the word 'married'. There, right there, was an unforgiveable difference between the two of them. He would have expected better from a former Catholic school girl. "So, you are saying that my own website is going to be promoting the man who's trying to destroy this paper?"

"No, Leonard, I'm saying that *my* website will cover the story if and when it needs to. But I will not be launching an online campaign against Adam Jaymes. Nor will I stop writing stories about *Glee* just because he's in it. My audience is different to yours, Leonard. It's about time you began to understand that."

By the time Oonagh had finished speaking, Twigg was drumming his fingers on the desk. It was a passive-aggressive gesture that would have most staff at the *Daily Ear* running for cover. Oonagh knew she was supposed to be intimidated, but she'd grown up in a family of men – she had nine uncles and seven older brothers. Leonard Twigg couldn't hold a candle to any of them. "You have very nice finger nails, Leonard," she observed, sweetly. "Where do you have them manicured?"

He stopped drumming and glared across the desk at her. "Do you know the point of a *Daily Ear* story, Oonagh?" he asked. "Do you know what we try to achieve with every single article we print, whether it be a four-page feature or a NIB?"

"As a newspaper I'd imagine, first and foremost, we are trying to inform," Oonagh replied, beginning to sound a little bored by the conversation.

"Wrong!" Twigg snapped. "Completely and utterly wrong."

With a weary sigh, Oonagh slumped back into her chair, shaking her head ever so slightly. "Then please tell me, Leonard, what is the point of a *Daily Ear* story."

"Every single story the *Daily Ear* prints should achieve one of two outcomes. Either it leaves the reader angry about some*thing*, or it leaves them hating some*one*. Any story that leaves a reader happy or optimistic has failed."

Oonagh collected her things and stood up. "You're an idiot," she said, as though stating a fact. "And I don't have time for this nonsense."

Twigg was seething and continued to glare at Oonagh as she casually made her way to the door. "But I think you raise a valid point, Leonard, about the editorial lines of the print and online editions of the *Ear*," she said. "I'm having brunch with Sam in an hour so I'll let him know we had this conversation and take a view from him."

She left the office and closed the door behind her. 'Take a view from him'. The words sat uneasily with Twigg. Oonagh had been clever. She had given the impression she had taken his concerns on board whilst, at the same time, highlighting her working relationship with the new chief executive. He knew what she would do next. She would drop him an email, outlining their conversation and the action she had agreed to. She did that a lot. It made it difficult to catch her out.

Almost without hesitation, Valerie popped through the door and closed it behind her. "So, what does the fat Irish whore have to say for herself?" she asked, and sat down.

"Nothing, as usual," Twigg replied, refusing to acknowledge anything Oonagh had just said to him.

"Well, if this isn't a good time to get rid of her I don't know when is. You might as well take advantage when it's all hitting the fan." Valerie gestured toward their colleagues on the other aside of Twigg's glass wall. "People expect a few heads to roll. I mean, every single bastard sat in that newsroom is expecting this to be my final day. I'm sure Felicity's been asked to do a collection for me, just in case."

Twigg had been asked to contribute to Valerie's leaving collection, but decided to keep that to himself. "We're all set, though," he replied, as reassuringly as he could. "I believe we've got you covered. We're still the biggest selling daily. We're very strongly placed to influence public opinion off the back of anything Jaymes does. They'll look to us to respond, and we will."

"Oh, I'm not worried anymore," Valerie declared, and then relaxed back into the old leather chair and crossed her legs. She was almost excited at the prospect of being Adam Jaymes' next victim, especially since they had already worked out what his exposé would be and prepared for it. "You can explain anything away, if you know how. It's just more difficult when there are other people in the firing line."

"You're talking about Fiona, I assume," Twigg said. "Is there any word?"

Valerie shrugged. "I understand she's left town for now. Colin thinks she's gone to stay with her family in Edinburgh. Apparently she wanted to put as much space between them as she could."

"Is he going to stay at the hotel?"

"Only for a few more days, and then he's moving back to the house. Assuming Fiona hasn't changed all the locks."

"You saw him last night, didn't you?" Twigg enquired. "Still drunk?"

"Oh, beyond drunk, the poor darling," Valerie replied. "But he'll be back at work soon. One of our wounded soldiers hobbling back into battle."

Twigg noticed she had produced a packet of cigarettes, and was restlessly turning it in her hand, as though waiting to be given permission to smoke. But Twigg hated cigarettes. He had banned smoking in the building long before he'd been required to by law, and wasn't about to let Valerie stink out his office. He knew how much the smell would hang in the air, for days afterwards.

"Completely different for me, of course," Valerie continued. "My husband's dead and my daughter stopped talking to me years ago. Who's Adam Jaymes going to offend, my bloody Labrador?"

"Your husband was a good man," Leonard said. And he meant it. Jeremy Pierce had been a Tory MP for two terms under Thatcher and one under Major. A dashing, unrelenting, unapologetic right-winger and the closest thing to a best friend Leonard had ever had. He remembered how proud Jeremy had been at serving in the House of Commons, and his terrible pain at being one of the many Tories swept from power in the Labour landslide of 97. "He would have stood by you, come hell or high-water. He was a man of honour. The sort of MP we don't have nowadays."

"Oh, I know, I know," Valerie said. She had fond memories of Jeremy, and those exciting years she had spent as the wife of an MP. He hadn't been the love of her life, but they'd been great pals and had a perfectly healthy and happy marriage that had served a purpose for both of them. They'd even had a daughter together. She had enormous respect for him as a husband, father and politician and was genuinely heartbroken when he died. "When I was at the hotel last night, looking after Colin, it made me remember how good the pair of you were when Jeremy was dying," she said. "Those dreadful final months and all those car journeys up and down to that blasted NHS hospital. All those hours and days sat at his bedside on that horrible wooden chair, drinking god-awful tea from plastic cups and getting endless text messages from people who couldn't be bothered to actually call. And poor Jeremy was on so many pain killers, it was as if … . well … it was like he was already gone. That brilliant mind of his, all that knowledge and wit. This man I was visiting, this person lying in the hospital bed, well … it was like I was visiting a senile old uncle rather than my husband. I don't think I'd ever felt so lonely."

"I know," Leonard said, partly because he remembered that period of Valerie's life and partly because she had written about it, in great detail, so many times in the eleven years since Jeremy's death. But there was a sadness to her voice which seemed genuine rather than affected and he wondered if she was beginning to feel uneasy at exploiting Jeremy's cancer to explain away a drink-drive conviction.

"I remember all those phone calls, and the visits, and the silly little presents you and Colin sent me to cheer me up, right from the moment Jeremy was diagnosed," Valerie said, and smiled at him. "And it made such a difference to me."

Twigg nodded his head, acknowledging Valerie's gratitude in a typically understated way. He did *angry* very well. And exasperated, and indifferent. But the softer emotions didn't run smoothly for him and he liked to keep all the fluffy stuff at arm's length. He was concerned, however, that Valerie was too confident about that evening's exposé. But he decided not to raise his concern and, instead, make sure she had all the support she needed for whatever was to come, especially if public reaction to her drink-driving conviction was stronger than anticipated. "We had some response to yesterday's column," he said, moving the conversation on. "Have you reviewed it yet?"

She groaned. "Not yet, but I guessed Adam Jaymes' fans might take a short break from bumming each other to send a few emails."

"Actually, it was the section on single mothers that set them off."

"Oh, good lord." Valerie rolled her eyes and slumped back dramatically into the chair. "There are too many bleeding heart liberals in this country who've put single mothers on a pedestal and make a pariah of anyone who dares to take a more critical view. I stand by what I wrote. They need to stop bleating on about how tough they think their life is and take responsibility for their predicament. If you are a single mother it's because you *chose* an unsuitable partner to have a baby with. Deal with it!"

Leonard had always suspected that Valerie secretly enjoyed the notoriety that came with her outspoken opinions. He had seen her, week after week, edge closer to that fine line between valid debate and pure attention-seeking. Valerie always defended her work as a discussion of unpleasant truths, but for many it often seemed she was simply writing whatever would get the greatest reaction. Oonagh had once admitted to Twigg there was a direct link between the level of offence in any of Valerie's columns and the amount of traffic it brought to the website. Angry readers would tweet the column to their followers, who would read it and be equally outraged and then tweet it to their followers too. And the whole time they would unwittingly drive up the hits on *dailyear.com*.

"I think," he said, "that our readers see a significant difference between a woman who's a single mother through divorce, and some squawking, chain-smoking teenager who got knocked up on purpose to get a council house."

Valerie huffed. "So what you are saying is ... ?"

"Well, to be clear, in the future I want you to steer clear of attacking any single mothers who, say, wrote the *Harry Potter* books." Twigg had seen the research. He knew who his readers did and did not want the *Ear* to criticise. And he was enough of a businessman to allow this research to influence some of his editorial decisions.

Of all the people Felicity had met during her time at the *Daily Ear*, Derek Toulson was the one she liked least. She had only spent a few weeks in his PR department and quickly realised it was not the sort of environment where she could ever feel comfortable. Derek's outward charm and good humour masked a vindictive nature, a man who revelled in bullying his staff knowing he exercised just enough influence at the company to get away with almost anything. Felicity had seen him change the team's entire rota at the last minute just to scupper a PR manager's plan to attend a family wedding. She had seen him threaten to sack a press officer if he left before the end of his shift, even though his wife had gone into labour. She had seen him nit-pick over the exact details of compassionate leave and then order a graphic designer back to work less than a week after the death of her father. Usually he would target one person in the department, someone who'd been in his good books for a little too long and who needed to be reminded who was boss. There would follow weeks of vicious personal emails and phone calls and threats of disciplinary action. They would be singled out for degrading comments in team meetings or department emails, until they were barely able to come to work anymore. And then suddenly and unexpectedly they would be restored as one of his favourites, as if nothing had happened. Each member of the team was relieved and grateful for the good days when his venom was aimed at someone else, but terrified of the bad days. Breaking people, Felicity realised, was Derek's hobby.

For the women there was the added risk of sexual harassment. He wasn't a good-looking man: in his mid-forties and of average build with thinning hair and very little by way of a chin. But regardless of this, he would flirt endlessly, aggressively in fact, with his female staff and absolutely expected his interest to be reciprocated. HR had a list of complaints so long that no one even bothered counting anymore. But the high turnover of staff ensured few were there long enough to see their complaints through to the end, and there was never enough cross-over between victims for a joint complaint to be lodged. Felicity was a modest girl who knew she was attractive simply because other people kept telling her she was. But it didn't sit comfortably with her, and she had never enjoyed the attention it brought. Over the years she had developed a façade of plainness which prevented any unwarranted interest and this had somehow enabled her to pass quietly under Derek's radar. He also knew she worked directly with Gayesh, Twigg, Valerie and Colin and so had always afforded her the sort of everyday pleasantries his other staff could only look at in wonder. But Felicity had seen how he behaved towards everyone else in the team and often felt sick with nerves whenever he was in the same room.

As she entered his office to deliver a pile of documents from Sam, she could feel her heart beginning to beat faster. She had hoped he would be busy on the phone or face down in a report. But he wasn't. He was seated at his desk, looking straight at her with a huge friendly grin on his face. Felicity could tell his smile was hiding more than his usual bile. It was the only time he had ever really acknowledged her, and she knew why. Derek was aware that she was working with Sam, and had clearly decided to pay her more attention. Of all the senior staff, she knew the change in management would have alarmed Derek the most. Gayesh had never involved himself in staffing matters, and Derek had kept close enough to Howard to make the other directors think twice about taking him on. But Sam was in charge now, and Derek didn't know him at all. He needed some reassurance about the way their new boss operated, and saw Felicity as his 'in'.

"Hello stranger," he chirped. "Long time, no see."

"Sam's asked if you can look over these and report back to him by 2pm," she said, trying not to let her voice waver and reveal her nerves. She placed the paperwork on his desk, and pulled her hands quickly back to her sides so he wouldn't see them shaking.

"2pm," Derek replied. "Well, I shall do my best."

Felicity turned and went to leave his office as quickly as she could, but he called her back and asked her to sit down for a moment. She did as she was asked, cursing herself for not being a little quicker on her feet as she had headed for the door.

"So, you're working for the new chief exec. How's life on the top floor?" he asked.

"I'm only there some of the time," she replied, trying to sound humble. "But it's good. He's very nice."

There was a brief flash of sourness across Derek's face, as though he had reacted badly to the word 'nice'. But then his smile returned. "Well, you can tell Sam from me that you were a real asset when you worked in the PR team. I'm happy to say that. You worked very hard and did a really good job. I'm more than happy to say that for you."

Felicity knew she was expected to smile and say thank you, but was so anxious that all she could manage was a polite nod.

"I wonder," he said, as though an idea had just popped into his head. "I wonder if you might want to share with Sam some of your experiences of working in the PR team."

"Goodness," Felicity thought to herself. "*Really?*"

"I put you onto quite a few very interesting projects, as I recall. I think it would be terrific if Sam could hear from someone like you about the important work we do here. Beyond the day job, I mean."

Against her best efforts, Felicity could feel herself complying and nodding her head. She hadn't wanted to. She had wanted to just sit there and stare in obvious amazement at his cheek. But her internship was important and she knew she couldn't do anything that would put it at risk.

"Perhaps you could tell him about the community investment scheme that I run," he suggested. "Pound-for-Pound. I think you gave some support for that, didn't you? It's a great scheme. There are hundreds of community projects up and down the UK that have benefitted from our investment. And you can't buy that sort of goodwill."

Felicity managed a smile and nodded again. "Of course," she said. And then she lied. "I really enjoyed my time here. It was a really fascinating part of my internship. I'll make sure Sam knows all about the Pound-for-Pound scheme." She left Derek's office feeling degraded. And as she walked past the grey, unhappy faces of her former colleagues, she felt ashamed at having put her own needs ahead of the team.

During his time in LA, Sam had returned home to London regularly and during every visit Audrey had spoilt him rotten. And so, in retrospect, he should have realised there would be more to a lunchtime visit from his mother than a cup of tea and a chat. She had turned up with a picnic hamper filled with homemade food including cakes, breads, tortilla, potato salad, a very solid chicken and ham pie and a flask of tea. As they sat happily chatting and eating, Audrey had updated him on family and friends and talked about her charity work and other projects. But he could tell there was something bothering her and guessed she was waiting for the right moment to ask about the previous night's row with his father. She would know about it, of course. Sam knew Howard would have called her first thing to tell her all about it. After all those years, his father still appeared to be a little fearful of Audrey's sharp tongue and would rather she hear about their exchange from him rather than Sam. "Are you keeping your father up to date with everything you're doing?" she eventually asked, casually. "I think he likes to know what's going on." Sam smiled at his mother, a big funny smile, and she frowned at him. "What's that for?" she asked.

"You," he replied. "I could tell you were waiting to ask me something. I guess Dad told you about our row."

"Well, it didn't sound like a row to me. It sounded like he was just very rude to you, and in front of Estelle too. I had a choice few words for him this morning when he told me."

Sam found it strangely comforting that, in many ways, his parents' relationship had continued unchanged by their divorce. Audrey was still the first person whose advice Howard would seek and the only person who could genuinely upset him with a proper telling off. Estelle might well be Howard's wife, but Audrey had remained his confidante. His parents had separated 10 years earlier, just shy of their 30th wedding anniversary. At the time, Sam had only been in LA a few months and was overwhelmed by the size and complexity of his new job. He found himself on the side-lines of his parents' divorce, being offered scraps of information by his father and endless reassurances from his mother that it would all work out for the best. Even now, he still didn't know for certain the cause of their separation and he wondered if he ever would. Howard felt the matter was now closed and Audrey wasn't a great sharer. Typically she would only say what needed to be said, and belonged to a select group of lifelong friends who all had a similar disposition. Common people wore their hearts on their sleeve, she said.

"You know, it would make perfect sense for Adam Jaymes to target the family," he said. "We're all expecting it to be one of the staff, but I know he's going to go for me or Dad at some point."

"Oh, what would you have to worry about?" Audrey asked, defensively, as though her son's honour was beyond reproach. "But I'm sure he'll have a go at Howard. Your father's a strong character though. He's made tough choices over the years and I know he'll stand by all of them. If Adam Jaymes tries to take on Howard, well, my money's on Howard. My money would always be on Howard." Audrey seemed to realise there had been a little too much fondness in her tone and so neatly moved the conversation along. "Anyway, you've yet to tell me what happened with Nevaeh," she said. "After all this time I was beginning to think I'd need to buy a new hat. It was quite a shock when you said she'd moved out."

Sam didn't quite know what to say. Audrey had only met his girlfriend the once and taken an instant dislike to her, and there was the slightest hint of 'I told you so' in his mother's voice as she probed for details about how the relationship had ended. Sam and Nevaeh had met at a charity event in New York two years earlier. He was the young heir to an international media empire and she was the breathtakingly beautiful model who had seemed funny, smart and down to earth. But over time, as she had embedded herself deeper and deeper into Sam's life, the veil had gradually slipped. His mother's critical assessment had been spot on, and Nevaeh revealed herself to be both devious and vindictive. Rather than bolstering Sam's delicate self-confidence, she had done everything she could to grind him down and isolate him from other people. She bought him new clothes that were obviously too small so she could criticise his weight. She would watch him collapse on the settee after a particularly long and stressful day and then demand he take her out dancing, so she could tell him how much he bored her when he said he was too tired. And she would casually ruin a dinner party by taking offence at an innocuous comment from one of Sam's friends, elaborate an entire argument out of thin air and then demand Sam support her by sending his friends home. Sam had lost a lot of friends during his relationship with Nevaeh.

The final straw had come when Nevaeh had logged onto Sam's laptop to find evidence of an affair only to find, instead, his extensive collection of pornography; hundreds upon hundreds of videos that he had downloaded over the years, all meticulously filed by specific genres including British, inter-racial, Milf, midget, MMF, swingers and vintage. When confronted by Nevaeh, Sam had attempted to defend himself by making a half-baked argument that there was an important cultural context she was missing and that it was simply his personal collection of adult erotica, a bit like an art collection. But she had revelled in her find, throwing horrendous accusations at him to make him seem little more than a mac-wearing pervert. Nevaeh stormed off to stay with friends for a few days, expecting her weak boyfriend to do what he usually did after a row and lavish her with apologies and gifts to win her back. But Sam had finally had enough. Rather than pursuing Nevaeh, he locked down his apartment, changed his contact details and handed the issue to his legal team so he would not have to deal with her again. Within 24 hours she was out of his life with a pay-off and a gagging contract. He couldn't have been happier. Sam could not tell his mother the truth, of course, and so fudged the details as much as possible and gave Audrey the public line that he simply hadn't been ready to settle down. But the conversation prompted a worrying realisation that, back home in LA, there was a woman who knew his most embarrassing secret and who was more than vindictive enough to have shared it with Adam Jaymes.

The Project Ear deadline was approaching and Valerie could feel the atmosphere grow increasingly electrified across the *Ear*'s enormous newsroom. The phones were ringing far more than usual and there was a boisterousness amongst the staff that made the world on the other side of her glass wall seem little more than a playground. She could see groups of reporters and sub-editors gather in huddles for excited conversations before returning to the desks, only for other huddles to briefly form and then disperse. And the whole time, she could see everyone glancing in her direction, as though hoping to catch the exact moment she received her phone call. One of the giant screens above the newsroom was streaming *Sky News* and another was showing the BBC. Both were counting down to 9pm and had spent the previous hours interviewing a revolving door of celebrities, commentators, bloggers, journalists and legal experts. The BBC was obviously trying to keep its glee reigned in, with lots of thoughtful questions and furrowed brows. But Sky was having a bit more fun with the story, and had opened a phone poll on who would be next. Valerie was top of the list with 63% of the vote. "Oh," she said to herself, "my odds are shortening."

The third screen, the one Valerie had the clearest view of from her desk, was showing Adam Jaymes' website with its clock ticking down to 9pm. She could see the irony in that Adam's website was quite literally hanging over everyone's heads. She decided it was time to face the music, and so transferred her phone to Twigg's office and joined him at his desk along with Sam, Oonagh and Derek. They were going to record every moment of what happened next, capture Adam's exact words and the flurry of activity that followed. And they had Valerie's rebuttal all powered up and ready to go. "It's funny how we're all expecting it to be me," she said, trying to sound pragmatic just as she was beginning to feel genuinely uneasy. "I mean it probably will be me, but it seriously could be anyone of you or anyone of those bastards out there in that newsroom." She noted Oonagh's serene expression, a calmness that annoyed Valerie intensely. It was as though Oonagh was saying "Well it won't be me". And Valerie instantly wished it would be. She'd like nothing more than to see that smug smile wiped off her face.

"Whatever it is, and whoever it is, we will deal with it, Valerie," Sam replied. "We will not be another *News of the World*." He was pleased that, for once in his life, he felt genuinely up to speed with what was going on. He now knew the company line on most of their potential scandals, although suspected Derek hadn't briefed him on absolutely everything. Derek, he suspected, had a good few secrets of his own.

As 8.55pm arrived, all eyes fell on the conference phone that had been installed especially on Twigg's desk. Valerie noticed the hum of noise from the newsroom lessened noticeably, like that pause on New Year's Eve when everyone's waiting for Big Ben to strike twelve. "Come on you bastard," she said.

"Don't tempt fate, Valerie," Twigg said, sounding very sensible. By 8.56pm everyone in the room began to feel somewhat deflated.

"Where the hell is he?" Valerie asked. "Is he calling someone else?"

There was a knock at the door, and everyone turned to see Felicity standing outside Twigg's office. He put his hand up to show her the office was off limits, but she was holding something in her hand and was pointing at it anxiously.

"What is that girl doing?" Oonagh asked. "What has she got in her hand?"

Boldly, Felicity opened the door and stepped inside. "I'm very sorry but - "

"Not now, Felicity. Out!" barked Twigg.

To everyone's surprise Felicity ignored his instructions and walked over to Valerie to hand her a mobile phone. "I was waiting in your office and your mobile started ringing about a minute ago. I thought it might be important. The number's blocked so you can't call him back."

"Did you answer it?" Twigg asked.

"No, no ... I just assumed ..."

Valerie looked at her mobile as though it was the first time she had ever seen it. "Thank you dear," she said. And then Twigg ushered Felicity out of his office again. "Keep an eye on the screen," he told her. "Tell us when it changes."

Felicity left the office and joined the masses outside who were now all on their feet, gazing at Adam Jaymes' website as it hung above their heads, counting down to 9pm.

Suddenly, Valerie's phone buzzed into life again. She could feel a wave of cold panic sweep across her entire body as she realised it really was her. "What do I do?" she asked.

"Answer it, but put it on speaker so we can hear exactly what he says," Oonagh replied.

Valerie shook her head, suddenly looking like a confused old woman. "I don't know how to do that," she said.

Oonagh took Valerie's phone and clicked the answer key twice. She then handed it back and silently gestured for Valerie to start speaking. Meekly, Valerie held the phone towards her mouth and politely said: "Hello, this is Valerie Pierce."

"Hello Valerie Pierce. This is Adam Jaymes."

It may have just been the familiar sound of his voice, or perhaps the unbridled cheerfulness with which he greeted her. But whatever shock or fear had been holding Valerie's unforgiving character at bay suddenly evaporated with an explosion of foul language. "Oh, you fucking piece of shit!" she screamed, to everyone's surprise. "How the hell did you get this number? No one has this number. How dare you call me on this number. You worthless, talentless, revolting little wanker!"

Oonagh was open-mouthed at Valerie's unexpected outburst, and Twigg reached over to hold her hand in an attempt to quieten her down.

"I just called to let you know it's your turn," Adam concluded, still cheerful, and then the line went dead.

"What was that? What did he say? My turn? Did he say it was my turn?" Valerie was no longer anxious. She was just angry that someone had turned the tables on her, especially *him*, Adam Jaymes. "How dare he? Who does he think he is? My turn. The fucking little shit."

"Valerie!" Twigg boomed. "Enough. We're covered. We knew it would be you and we're prepared. We can turn this whole situation around right here, right now."

A buzz of conversation began to grow louder from outside Twigg's office, and all five glanced towards the newsroom.

"The site must have updated," Oonagh said, and she stood and walked towards the glass to see if she could see the screen. But it hung at an obscure angle to Twigg's office and they couldn't make out what it showing. But they could see Felicity was scribbling notes onto a pad, and waited quietly as she walked back towards them.

"So, what's the headline?" Valerie asked, as Felicity came back into the office. She was relieved it was done, and was now almost blasé about what would happen next. The waiting was the worst part of it, Valerie thought. The reality wasn't going to be so bad. "Oh, let me guess. Valerie Pierce in drink-drive shame? *Ear* columnist in booze scandal? Am I close?"

"Er, no. Not really," Felicity replied, looking perplexed. "It's not a story about drink-driving."

Twigg stood up, alarmed that their neatly organised plan had been trumped. "What is it then?" he asked. "What's the story?"

Felicity looked at her notes and then back to the five horrified faces staring directly at her. "It's an exclusive interview with Valerie's first husband."

Valerie's chin dropped.

"What?" Twigg shouted. "*First* husband? What?!"

"No," Valerie whispered, her heart pounding so hard in her chest she thought it was going to burst. "He wouldn't. He absolutely wouldn't."

"Valerie, *FIRST* husband?" Twigg yelled. But when Valerie didn't respond, he looked back to Felicity. "First husband?" he asked again.

"Yes," Felicity replied. "It's an interview with Valerie's first husband. And his boyfriend."

8

VALERIE DIDN'T WAIT for the shock or humiliation to set in. She marched from Twigg's office, collected her things and left the building as quickly as she could. She ignored the protests from Twigg and Oonagh, the appeals to stay and explain what was going on. She saw the faces of all those reporters, her colleagues, who seemed relieved, jealous and amused in equal measure. And she saw the triumphant headline on the Project Ear website, hanging over the newsroom: "Ex-Husband Exclusive: Valerie Pierce turned me gay". She knew she would have to give the *Ear* her rebuttal at some point, but even the security guard in the lobby (who had been told to stop her leaving the building) knew it was not that time. Valerie was driving down to Kent to see her ex-husband and his boyfriend, and nothing was going to stop her. Her mind was set and everything else blurred around her. In what seemed like just seconds she had swept down the stairs to the underground car park, found her car, programmed her satnav and sped up the ramp to the road outside. A few photographers had been smart enough to loiter by the exit, and rushed over to snap pictures of her as she accelerated away. Valerie didn't notice. She was too busy blurting out random expletives and cursing the day she had ever met Raymond Vaughn. How could he? After all those years, everything they had agreed, all the things she had generously failed to share with her readers. With anyone, in fact. Even poor old Jeremy hadn't ever heard the whole story, and her daughter didn't have a clue that her mother had been married before.

"Married? Pah! Bollocks!" she howled as she swerved around a bend, momentarily mounting the curb as she did. "Fucking stupid lying cheating devious stupid idiot!" she screeched. She tried to rationalise what had happened, and the more she thought about it, the more obvious it seemed. "Oh, of course he would spill the beans to Adam Jaymes," she sneered, her tone brimming with disgust. "He probably asked for a quick grope, came in his pants and then told him everything. And that's a better sex life than he ever gave me." The rest of the journey continued in a similar fashion. Valerie hit 100mph for most of it and screamed and shouted as though her ex-husband were sitting in the passenger seat next to her. She knew, of course, what the exposé had done. It had ridiculed her, it had undermined every single article and every single argument she had ever made against gay rights, gay marriage and Adam Jaymes. It had made her look like little more than a bitter, shrieking ex-wife and made it virtually impossible for her to write anything on the topic in future. As her journey drew to its conclusion, Valerie turned on the car radio. She knew Five Live had late night phone-in shows and decided to see if her humiliation would get a mention. Of course it did. In fact, it was *the* topic of conversation. The host had been joined in the studio by a collection of old hacks and celebrities, and a spokeswoman from Stonewall had been shoe-horned into the discussion by phone once the details of the exposé had become clear.

"So, in a nutshell, you're asking Valerie Pierce for an apology?" queried the host.

"I'm not sure we're talking about an apology, but certainly an acknowledgement that this unfortunate personal experience has been the driving force behind years of relentless homophobic campaigning," the spokeswoman replied. "We have challenged Valerie

Pierce's anti-gay rhetoric for the better part of two decades and her particular obsession with Adam Jaymes is well-documented."

"Obsession? What?" Valerie squawked.

"She has always presented herself as some sort of moral guardian, willing to put herself in the firing line to stand up for Middle England," the spokeswoman continued. "But should this revelation be true, I think the *Daily Ear* will have to admit it's done little more than hand a scorned woman endless resources to vent her personal frustrations. It's not as if Valerie Pierce likes to keep her own life private. This is a woman who is paid to share, some might say *over-share*, every detail of her private life. The fact she has kept something as fundamental as a marriage to a gay man a secret for all these years demonstrates - "

Valerie switched the radio off. Her fears had been confirmed. Her opinion, which was her livelihood, was now worthless.

"You have reached your destination," the satnav told her. She hadn't been to Ray and Pete's house before. But once, years ago, she had allowed her curiosity to get the better of her and typed their address into Google. She had quickly found they had created an entire website dedicated to their cottage renovation and the landscaping of the surrounding grounds. She had sneered at their gay attention-seeking, but still saved the web address under her 'favourites' so she could keep track of any on-going work. Valerie screeched to a halt, stepped from the car and slammed the door. And there it was, Ray and Pete's twee little country cottage. Picture postcard-perfect, with the sort of garden that would make Alan Titchmarsh jealous. She stormed up the little garden path to find the front door was already open, and could see Ray's tall muscular physique silhouetted in front of her. Even after so many years, she recognised him immediately.

"I thought you'd show up," he said, glumly.

"I bet you fucking did," she replied and stamped straight past him.

The inside of the cottage had been completely refurbished. It was modern and open-plan, with a huge extension at the back that couldn't be seen from the road. Valerie looked around the room, a sneer on her face. It was exactly the sort of ostentatious home she would expect from a *gay* couple. Ray followed her into the room and she turned to face him. He hadn't changed, not really. He'd obviously been working out and his hairline had receded a little. But he was still ridiculously handsome with the same brooding matinée idol looks she had fallen head over heels in love with, the same man she had foolishly married when they were both just 18. At the time they'd joked about being a modern-day Katharine Hepburn and Cary Grant, but now she knew they had been more like Doris Day and Rock Hudson.

"I want you to calm down," he said.

"That would be nice for you, wouldn't it?" she replied. "A nice, calm conversation with the woman whose career and life you have just destroyed."

"Can I get you a drink, a merlot?"

Oh, she thought, he remembered. Clever. "I don't want a drink. I want an explanation."

"Will you sit down?"

"I'm not staying. I don't want your hospitality. I just want you to explain how you could have done this."

Ray shrugged his shoulders, and looked defeated. "I had no choice," he said. "Honestly, it was completely out of my control."

There was a noise from the other side of the room. Valerie peered through the opening to the kitchen area and saw Pete drying a plate, as though nothing interesting was going on. She was pleased to see he had put on a good few stone and lost his hair almost completely. "Val," Pete said curtly, with a nod. He had been part of their group of friends, and had even attended their little wedding ceremony and acted as one of the witnesses. It had been difficult enough for Valerie when Ray had told her their marriage was over after less than a year, but was even harder when he left their home hand-in-hand with Pete. She was still angry with Ray, but she despised his partner.

"This is between Ray and me," she said and turned her back on him. To her annoyance, before the conversation could continue, Pete went to Ray's side and took his hand.

"Actually, sweetie, this is my house and my partner. You want to talk to him, you talk to me too."

"Oh," Valerie groaned, and looked scornfully at Ray. "The missus and the ex, fighting for your attention. It must be like you're *living* a Bette Davis movie."

"God, she hasn't changed has she?" Pete said.

Valerie looked him up and down. "I couldn't say the same for you, Pete darling," she purred.

"Val, if you want to hear how this happened, that's fine. I will tell you," Ray said. "But let me make it clear to you now. We don't buy your rag of a newspaper because we won't have your homophobic bile in our home. The same goes for you. One more snide comment and you can get back in your car and piss off back to London. Is that clear?"

Valerie wished she had taken his offer of a drink, so she would have something to throw in his face. As it was, she knew he had her at a disadvantage. "Fine, I'll behave," she conceded.

Ray and Pete sat down together, and although Valerie would have preferred to stay standing she forgot herself for a moment and sat down as well. She couldn't believe how many years had gone by since she had last seen them. What was it, she wondered, 30, 35 years? She had not seen Ray, face to face, since the day he had left and yet it was like they'd seen each other just the week before.

"I assume you were both thrilled when Adam Jaymes turned up at your door," she said. "I'm surprised you haven't got a signed photograph framed on the wall."

"Oh for Christ's sake, Valerie," Ray snapped. "We never met him. We didn't even know this had anything to do with him. He's got people working for him. He's got his own team of journalists."

"Funny that, isn't it?" Pete said, sarcastically, "Reporters screwing over other reporters. It's almost as if people in your profession have no ethics."

Valerie glared at Pete and wished he would die, right there in front of her. But she knew he was probably right. The previous years had not been kind to the newspaper industry, and there were likely to be thousands of out-of-work journalists happy to take money off anyone to do pretty much anything. "So, did you meet anyone at all?" she asked.

"Yes," Ray said. "A woman and a photographer turned up at our door a couple of months back. They said they were doing a piece about country homes and had seen our website."

"We have a website," Pete interjected, proudly. Valerie wasn't about to let them know she'd seen it, so faked a totally uninterested expression and gestured for Ray to continue.

"They took loads of photographs of us, all over the house and in the garden. It seemed really legitimate. But once the photographs had been taken it all, well, the woman changed tack completely. Suddenly, she was telling me how she knew I was your secret ex-husband and how they were doing a piece about you for some new publication."

"How did she know?"

Ray shook his head. "She wouldn't say. She wouldn't even tell us which newspaper she was working for. We had no idea it was anything to do with Adam Jaymes until that *Newsnight* episode, and then we put two and two together."

Valerie stood up and walked to the window, quietly pondering the situation. "I can't believe they could have offered you enough money to sell your story," she said, sadly.

"It wasn't money," Ray replied. "It was blackmail. They told us if we didn't agree to an interview then they had a much worse story they were going to run. They had evidence of a court case that had been hushed up. That you had been caught drunk at the wheel of your car with your granddaughters in the back seat."

Valerie span round. "What?" she yelled. "But we *knew* about that story. We had *prepared* for that story. I could have handled that story coming out."

"Well, I didn't know that," Ray said, defensively. "They told us it was far worse, that they could prove the whole story had been covered up and the repercussions were more serious. Much more serious."

Valerie was clenching her fists and looked as though she was about to stamp her feet with rage. "Oh for God's sake, how could you think that would be worse? You stupid bloody idiots."

Pete shot to his feet. "Get the fuck out of my house, you evil old witch!" he shouted. "We tried to help you, and this is how you treat us? Fuck off!"

Ray gently tugged at Pete's hand and tried to ease him back onto the couch, but Pete pulled his hand away. "No, no, I'm not having it," he said. "All these years we've seen the evil crap she's written about gay people, and we still tried to do the right thing by her. Keep your marriage a secret."

"Why, out of guilt for stealing my husband?"

"Guilt? Why would I feel guilty? You're the one who pushed a man into marriage when he was clearly gay."

"*Clearly* gay?" Valerie yelled back. "According to the headline, it was that year he spent married to me that *turned* him gay."

Ray stood up, and put his hands arms out, like a teacher trying to break up a playground fight. "Stop it, the pair of you," he bellowed. "Enough."

After a moment of silence, Pete stormed back to the kitchen. "Tell me when she's gone," he said. "I'll open the fucking champagne."

"For the record," he said, "I did not say you turned me gay."

"Well, you must have said something like that," Valerie replied.

"No, I didn't. I just said that during our marriage it became obvious to me that I had made a mistake. That I could never be with a woman, not honestly. And the more months that went by, the more I realised I was being unfair to you. That I could never be the husband that you deserved."

Valerie huffed. "That's all they would have needed from you. A year married to me turned you gay."

"But it's not what I said."

"But you said enough that they could write that headline," she replied. "That's how they operate, how they … " Valerie realised what she was saying and quietly decided not to continue the sentence.

"How they … twist things?" Ray suggested, eyebrows raised. "Well, I guess you would know."

Valerie folded her arms and stared at her ex-husband, with a lonely coldness in her veins she hadn't felt in a long time. How wretched, she thought, that all these years later she could still feel so utterly rejected by Ray. And to make matters worse, she knew she had let herself down that evening and behaved like some parody of the bitter ex-wife. It was as if she had gone out of her way to show Ray how right he was to leave her.

"You still could have warned me," she said, quietly. "Come on now, you could have picked up the phone and warned me. Even after all of this time."

"I couldn't," he replied. "They said they would know straight away if I told you. And if I did tell you, they would run the drink-drive story too. Honestly, Val, I was just trying to minimise the harm. I know you think I made the wrong call but everything I did, I did with the best of intentions. And believe it or not, that goes for Pete too."

Valerie knew all the tricks in the book, and certainly knew how a good journalist could easily get a decent man like Ray to make a bad choice by convincing him he was doing the right thing. This situation was not Ray's fault and as much as she hated to admit it, it wasn't Pete's fault either. But at least she had the truth, and all she needed now was a dignified way to end the dramatic scene she had created and extract herself from Ray's life once more. She noticed the half-empty wine glasses on the coffee table in front of the TV, and the heavy aroma of Italian cooking and garlic bread that was still hanging in the air. It was the sort of simple, warm luxury she knew many couples enjoyed together during a quiet Friday night in, the sort of private moment she had shared with Ray during their time together. But there and then she felt very much an intruder, the unwanted guest storming into someone else's personal space. It was time for her to leave.

"I'm sorry you were dragged into this," she said softly, and although she didn't mean it, she then added, "and I'm sorry for Pete too." She was determined that Ray's last memory of her would not be the screaming harpy he had clearly been expecting, but instead a composed if heartbroken woman who walked from his home with her head held high. And as she made her way back to the entrance she heard Ray gently call her name. She turned and stared at him, desperately hoping his parting comment would be some gesture of kindness. "Be careful, Val," he said. "This was a real operation. There's money behind it. I know tonight is a bad night, but I honestly think the worst is yet to come."

Valerie gently nodded in agreement, and then returned to her car and drove away knowing she would never see Ray again. She had taken the precaution of packing an overnight bag so she could go straight to her flat in Leigh-on-Sea if the worst happened. It was a much longer drive than back to her house in Barnet, but too many journalists knew her London address and she had no intention of pushing her way through a media throng just to get to her own front door. Her journey to Essex was a very different affair from her drive to Kent. She was silent and introspective after seeing Ray again after all those years. Beyond the intensity of their confrontation she could see how happy, how content he was with his lot. And it was the fact that Ray could still make her feel so inadequate, so rejected, that had troubled her the most. It was that cold and unwelcome greeting as she had arrived at his door, and the relief on his face as she had left. He clearly hadn't wanted her there, and was happy for his life to continue without ever seeing her again.

But it had never been that way for Valerie. For her, Ray had always been there in the back of her mind, in the background of her life. She had often wondered where he was, what he was doing and if he ever thought of her. But the kind memories, those moments of gentle reflection, were only ever fleeting. Mostly she hated him, him and his big gay life. And then there had been Pete, loitering in the kitchen and clearly amused by her pain and sense of betrayal. Pete, the dreadful little queen who had stolen her husband all those years ago and who, that very evening, had the gall to behave as though he somehow had a role to play in the drama of her predicament. But just as her fingers tightened around the steering wheel and her temper was about to flare up again, she remembered the phrase *"pretended family relationship"*, and she smiled. It had been a slogan of 80s right-wing electioneering, something her late husband Jeremy had always claimed was his. She remembered how delighted he had been at putting those very words into law, to prevent gay couples from ever claiming recognition. And she remembered how spitefully thrilled she had been about it at the time. She had written extensively in her column about the wonders of the Local Government Act 1988 and how Thatcher's government was protecting *real* marriage and family values from the onslaught of perverted, political correctness.

And when the act became law, she had been sorely tempted to mail a copy of her column to Ray and Pete, with the phrase *"pretended family relationship"* highlighted in marker pen. She dearly wanted to tell them they would never have what she and Jeremy were enjoying, a normal and legal marriage. But she hadn't, because she needed them both to keep quiet. And whilst she knew the content of her columns would likely antagonise the pair of them, she also knew they would keep their heads down unless she antagonised them personally. Her journey ended at a dark and quiet row of large Victorian houses, elevated on a hillside and overlooking the estuary with a rail line crossing the land in between. There were no reporters or camera crews waiting for her, and she smirked as she imagined them all standing outside her house in London, not realising their wait was futile. She collected her bag from the boot of her car, and then made her way to her flat on the second floor of the largest house in the road. It had been her mother-in-law's home, and had passed to Valerie when Jeremy had died. She'd always intended to have the place redecorated, but had never gotten round to it, so it still looked like an old lady's house, with large orange-print floral wallpaper from the seventies and clashing brown patterned carpets throughout.

But the view from the balcony was good and the furniture, at least, was relatively new. She turned on the lamps in the sitting room, dropped her bag to the floor and slumped down onto the couch. She was already missing Jasper, her Labrador. He would have been on the couch with her by now, licking her face with joy and whining with the excitement of seeing her again. She hated that he was in a kennel, and blamed Adam Jaymes for that too. Her gaze drifted across the room and settled on a bookshelf above the television. There, wedged between a pile of women's magazines and her 1989 Press Award, was a copy of her book *Reclaimed Womanhood*. She'd written it 15 years earlier and it had been released with a blaze of publicity, positioned by her publisher as a "modern, intelligent response to *The Female Eunuch*". Valerie had wanted to be the anti-Germaine Greer, helping women to rediscover their femininity and traditional roles, and to celebrate the importance of simply being a man's wife. She'd expected the book to become a number one best seller around the world, and that she would have been elevated above her peers in the newspaper industry to the must-have guest for chat shows and radio discussion programmes. But despite a massive boost in publicity from the *Daily Ear*, the book had been a mortifying flop. In fact, it was laughed off the shelves of bookshops up and down the country and so damaged her reputation that, for many years, she was barred from pretty much every chat show in the land. So public was her failure that, for a time, Valerie allowed herself to be defined by it. She ran back to her day job as a newspaper columnist and hid there. It became her sole enterprise, her everything, and her dreams of touring the world as an international bestselling author faded into obscurity. If truth be told, the evening's events had left her feeling as vulnerable as they had angry. If Adam Jaymes' exposé had robbed her of her column, Valerie knew she was finished.

A few moments passed, and she wondered if she could simply fall asleep where she was, fully clothed on the couch. But her anxiety was beginning to stir and she could feel a tension in the pit of her stomach that wasn't about to go away. With a sigh, she sat up and pulled her mobile phone from her handbag. She had switched it off hours ago, and knew she would be inundated with voice mail and text messages the moment it was switched back on again. "Come on then, you bastards; let's be having you," she whispered to herself as her phone lit up in her hand. Moments later, 43 text messages had plopped into her inbox (20 of them from Twigg) and she had 16 voice messages waiting for her too. She couldn't quite face the voice messages, not straight away, and so scrolled through the texts first of all. Leonard; Leonard; Leonard; Colin (oh, bless him); Leonard; Don't Know; Audrey; Fat Irish Whore; Leonard; Don't Know; Leonard; Leonard; Fat Irish Whore; Sam; Leonard; Don't Know; Don't Know; Alice; Leonard …

Alice? Alice!

After years of silence, of angry non-communication, her daughter had finally taken that first step to get back in touch. Here, in her darkest, loneliest moment was a message from her little girl. Valerie felt a wave of happiness, of relief, that perhaps this awful exposé could bring the two of them back together again. She clicked on the envelope and read the short message her daughter had sent, three simple words: "What. The. Fuck?"

9

Ding dong, the witch is dead #ValeriePierce - let's just hope someone follows it up with a bucket of water

"**AND TRUE TO** his word, his second exposé was published last night at 9 o'clock on the dot. As had been widely anticipated, controversial *Daily Ear* columnist"

three decades of obsessive, uncompromising anti-gay rhetoric has been exposed as little more than the spiteful cries of a vengeful ex-wife

@RealAdamJaymes Brilliant! Some justice for Pearl Martin at last #WellDoneAdamjaymes

"had the unenviable task of being sat next to Valerie Pierce for an entire evening at last year's 'Woman of the Year' awards. How strange, I thought, that a woman who sees so little value in her own gender should attend an event which celebrates the fairer sex. Indeed it must represent the antithesis of all her beliefs. And yet I'm certain she sat there throughout the entire ceremony fully expecting to be the surprise recipient of the 'Lifetime Achievement' award"

> *@RealAdamJaymes defeated an entire Sontaran army single-handed on #DoctorWho. The Daily Ear? No problem!*

> *but I bet Valerie isn't wearing her signature purple suit today. Instead she'll be covered in shame from head to foot*

"And on that point, Janet, if I can come to you. Stonewall says this revelation will forever undermine Valerie's credibility as a columnist, particularly on the issue of gay rights. Do you agree?"

> *#ValeriePierce – the picture at the top of her column turned me gay. I didn't even have to marry her*

"known Adam for many years, and I have to be very honest here, and say that I am increasingly worried for his mental health. To have spoken so passionately and coherently about privacy issues in the past, and then to resort to this despicable and hypocritical course of action"

> *fell victim, at a vulnerable age, to a selfish and duplicitous gay man. This exposé does nothing but show that the best writers draw on their own personal experiences to guide their view of the world and Valerie Pierce remains one of the best, if not the best, in the newspaper industry*

> *I notice @TheDailyEar is the only paper – yet again – not to cover this story. Cowards! #WellDoneAdamjaymes*

"hard to feel any compassion for a woman who so publicly and gleefully danced on the grave of an actress who, some have claimed, was driven to suicide by Valerie herself"

> *However, as often happens with newspaper columnists, Valerie has talked herself into believing that she is an academic; if she*

announces her opinions with enough vigour it somehow gives them gravitas. But she is most certainly not an academic. Indeed, she often reveals herself to be a person of limited intellect

@RealAdamJaymes I'm such a fan of yours, Adam. PLEASE stop this horrible project. You're making yourself no better than them.

"has retaliated with a surprisingly robust statement which says, *'It is regrettable that this personal matter should now be the subject of an orchestrated Twitterstorm, fanned by individuals – including members of the Labour party – with agendas to pursue'.*"

and the entire country is now hooked on this bizarre Whodunit. The only difference is that we know *Whodunit*. It was Adam Jaymes. We're just waiting to see who his next victim is.

@RealAdamJaymes I'm really excited about your appearance in #Glee.

"Thank you for joining us, Brenda. It was great to talk to you. Some really interesting points there. And next on the line is Robert from Aldershot. Good morning Robert. So, you take a completely different view on this from Brenda and think Adam Jaymes is in the wrong. Why's that then?"

@RealAdamJaymes Get some help, you evil twisted pervert.

10

"TOXIC", ANNOUNCED TWIGG, and the room fell silent. No one in the morning meeting seemed quite sure where their editor was taking the discussion, and none of the assembled group of senior journalists was keen to question him. Nobody, that is, apart from Oonagh who repeated what Twigg had said and then shrugged. "In what way 'toxic'?" she queried.

"We have become too much the focus of this story," Twigg replied. "But I've noticed a small sea-change, a few more people speaking out against Jaymes and in support of us. So we need to start rowing in that direction, turn the spotlight on Adam Jaymes, look at the repercussions on his career and his reputation. The public is beginning to realise he is not a hero but a bully. He's becoming unpopular. Unlikeable. Unemployable. His *brand* has become toxic."

"And do you have one of your *funny* little graphs to prove this, Leonard?" Oonagh asked with a slight rasp to her voice as she attempted to contain a laugh. The atmosphere in the meeting shifted immediately. No one uttered a word, not a gasp and definitely not a chuckle. Ever so slightly, the rest of the staff drew back in their seats as though waiting for Twigg to explode. They'd never seen him mocked before, certainly not to his face. In fact, so unpredictable was his temper that none of the *Daily Ear* staff even tried to engage him in light-hearted banter.

Twigg could see a change in Oonagh, and it was a change he didn't like. Gone was the façade of mutual respect, of not speaking out of turn in front of the staff. It appeared their unhappy exchange the previous day had altered their relationship. Or, he wondered, perhaps it was her brunch with Sam that had left her with the impression she was in a strong enough position to take him on. Whatever it was, Twigg took this to be a public announcement of her intention to challenge him. "Better men than you have tried," he thought to himself. "We've got a team with Valerie now, so we'll also have her exclusive story. I want it up on the website by this afternoon and we'll run a longer piece in our print edition tomorrow."

Oonagh went to ask another question, but Twigg got in first with, "That's it, back to work!" and the senior staff quickly mumbled and whispered to their feet and left the office. Twigg was pleased to see Oonagh stand and leave with the rest of them. He was usually happy to spar with her, with anyone in fact. But it had been a long, challenging night and Twigg had managed little more than a power nap. He wasn't on top form and could feel a sluggishness in his mind that he didn't like because it felt like a weakness. He needed to freshen up. His office had a private en suite, a small bathroom he'd had installed many years ago during the multi-million pound refit of the *Ear* offices. Gayesh had been in charge at that time, and Twigg's keen eye quickly spotted that a disproportionate amount of the refurbishment budget had been siphoned off for the top floor. Once Gayesh was aware that Twigg had noticed this irregularity, he quickly decided the *Ear*'s editor worked such long hours that a private bathroom was a necessity. It had been a perfect pay-off for Twigg. He didn't like using the same lavatory as other people, and his obsession with hygiene and personal grooming made his en suite a good personal investment. Now he could always look and feel perfect. Not a hair out of place, not a crease in his shirts and minty-fresh breath 24 hours a day. He had also been told by Valerie that the en suite made him a less unpleasant manager, something she had put down to a reduction in his stress levels as a result of having his own bathroom. He went inside and locked the door behind him. It was a well-designed space for a room that wasn't particularly large. It had clean white tiles from floor to ceiling and a toilet, sink, shower and chair with enough floor space to hang clothes and get changed and dried. It was also a place where, every now and again, Twigg could withdraw, sit and be quiet without the constant eyes of a horde of journalists watching him. And it was during those quiet moments that he often had some of his best ideas. Fifteen minutes later, Twigg returned to his desk and buzzed through to his PA. "Get me Chris Lackie on the phone," he ordered.

Felicity had spent most of the journey to Leigh-on-Sea trying not to stare at Jason Spade, but she had never been so close to someone so extremely overweight before, and found herself looking at him with a morbid fascination. Her mum and dad would not approve, she thought. They'd raised her to be respectful and to treat everyone the same. But every part of his body, from his plump fingers to the back of his neck, seemed bloated and rounded, and he even had to reach around his own belly to control the steering wheel. She knew he was relatively young (in his late thirties or early forties) but the weight distorted his face and he made a wheezing, rasping noise as he breathed which made him seem at least twenty years older. But he still appeared to be highly charged when it came to the opposite sex. From the moment she had climbed into the passenger seat, he had started to make jokey comments about her pert bottom and fresh face. But she knew the jokiness was a façade and that he was using humour to check her out, to see if he could entice her into a conversation that would quickly deteriorate into a bombardment of personal questions and smutty requests. There was no way Felicity Snow was going to allow herself to end up in Jason Spade's wank-bank and so she had talked about her parents and her school and her fondness for cooking and as many other dull, every day topics as she could think of. Each time Jason made an innuendo she took it at face value and started to talk about something unexciting.

"So, this cookery course, did they teach you how to make a *sausage hot pot*?"

"No, we didn't really do British cuisine. It was mainly Italian. I learnt how to make an amazing risotto, though. White wine, garlic ... "

"So, you like a bit of Italian, eh?"

"Well, mum and dad wanted me to go into catering originally. I think they were hoping I'd be the new Delia Smith."

"Nah, I see you more as a Nigella Lawson."

"I'm probably more of a Mary Berry to be honest."

Having spent months in the bowels of the *Daily Ear*, Felicity had become hardened to the casual swearing, rude stories, sexism and veiled racism that seemed to run through the veins of a large, busy newspaper. But Jason was a different beast entirely. She knew there was more to him than the ambling, simple, lonely underdog he pretended to be. Beneath it all was a very clever man who knew exactly what he wanted and who wasn't about to let ethics, the law or a conscience get in his way. Felicity knew his reputation, of course. Jason was the creator of the 'panty-less up-skirt', a particularly unpleasant practice of some paparazzi, who would throw themselves into the gutter to snap pictures of female stars as they climbed out of limos and taxis. It was a method of exposing those ladies who avoided a VPL by going commando. The *Ear* would often run censored versions of the pictures and be highly critical of any woman who was caught without her knickers on. Those pictures deemed unsuitable by the picture desk would end up on less salubrious websites (Jason wasn't picky who his customers were).

Pearl Martin had been a regular victim of Jason's, but not just of his up-skirt photographs. For years, he had pursued her from home to work to celebrity event and back again. Jason had fed the *Ear*'s entire Pearl Martin obsession with dozens of photographs every week, and every picture telling an increasingly negative story. If she was drinking coffee outside a Starbucks it was because she was suffering another hangover. If she was shopping for clothes, it was because the drink had made her bloat and she needed larger outfits. If she was holding a glass of champagne at a gala event, it was (at least) her 12th glass. And if she was crying in the street, it was because she was having a drink- or drug-induced break down. Although, in truth, any photographs of Pearl crying were typically the result of Jason hurling abuse directly into her face. It was a little trick he used to make sure female celebrities would cry when he needed them to. Pearl's friends, and in particular Adam Jaymes, had singled out Jason for criticism at her inquest. As far as they were concerned, Jason had provided the ammunition and Valerie had fired the gun. But although in his summing up the coroner made references to the *"unhelpful and often irresponsible behaviour of some members of the press"*, he still recorded a verdict of suicide which is not what Pearl's family had wanted. But Felicity had found the most contradictory aspect of Jason's character was that, in truth, he was an extremely talented photographer who could easily have made a decent living in a far more legitimate way. However, he thrived, perversely, on pursuing and preferably destroying the rich and famous, and he had a very lucrative deal with the Harvey News Group that kept him happy.

By the time they arrived, Felicity felt grubby and couldn't get out of the car quickly enough. Valerie was waiting on the pavement for them, looking far more relaxed than Felicity had been expecting. She was in black trousers and a mauve, cowl neck sweater, and had her arms folded across her chest with a cigarette in her hand. Behind her, the horizon was a dramatic view of the estuary beneath a dark, bleak sky. It conjured up the memory of an old Joan Crawford movie that Felicity had watched as a girl with her uncle. It certainly wasn't the panicked or humiliated Valerie she had been expecting. Whatever Valerie had done overnight, it appeared to have cleared her anxieties. Forgetting herself for a moment, and perhaps simply out of the relief at seeing someone else, Felicity walked up to Valerie and greeted her with a kiss on either cheek. It was an act of familiarity she would never have performed in the office, and she took herself by surprise. But Valerie simply grasped her arm and smiled. "You survived a whole car journey with Jason Spade. I'm impressed," she said. "Most young women would have jumped out onto the motorway after five minutes. Tuck and roll, dear, tuck and roll."

"It wasn't the best car journey," Felicity admitted.

"Don't worry. I'm 10 minutes from the train station. Perhaps you might consider a different mode of transport for your journey home?"

"Hello Val," Jason said breezily as he unpacked his bags and equipment from the boot of his car. He was wearing jeans that kept slipping down at the back, and an XXXL black t-shirt with a slogan printed on the front in big white letters; "F**k you, F**k *Newsnight*, F**k the BBC". Although Valerie didn't find it amusing, she did admire his gall. "This has got to be a quick job, I'm afraid," Jason said. "Twigg wants this double-fast, a few shots of you looking brave and thoughtful. Has your place got a balcony?"

"Yes, it's that one," Valerie replied, and pointed to her first floor apartment.

"Excellent. Well I thought we'd make the most of the miserable weather, so I'll have you lit at the front. You'll be in a column of light and we'll have the dark clouds behind you. Like a storm has come and gone and you've survived it. And are all the better for it. I don't want you looking weak, more reflective and strong."

"I have no intention of looking anything other than furious," Valerie replied. They made their way to her apartment and made the mistake of letting Jason walk up the stairs ahead of them, giving both Valerie and Felicity a disturbingly close view of his builder's bum.

"Be brave," Valerie said, smirking. "At least he's wearing pants today."

As they reached the sitting room, Felicity was surprised to find someone waiting for them. A woman was perched on the couch with a large mug of coffee in her hands. There was something familiar about her, and it took a moment for Felicity to realise what it was. Facially, the woman had the same sharp angles and severe stare as Valerie. Without a doubt it had to be her daughter, Alice. Valerie had spoken of her estrangement from Alice and although she had never specified a single event that had caused their rift, Felicity wondered if the 'drink-drive' incident had been the final straw.

"Are you ready for us, Alice?" Valerie asked, all sweetness and light. "This is Jason and Felicity."

Alice barely acknowledged them, and continued sipping her coffee. Although she was the image of Valerie, she had obviously gone to great pains to minimise the resemblance. She had short-cropped, bleached-blonde hair and seemed to make a point of dressing androgynously. She was slightly plump, possibly just to spite her mother, and didn't wear any make-up. "What do I have to do?" she asked, and Jason quickly started to organise the pair of them.

"Can we have the two of you leaning over the balcony, but half facing me with a smile on your face?" Jason said. "Maybe an embrace? You know, standing strong together. That sort of thing."

Felicity found the next 10 minutes excruciating. The discomfort between Valerie and Alice was obvious to the point that Jason had to physically place their arms around each other and guide the direction of their faces. Felicity watched in wonder as he artfully, masterfully, created images that would tell the story of a loving, close-knit, middle-class family reunited in the face of adversity. They would convince the *Ear*'s readers that the exposé had somehow strengthened Valerie's resolve, and not weakened her in any way. But Felicity could see the truth. This was the story of a selfish, difficult mother and her estranged, complicated daughter. Far from being reunited in the face of adversity, they were simply putting on a front because it didn't suit either of them for the public to know the truth about their relationship. And Felicity knew that meant Alice would have to agree to more than just some awkward pictures. She would have to allow her mother to spin a version of events and never say a word to suggest anything different.

Once the shoot was over, Alice simply collected her things and left. There was no big scene or strained goodbye. She simply said, "Right, I'm off" and went. In fact, she seemed to get some pleasure from suddenly blanking her mother again, and making it clear their estrangement was to continue. And as she disappeared down the stairs there was a moment, just a brief moment, when Felicity was sure she caught a flicker of sorrow on Valerie's face and she realised that, for all of Valerie's bravado, she had hoped her daughter was going to stay for more than just the photocall. Jason pulled his laptop out of his satchel and then took himself off to the kitchen to edit the pictures and upload them to the picture desk's cloud. "Don't worry, Val, I'll get rid of your bags," he laughed as he went. And Felicity thought she and Valerie would have a few moments alone which was perfect, as she desperately wanted to know how Valerie was going to handle her response to Adam Jaymes' exposé. But then she heard Jason say "hello" in the corridor on his way to the kitchen and, without warning, someone else appeared in the sitting room.

"How lovely," Valerie said, and gave her colleague an embrace. "You're looking much better than the last time I saw you."

And there stood Colin Merroney, smartly dressed in a suit and tie with his hair all brushed and his face freshly shaved. "Well, I couldn't let you have all the attention could I?" he said, wryly.

"You remember Felicity don't you?" Valerie enquired, and gestured towards her.

"I do," Colin said and smiled at her. "I have a vague memory that I either need to say thank you or sorry. I can't quite work out which."

Felicity was a little startled to see Colin looking so well and so refreshed, especially after the state she'd left him in just a few days earlier. But she remembered her manners and smiled back at him. "No, we're good," she said.

Valerie guided Colin to the couch and sat down with him, stroking his arm reassuringly. They chatted quietly for about 20 minutes, catching up with each other's stories. Valerie enquired about Fiona. Colin asked for gossip from the office. They exchanged views about who was next on Adam Jaymes' hit list. Valerie gave her view on how Sam Harvey was doing, and Colin shared a rumour that Gayesh was trying to get the job as Channel 5's new chief executive. Felicity hovered on the outskirts of the room, not sure where to put herself. She didn't want to venture into the kitchen where Jason was at the counter managing his laptop, but she was worried that if she went back to the balcony it would look like she was trying to draw attention to herself. And there was something almost hypnotic about watching two old hacks completely lost in conversation with one another. Being journalists, they clearly had much more pleasure in sharing stories than listening. And she could see the joy they took in every little nugget of information they bestowed, every piece of gossip no matter how far-fetched or unlikely.

And then Colin produced a note pad and pencil from his pocket and a digital recorder. "But we're not here to talk about me, Valerie. So, shall we get cracking?" And there he was, Colin Merroney, interviewing another reporter. Felicity sat down, and listened as Valerie and Colin worked together to concoct a response to the latest story. "This all happened more than 30 years ago. Ray and I were both young and we rushed into something without really thinking. It was very silly and immature, but that's as far as it goes. We realised it wasn't right, for either of us, and very amicably agreed to go our separate ways ... The truth is I was always very fond of Ray. And, indeed, I still am. And I feel entirely responsible for Ray and his lovely partner, Pete, being targeted by Adam Jaymes in this cruel, cruel fashion ... poor Pete has been comfort eating, he's put on so much weight . . . When Ray and I separated, he still wasn't openly homosexual. So I had to respect his privacy ... Jeremy's parents came from very privileged backgrounds. They would never have allowed our marriage if they had known I was already a divorcée by the time I was 20 ... And then it was the 80s and I just didn't want to get Jeremy and Alice caught up in nasty speculative stories about AIDS ... I had to keep Ray and Pete safe from public attention. They were living a very quiet and private life together, a life that has been destroyed by Adam Jaymes ... Alice asked me to keep this a secret. She thought it was disrespectful to her father's memory if it came out after he died ... If I'm honest, my first marriage was a good experience for me and I have no regrets ... I grew up with very strong views about family values and, if anything, my first marriage tempered my attitude towards other lifestyles and sexual preferences ... Adam Jaymes has no moral justification for his behaviour. This isn't public interest; it's public revenge."

Two hours later, Valerie's rebuttal was laid bare for all to see. The story was on the *Ear*'s website, with the promise of the interview in full in the printed version the next day. "There, you see? You can explain anything away," Valerie said, smiling at Felicity, "if you know how."

Derek Toulson was supposed to have cancelled all his meetings. He was told to stay in the office and manage the fall-out from the latest exposé. But his borough council appointment was only a short train journey from London, and he simply couldn't bring himself to postpone. The 'Pound-for-Pound' community investment scheme was his baby, his creation, and he simply enjoyed these meetings too much to let anything get in their way. After all these years he was still drawn to local government, the place where he had started and ended his career in politics.

He had been an elected Tory on a district council in Hertfordshire and eventually served as council Leader, which sent him on a heady power trip for the better part of 10 years. He looked after the top team, of course, whose salaries more than doubled under Toulson. He even let them design their own extremely generous pension schemes. But in return they had to manage an endless stream of staff complaints about Cllr Toulson's bullying, threats, attempts at coercion and generally inappropriate conduct. For a decade, an endless stream of grievances were brushed under the carpet.

But one day Derek picked on the wrong man. In the midst of a nasty and hard-fought local election campaign, he sent a threatening email to a young council officer who was frustratingly meticulous when it came to local government legislation. *"If you mention purdah to me one more time, I will kill you"*, the email stated. It wasn't even the worst threat Cllr Toulson had made, and he had expected the senior team to quickly resolve the situation. But the officer bypassed the executive team completely and took his complaint direct to the police, and before he knew it Cllr Toulson was back to being simple Mr Toulson again. The Pound-for-Pound scheme had given him a path back into that world, and he knew it was the reason he was treated as something of a star on the local government circuit.

"Gentlemen," he said as he entered the meeting chamber where half a dozen heavy, tired, middle-aged men were waiting for him. The officers and councillors sat on opposite sides of the table; the officers were smart and business-like and moneyed, and the councillors were far less polished in their appearance. It was a peculiarity of local government that Derek was well aware of. The cabinet members had the power but the senior staff were paid the six-figure salaries. The resentment from both sides of the table was always palpable.

He handled the introductions quickly and efficiently, and then set about his presentation. "I'm not doing a PowerPoint," he said, dismissively. "You know the deal. I have £50,000 to invest in your local community. All you need to do is tell me how you would like to spend it, and then match that offer pound for pound. The *Daily Ear* gets good PR, and your local community gets a hundred grand of investment. It's win-win."

Over all, the response was positive but one councillor (who Derek had suspected was a bit of a know-it-all the moment he clapped eyes on him) said, "But why would we want to promote your paper here? I don't understand the point of this meeting. The *Daily Ear* is dirt. Adam Jaymes is ripping you to pieces. Why should this council be linked to your organisation?"

Derek could tell the councillor had been itching to speak from the moment he'd entered the room. And he knew the type: opinionated but actually quite dim. Liked the sound of his own voice but hardly ever said anything worthwhile. Has a position of authority and so is rarely told he's an idiot.

"Councillor ... ?" he enquired.

"Oh, I'm Cllr Inkley."

Derek smiled. "You're an idiot," he said. "I'm so bored of having to deal with wankers like you. You make me sick."

There was a brief pause as the officers and members tried to work out what had just happened. Was it a joke? Was it some kind of bizarre sales pitch gone wrong? Cllr Inkley looked around the room for support, but between the smirking officers and his own disapproving cabinet colleagues, he realised he was on his own. "I ... I don't think that's acceptable," he stuttered.

"Fuck off," Derek replied. "Seriously. Fuck off out of this meeting." He pointed to the door and then leaned in across the table to be as close to Cllr Inkley's red face as he could. "I have fifty grand that I can give to you, or to someone else. I couldn't give a shit who gets it, as long as my newspaper gets good PR out of it. You don't think my money is good enough for you? Fine. Go fuck yourself."

"Now wait a moment," the Leader of the council intervened. "No one has said we don't want this investment." He turned to Cllr Inkley and glared at him. "No one!" he repeated.

Derek sat down and looked at his watch. "You have another 15 minutes of my time. I suggest you don't waste it." He then turned to the officers. "Gentlemen, perhaps I can have some time alone with your cabinet members to iron out our differences."

With the Leader's acknowledgement, the three officers left the room and closed the door behind them.

"It's not that we don't want the investment," the Leader said. "But we're like every other local authority. We've already made huge cuts to our budget. We can't just pull £50,000 out of thin air."

Derek offered them a half-smile, and rested his palms on the table. This was the bit he liked best. "Gentlemen," he said. "My name is Derek Toulson. My heart is cold and black. I am the voice at the back of your head, the nagging voice that reminds you of your true blue roots."

He reached into his jacket pocket and removed a slip of paper. "My team has already looked into this council's commitments. Here are the savings I would suggest you make to match my £50,000." He placed the sheet of paper on the table, face down, and then pushed it towards the three councillors. "It's that simple," he said.

11

CHRIS LACKIE HAD taught himself never to hurry. No matter how urgent the request appeared to be, he would always walk slowly and methodically. He felt it gave him an air of gravitas, that he would always look composed and organised and that his attendance would be that much more anticipated. As the City of London Police Assistant Commissioner, he had to maintain the appearance of certain standards and a refusal to rush was a big part of that.

Besides, he knew who was waiting for him in the interview suite and he was in no hurry to get there. He could usually count on Constables Barnet and Sly to cope with most situations and had been disappointed when they had called him for assistance. Normally, he would have told them to grow a pair and deal with it. But there was a hint of desperation, perhaps even panic, in Barnet's voice which was unusual. He and Sly were tough as old boots, but this situation was clearly out of their comfort zone. It was more political than police work and Lackie had to accept it was ultimately his doing, not theirs.

It was 11am and he hoped to clear the matter up and still make his lunchtime appointment with the Women's Institute. As he reached the interview suite, he was greeted by Barnet and Sly. "We're sorry sir," said Constable Sly, looking surprisingly shaken. "He came in, and it looked like he was going to cooperate. He just sat listening, seemed quite agreeable. But then he said he wanted to see you, and when we said no, it all changed. He started making threats and we didn't know what to do."

"He ... he knows things, sir," Constable Barnet added. "He knows lots of things. We thought it best if you spoke to him."

Lackie nodded and did his best to look un-fazed. "Leave him to me," he said. "Which room is he in?" Although Lackie had never met him before, their paths had almost crossed on numerous occasions over the years. Indeed, they had *almost* met so often that it didn't feel like it was the first time they were coming face to face. As he entered the small, beige room he found Adam Jaymes looking directly at him. He was wearing a beautifully fitted, crimson three-piece suit and was sitting behind a desk with his legs crossed and one arm relaxed across the back of the chair. The air was gently perfumed with a spicy scent of lime, nutmeg and vanilla, a fragrance Lackie didn't recognise and suspected he couldn't afford, even on his inflated police salary.

"I'm only here because of the unusual nature of these complaints and the high profile of this case," he said, feeling the need to explain straight away why he had answered Adam's summons.

"There is no case," Adam responded immediately, his voice soft but clear. It was the same calm tone with which he had casually destroyed Colin Merroney's marriage on live television.

Lackie tried to maintain an air of control but he suspected the situation was well beyond his grasp. He knew the *Ear*'s photographer was already positioned outside the station, ready to take photographs of Adam as he left. And he knew Leonard Twigg was waiting for his call, ready to publish the exclusive story about Adam Jaymes being questioned by the police. "We've received serious complaints from members of the public that you have used blackmail and intimidation to gather information to use against the staff at the *Daily Ear*," he continued.

Adam nodded his head. "So I understand," he replied.

Lackie stared down at Adam. "Perhaps you don't appreciate how serious these allegations are," he said sternly, in an attempt to position himself as the authority in the room.

"Allegations," Adam repeated back to him wistfully, as though quietly pondering Lackie's use of the word. "It is interesting," he continued, "because your two colleagues admitted these *allegations* were made anonymously. Although, I'm told, the complainants did stay on the phone just long enough to deny they were staff from the *Daily Ear*."

Lackie didn't respond. He knew he was on thin ice and Barnet and Sly clearly hadn't helped matters. He sat down at the opposite side of the desk, back straight, hands palm-down on the table top. "I see, I see," he said, "so you've bought into that nonsense, have you? You don't want to consider that you're here simply because there are genuine public concerns that you have been breaking the law?"

With that comment, he had expected Adam's demeanour to shift. Perhaps there would be a sarcastic smile or a roll of the eyes. Perhaps, being an actor, there might even be a hearty guffaw. But there was no change. Just those dark brown eyes and that sparkling stare. "The truth," Adam said softly, "is that no one from the *Daily Ear* is in a position to complain to the police or the courts about what I'm doing, because the public would scream hypocrite. That's why you agreed to make it look as though these complaints have come from ordinary people."

Lackie wasn't about to relinquish control of the interview so easily, or start to deny accusations. It was his job, as the police officer in the room, to make the accusations, not to respond to them. "For the record," Adam continued, "my team has used exactly the same techniques to investigate the Harvey News Group as the *Daily Ear* uses to investigate celebrities. If my team is breaking the law, then so is the *Daily Ear*. Do you intend to arrest your friend Leonard Twigg, too?"

"You haven't been arrested," Lackie said, defensively. "You *haven't* been arrested," he said again. His heart began to pound in his chest as he realised the two constables had been right to panic. There was a genuine risk the situation would get out of control very quickly, and so he attempted to draw it back down to his own level. "So who is this team? Perhaps I should be talking to them," he suggested. He hoped Adam would respond like any other suspect, and just begin to answer his questions. But after a moment of silence, Adam replied, "How is that grandson of yours?"

Lackie attempted to maintain his poker face, but he knew what Adam was talking about and that he had been rumbled. "My family has got nothing to do with - "

"I hear his work experience in the *Ear*'s sports department is going very well. I doubt anyone is aware he's your grandson, what with him having a different surname, but what an amazing opportunity for the boy. There can't be many sixteen-year-olds who get a chance like that."

Lackie's poker face was fading. He wasn't used to this, to losing control of an interview so quickly and so entirely. Adam Jaymes was driving the conversation with accusations and, worst of all, Lackie knew those accusations were all true.

"And I hope it isn't made public," Adam continued, "because it might be seen as something of a personal favour. And that would only fuel all those rumours, wouldn't it?"

Lackie didn't respond.

"You know, *those* rumours?" Adam said, smiling. "Because a lot of people think you are, at best, mediocre. A bit of a lightweight in fact, too concerned with image and policy announcements. Or lunch appointments with the WI. And yet you've done remarkably well for yourself."

"It's almost as if, over the years, someone has been helping your career. Someone rich and influential, who's been there at all those crucial moments, nudging you along. Ensuring you got the promotions, even when there were other candidates who were clearly better qualified. And in return you've given tip-offs or confidential information. Or you turned a blind eye to complaints of press harassment. You know, *those* rumours."

Lackie leaned forward and knitted his fingers together. He doubted the revelation about his grandson, on its own, would damage his career. But it was a politically sensitive time, what with the inquiry's spotlight on some parts of the media and its relationship with the police. And Adam was correct; it could fuel enough speculation about Lackie's personal relationship with the *Daily Ear* to bring about an investigation.

And he knew there were plenty of paper trails leading straight back to him. He had sometimes been too quick to ask Twigg for help or, indeed, too quick to help Twigg in return. And, as a result, he had been sloppy and left incriminating evidence all over the place, going back years. His text message conversations with Twigg alone would put him out of a job. And if his wife ever saw them she would probably have a few sleepless nights too.

"I suspect you were a good man once," Adam said, leaning forward. "You became a police officer for all the right reasons and probably made a difference. To some degree, you probably still do. But once you get into bed with a man like Leonard Twigg, there's no going back, is there?"

Lackie felt like a silly old fool. Yet again, he had allowed Twigg to rush him into another situation and hadn't given a moment's thought to the jeopardy he was placing himself in. He hadn't stopped to consider the possibility that Adam Jaymes might turn his attention away from the *Daily Ear* for a few moments and focus on the senior police officer foolish enough to get in his way. "Is this why you asked to see me? To threaten me?" he asked.

"I don't recall asking to see you," Adam replied, and reclined back in his chair again. "I remember being very surprised that Assistant Commissioner Lackie took time out of his busy day to come and see me while I was being questioned. I think my seven million Twitter followers. Oh wait ... ". He pulled his iPhone from his jacket pocket and checked it. "Sorry, my seven *point five* million Twitter followers would very much like to hear about your visit to the cells."

"These aren't the cells," Lackie said. He missed the old days, when the police and their friends in the media had control over the flow of information to the public. Now every Tom, Dick and Harry had a Twitter account or Facebook page and could upload anything they wanted, from snotty criticisms to incriminating video clips. Nothing was straightforward any more, he thought. Too much transparency, too much accountability, and too many questions.

"I was asked if I would attend the station here this morning, voluntarily, to assist you with some concerns that have been raised," Adam said. "And, of course, I am always happy to help the police with their enquiries. But no one knows I'm here. Nobody. I just came. So what do you think my Twitter followers would think if I were to set foot from this police station and come face to face with, say, a photographer from the *Daily Ear*? What do you think those seven and a half million people would think about that?"

"I think, young man," Lackie said, making one last attempt at sounding authoritative, "that you should remember where you are and the very grave situation you are in. You would do well to avoid throwing around accusations that could land you in even more trouble."

"Oh, for goodness sake," Adam muttered. "You can keep that nonsense for teenage shoplifters." And then, suddenly, he leaned forward onto the desk again and knitted his fingers together, mirroring Lackie's position and staring him directly in the eyes. "I'm going to explain something to you now, Assistant Commissioner," he said, quietly, "and I hope you will listen carefully because, as I've said, I am sure you were once a good man. I am represented by the best legal team on the planet. If you do anything to intervene with my project, or take false action against me again, I will make a phone call to that legal team. Just one phone call. And they will rip through this grubby little police force brick-by-brick, email-by-email, padded envelope by padded envelope. By the time they have finished, you will not have a job, reputation or pension worth talking about."

And, right then and there, the reality of the situation smacked Lackie right in the face. After all these years, decades in fact, Leonard Twigg was finally facing someone bigger, richer and smarter than he. And at that precise moment, Lackie wished more than ever that he'd never gotten into bed with him. "You're free to leave whenever you want to go. You know that don't you?" he said, defeated.

"Yes," Adam replied cheerfully, and stood up. He buttoned his jacket and walked slowly towards the door but stopped. It was likely to be the one and only time the two men would ever meet, and Lackie realised Adam had one final thought to share with him.

Without turning back to look at him, Adam started to speak, a sad tone to his voice. "Years ago a friend of mine came to you for help. She was being stalked by this man, a really vile and cruel monster of a man. He was everywhere she went. He camped outside her home. He would follow her to work. He would wait for her outside restaurants or shops. Sometimes he would decide that she looked too happy, that he needed to make her cry, and so he would just walk up to her in the street and shout abuse in her face, *right* into her face, and then take photographs of her crying. And that's when he wasn't lying on the ground trying to look up her skirt and take photographs of her vagina. But month after month you sent her away, and told her there was nothing you could do. You told her that the man was 'just doing his job', and that it had been her decision to become a famous actress and that she needed to live with the consequences of her decision. Do you remember that case, Assistant Commissioner?"

Lackie sat perfectly still, staring at the wall. He didn't do anything to indicate he had acknowledged what was being said.

"I could have come after you, Lackie. It would have been easy. And I have good reason to. You know I have good reason to," Adam said and gently pressed down on the door handle. "You should count your blessings." And, with that, Adam Jaymes was gone.

Lackie waited a few short moments and then jumped to his feet and hurried out into the corridor where he found Barnet and Sly waiting for him, looking anxious. "Get outside now and tell the photographer from the *Ear* to come in straight away so I can see him," he said. "We need to draw a line under this now."

His constables hurried after Adam Jaymes, and Lackie returned to the interview room and sat down again. He rested his face in his hands and an enormous sigh escaped from his mouth. Pearl Martin's suicide had haunted him for years. Even now, he could still clearly picture her ghostly pale face and big, pleading eyes. And he knew he hadn't done as much as he could to help her. His commitment to Leonard Twigg had come first, and so he had protected the hunter rather than the prey.

After her death, there had been a public outcry the like of which no one had ever seen before or since. Lackie had taken a step back and allowed Twigg, Valerie, Jason and the rest of the *Ear* to take all the heat. He had genuinely thought the *Ear* would fall and that he would never hear from Twigg again.

And while the *Daily Ear* had been under attack from all sides, Lackie had busied himself with a few internal reviews. He had been asked to appease concerns that the police didn't respond strongly enough to complaints of stalking. And without any help from Twigg, he smoothed the whole situation over and managed to keep his job. But once the dust had settled, he realised the *Daily Ear* was still there. And, before long, Twigg was back in touch. Adam was right, once you make a deal with the devil there was no turning back.

With a sense of dread, Police Assistant Commissioner Chris Lackie pulled his mobile phone from his pocket and called the editor of the *Daily Ear*.

Jason Spade was waiting for Adam Jaymes and pounced the moment he stepped from the police station's revolving doors. "That's it, Adam, you know the routine. Just doing my job," he said, cheerfully snapping dozens of pictures. There was a glee to Jason's tone and a familiarity to his demeanour, as though he and Adam were old mates who hadn't seen each for far too long. He then hot-footed it from side to side, trying to capture Adam's elusive bad angle (no photographer had so far been able to find it). For a man who was morbidly obese, Jason was surprisingly nimble on his feet when chasing a celebrity. But, to his surprise, Adam Jaymes didn't rush off. Instead he stood still and stared directly into the camera lens. "Yeah, a bit close, Adam," Jason said. He then lowered his camera and found the star looking him directly in the eyes. After a moment, Adam said, "You were the one who got the pictures of me and my husband on the yacht."

Jason grinned, proudly. "Oh yes," he said, "and I made a small fortune out of those pictures, thank you very much. They were everywhere, nearly crashed the internet when we put them up."

"I suppose it must have made a nice change, taking photographs of two gay guys in swimming trunks instead of lying in the gutter trying to take photographs up women's skirts."

"Funnily enough," Jason said, brazenly, "most of the hits we got for those pictures were in America. Your husband is a lot more famous than you. I bet that hurts."

In spite of Jason's taunting, Adam's expression didn't change. There was something threatening about him, Jason thought. Not physically threatening but there was something behind those dark eyes, something that seemed a little too self-assured. And there was the tiniest hint of a smile on that handsome face. It was as if Adam wanted Jason to know that he wasn't safe. "I'm not scared of you," Jason said defiantly, his face curled up with hatred.

"No?" Adam enquired.

"No!"

Adam inhaled through his nose. "Do you just always smell of shit then?" he asked. He then continued to his car and was driven away. Jason turned and found Barnet and Sly standing just behind him. "Inside, now!" Barnet hissed.

EXPOSÉ

Leonard Twigg wasn't happy. His phone conversation with Lackie had ended badly. He had lost his temper, told the Police Assistant Commissioner he was a failure and then slammed the receiver down. He knew he would call him back at some point, not to apologise but to make things good again. When all was said and done, Lackie was a useful contact and an important part of Twigg's limited social life. But he also knew Lackie's argument held water. If the *Guardian* or the BBC realised Lackie's grandson was in the *Ear*'s sports department it could open up an entirely new stream of questions at the inquiry. And things were tough enough as it was. And so Twigg had agreed to drop the story about Adam Jaymes being questioned by the police, but not before he had bombarded Lackie with a barrage of angry insults for not controlling the situation. Twigg knew he would likely send him a text later to apologise for his rant, but for now he was too busy seething. "We just can't get a break," he muttered angrily to himself.

He wasn't used to this, to not being in charge of a situation. His entire life had been an exercise in control, from taking over the management of his parent's bank account when he was 12 years old to planning and manipulating the UK's news agenda for more than 20 years. Everything had to be neat and tidy, boxed and labelled and prepared in advance. This Adam Jaymes situation was messy and that was largely because Twigg didn't know who would get the next call. He knew the *Daily Ear* was riddled with scandals, and he doubted he knew even half of them. Whilst he hadn't been at all surprised to discover Colin had been having an extra-marital affair, the revelation of Valerie's first marriage had been a horrible shock. It had shown Twigg that even the people he thought he knew best might have secrets that could damage the *Ear*'s reputation further.

It hadn't been all bad news, however. He was happy with Valerie's interview and that day's printed edition of the *Daily Ear* had seen a healthy boost in sales as a result. And although the readers' comments on the website had remained mostly negative, Valerie had received a fair number of supportive comments too. It wasn't an overwhelming show of support by any stretch of the imagination, but not as bad as expected. And he was very happy with his 'Toxic' story. He hoped it would be remembered as a classic tabloid front page, right up there with 'Gotcha' and 'Freddy Star Ate My Hamster'. He loved the idea of it sticking to Adam Jaymes' reputation for the rest of his life. Whenever anyone talked about Adam, the word 'toxic' would be in the back of their mind. Oonagh appeared at his office door, and walked in without knocking.

"Enter," Twigg said, to make a point.

"We have a problem," she said, and sat down in front of him. "Your 'Toxic' story isn't working. In fact, it's become something of an embarrassment."

Twigg glared at Oonagh. He could tell she was happy to deliver the news, but was going to need a lot of convincing that she was right. "Explain," he said.

Oonagh flicked through several sheets of A4 paper she had printed up. "Well, one of the executive producers of *Glee* tweeted this morning. He's says it's completely untrue that they've cut Adam Jaymes' scenes and that the episodes are being broadcast without any edits. In fact, he says they've invited him back and hope he will guest star again in the future."

Twigg shrugged.

"Adam Jaymes' agent has confirmed that he hasn't been sacked from *True Blood* and has actually just signed a contract for the new season."

Twigg didn't reply. He just sat and listened and looked increasingly glum.

"M&S has denied it has dropped Adam from its upcoming menswear campaign and the children's charity Barnardo's says he is still one of their celebrity ambassadors. In fact everything you claimed in your story has now been flatly denied. And, to rub salt in the wound, Maroon 5 have announced they are duetting with him at tonight's Brit Awards and E!'s *Fashion Police* just named him Best Dressed Celebrity of the Week. Like I said, it's become something of an embarrassment." Oonagh relaxed back in her chair, clearly pleased with herself. "So, what now?"

Twigg wasn't about to give her the pleasure of seeing him rattled or upset. And he certainly wasn't going to let her think he doubted his own judgement. "So, amid this melodrama you've just inflicted upon me, all you basically have to report is that a few people have denied our story," he replied. "Which is what we expected anyway."

"We look foolish and desperate."

Twigg smiled, opened his laptop and started to type. "He'll be booed off the stage tonight," he said, without looking up. "And all this negative publicity has created a rift with his partner. He's not back in London just for the Brits. He's here because he and his other half have separated."

Oonagh's eyes grew wider and wider. "What? What on earth are you saying?" she asked, with obvious frustration. "Booed off stage? Separated? Says who?"

Twigg sat back in his chair and crossed his arms. "We will. Tomorrow," he replied, cheerfully.

12

DEREK TOULSON HAD despised Jason Spade from the moment they first met. He had nothing against the paparazzi in general, but it infuriated him when poorly educated people earned more than he did. And Derek knew Jason earned a lot more. Indeed, he suspected Jason had amassed a personal fortune that ran well into seven figures. During the late 90s, when Jason's infamy was at its peak, there had been a well-publicised bidding war for his services with a flood of offers from across the world including tatty US celebrity magazines and European tabloids. But Howard Harvey put a stop to all attempts to poach his star photographer by agreeing an exclusive and extremely lucrative contract the likes of which no photographer had seen before, or since.

Derek, on the other hand, had joined the company only a few years earlier and hadn't negotiated a particularly good deal for himself. He couldn't bear the thought that he earned less than a man he considered little more than a fat, flatulent, badly dressed pervert who seemed to do little else but lumber around the building leaving the pungent pong of body odour in his wake. But he didn't hate Jason just because of the money. It was also the disproportionate amount of clout that Jason had within the Harvey News Group. He resented the way that Jason's name was spoken with reverence by most of the staff at the *Ear*. It was the sort of respect, perhaps even dread, that he liked the mention of his own name to generate.

But Jason was a big hitter at the *Ear*: he was in another league to Derek and Derek knew it. Jason had a special relationship with all the key players like Howard, Twigg, Valerie and Colin, and no matter how hard he tried, Derek had continually failed to elevate himself above a supporting role. Twigg merely tolerated him, Howard would often get his name wrong and Gayesh had used him to write his kids' CVs and job applications. Even recently, Sam Harvey had refused his requests for a one-to-one, instead meeting him en masse with the other senior staff.

That scalding sense of irrelevance was the main reason Derek took so much pleasure in bullying his own staff. It sickened him to feel so unimportant while a pleb like Jason swanned around like he owned the place. During his years in local government, he had been at the centre of everything. He had sat at the top table, been a part of all those meetings which took place behind closed doors and influenced pretty much every decision across the authority, and he made sure the Jason Spades of the world knew their place and stayed there. That was not the case at the *Daily Ear*, however, and Derek knew it wasn't a situation that could be easily changed. Together, Jason and the others had been bonded by a blaze of public fury and one of the fiercest media storms the UK had ever witnessed. The uproar that followed Pearl Martin's suicide had been unprecedented and almost everyone believed it would close the *Ear* and potentially land some of its senior staff in prison.

Just as it looked as though the game was up, Twigg had engineered the most astonishing fight back. He booked Colin onto every daytime TV show that would have him, set Valerie loose against the presenters of *Newsnight* and *Today*, publicly appointed Jason as chairman of a new photographers' standards committee and then called in every favour the paper had. Rumour had it Twigg had even pressed the Prime Minster into pulling a few strings to stop any criminal charges being brought. In the end, the storm passed and they all survived to fight another day. It was a unique experience that had linked Jason with the others in a special way and it had all happened several years before Derek had joined the company. The inner sanctum had remained closed to him ever since.

But Adam Jaymes' Project Ear had provided him with hope. It had given him the opportunity to put himself at the centre of the drama and finally infiltrate the top team. By the time Adam Jaymes had uploaded his final exposé, Derek fully intended to have the keys to the inner sanctum and blocked entry to Jason Spade forever. "You're the biggest risk we have," he growled at Jason, who was sitting on the other side of his desk looking barely awake. "A great big, fat, stinking risk." Derek's office door was closed, but he knew his voice carried beyond the wall of glass. He wanted his team outside to hear him and not just so they would know he was putting Jason Spade in his place. He wanted them to see him taking on someone many considered untouchable. No one, Derek had decided, was beyond his grasp anymore.

He leant over his desk and pointed his finger within inches of Jason's face. "So," he continued, a dribble of hate-filled saliva escaping from the corner of his mouth. "You need to tell me now, anything you have that Adam fucking Jaymes might use against us. Anything at all, I need to know it now."

Jason didn't flinch. He sat, a mountain of flesh slumped onto a chair, and stared at Derek with a puzzled expression as though he couldn't quite understand why some jumped up PR guy was even speaking to him. A few moments passed quietly and nothing was said. The only noise was Jason's crackling, rasping breath and the occasional creak of his chair. And just as Derek was about to enquire if Jason was having a stroke, the photographer replied with a stern voice, "I don't like people poking their finger in my face."

"Perhaps you'd respond more effectively to a cattle prod," Derek replied, withdrew his hand and sat down. "You clearly haven't been paying attention. I would have expected you to be the first person through my door when Adam Jaymes started his campaign against us. I did not expect to have to chase after you."

"I've been busy," Jason said, gruffly.

"Too busy counting your money?" Derek replied through curled lips, unable to keep his resentment at bay. But he'd given himself away, and Jason's sudden smile made him immediately regret what he had just inadvertently revealed.

"No, some of us have work to do," Jason said, "and real work too, not just poncing around with a flip chart."

"You fat wanker!" Derek screamed and lurched out of his seat so he could yell directly into Jason's face. But before he could get his feet solidly onto the floor, Jason shot up from his chair, grabbed Derek's arm and in a single, lightning fast move spun him around and wedged him face down onto the desk with his hand pushed tightly up his back towards his shoulder blades. Derek screamed again, this time in pain as he felt his joints in his arm and shoulder squeezed and stretched so far it seemed like they would snap. "No, no don't!" he squealed, through the half of his mouth that wasn't jammed against the surface of his desk.

Through the big glass wall, he could see his team pretending they weren't watching what was going on presumably, he thought, so they would all have an excuse for failing to come to his aid. But he could see at least three of them surreptitiously taking pictures on their phones.

"You listen to me," Jason wheezed into Derek's ear. "I don't put up with shit like this from some jumped up Johnny-come-lately like you." He pushed Derek's arm even further up his back, and smiled as he heard a gentle clicking noise from Derek's shoulder.

Derek squeaked, his voice high-pitched and frail. "I … I think you just dislocated my shoulder."

"You speak to me like that again … in fact, you so much as look at me again, and I'll rip your fucking arm from its socket and beat the living crap out of you with the stump." With that, Jason pushed himself off Derek's back, stood upright and brushed his podgy hand through his own hair.

Derek turned round, rubbing his shoulder, and sat onto his desk, gently shaking with the shock of what had just happened. "I'll have you fired for this," he snivelled. "I've got witnesses. A whole fucking office of witnesses."

But with an alarming calmness, Jason just grinned at him. "Go ahead. Make your little complaint. See how many seconds pass before you're asked to clear your desk." And then, with a deep growl from his behind, he released the most nauseating stink into Derek's office which he then tried to wave in Derek's direction. "A little something to remember me by," he said with a big smile and left the room, closing the door tightly behind him.

Derek covered his mouth and nose with his hand and remained on his desk, unable to move. He knew he had nowhere to take his complaint. All of those HR barriers that had protected him from staff complaints over the years were there four times over for Jason. Derek knew he was dispensable, and that Jason was not. And if he complained to the police he'd effectively make himself unemployable. Twigg would make sure of that. His one consolation was the knowledge that Jason was definitely going to be on Adam Jaymes' hit list. How could he not? And at least Derek could make it clear to Twigg and Sam that he had tried to prepare for that eventuality but had, instead, been brutally assaulted. He then shifted round on his bum ever so slightly, and glared through the glass wall at his team. He knew that for the rest of the week, he was going to make their lives a living hell. Every single fucking one of them.

Everyone in the newsroom was on their feet applauding and cheering as Colin and Valerie made a heroic return, hand-in-hand. It was a perfectly orchestrated moment, devised to send a strong message of defiance to Adam Jaymes and the outside world that the *Daily*

Ear, once again, was down but not out. Twigg had made it clear at the morning meeting that he wanted to give Colin and Valerie a big welcome back, and that he expected nothing less than a standing ovation. Derek had then briefed the staff about what they could and could not do. And on this occasion, just this once, they were allowed to take pictures and tweet them but only if they used the specific hashtag *#pressfreedom*.

It was a moment of triumph that briefly lifted the spirits of the *Ear*'s editorial team. With Sam Harvey at his side, Twigg shouted across the newsroom and requested quiet. Apart from a few ringing phones, the enormous office and its dozens of reporters fell silent. "Colleagues," he bellowed, "I'm not going to lie to you! It's been tough. And I believe we have some great challenges yet to come. But this is a great newspaper, with great staff. The best. And we have been through far worse than this in the past. We have a job to do, and we're going to keep on doing it. Whatever Adam fucking Jaymes throws at us!"

Then, with the newsroom applauding once more, he and Sam officially welcomed back Colin and Valerie and they all retired to the editor's office. "Oonagh's got her team monitoring Twitter and the newsfeeds," Sam said, as the four of them sat around Twigg's desk, "so we'll see how it goes". Valerie managed to stop herself from rolling her eyes, but did let slip a quiet groan at the use of Oonagh's name.

"I think it's time we turned up the heat on Jaymes, and some of our competitors who are enjoying this far too much," Colin said. "The BBC's all over it like a rash. Usual bollocks, of course. Too many BBC journalists with too much time to think up too many stupid news angles. But they started it, with that fucking *Newsnight* episode. We haven't done enough to question what the BBC's role is in all this."

"We're looking into that at the moment," Twigg replied. He could see Colin was champing at the bit, ready to dive straight back into a face-off with the BBC. But he needed his senior team to be prepared and clever. Twigg knew he had made mistakes over the previous few days. He had allowed his anger and frustration to get the better of him, and as a result he had forsaken his methodical way of working in favour of knee-jerk decisions. As much as he hated to admit it, Oonagh had been right to question his judgement. His attempts to turn the tables on Jaymes had failed miserably and, prompted by his confrontation with Oonagh the day before, he had taken some time out to review public opinion, the mood in Parliament and the feedback from their own readers. Felicity had pulled the information together for him, and it had not made pleasant reading. It was clear, on this occasion, that there was no margin for error. The public was enjoying every second of Project Ear and was waiting with baited breath for Adam Jaymes' next exposé. The *Ear*'s own readers were only slightly more on side, but largely seemed to think it would be good for the senior staff to eat some humble pie for a change. And most disappointing of all was the realisation that his closest allies in the police and Parliament were keen to keep the scandal, and Twigg himself, at arm's length. The *Daily Ear* was on its own. "Sam and I have discussed this at length, Colin. We have to be seen to be taking this on the chin, and then carrying on as normal," he said.

"Are you mad?" Valerie said, with an uncharacteristic tone of dissent. She and Colin stared at Twigg, as though he had committed the worst of betrayals.

Twigg waited a moment, expecting Sam to wade in and support him. But, as usual, Sam sat quietly on the side-lines waiting for the conversation to happen around him, not with him. "I don't want to get involved in a wider argument with the rest of the media," Twigg said, "because we will lose that argument."

"You don't know that," Colin argued, clearly frustrated. "If we don't widen the discussion, the focus will stay on the *Ear*. And this isn't just about us, it's about press freedom."

"No one is on our side, Colin," Twigg stated, loudly. "Like it or not, Adam Jaymes' rationale for Project Ear has won enormous sympathy with the public and, shamefully, with many parts of the media too. We cannot allow ourselves to look like hypocrites and if we kick up too much of a stink about Project Ear that is exactly how we will look. So they'll be no legal action, no injunctions, no more editorials." Twigg paused and then with a sigh added, "And, for the time being, no more negative stories about Adam Jaymes."

"We'll look like fools," Valerie said, her voice beginning to grate with dismay and anger. "Did you see the newsstands after that horrific *Newsnight* episode where they sandbagged poor Colin? Every single paper had the story on their front page apart from the *Daily Ear*. Our lead story? More tripe from our royal correspondent and his obsession that Princess Diana had Dodi Fayed's love child. I have to say, Leonard, that I think you and Sam would see things differently if you were sitting where Colin and I are sitting right now."

Twigg stared at her, and nodded to acknowledge her point. "Well, perhaps in a few days that's exactly where I'll be," he replied. "But for now, my decision stands. Now go on, the pair of you, back to work."

Valerie and Colin returned to the newsroom. They didn't speak, but as they went their separate ways they exchanged a look of sadness that exposed their mutual feeling of complete betrayal. Valerie could feel an anger swelling through her veins and decided to channel it into her next piece of work – an annual round-up of the top ten women she believed were too ugly for TV.

"Tough, but I think you handled that very well," Sam said.

Twigg huffed. "Yes, *I* did, didn't I?"

Sam went to stand up from his chair, but shuffled back down and then looked towards Twigg for an indication that he was willing to hear a suggestion. Sam wasn't used to this, playing fast and loose with his own ideas, but he knew the stakes were high for the *Ear* and himself and was willing to stick his neck out, just this once.

"You want to say something?" Twigg asked, a little surprised to see Harvey Jr putting his head above the parapet for a change.

"A proposition, actually," Sam replied. He paused for a moment, and hoped his voice wouldn't waver while he delivered his idea to Twigg. It wasn't entirely his idea, of course. He'd had a phone conference with some of his old team in LA to brainstorm the situation. But he had organised it on the hoof, with little time to properly brief them about the history behind Project Ear and Adam Jaymes' grievances against the Harvey News Group. They also didn't completely understand the complexities of the British media and its relationship with the cult of celebrity. So, on this occasion, he was taking a risk and putting forward an idea that was mostly his own. Because he knew that, apart from his father, Twigg was the one person he had to convince of his worth. Without his endorsement, Sam would not be able to maintain his reputation in London as a credible business person. "As you made clear, we have no supporters. None of any value, anyway," he said. "And I know our sales are, quite bizarrely, going up at the moment but that's just in the short term. Those extra readers are just here to gawp, not remain loyal."

"I don't disagree. Your point?"

"Adam Jaymes has us on the ropes. And, by the sounds of things, he's barely started. I've looked over the reputation management reports Derek has prepared. And Leonard, if I'm honest, they worry me greatly. There are a few in there that could close the *Ear* tomorrow, and land most of its senior staff in court."

Twigg didn't respond. He knew what Sam was talking about. Those historical indiscretions that had seemed routine in their day but, in these more enlightened times, would now be considered criminal.

"The only way to close this situation down now, and quickly, is to invite Adam Jaymes in to meet us. We can listen to everything he has to say and find out exactly what he wants us to do. I'm not talking surrender, just an amicable truce."

Twigg glanced to the ceiling as though drinking in Sam's words and giving them great consideration. But as he turned back to Sam, it was clear he had simply taken a moment to calm himself before responding, and had the look of a strict schoolteacher who had caught a boy talking at the back of the class. "I'll be speaking to your father about this later today," he said, his voice filled with contempt. He waved his hand towards the door and then opened his laptop and started to type, dismissing Sam and his hare-brained scheme without a second thought. Sam had never been on the end of Twigg's anger before and he suddenly understood how such a little, unassuming man could carry so much gravitas. There was something inexplicably frightening about being in Twigg's bad books. As he left the office and made his way through the newsroom, he began to understand why so many hard-nosed journalists suddenly became speechless in the man's presence through a profound fear of saying the wrong thing. Over the years the news team had even created a new word, *Twanic*, which described a sudden uncontrollable fear or anxiety resulting from a missed call from Leonard Twigg. This reaction was so commonplace and well documented that the news desk just used the word like it was an everyday thing. "Dave's on the phone, having a Twanic attack. Anyone know why Twigg wants to speak with him?"

Sam returned to the reassuring seclusion of his own office and sat at his desk with his head in his hands. He knew another exposé was due that evening and he knew his father would be expecting Sam to quickly and effectively deal with whatever it was. In fact, the world would be watching to see how he handled it. He stood and walked to the window, looking at the grand view up the Thames to Canary Wharf. "All those people," he said to himself, "all those people waiting for me to fail." It suddenly felt as though the rest of the day was just going to evaporate and he would find himself rushed towards 9pm without feeling in any way prepared. Project Ear was counting down to victim number three and even though Sam had been briefed about the many secret shames of his newspaper and its staff, he had begun to genuinely worry that his own name could be next on Adam Jaymes' hit list.

13

THERE WAS AN obvious shift in the atmosphere of the *Daily Ear*'s newsroom as 9pm approached. The staff busied themselves with an intensity that had more to do with dread than workload. Keyboards were typed ever so slightly harder and phones were answered ever so slightly quicker, snatched up before they were able to ring more than once. But despite the frenetic tension, the enormous area was quieter than normal. Apart from business-as-usual phone conversations, the routine banter and chit-chat had dried up. Each and every member of staff was focusing on their work, nervously wondering if they could be the recipient of Adam Jaymes' next phone call. The indiscretions of an entire newsroom of reporters were as plentiful as they were varied. No one felt safe and everyone hoped it would be someone else who got the call. But every now and again, the reality of the situation became too great and each member of staff would glance up at the screen that was streaming Adam Jaymes' website and its ominous countdown clock. And it felt as though it was counting down just for them.

Leonard Twigg's office seemed tranquil by comparison. He had gathered the key players together as he wanted to make sure they were all in one place so they could quickly work together to dismiss the next exposé, no matter who received the call or what the scandalous story entailed. Valerie was reclining in a leather armchair, quietly drinking tea and reading *50 Shades of Grey*. She had decided to write an article criticising the author but thought she should at least read it first. Colin sat angrily, arms crossed, muttering under his breath. Sam was doing a sweep of news websites and social media on his iPad, assisted by Oonagh. Felicity was making herself useful, delivering refreshments around the office, and Jason was slumped on one of the larger chairs, chin on his chest, snoring.

Twigg was pacing the room, anxiously staring through the glass wall at the enormous screens hanging over his newsroom, waiting for any change that would indicate who at Harvey News Group was next. Once again it was the lead story on *Sky News* and the BBC News channel with the usual mix of media experts and tarnished celebrities airing their views. With Valerie and Colin out of the way, Twigg knew he was now the bookies' favourite to receive Adam Jaymes' call, with Jason a close second and Howard Harvey third. As he looked around his office, he suddenly realised someone was missing. "Where's Toulson?" he asked. There was a group shrug. "Oh, give me strength. The man spends all his bloody time trying to be involved and then doesn't show up when he's actually needed."

"Shall I get him on the line for you, Mr Twigg?" Felicity asked. "I think he was dealing with some staffing issues."

"Staffing issues?" Twigg bellowed. "Nothing is more important than this." He realised he was shouting at the wrong person and so found a kinder tone for Felicity. "Yes, please, get him on the line."

Derek was rushing to the newsroom from the HR department, having spent the previous five hours sacking three members of his team and bringing disciplinary action against four others. The red mist had got the better of him after his humiliation at the hands of Jason and he'd had to punish those who'd failed to help, or smirked, or just watched. As he hurried into the lift and the doors closed in front of him, he could feel his Blackberry vibrate in his jacket pocket. "Oh shit!" he muttered, knowing full well it would be Twigg screaming at him for being late. He wondered for a moment if it would be best not to answer it, and to just arrive at Twigg's office in the hope that the inevitable pandemonium of Adam Jaymes' call would deflect attention from his tardiness. But he knew Twigg's memory was long and a bollocking was on the cards either way, so he bit the bullet and answered his call. "Derek Toulson," he said, and braced himself. But the voice at the end of the line wasn't angry. It was calm and polite. And it certainly wasn't Twigg.

"Hello Derek Toulson, this is Adam Jaymes."

Derek's blood ran cold and he stood absolutely still.

"I just called to let you know it's your turn." And then the line went dead.

Derek heard the lift hum into life as it began its descent to the newsroom. His mind was racing, a blur of questions and images and voices. "What was that?" he gasped. He looked at his phone to check he hadn't imagined the call. But it was still lit-up. Adam Jaymes had called him. As he continued his ascent to the newsroom, he prayed it was nothing more than one final, malicious prank by one of the employees he had just fired.

"I'll try again, he was engaged," Felicity said, but before she could dial there was a roar from the newsroom and the entire floor took to its feet to look at the screens above.

"What's that? What's happened?" asked Oonagh, as everyone in the office looked through the glass wall. "No one's phone has rung. Have they? Has everyone got their phone turned on?"

Twigg opened his office door and marched out into the newsroom, pushing his way through the crowd and looking aloft to see what was going on. The others followed, apart from Jason who remained dozing in his chair. The Project Ear website was showing a humorous picture of a horse's face with the headline "Naaayyyy!

I'm not gaaaayyy!!" and underneath the more damning sentence, "Bungling *Ear* exec shuts 'gay horse' sanctuary."

"It's Derek," Valerie gaped, recognising the top of Derek's head poking out from the bottom of the screen.

"Who's in charge of that screen?" Twigg hollered. "We need to scroll down."

A young technician waved at Twigg, and quickly vanished into a small alcove at the edge of the room. They all looked up again as the technician brought the rest of the page into view.

"But that doesn't make sense," Colin said. "He wasn't even here back then. He's no one. Why would Jaymes bother with him?"

And then, at that exact moment, the lift pinged and the silver doors slid apart. All heads turned as Derek stepped from the lift to see his name and face presented for all to see across Adam Jaymes' website. "He ... he just called me," Derek said, almost proudly. "I got the call."

With that, Twigg grabbed Derek by the arm and marched him into his office. And then the phones started ringing like they had never rung before.

Derek sat in Twigg's chair with the entire senior team in front of him, staring down at him. Even though the situation was far from perfect, a small part of him was thrilled. He was finally part of the *Ear*'s inner sanctum. He was with all the big hitters – Twigg, Sam Harvey, Valerie, Colin, Oonagh. He was part of the fire and heat that would bond them all forever. After all these years, he had finally arrived. He didn't even care that Jason was lurking in the background, grinning at him. "It's a simple scheme," he said. "We put up £50k and they put up £50k. That's all. It's win-win. We get publicity, they get investment."

"Oh Derek, you fool. That's not all," Oonagh said, reading the full story from her iPad.

"Perhaps Oonagh can tell me the whole story," Twigg said, and turned his back on Derek. "Oonagh?"

"According to Project Ear we've only ever invested in Tory-run councils. They have no money to match our offer of fifty thousand pounds so Derek gives them a list of local charities the council supports. These are charities that, apparently, the *Daily Ear* doesn't approve of. The Council cuts its funding and uses the saving to match our fifty grand."

"And why is that so unreasonable?" Valerie enquired.

"Because," Oonagh said, "all the projects on Derek's list are aimed at ethnic minorities or single parents or gay teenagers or families living in poverty. We are responsible for the closure of more than 100 charities across the country which supported some of the most vulnerable groups in society. People living in the most deprived areas have lost vital support so residents in more wealthy areas can have a hundred grand invested in their local swimming pool, or park."

"I still don't see the problem," Valerie said, and then shrugged. "Maybe it's just me."

"And the gay horse sanctuary?" Twigg asked.

"Well, clearly Derek got his wires crossed. He thought it was some sort of animal sanctuary for gay horses and so had it closed. But of course it's not a gay horse sanctuary. It's *Gay's* Horse Sanctuary. It was named in honour of Sally Gay who built the sanctuary up from scratch during the 1980s."

Valerie pulled a face and shrugged again, to reinforce how little she cared.

"Sally Gay died of cancer 10 years ago," Oonagh concluded, "and we closed her horse sanctuary." And then she gave Valerie an old-fashioned look in return.

Sam sighed. "That's going to be our duck house, isn't it?" he said.

"The problem," Oonagh continued, an angry tone beginning to strain her usually composed demeanour, "is that it reinforces an image of the *Daily Ear* as a racist, homophobic newspaper that despises the poorest families simply because they are poor. Not only is our reporting on these issues now going to be called into question, but we are going to be seen as having actively campaigned to have services for these groups cut in a most underhand manner."

Valerie was beginning to get cross that Oonagh's view was proving so central to the conversation and so decided to interject. "Why is this a problem?" she asked, loudly. "Honestly? Is anyone going to be surprised, *really* surprised, that we don't want public money wasted on these types of services? It's bad enough when loony left-wing councils are giving our money hand over fist to every black, lesbian, disabled, unemployed, single teenage mum who comes along. But it's downright shameful when its Tory councils doing it. We shouldn't be embarrassed by this. We should stand up and be counted. Frankly, I think Derek deserves a pat on the back."

Derek, although still slightly dazed, smiled at Valerie and nodded to show his appreciation but felt it best not to add his penny's worth at that point.

"Colin?" Twigg said. "Do you have anything to say? Do you think we're in the clear on this one?"

Colin had stayed by the entrance to Twigg's office and was leaning against the door with his arms tightly folded across his chest. As all eyes fell on him, he rolled his eyes and groaned out load. "Oh for fuck's sake," he said. "This is absolute bollocks."

"Not helpful," Twigg snapped. "I want your opinion. Do you agree with Valerie? Do you think we have nothing to worry about?"

Oonagh went to speak again but Twigg raised his hand to make clear he did not want her opinion. Colin looked at Valerie and remembered what a good friend she had been. Not just over the past week, but over the years. She had been one of the few journalists who'd been respectful to him from the start. She had been one of the few women who'd never had the slightest interest in him sexually, who had always treated him like an equal and given him good advice when he'd needed it (which he often did). He wanted to support her and agree with her, to back her up in such an important meeting. But he also knew, on this occasion, that she was entirely wrong. Colin was experienced enough to see beyond the walls of the *Ear* and how the story could easily steam roll out of control. This wasn't a simple tale of infidelity or a secret marriage. This was something that affected real people, out there in the real world.

The tabloids would have fun with the 'gay horse' sanctuary, but the BBC and the broadsheets would push the broader issues. It would lead to investigations, and enquiries, and *Panorama*s, and Prime Minister's questions. And beyond the national media there would be a thousand local newspaper reporters following up the story in their patch. There would be endless dissection, analysis and comment. Local authorities would be inundated with Freedom of Information requests and the drip-drip-drip of detail and new angles would keep the story going for months. If Derek's scheme wasn't seen as corrupt, it would certainly be seen as unethical and dishonest. More than that, Colin knew how he would cover the story if he worked for another paper. He knew how relentlessly he would pursue the *Daily Ear* until someone, *anyone* had been fired and he could claim their scalp as his own. The *Daily Ear* needed to act swiftly.

Colin unfolded his arms and the look of anger on his face gradually faded and for a brief moment he looked genuinely remorseful. He looked at Valerie, gently shook his head, and then gazed at Twigg. "Derek has to go. Straight away," he said. He looked at his editor and tried to work out from his expression whether he agreed or not. There seemed to be a hint of a smile on Twigg's face as though Colin had just passed a test. He looked beyond Twigg and noticed a few nodding heads that seemed to indicate everyone else had acknowledged the need for a sacrifice. And then his eyes dropped back down to Derek, who was still smiling and looked somewhat tickled at being centre of attention.

"I agree," said Sam, the first to speak up. He was taking a chance by voicing his opinion ahead of Twigg's, but had never felt comfortable with Derek and was pleased to have a reason to fire him. "On this occasion, I don't see we have a choice."

"Agreed," said Twigg. And Derek's fate was sealed. "I'll have a car ready to take you home, Derek. Felicity will clear out your desk and we'll send on your personal possessions. Sam will organise an exit package for you. But I hope I don't need to remind you that if you break the confidentiality clause in your contract, you will leave with nothing."

Derek nodded. "No, no, you're right. I should take some time off. Maybe a few weeks. Just while this all dies down." In his head, Derek was still in the inner sanctum, still one of the key players. It simply hadn't registered that he had just been sacked.

"What?" Twigg snapped. "What's wrong with you, man?"

Oonagh reached down and gently helped Derek to his feet. "Come with me, Derek. I'll see you out and I'll explain on the way down what's going to happen next. Have you left anything in your office that you need urgently?"

With the penny finally dropping, Derek looked around at his former colleagues, suddenly feeling very alone. They were not his friends. They were getting rid of him. He was not one of them, and never had been. He was disposable, and Jason was still sitting in the corner of the room and was still grinning at him. "My coat. My briefcase," he said meekly. "I will need my briefcase."

"I'll fetch it for you, Mr Toulson," Felicity said and followed Derek and Oonagh from the office.

Standing at the glass wall, Twigg and his remaining colleagues watched as Oonagh and Felicity escorted Derek to the lift. The staff in the newsroom watched silently as though a funeral procession was passing by. Few really knew who Derek Toulson was or what he did at the *Daily Ear*. They certainly didn't understand why an industry no-one had been targeted by Adam Jaymes, but they all suspected they would learn an awful lot about him over the coming days.

14

the most disgusting hypocrisy. In March last year, Valerie Pierce used her *Daily Ear* column to grandstand on the issue of knife crime. Whilst not identifying black communities directly, she attacked 'inner city families' and lambasted them for failing to tackle the problem. However, the article was illustrated with a picture of a black youth. But unbeknown to her readers, at the exact same time the *Daily Ear* was working behind the scenes to have funding cut for vital youth mentoring schemes in those very inner city areas. Charities like *Start Again*, which had an incredible success rate in getting Black teenage boys off the streets and back into education or training. This was one of the schemes axed so the local Tory council could, instead, spend £100k installing a coffee shop in a local library. A coffee shop!

I don't have a gay horse, but I have suspicions about my dog. Anyone know of a gay kennel that #TheDailyEar hasn't shut down? #ProjectEar

"**HAS BEEN BLAMED** for the closure of more than 100 charity-run services across the country, services – according to the actor Adam Jaymes – which were aimed at helping the country's poorest and most vulnerable families. The *Daily Ear* released a statement a few hours ago, stating it had suspended the Pound-for-Pound community investment scheme and launched an internal investigation. And the *Today* programme has learnt that the man behind the scheme, Derek Toulson, left the Harvey News Group last night shortly after the story was uploaded to Adam Jaymes' now infamous 'Project Ear' website. Joining me in the studio to discuss the implications for the councils involved, I have the chairman of the Local Government Association"

Council leader was just on BBC Radio Northampton breakfast show. Tried to defend taking #TheDailyEar's blood money #Failed #ProjectEar

Derek Toulson wasn't even at #TheDailyEar during the #PearlMartin years #confused #ProjectEar

Today, the *Sun* is starting a campaign to re-open Gay's Horse Sanctuary, a safe haven for horses of all sexual orientation

"but, with all due respect Cllr Hislop, you could have said no to the money. That's the point a lot of our listeners have been texting us about this morning. No one at the *Daily Ear* forced you to withdraw funding from those charities"

@RealAdamJaymes I waited 3 days for this? Boring! Next time, I want Colin Merroney bumming a member of the royal family. Preferably Harry.

"decision to close these services were all taken by the democratically elected Council members. The fact they were nudged in the right direction by a well-meaning newspaper executive is neither here nor there"

We collected 2000 signatures to keep Gay's Horse Sanctuary open. The Council still cut the funding. Now we know why #Disgusted #ProjectEar

@RealAdamJaymes AMAZING 'Singing in the Rain' routine with Mr Schue in #Glee but I wish Mr Schue hadn't rapped in the middle of it #Cringe

After two exposés that were little more than salacious fun, the actor Adam Jaymes has (rather surprisingly) delivered a news story worthy of the *Telegraph*'s own 'MPs' Expenses' exclusive. And while media attention currently focuses on the hilarious gaffe that saw a horse sanctuary closed because it was named after a woman called Gay, the more disturbing aspects of this project are becoming clearer

I used to work with Derek Toulson when he was in local government #MassiveTosser #ProjectEar

"so important, just to have somewhere to go for help and advice, where no one was judging me or looking down on me. The people at the centre really made me feel good about myself, and there were times when I even felt happy. It felt like it wasn't all just pointless. But then they closed it, and before I knew it, everything just went back to how it had been before"

@RealAdamJaymes So what? It was still the councillors who made the cuts. If you don't like it, vote for someone else #ItsDemocracyStupid

I've been inundated with emails from constituents. Keep them coming! I'm attending an emergency meeting with the Council at 11am #ProjectEar

Is #TheDailyEar editor really trying to convince us he knew nothing about this scheme? If so, how come @RealAdamJaymes knew? #SackHim

has not affected the actor's popularity here or in America. His appearance in *Glee* boosted the show's viewers to their highest level in three years, and his performance with Maroon 5 at the *Brits* got the biggest cheer of the night. In fact, even the *Daily Ear* appears to have given up trying to convince its own readers they should hate him. I guess that, as idiotic as the *Ear*'s editorial staff must be, they know a losing battle when they're in one. You see, the Americans love Jaymes because he's a talented and diverse performer. They don't even seem to mind that he's gay, or that he's bagged one of the country's most eligible bachelors. But the British love him because he grew up right in front of us, on telly. We were with him from his early days as a soap star, playing Pearl Martin's awkward and spotty little brother. And years later, we proudly watched him blossom as Doctor Who's plucky assistant Joe. And it was as Joe that he had his shining moment, bravely sacrificing his life to save the Doctor and Donna from certain death. Fiction, yes, but 14 million of us watched that episode of *Doctor Who*, and cried into our hankies as he breathed his last in his beloved Doctor's arms

"All I'm saying is that many people will look at the list of services and they will wonder why public money was being wasted in such preposterous way. I mean, a soccer team for gay teenagers? Why can't they just join a normal football club like everyone else?"

Leonard Twigg is 55. He never married and still lives with his mum. Just saying #ProjectEar

15

AFTER 48 HOURS of frenzied fire-fighting, Sam Harvey left the *Daily Ear* offices and withdrew to his mother's house in Campden Hill Square. He wanted to cocoon himself in the family home and hide away from the world and all of its staring eyes and pointing fingers. His father had given him a lot of responsibilities from an early age and he'd had to deal with some tough situations in the past, but nothing could have prepared him for Project Ear and the seemingly endless mauling being delivered by the rest of the media. The amusement created by the gay horse sanctuary blunder hadn't bought them as much time as they hoped. The finer details of the Pound-for-Pound scheme were now in the public domain and created such a blur of activity that Sam couldn't even remember when he had last eaten or washed.

Earlier in the day a photographer from another paper had caught him unawares as he'd headed across London to meet with lawyers. He knew the picture would show him looking dishevelled and tired, and that it would likely be used to support a story which would doubtlessly suggest he was cracking under the pressure. And he knew that, in truth, he was sinking fast. Howard had sent him an email demanding to see a strategy for dealing with Project Ear but Sam didn't know how to write a strategy. He had tried to write one once, a few years earlier, but been told by his team that it was a plan and not a strategy. He had never been able to work out the difference between the two. So until recently, he had always had other people write them for him. Howard had made it clear he expected Sam to close down Project Ear quickly, but Project Ear wasn't dying, it was blooming. If anything, the Pound-for-Pound exposé had given it credibility. This was no longer just about sensational stories and revenge. It was about local government corruption and social injustice.

It was in the regional press where the story had really found its legs, with hundreds of local reporters quick to track down disenfranchised service users, irate opposition councillors and bemused ex-volunteers across the country. Now the truth was out, each and every story had led to the formation of a large group of angry and extremely vocal campaigners demanding more than just Derek Toulson's scalp. Sam knew these were the days that would genuinely separate the men from the boys.

"You look like you need a mug of hot milk and some apple crumble," Audrey declared, as she walked into the kitchen to find her son dramatically slumped over the table.

"That would be nice," Sam said, not quite managing to lift his head as he spoke. "It's been the worst day of my life. Literally the worst day of my life. Everything that could go wrong, did go wrong."

Audrey ruffled his hair and kissed him on the forehead. "Sit up, sweetheart, and just remember that this isn't a problem you created. I think your father has been very unfair, bringing you back from LA and handing you responsibility for this."

Sam sat up. "He wants me to prove myself, Mum," he said.

"Perhaps," Audrey replied. "Or perhaps he's just putting himself in the clear."

Sam was puzzled by what his mother had said. She rarely ever uttered a bad word about her ex-husband, even when justifiably she could have said an awful lot. And yet here she was, out of the blue, implying that Howard Harvey had sacrificed his only son in order to avoid the blame for his company's wrongdoings. Sam turned and leaned over the back of his chair and watched as Audrey prepared his supper. "You OK, Mum?" he asked, softly. "It's not like you to speak so frankly like this."

Audrey paused for a moment. Her usually bright face was suddenly ashen and tired. For the first time in many years, Sam thought he might actually see his mother cry. "I'm just so angry with your father," she snapped, choking the final few words as she struggled to conceal her resentment. "I can't believe what he's become. What he's doing to you, jetting off to New York in the middle of all this."

"Dad's working, Mum," Sam said. "He's trying to close a deal he's been chasing for years. Besides, this is what he does. He's spent his entire adult life jetting off to other parts of the world and leaving other people to sort out his problems. He's not a problem solver. He builds things, makes them a success and then expects other people to run them for him."

"But this is different, Sam," Audrey replied, sternly. "All of this casual bravado about the *Daily Ear* being disposable, that it's *just* another newspaper. Well, it's not. He knows it's not. And you're not *just* another executive, either. You're his son. He should be here to support you, not shopping and lunching in Manhattan with that ... that girl."

Sam chuckled. "That girl?" he said. "Estelle's hardly a girl, Mum."

"Oh Sam!" Audrey cried and suddenly lifted her hands to cover her face. Sam realised he had misjudged the conversation. His mother was genuinely upset and a few light-hearted quips weren't what she needed to hear so he stood up, wrapped his arms around her and let her sob into his shoulder. "I can't believe you've let it get to you like this," he soothed. "Come on, Mum. I'm fine. Really. I'm just tired. And Dad *is* supporting me. We talk on the phone every day. But there's a bigger picture. He's trying to buy a big chain of newspapers in America and it's a deal he can't put off. It's now or never. He really hasn't abandoned me, I promise you."

After a few moments Audrey gave her son a quick squeeze and then stepped back, pulling a hanky from her sleeve as she did. "Sorry," she said, looking ashamed of herself.

"You don't have to say sorry, Mum. I'm just a bit surprised, that's all. I hadn't realised you were so upset."

Audrey blew her nose and then pushed the hanky back into her sleeve. "How can I not be upset?" she asked and then groaned, as though frustrated by her own behaviour. "Oh for goodness sake. Hot milk indeed. We need a bloody drink," she said. "Port?" She took the milk pan off the heat, turned off the stove, produced a bottle of vintage port from one of the lower cupboards and poured them both a teacup-full. She then quickly threw together a board of cheeses and biscuits.

As they sat together at the kitchen table, Sam found himself a little startled that his mother's mood had changed so much. "Has something happened that I don't know about?" he asked.

Audrey threw back her port and poured herself another. "No," she said with a sigh. "No, nothing. It's just been so upsetting, watching this unfold. Unravel. And the things I've seen written in the *Telegraph* about you. All my friends are falling over themselves to be supportive and say the right things. But it's all so unfair and untrue."

"Mum, I've seen the stuff in the *Telegraph*. And the *Guardian* and the *Mail* and the *Sun*," Sam replied. "Felicity's in early every day and puts together a cuttings folder for me. And, believe me, she doesn't hold anything back. I told her not to." He kept his tone gentle and composed because, although some of the comments had struck at the heart of his own anxieties, he didn't want his mother to know the pressure was already getting to him. "And it's all fine," he continued. "This is my job. If I'm not prepared to take the flack, I have no business being chief executive."

"But it's ridiculous," Audrey said, "It's like they think you should be some kind of wizard. That you should be able to wave a magic wand and make Adam Jaymes vanish. But there is no quick answer to this, why can't they see that? And your father, Sam. I am so ashamed of him. This is *his* doing but he's put *your* reputation on the line." Audrey slammed her palm loudly down onto the table and the kitchen fell silent. She put down her tea cup and covered her face again.

It was rare for Audrey to lose her temper or raise her voice. For Sam this was an entirely new side to his mother and, in a strange way, he found it oddly refreshing. "Goodness," he said eventually, with a humorous tone in his voice. "This is quite an evening we're having here." He paused and waited for Audrey to remove her hands from her face, to give some indication of her mood. After a few moments he thought he heard a chuckle and, as she revealed her face again, and smiled wobbly, he was relieved to see that perhaps her distress was beginning to wane.

"Oh, I'm so sorry," she said, and grasped his hand. "I don't think I'm coping with this as well as I should be."

Sam wanted to put his mother back in a comfortable place. He didn't like seeing her with her heart on her sleeve because he knew that wasn't her, and he knew she would regret any further outbursts in the morning. So he started to help himself to some food, and asked Audrey to help him navigate the cheeseboard by telling him what all the different cheeses were. It was home territory for Audrey and she quickly began to feel more relaxed. As Sam began to eat his supper, Audrey polished off another port and refilled her cup. "I really am sorry, darling," she said. "I just think that no matter how important this business trip to New York is, Howard should be here helping you. You're his son and heir, his *only* heir. I know he's made provision for Estelle in his will, but when he dies his empire is yours. *Your* reputation is important to Harvey Media International and I just think he needs to do more to support you, not throw you to the wolves and watch to see whether or not you survive."

"Mum, please don't worry about me. I'm a big boy now and I'll be just fine," Sam replied. "Adam Jaymes' got a few more exposés up his sleeve and then he's finished with the *Daily Ear*. The very worst thing that will happen is that I'll have to close the paper. That would be a shame but, to be honest, we *can* take the hit. It wouldn't be the end of the world."

"I just feel so useless, so out of the loop," she said. "Your father used to confide in me much more than he does now. If there were any business problems, I'd know about them before his own staff did. I knew everything. But now I feel as if he's expecting me to just sit helplessly on the side-lines and watch this ... this *horror* play out in front of me." Audrey swigged back her port, and again refilled her cup. "This isn't just about the business, it's about my son. *Our* son and I cannot be expected to just sit here and watch."

Sam took his mother's hand and gave it a reassuring squeeze. "Mum," he said, gently, "I know the role you played helping Dad build his business. You and Gran and Granddad. But you're divorced now and as amicable as that was, at some point he was bound to start drifting away from you. It's just what happens."

Audrey topped up Sam's tea cup and shook her head. "I've seen friends divorce over the years," she said, sadly, "and with such bitterness and anger. They've fought over children and property and money. Often, they've ended up living thousands of miles apart and never speaking again, unless it's through a lawyer. Divorce can be so destructive. It can ruin decades of happy marriage, of friendship, and leave nothing but resentment."

Sam could tell his mother was somewhat tiddly, which was making her speak more freely than she usually would. And although it felt as though he was taking advantage of the situation, he decided it might be an opportune moment to do some probing about her divorce from his father. "But that's not what happened with you and Dad," he said.

"Oh no, not your father and me," Audrey agreed, with a hint of pride in her voice. "When we decided to separate, we knew that wasn't going to be for us. Oh no. We were going to be different. Our divorce was going to be like our marriage, kind and thoughtful and civil. We weren't going to give the media anything interesting to write about.

We weren't going to give our friends anything to gossip about. We agreed a way forward and stuck to it. And at first things really didn't seem so different. We saw each other as much as we ever did. We still talked and joked, occasionally had dinner together in town. He took my advice when he needed it, and he let me use the *Daily Ear* to promote my charities and events. If anything, being separated relieved all the stress. All those things that were putting pressure on us as a married couple weren't there anymore. So we just had the good stuff, the friendship."

"Mum, why aren't you and Dad still together?" Sam asked, as though casually pondering one of life's great mysteries. "You were together for 30 years and it just all seemed to end so suddenly. I know I was in America at the time but I just don't remember there being any problems. You both always seemed perfectly happy, content. The fact you're still so close must say something to you both." His words stayed in the air and for a moment he thought his mother might simply change the subject.

Even after a good few drinks Audrey didn't feel completely comfortable talking about the way her marriage ended, particularly to her own son. But as angry as she was with Howard she didn't want Sam blaming him for their divorce and so, after a moment of quiet reflection, Audrey smiled and asked, "Darling, did you ever consider that your father and I were able to remain close *because* we are no longer married?"

Sam shrugged and sipped his port. "What do you mean?"

"What I am saying is there weren't any problems, not really," Audrey continued. "But when you are married for a long time you get into a routine. Or perhaps a rhythm is a better word. Your father and I had a *rhythm*. He had his empire to run and flew all over the world, often for months on end. I had my own projects and charities to keep me busy. And I had the house to run and all my friends, of course. There was always someone to meet for lunch, or afternoon tea or for dinner. And I could pop home to the estate whenever I wanted to see the family. Your father and I spoke on the phone regularly, of course, and he was always very thoughtful. He would send me flowers and gifts two or three times a week. And then he would come home for a few days or a couple of weeks, and we would have some time together. But then he'd jump on a plane and fly off again and I would have the house to myself. We were both used to that and it worked for us. That was our rhythm."

"So what changed?"

Audrey settled back into her chair and a sadness etched across her brow. "We made a silly agreement, many years ago. Oh, I wish we hadn't."

Sam could hear more than regret in his mother's voice. There was a sorrow that he'd only ever heard a few times, the last being many years earlier when she had phoned him in LA to tell him his grandfather had passed away.

"We decided," Audrey continued, "that when we reached our fifties your father would slow down and we could enjoy a bit more time together. And rather foolishly we never reconsidered that agreement. So the year your father turned 50, true to his word, he promoted some of his best people to run all these companies he owned and went into semi-retirement."

"That's when he sent me to LA," Sam said. "Although I actually *asked* to go in case he was planning to offer me the *Daily Ear*. Ironic really."

Audrey smiled. "So you flew off to LA and Howard started to live at the house almost full-time. But we realised very quickly that we had a problem. I had become too used to my own company. Oh, I had enjoyed it whenever Howard came home for one of his visits, but I also liked it when he was gone and I had the house to myself again. Having him there all the time, well, I just found him irritating - crashing about the house, arguing with people down the phone. It wasn't what I wanted."

"And so it was you? *You* decided to end the marriage?" Sam probed.

"It was a bit of everything," Audrey replied. "Your poor father wasn't any happier than I. Suddenly he had all this time to think, time he'd never had before. But he started to think about things a bit too much and ended up having … well, I wouldn't say a breakdown exactly. But certainly a belated mid-life crisis. He got very depressed and frustrated and started to feel he wasn't needed anymore. And then one morning he woke up, rolled over in bed and he … ". Audrey's voice trailed away into silence.

Sam waited for his mother to complete her sentence, and when she seemed to have decided not to say anymore he prompted her. "And he … ?"

Audrey sighed, and looked a little ashamed at having revealed a little too much. "Well, that was the morning our marriage ended," she said, clearly beginning to close the conversation down. "Howard got out of bed, showered, dressed, packed a suitcase and left the house. And that was that."

Sam knew that would be it for the night, but there was a nagging voice at the back of his mind, something telling him he was still missing a vital point. There was something about his parents' separation that neither his father nor mother had chosen to share with him and he began to wonder what Howard had admitted to his mother in bed the morning their marriage had ended. He tried once last time to nudge his mother towards a disclosure.

"But then Dad met Estelle?" he asked.

Audrey nodded and looked a little uncomfortable. "I do feel ashamed," she said. "Estelle's a nice enough girl. A bit rough around the edges, of course, although she's always been perfectly polite to me. But I cannot tell you, Sam, how much it hurt when your father told me he had started seeing someone else. It was less than a year after we separated. Technically we were still married and suddenly this young woman was on his arm. The morning your father told me he was leaving me, well, that was difficult. But it was when he started seeing Estelle, that's when he truly broke my heart."

Sam suddenly felt terribly guilty at having taken advantage of his mother's vulnerable state, and so quickly concluded her tale for her. "You've always handled yourself beautifully. I'm so proud of you, Mum." Thinking it time to move on to a different topic, he decided to share some stories from work. "You know, I did suggest something very silly to Twigg," he said. "A few days ago I said we should call Adam Jaymes in for a meeting, try to barter a deal with him, come to an agreement."

Audrey smiled. "And Leonard, in that indomitable way of his, said you were wrong and made you feel like a complete idiot?"

Sam nodded.

"Yes, he does that a lot, darling," Audrey said, her tone hinting of disapproval. "Leonard has a way of closing down conversations when he hears something he doesn't like. He tried it with me once. Needless to say, he didn't try it again."

"But I have to respect his opinion, Mum. He knows what he's talking about."

Audrey sipped her final cup of port and smiled at her son. "Sam, let me tell you something about Leonard Twigg. He's the most successful newspaper editor of the past thirty years, bar none. He puts the likes of MacKenzie and Dacre in the shade. They can't touch him. But – and this is an important *but* – when he makes mistakes, they're big. And believe me, he's made mistakes and plenty of them."

"Like Pearl Martin?"

"She was the tip of the iceberg. There have been many, *many* others along the way." Audrey could tell her son was anxious about having a disagreement with Twigg. She liked Twigg and had enormous respect for him, but whilst others spoke of him with awed reverence she simply considered him to be an employee who had done a mostly good job. "Let me just say this," she continued. "Behind all of Leonard's bluster and pomposity, there's a little man in his fifties who still lives at home with his mother. Perhaps you should remember that the next time he tries to make you feel like a fool."

A characteristic of Audrey's that Sam had always cherished was her inability to be impressed by anyone simply because of their title, job or position. She could walk into a room of judges, cabinet ministers and lords and have them all eating out of the palm of her hand within a matter of minutes. She proved, more than anyone he knew, that you really cannot buy class. "So you think I should follow up my idea? Invite Adam Jaymes in for a discussion?"

Audrey lifted her hand and gently brushed Sam's hair from his brow. "I think it's about time that Leonard was reminded who's boss," she replied.

It was 5am and Felicity Snow was standing alone in a dimly lit London street, not far from the *Daily Ear* offices, watching as a newsagent put the morning papers in the display bins at the front of his shop. Almost without fail, each paper had a front page story about Adam Jaymes, Project Ear or the Pound-for-Pound scheme. The *Sun* had proudly splashed with the announcement that it had successfully re-opened Gay's Horse Sanctuary, thanks to a swell of donations from its generous readers. The *Mirror* had tracked down Colin's pregnant wife to her family home in Scotland. Although there was no interview, there was an exclusive picture that said it all: a young, pregnant woman sitting on her own in a café and clearly broken-hearted. The *Mail* had a front page photograph of Sam, looking dishevelled and tired as he hurried from the *Daily Ear* offices. *"Fears grow for Harvey Jr as Adam Jaymes turns up the heat"*, the headline read. The *Telegraph* said the on-going scandal had scuppered Howard Harvey's attempts to buy an American newspaper chain, and the *Guardian* said the Met was under increasing pressure to re-open the case surrounding Pearl Martin's suicide.

In fact, the only paper not to have the story on its front page was the *Ear* itself. The *Daily Ear*'s splash was an altogether more traditional affair, exposing a young Olympic gold medallist who had allegedly slept with a 57-year-old prostitute. *"Olympic hero's night with granny hooker"*. An exclusive by Colin Merroney.

Felicity found herself smiling because although it seemed so unwise for the *Daily Ear* to carry on as normal, she could understand how the editorial team would find it hard to do anything else. Olympic stars paying ageing prostitutes for sex was exactly the sort of story that had made the *Daily Ear* Britain's best-selling daily. Those were the stories that were the adrenalin for every journalist at the paper, the driving force that got them out of bed every morning and kept them running at breakneck speed all day until they finally crashed back into bed at silly o'clock. That sort of passion and commitment and obsession made the *Daily Ear* more than a job or career, it was an addiction. And for anyone who did their time and was able to survive the pressure and the workload, the benefits were vast.

Felicity knew that Colin Merroney could click his fingers and organise a meeting with almost any politician, company director or celebrity agent in the country. Jason Spade travelled the world first class and was front and centre at pretty much every major celebrity event, award ceremony or wedding. And Valerie Pierce could waltz into any busy London restaurant and get a table straight away, even if it was fully booked. Working at the *Ear* gave even a humble intern like Felicity a certain amount of gravitas and power. Her university friends now treated her like a precious commodity who could offer them tiny insights into a world they would never know. In years to come, they would name-drop Felicity Snow and share her inside story about the *Daily Ear*'s fight with Adam Jaymes. Felicity, within her own modest social circle, had become a star. And she detested it.

"You want your papers, sweetheart?" the newsagent called to her, as he finished putting out the morning editions. He was middle-aged, white, balding and plump and, despite the unbearably early hour, was always cheerful.

Felicity smiled and nodded at him. "Please," she replied and he quickly brought out her papers, tied together with thick string, and handed them to her. "Here you go," he said as he passed them over.

And then, as she manoeuvred them into her grasp, she noticed that he was staring at her.

"Is something wrong?" she asked, suddenly aware that she had stumbled from her flat without checking for the basics, like toothpaste streaks or bed hair.

The newsagent suddenly looked uncomfortable. "Yes, sorry, it's just you're about the same age as my eldest daughter. And, to be honest, sweetheart, if my daughter was being sent out onto the streets of London on her own at this time of the morning, I'd have a few things to say about it."

Felicity thanked him for his concern and said, "Well I think your daughter is a very lucky young lady," and then walked off. As she made her way towards the office she began to think of her own parents. She knew they would still be fast asleep, tucked up in bed in their warm little terrace house in Upminster without a clue what she was up to. They weren't fans of the *Daily Ear* and would be furious if they knew she was working there. Felicity had told them her placement was at the *Guardian* and the few friends who knew the truth had been sworn to secrecy. She hated lying to them, but an internship at the *Daily Ear* was an opportunity she couldn't turn down. And even though it had been hard work and sometimes extremely unpleasant, she knew it would all be worth it in the end. And when it was all over, and she was back at university, she would tell her parents what she had really been up to. Felicity had convinced herself that lying to her mum and dad wasn't so bad if she planned to eventually tell them the truth.

16

"I CANNOT BELIEVE that conniving, evil son of a bitch is being welcomed into *our office* like he's some kind of ... of ... "

"Star?" Felicity suggested, a well-meant attempt to help Valerie finish her sentence.

Valerie span round on the spot and glared at the intern. "Peace envoy!" she spat, blowing cigarette smoke into Felicity's face. "Star indeed," she grumbled.

"Well he is a star," Felicity said with a matter-of-fact tone and waved her hand in front of her face to disperse the smoke.

"Nonsense, he's just an actor," Valerie replied, and did air-brackets around the word 'actor'. "Felicity, you're not a star just because you're on the *telly*, or in a movie. There are celebrities and then there are *stars*. It's the difference between Joan Collins and Liz Taylor. Paul McCartney and John Lennon. Tony Blair and Margaret Thatcher."

"Margaret Thatcher?" Felicity enquired.

"Oh yes," Valerie replied. "That's why Hollywood made a film about her. Blair will be lucky to get a made-for-TV movie."

"Well, I think a lot of people would call Adam Jaymes a star," Felicity replied.

Valerie looked her up and down and then waved a finger at her. "What's all this?" she asked. "All of this attitude all of a sudden. Where did this come from?"

Felicity realised her excitement was getting the better of her and that she was not being as affable as she should be. "I'm sorry," she said regretfully. "I didn't mean to be rude. I came in at 5am to do the papers. I'm feeling a bit frazzled."

"You weren't being rude," Valerie said, with a chuckle. "You were being assertive for the first time and good for you. A little of that goes a long way. Especially round here." Valerie checked her watch and sighed. "And you'd better not let your university know we've been making you do 16-hour days. They'll never place anyone with us again."

"I'm fine, honestly," Felicity said. "Mr Twigg told me to go home hours ago, but I wanted to stay on to … well … to … "

Valerie beamed at her. "Busted," she said. "Oh, I think we all know why you're still here. You want to catch a glimpse of the famous Adam Jaymes as he attends historic peace talks with the *Daily Ear*."

Felicity felt very uncomfortable that her true intentions had been exposed by Valerie. She had wanted to prove herself to be reliable, flexible and willing to work long hours but now she just looked like a silly girl staying late to catch a glimpse of a famous actor. Valerie drew on her cigarette but continued smiling at her, and then prodded her shoulder. "And who could blame you?" she said, playfully. "You want to work in the media? Of course you're here. I'd have thought less of you if you'd gone home."

With that they both turned and stared through Valerie's glass wall into the main office. There was a buzz in the newsroom that had been missing for the past week, an energy and excitement that hinted at a return to business-as-usual. But though it pained her to admit it, Valerie knew the real reason there was such liveliness. Everyone knew that Adam Jaymes was about to make an appearance and although he was at war with the *Daily Ear*, the staff were still excited that he was just minutes away. "Why's he coming here?" Felicity asked. "Surely it would have been better to meet in the chief executive's office, or somewhere more private."

Valerie shrugged. "Leonard said he insisted he meet in the editor's office. Said he wanted to see the *Daily Ear*'s newsroom while he was here. It all sounds very suspicious to me. And it's very late in the day for peace talks. I cannot see any good coming from this, neither can Leonard. But 'Harvey Jr.' ordered the meeting so we have to oblige."

Twigg, Oonagh and Sam had been in deep discussion in Twigg's office for more than an hour. Valerie understood why she and Colin had been excluded from the meeting, but was increasingly unhappy at the high-profile role Sam had handed Oonagh. With every day that went by, Valerie could see Oonagh commandeering more attention from the senior staff and manoeuvring herself into a position of influence and power. The fact Oonagh had been handed a pivotal role in the 'Adam Jaymes meeting' made Valerie uneasy. "I don't like it," she said. "This is a mistake."

Colin joined them in Valerie's office and closed the door behind him. "Twigg has instructed me to be out of the newsroom when Adam Jaymes walks through," he said, exasperated. "He reckons I'm going to punch him."

"Well no one would blame you," Valerie replied and smiled. "Likewise, I've been instructed to stay in my office. Clearly I'm good enough to get a phone call from Adam Jaymes but not good enough to actually meet him. Although, to be honest, I would probably stub my cigarette out on his smug face, so it's probably for the best." Valerie dropped into her seat and Colin pulled up a chair next to her. They sat, side by side, watching as the newsroom continued to hum with excitement.

"Would you like me to get you a tea or coffee?" Felicity asked, desperately trying to appear helpful.

Valerie shook her head. "This really isn't a tea or coffee moment, dear," she declared and produced a bottle of wine from her desk along with three glasses. "You do drink, don't you?" she asked.

Felicity nodded and the three of them settled down with a glass of red to watch the show. And at 8.50pm on the dot, precisely on time, Adam Jaymes arrived in the *Daily Ear* newsroom. There was no fanfare, no swarming army of body guards or sycophantic entourage. Dressed simply in jeans and a grey sweater, the actor was shown through the newsroom in such an unassuming manner that most of the journalists missed him completely. The route from the lift took him directly in front of Valerie's office and as he passed by, Felicity's eyes widened and time seemed to slow down as her mind tried to capture every detail and commit it to memory. Whatever Valerie's views on Adam Jaymes, all Felicity could see was a star. From the graceful and confident manner he was walking to the glistening of his thick, dark hair under the office lights. There was something about the man that elevated him far above the ordinary. Even in such casual clothing, it looked as though he had come straight from a GQ photo-shoot. Adam didn't notice the three of them on the other side of the glass office wall, and so didn't see Valerie and Colin glaring at him with all the hatred they could muster or Felicity gazing at him adoringly. "Wonderful," she breathed, softly. Valerie and Colin turned their glares in her direction and she apologised. "Sorry," she said meekly, "it just slipped out."

"Adam. Thank you for coming. I'm glad you're here," Sam said. His voice was rich and friendly and his hand was extended in a gesture of welcome. For a moment it looked as though Adam would ignore the gesture but after an awkward pause he politely extended his hand and the two men shook. "I hope we can have a good conversation this evening," Sam continued, knowing that he was sounding cringingly earnest. He closed the door and led Adam into the office, towards four leather armchairs that had been positioned specifically so there was no desk or coffee table separating the discussion.

"I'm Oonagh Boyle, editor of the website," Oonagh said, a warm smile on her face. "And can I just say that, even under these difficult circumstances, it's still very much a pleasure to meet you at last."

Adam took her hand, but had a frown on his face. "I think we have met before," he said. "Surely?"

It was an unexpected comment which alarmed Sam and Twigg. They exchanged concerned looks and wondered if Oonagh was about to fall victim to a Project Ear revelation, right there in front of them. But her smile didn't fade, and she broke the tension with a cheerful laugh. "You cannot possibly remember that!" she exclaimed.

"I never forget a face," Adam replied. "Stratford-Upon-Avon. Hamlet. Am I right?"

Oonagh nodded. "That's astonishing," she said, almost giggling at the thought that he remembered her. "We met for about 20 seconds. I cannot believe you remember that."

Twigg's patience had been stretched enough that day. He had remained towards the back of his office so he would not be expected to shake the actor's hand. Having his place of work soiled by the presence of Adam Jaymes was bad enough, but having to watch Oonagh Boyle flirt girlishly with him was beyond the pale. "Much as I hate to interrupt this happy trip down memory lane, we are here for an important reason," he snarled, immediately undoing the efforts of Sam and Oonagh to create a welcoming atmosphere.

Adam did not respond to Twigg's angry interruption. In fact, he seemed to make a point of not acknowledging Twigg in any way and so Sam quickly intervened in the hope of getting the meeting back on track. "Yes," he said, "we should get on."

"Time is of the essence," Adam said, and then smiled at Sam as he took his seat.

"What do you think they're saying?" Valerie asked, sounding very cross and squinting as hard as she could to try to lip read the conversation underway in Twigg's office. "This is so frustrating."

Colin had reclined into his seat and was sipping from his wine glass. "At least the heat's off us, Val, we've done our bit," he said, trying to stop her temper from flaring.

Valerie sat back and sighed. "I suppose," she said. "We've each taken a bullet for the *Daily Ear*. It's time our generals try to negotiate a peace treaty. And if they can't, well, I guess one of *them* will be in the firing line this time. Although it does beg the question why didn't they call him in for talks straight after *Newsnight* or after the story about me?"

Colin could hear the anger beginning to swell in Valerie's tone again. "I think this was Sam's suggestion. Twigg was set against it."

"I don't care whose idea it was, I just care about the timing," Valerie snapped. "The truth is, they didn't really care when Adam Jaymes was humiliating me and you. But the story about Derek changed all that. With three down, Sam, Howard and Oonagh have suddenly realised they're shuffling towards the front of the queue. This meeting isn't about a peace treaty. It's about trying to stop Jaymes before he does to them what he's already done to us."

Colin gently shook his head and discreetly gestured with his hand towards Felicity. "Not in front of the girl," he whispered. He had no reason to distrust Felicity but he didn't think it was the sort of conversation an outsider should be privy to. Valerie realised Colin was right, especially since her book was going to present the staff as having had a united front during Project Ear. It wouldn't suit the narrative if there were witnesses to suggest there had actually been conflict and infighting. And so Valerie released a deep, irritated sigh and nodded. "Quite right," she said.

In truth, Colin was equally frustrated and knew a big part of that was the unfamiliar sense of helplessness. For all these years, the *Daily Ear* had empowered its staff and protected them from the repercussions of their behaviour, only now Colin had been publicly humiliated and Valerie's career and reputation could still go either way. He had seen his editor, the invincible Leonard Twigg, unable to navigate a clear path through the troubles and at every turn they had been reminded how little support they could expect from pretty much anyone else. But at the heart of his despair was the image of Fiona he had seen in one of the other newspapers, a sad figure alone with her thoughts. Her attempts to go into hiding had been foiled by another tabloid and whilst he didn't think for a moment that she would choose to speak to a reporter, he knew how to pressure even the most resolute character into an exclusive interview. Added to that was the loss of his best friend and even his own parents, so often proudly bragging of their successful son, had left the country to stay in their apartment in Cyprus. In fact, outside of the *Ear*, Colin didn't have any friends left.

But perhaps worst of all for Colin was the impact of Project Ear on his work. The Olympic star and the prostitute should have been a straightforward kiss-and-tell. But as he had sifted through the rumours and tip-offs, and interviewed numerous people along the way, he had found himself being ridiculed and challenged. One prostitute had even disputed his moral right to investigate the story; it had been something of a shock for Colin to have a hooker question his integrity. He also had to deal with a member of the Olympic committee laughing at him down the phone, and asking if he saw any irony in his situation. But the truth was that, no, Colin didn't see any irony. All he felt was a deep, burning sense of injustice that *his* private life had been thrown into the public arena, as if he was some kind of cheap celebrity. On his return to work, he had set up a Google alert under his own name so he could keep abreast of what was being written about him. But within a matter of hours his inbox had swelled to unmanageable proportions, and so he had switched the alert off again. No one, it seemed, had any sympathy for him. Even his gay fans appeared to have abandoned him, although a few had emailed to offer him a shoulder to cry on.

He finished his wine and Valerie refilled his glass. "I've two more bottles in there, just in case it turns into a long one," she said. They then settled back into their seats and silently watched the newsroom, waiting for the meeting to conclude and for Adam Jaymes to leave. "You know, Leonard absolutely despises Adam Jaymes," Valerie said. "He struggles to keep his temper at the best of times. Goodness only knows how he's going to keep it bottled for a whole meeting."

And then, as though watching a car crash gently unfold in front of their very eyes, they noticed Jason Spade walking across the other side of the newsroom, marching keenly towards Twigg's office. "Shit!" Valerie shrieked and leapt to her feet. "It's Jason. Does he know Adam Jaymes is in Twigg's office?" She turned and looked at Felicity. "Was Jason told?"

Felicity shrugged. "I don't know if he was told personally, but he would have received the same email as ... "

"Colin, for God's sake stop him!" Valerie howled, with such a sense of urgency that it sent her colleague rushing out of the door and across the newsroom. Colin sprinted around the expanse of desks and floor cables in an attempt to head off Jason before he reached Twigg's office. Even with Valerie's voice still ringing in his ears, he knew he couldn't shout over to Jason. He couldn't do anything that would draw Adam Jaymes' attention. But as he reached the far side of the newsroom his foot caught on the edge of an open drawer and he took to the air like he a rugby player tackling a giant prop forward. He crashed into Jason's legs and the two vanished with a loud thud behind a cluster of desks.

"Oh God!" Valerie squealed as a group of reporters jumped up and rushed over to help. "Oh my God!"

Jason was an enormous man, tall and obese. Colin was short and slim and Valerie feared he would not have fared well if Jason had landed on top of him. But, much to her relief, Colin quickly sprang back up onto his feet and reappeared amid the bustle around the incident.

"I'm a first aider," Felicity said. "I'll go and help."

"Oh, yes, of course you are," Valerie said and rolled her eyes.

Felicity hurried over to see if she could offer any assistance. She arrived to find three journalists struggling to heave Jason from the floor and onto a chair whilst Colin was explaining to him, quietly but sternly, why Twigg's office was currently out of bounds.

"Is something going on outside?" Adam enquired. Everyone in Twigg's office had heard the commotion from the newsroom and felt the vibrations when Jason hit the floor. But whilst Twigg, Oonagh and Sam could see – to varying degrees – what had happened, Adam was sitting with his back to the newsroom and so had missed the entire incident.

"I think someone dropped something," Sam replied, trying to sound nonchalant so as to discourage Adam from asking any further questions about it. "So, thank you again for coming," he continued, afresh. "I did just want to start this discussion by saying that I don't think anyone in this room is going to challenge that you may feel you have reason to take issue with the *Daily Ear*. But we've never actually sat down together, like this, before. And I felt that perhaps, going forward, a direct conversation was a more positive and constructive approach." Sam was using the agreed rhetoric that acknowledged Adam's grievance without admitting liability. He knew it sounded stilted, but hoped it would be enough to put Adam at ease and keep him open-minded.

Sitting just feet away from the actor, Sam suddenly realised a quick resolution was genuinely within his grasp. As aloof and unreadable as Sam found him, Adam Jaymes was still just a man who could be reasoned with and hopefully won over. If he handled the next few minutes correctly, Project Ear could be done and dusted by 9pm. "So," he continued, "I thought a good way to begin would be to open the floor and really just give you the opportunity to tell us why you've started this ... erm ... project, and what you think would be the best outcome from this meeting."

There was a pause in the conversation and Adam didn't respond. In fact, he didn't do anything at all. He just continued to stare with his dark brown eyes and Sam's sudden optimism immediately drained away. There was something about Adam that was unnerving, something in his demeanour, a quiet confidence and cleverness that left little room for superficial pleasantries or public relations. Sam realised the actor could see the rotten truth at the heart of the matter and that truth, Sam knew, was that Adam Jaymes had the *Daily Ear* over a barrel and they had called the meeting so they could essentially beg him to stop. Sam swallowed hard, and glanced at Twigg and Oonagh for support. But Oonagh had been instructed not to intervene at this stage of the meeting and Twigg was clearly happy to leave the ball in Sam's court. It was, after all, Sam's meeting.

"Can I get you a refreshment?" Sam eventually asked, playing for time. "A bottle of water or a tea or a coffee?"

"If you want to talk to me about Project Ear then please do," Adam said, his crystal-clear diction drained of any of the friendliness he had initially brought to the meeting. "But be direct and honest. Just tell me what you want and save the corporate bullshit for someone else."

Sam recoiled slightly into his chair and, for a moment, was at a loss for words. He, Twigg and Oonagh had spent the previous hour rehearsing what they could and could not say. Robbed of the agreed language so early in the conversation, Sam found himself completely adrift. Oh, how he missed the security of his team in Los Angeles.

"Why don't *you* cut the bullshit and tell us what *you* want?" Twigg interrupted suddenly, his voice stern and angry. He despised Adam Jaymes but was even more furious that, since entering his office, the actor had completely blanked him. He had not looked at him or spoken to him since the start of the meeting and had behaved as though there were only three people in the room. It was as if Adam Jaymes considered Twigg unimportant, beneath his eye-line, but the editor of the *Daily Ear* was not about to be ignored. "Are you trying to make a point? Influence the Inquiry? Or is it simple revenge? It would help,

Adam, if you stopped wasting our time and got to the point." He had made no attempt to conceal the loathing in his words and his sudden outburst crushed any remnants of hope Sam had that the meeting might have a positive outcome. Sam knew Twigg was angry that he had been overruled, but had expected him to keep a civil tongue and certainly hadn't expected him to sabotage the meeting.

Adam turned ever so slightly and looked in Twigg's general direction but didn't actually make eye contact. He had the tiniest hint of a smile on his face, which made both Sam and Oonagh feel uneasy. "I'm grateful for your honesty," he said, smoothly. "We wouldn't want to pretend this is a friendly get together, would we? Your revolting story today about one of this country's Olympic heroes shows you haven't learnt your lesson yet."

"You're defending a man who used his fame to exploit a vulnerable woman for sex?" Twigg asked, his face curled up with disgust.

"I would certainly question whether *he* exploited her or if *you* did," Adam replied. "You really can't take the higher ground when you've spent your entire life in the gutter. Your rag does nothing *but* exploit women. I'm sure you'd print pictures of your own mother in a bikini if it would shift an extra thousand copies."

For a moment Sam and Oonagh both feared Twigg would lunge from his chair and attempt to grapple Adam to the floor. Attacking the paper was one thing, but they both knew defiling the good name of his beloved mother was something else entirely.

"Clearly we have some differences of opinion in terms of the nature of investigative journalism," Oonagh said, automatically raising both hands as if trying to separate two men who were about to brawl in a pub. "But it's those very differences that we hoped we could explore here this evening."

"Adam, this really is an open discussion," Sam added, making one last attempt to steer the meeting to a positive outcome. "We are very open to your concerns and any suggestions you might have about how we, as an organisation, can move on from this."

Adam glanced down to the floor and for a moment it seemed as though he was considering their comments. But then he quietly responded in such a way as to make it clear that the conversation was over. "You can't move on," he said sadly, and then lifted his face to look at Sam again. "We've been here before, too many times. We've had countless police inquiries, independent reviews, high court challenges and debates in Parliament. And each and every time you have promised new guidelines, better self-regulation and some kind of culture change. But the truth is that once the dust has settled, the *Daily Ear* just carries on as it did before. You carry on and you carry on, as if nothing ever happened. There is no change to be had here, because you simply don't believe you should *have* to change. You destroy people. You destroy their families, their careers and reputations. Let's be honest, Pearl Martin would still be alive today if it wasn't for this newspaper. And she isn't the only person the *Daily Ear* has driven to suicide."

"And how is that any different to Project Ear?" Twigg demanded, refusing to give up any moral ground to his opponent. "You're a little too quick to cast aspersions on the staff at this newspaper when you've spent the past week enjoying your little PR blitz."

But Adam couldn't be lured into a shouting match by Twigg. After a moment of reflection, he stood and turned his back on them to look out across the newsroom. "I should thank you all," he said. "This has certainly been a worthwhile discussion." His words and the cool way he delivered them left Sam with no doubt that the meeting was a failure. Far from helping to solve the problem, he feared Twigg's behaviour had actually offered further proof that Project Ear was a justified endeavour.

Adam slipped his hand into his trouser pocket and pulled out his phone and Sam assumed the actor was about to call for his car. But there, just yards away on the other side of the glass office wall, was the distinctive form of Jason Spade. He was sitting on a chair and was rubbing his knee, a strained expression on his face as though he was in pain. Colin was immediately next to him, bent down and speaking directly into his face in a firm manner. With a smile, Adam pressed a single key on his phone and then held it to his ear. After a moment, he spoke. "Hello Jason Spade, this is Adam Jaymes."

Sam, Oonagh and Twigg all shot to their feet. There in front of them, in the newsroom, was Jason. He was still on the chair but he had answered his mobile phone and the look of pain on his face and been replaced with one of confusion.

"I just called to let you know it's your turn."

"Wait!" Sam bellowed. "What was that? What did you just do? We're in the middle of talks. Whatever you have planned, please just delay so we can continue this conversation."

But the meeting was over. Adam slipped his phone back into his jeans, turned and for the first time looked Twigg directly in the eyes. "I'll be in touch," he said, and without uttering another word he walked from Twigg's office. Sam followed him through the doorway, fully expecting the actor to acknowledge Jason or perhaps even approach him. But he didn't. With dignity and composure Adam Jaymes simply walked past the dozens of stunned, statue-like journalists and back to the lift. The strange hush which had fallen over the newsroom lasted only until the lift doors closed behind him, and then there was a roar of questions and conversations. Twigg, Sam and Oonagh hurried over to Jason, who was sitting with his phone in his hand looking perplexed.

"What the fuck was that all about?" Colin asked, trying to be heard above the noise from his colleagues across the newsroom. "He was only in there a couple of minutes. What the hell did you do?"

"It's Jason," Oonagh said, clearly distressed at the way the meeting had concluded. "He stood there, bold as brass, and phoned Jason right in front of us."

They all looked down at the injured photographer, who shrugged as if he didn't care. "Fuck him, the stupid tosser," he said. "He's got jack-shit on me. What's he going to say about me that's hasn't already been said?"

"That you secretly took nude pictures of female swimmers during the London Olympics."

They all turned at the sound of Felicity's nervous voice. She and Valerie were standing just behind Oonagh, gazing up in dismay at Adam Jaymes' website. Jason was unable to see the giant screens from his seat, and could only watch as an entire newsroom of journalists fell into an appalled silence as they absorbed the information that was now hanging right above them.

"What does it say?" he asked, as a cold wave of panic spread across every inch of his enormous frame. "What does it say?" he yelled, when no one answered him.

"It says *'Peeping Tom shame of pervert Ear photographer'*," Felicity said, trying to keep her repulsion from affecting the tone of her voice. "He's got an old hard drive from your computer. It was damaged but he's got a team of specialists who were able to extract hundreds of images from it. These included pictures from the women's changing rooms at the London Aquatics Centre."

Jason was shaking his head. "Not mine," he said. "Not my hard drive. It's a lie. He's made it up." Beads of sweat started to burst from almost every pore on his head as, with growing alarm, he saw the expression of every single face in the newsroom change from shock to disgust. "You know Adam Jaymes," he said, pleading to be heard. "He hates me. He'd do anything to get me. Anything. He's made this up. I wouldn't be surprised if he took the pictures himself. To frame me. He's trying to frame me."

"For the love of God, shut up man!" Twigg growled. He then leaned in close and spoke directly into Jason's ear through gritted teeth. "It says the pictures must have been taken with a sophisticated spy camera. That's the equipment you bought last year, isn't it? My signature is on that purchase order. You got me to sign-off on this?"

Jason pushed Twigg away and then glanced urgently from face to face, all around the newsroom, desperately searching for someone, anyone, who looked as though they might believe him. But there were no reassuring smiles or comforting gestures of support. There was nothing but disgust. The only scrap of empathy came from Valerie and Colin, who gazed down at him with something that was halfway between revulsion and pity. "Jason, dear," Valerie said, softly. "There's no coming back from this."

17

"TRUE TO HIS word, he has now handed the hard drive to Scotland Yard. The Metropolitan Police say they are urgently reviewing its content, and have called in a team of specialists to help identify when and where each photograph was taken, and the identity of any of the women in the pictures. Although Adam Jaymes' exposé centres on images allegedly take during the 2012 Olympics, the BBC has learnt there are hundreds of images spanning a period of up to 12 years"

A man whose entire career consists of lying on the floor taking pictures up women's skirts. And everyone's shocked? Seriously? #ProjectEar

when almost 50 female television presenters and actresses threatened to boycott the National Television Awards in protest of Spade's conduct at the previous year's event. One called Spade 'an aggressive sex pest' and accused the police of failing to take appropriate action to protect

>> Two plus two equals bore <<
Has Adam Jaymes peaked too soon?

When Adam Jaymes started his hilarious crusade against The Daily Ear, we girded our loins ready for a few weeks of titillating fun.

It kicked off in superb style when pint-sized 'kiss-and-tell' muckraker Colin Merroney was whacked live on Newsnight. Jaymes' brilliant follow-up story involved gay-bashing battle-axe Valerie Pierce getting well and truly shafted by her secret gay ex-husband.

But now all the enjoyment's been sucked out of 'Project Ear' with two further revelations that are far too serious. Where's the fun gone? If the next exposé isn't an exclusive photograph of Estelle Harvey's long-lost man-bits, we're boycotting the whole thing!

@GaysHorseSanctuary Thank you @RealAdamJaymes & @TheSunNewspaper. We are now open again. Mum would be incredibly proud. Please RT

"took a more sinister turn, with the most disturbing revelation to date. Jason Spade is a man with a reputation for harassing female celebrities. He has been investigated by the police on a number of occasions, most recently after last year's National Television

Awards. But despite serious complaints ranging from stalking and verbal abuse to threatening behaviour, no charges have ever been brought against him. This latest development will doubtlessly put the apparent inaction of the police back under an uncomfortable spotlight"

The readers of Doctor Who Magazine just voted Joe the second greatest companion of all time. After Sarah Jane Smith, of course #DoctorWho

Remind me never to piss off @RealAdamJaymes

The car manufacturer Ford is the latest major company to suspend all advertising with the beleaguered newspaper, owned by the Harvey News Group. More than 30 companies, including M&S, Virgin and Barclays, have already pulled their advertisements from future editions of the paper and a raft of other firms are facing increasing customer demands to follow suit

"was made chairman of the short-lived Press Photographers' Standards Board, a working group that appeared to have no genuine remit or jurisdiction. In fact, some considered it to be little more than a PR stunt aimed at preventing a police investigation into the *Daily Ear* and – most notably – its star photographer, Jason Spade. Joining me in the studio is the Press Association's Pictures Editor"

@RealAdamJaymes you're as guilty of exploiting the women in those photographs as the pervert who took them.

no arrests have been made. In a statement Harvey News Group said: "We note the allegations made today concerning the content of a hard drive alleged to have belonged to a member of staff at the *Daily Ear*. We will work closely with the Metropolitan Police.

A member of staff has been suspended from his duties while the matter is investigated. We cannot comment further at this time". However, outraged members of the Olympics committee have threatened

Does anyone know where I can get one of those spy cameras? For purely legitimate reasons of course ;) ... #ProjectEar

"with growing pressure on the chief executive of the Harvey News Group, Sam Harvey, to close the paper which is due to celebrate its 50th anniversary in just two years' time. It's believed such a move could cost the group something in the region of half a billion pounds and put about 300 employees out of work"

The actor was spotted entering the building by the back door last night, ahead of private talks with the *Daily Ear*'s senior staff. Clearly, they believed direct talks with Jaymes were their last chance to avoid further damaging revelations. However, our sources suggest the meeting did not go well. It lasted a matter of minutes and ended when Jaymes published his latest exposé – something he apparently did while sitting in the editor's office. And so, with no deal to be brokered with Jaymes, what next for the *Daily Ear*?

18

LEONARD TWIGG WAS angry. His newspaper was haemorrhaging money, the NUJ was threatening a staff walkout and the police had just arrived with a warrant to search the *Ear*'s offices and computers. Amid everything else he had to manage, including a frenzy of media calls and interview demands, he was still expected to get his paper out. On top of all of that, the absolute cherry on his cake that morning, was the summons to the top floor from his jumped-up chief executive for an urgent meeting. It was not something he was used to; Twigg did not go to see people, people came to see him. As the lift reached the executive floor and its gleaming silver doors parted in front of him, he unhappily came face to face with Oonagh Boyle who had moved well beyond any pretence of camaraderie. "He's waiting for you in his office," she said with a knowing smile, before disappearing into the lift behind him.

Twigg marched straight into Sam's office and found him sitting behind his desk looking somewhat more professional than usual. Even his tie was correctly knotted for once. "I'm busy," Twigg said with great irritation. "Do you have any idea what's going on downstairs?"

"I believe the police have just arrived," Sam replied with a cool, matter-of-fact tone to his voice. "Please sit down."

Twigg needed to short-cut the meeting as best he could, so did as he was asked in the hope he could get it over and done with as quickly as possible. "And?" he snapped.

Sam had always been intimidated by Twigg; indeed, he was the main reason Sam had never wanted to work at the *Daily Ear*. There was something about him he found alarming. Even though technically Sam was the boss, Twigg's monstrous self-confidence and passive-aggressive manner easily eliminated any illusions of authority. But this day was different. Before he had even left the house, Sam had spent more than an hour on the phone to his father. Howard had been supportive and appeared pleased with the way Sam was handling things and was less pleased with the way Twigg had behaved. In fact, the call had been so good that Sam had arrived at work with his own self-confidence lifted. As a result, when Twigg entered his office Sam didn't feel the usual gnawing in his stomach or tightening in his throat. He no longer saw a powerful, frightening juggernaut of a man but just another *Daily Ear* employee who was seriously under-performing.

"Leonard, things have gone from bad to worse and right now I have two options. One is to keep the paper open and the other is to close it. It really is that simple. And right now, for Harvey Media International, option two is the most attractive."

Twigg didn't want to hear any nonsense about his newspaper, his beloved *Daily Ear*, closing down. It was everything to him. It was his power, his influence, his social life, his sense of worth. If the *Ear* closed, it would take everything with it.

"And to make matters even worse, Leonard, I now have reason to be concerned about your performance. Since this started, you have made a number of bad calls and your conduct in the meeting with Adam Jaymes was less than helpful."

Twigg was silent and simply stared at Sam in a manner that was clearly supposed to put him on edge.

"Leonard, we should have been able to draw a line under this whole sorry matter days ago. We should have responded sooner and in a more productive manner."

"Isn't retrospect a wonderful thing, Sam?" Twigg said, looking at his watch.

"This isn't about retrospect, Leonard. It's about making the right decisions, taking advantage of the right opportunities in the right way. I am increasingly concerned that your choices are not in the best interests of this newspaper or this company. Yesterday, you were baiting Adam Jaymes to such an extent - "

"That meeting was a mistake," Twigg cut in, showing a typical lack of respect for someone else's opinion. "Jaymes had no intention of finding any compromise."

"You were like a red rag to a bull. You may as well have published the story about Jason Spade yourself."

Twigg stood up and looked down on Sam. "I have a paper to get out," he said. "I shall speak with your father this afternoon and make it clear that your appointment as chief executive of this company has been nothing short of a - "

"You will not be speaking to Howard Harvey again," Sam stated, his voice surprisingly strong and clear. "I've agreed with my father that we need clarity in his communications with this company and so, from now on, I am the only person at the Harvey News Group he will speak to." As Sam's words cascaded through the air, Twigg could feel them stripping him of his advantage. In any management disagreement, his 'special relationship' with Howard Harvey had always been his trump card. Howard had entrusted Twigg with the authority to do pretty much whatever he wanted, from hiring and firing staff to changing editorial policy and, on occasion, political allegiances. That sort of power was not something he was prepared to surrender so easily, even if it put him in a direct fight with the Harvey heir. "I'll be speaking to your father."

"Sit down, Twigg," Sam ordered firmly and pointed at the empty seat so there would be no misunderstanding as to who was in charge. Twigg did as he was told but his mind was racing. This had come out of the blue. He hadn't spoken to Howard for a few days but there had been no indication that this was on the cards. Twigg wanted to leave Sam's office that second, get back to his own desk to call Howard and speak with him, and to make sure that this had all been a terrible misunderstanding. He did not, *would* not, believe that he could be cut off so completely after 30 years of loyal service.

"For the record, my father agrees with me that calling Adam Jaymes in was a good plan. And, like me, he is disappointed that you failed to make the most of that opportunity."

"He said that himself, did he?" Twigg asked. He hated that, for once, *he* was on the receiving end of a second-hand conversation involving Howard Harvey. He wondered if this is what it had been like for Gayesh and all the other senior staff he had dispensed with over the years.

Sam didn't waver. He didn't rise to the bait and remained impeccably cool and in control. "Yes, he said that himself," he replied. "And, to clarify, we have agreed that he will deal directly with me, and only me, on all matters regarding the *Daily Ear* and the Harvey News Group from now on. He will not accept phone calls or respond to emails from anyone else, and that includes you. I will of course pass on any relevant or important comments or questions. But any conversations you want to have with Howard, from now on, you will have with me."

Twigg had always known that this day might come, that his absolute rule at the *Ear* might eventually be usurped by the Harvey boy. But he hadn't expected it to be so soon and certainly hadn't thought it would be now. He knew the coming weeks were going to be tough but he had absolute faith that he and his paper would survive. Once Project Ear was done and dusted, he had hoped to get everything back to normal as quickly as possible. He planned to have a meeting with Howard where they would agree to send Sam back to LA and dispense with Oonagh Boyle altogether. But he now realised he had underestimated them both. Sam and Oonagh had headed him off at the pass.

"My father and I are also increasingly concerned that Adam Jaymes is finding stories about our staff that we are clearly unaware of ourselves."

"No one could have known what Jason was doing," Twigg replied, brusquely.

"And yet someone outside of this organisation found out. What's worse, you signed the purchase order. You gave a photographer who has a track record of taking indecent photographs the money to buy a camera specifically designed for spying." Sam dropped a sheet of paper across the desk. It was a print out from the website which sold specialist spy camera equipment. "It's a micro high resolution digital spy camera. It's called the PP-10 although, online, it's known as the Peeping Tom. And you signed it off."

Twigg leaned forward to look at the print out and gently fingered the sheet of paper. He remembered a rushed conversation he'd had with Jason years earlier. The pictures editor had refused to sign-off the purchase and so Jason had gone above her head and asked Twigg to approve it instead. Twigg remembered he had been a little uncomfortable with the idea of Jason having a spy camera. But he also remembered how Jason had made promises of all the affairs, hypocrisies and lewd behaviour they could expose with it. Twigg had allow himself to be won over. "I sign dozens of purchase orders every week. I will not be held responsible for this," he said.

"Really?" Sam asked. "But if not you, then who?"

Twigg chose not to respond. He sat back in his chair and folded his arms once more. "I did mention that the police are here, didn't I?" he said, petulantly.

Sam nodded. "Yes," he said. "And before I send you back to your office, you should know that I've made a few changes this morning to our management structure. They will be announced to the senior staff this afternoon."

"Changes?" Twigg asked. He had never felt so powerless in his life. It was not a sensation he intended to get used to.

"I've given Oonagh Boyle some additional responsibilities. Howard is very impressed with her and, I must admit, I am too."

"And what are these 'additional responsibilities'?" Twigg enquired, feeling the rug was about to be well and truly pulled from under him.

"I have appointed her executive editor for Harvey News Group. She'll be over all in charge of both the *Daily Ear* and the website and hold an editorial oversight of all of our regional media, too."

"What?"

"You will now report to Oonagh, not me."

"I will *what*?"

"I've also explained to Oonagh my concerns about your performance. I've asked her to do a piece of work with you, starting immediately, to try to help your professional development. We've agreed objectives for you, and linked them to some key performance indicators. I think it will be a very useful process for you, Leonard."

Twigg's face was screwed up with rage and hatred and he could feel the usual red mist rising before his eyes. "You have asked Oonagh Boyle to performance manage me?" he growled. His mind was racing, rapidly filling up with anger and violent thoughts. "Quit! Just quit", a voice was screaming in his head, "and tell the pompous brat to shove his job up his arse!" But even with the onset of a blazing rage, he knew the cold, sobering truth of his predicament. He had burnt too many bridges in the industry to foolishly think there would be a queue of offers waiting for him outside of the *Ear*. He had seen what had happened to his peers over the years, the other industry giants who had come and gone and – at best – found a place for themselves as commentators, columnists or lesser radio stars. If he resigned there would be nothing left for him. "I see," he eventually replied, almost as a hiss. "I'm sure her advice will be invaluable."

"If I choose to keep the *Ear* open, Leonard, then *business-as-usual* is not an option," Sam said. "Like it or not, I have to demonstrate that I'm listening to our readers and the public. I'm also under pressure from other newspaper groups to improve our performance. There's growing concern in the industry that the government might use this paper's conduct as grounds to legislate against press freedom. They want a sign from me that we can change, that we are responding to all the criticisms and anger that are being directed at us. I trust Oonagh to make that change."

Twigg had had enough. Without waiting for permission from Sam he stood and walked towards the door but paused at the exit as Sam spoke to him one final time. "Leonard, you're a newspaper man. You've covered dozens of stories like this, if not hundreds," he said. "You know that when a big organisation or company is in the shit, the first thing the *Daily Ear* does is demand the man at the top is sacked."

Twigg stood still, patiently waiting for the noise from Sam's mouth to cease.

"On this occasion," Sam continued, "you *are* that man at the top. You might want to bear that in mind."

Twigg didn't look back. He lifted his head high and left the top floor. He returned to his office and immediately called Howard on all the numbers he had for him, but every single call was re-routed to a new answering service. With a grinding sense of injustice, Twigg realised he had been cut off. He did not like this, being made to feel less than essential. He had played a major part in building Howard's empire but suddenly the Harvey family had closed ranks and he was left feeling little more than a minor employee who was ultimately expendable. Clearly the emphasis was now on Sam, the Harvey heir, and Howard was supporting his son at Twigg's expense. It was not a situation Twigg was going to accept lightly.

Audrey's *Amazing People Awards* had started in the early eighties as little more than a dinner and dance to honour her charitable friends, but the *Daily Ear* had played a major role in turning it into an annual TV event. At the time, Leonard Twigg had grown increasingly unhappy that all the other tabloids had their own annual awards and so had asked Audrey if the *Daily Ear* could sponsor hers. With a national newspaper on board everything changed and the event blossomed into a celebrity-filled ceremony watched by millions across the country.

But not everything had survived the previous few weeks and Project Ear. As Audrey stood alone in the middle of a huge television studio in Waterloo, she watched with a twinge of sorrow as an enormous back drop was lifted into place with the *Daily Ear* logo discreetly removed. All around her, lighting technicians, set builders, camera operators and sound engineers were working to create the *Amazing People Awards*. A frenetic noise of hammering, sawing and muffled backstage shouts filled the air, complemented by the occasional music stab or flash of lights from the gallery overhead. Audrey knew she wasn't really needed during the set-up but after the previous few weeks of doubt and complications she wanted to be there, to actually see it all coming together again. But this year had been different and after endless debate and pressure from the other sponsors involved she had finally caved in and agreed to drop the *Daily Ear* brand entirely. Even though both Howard and Sam had completely supported the decision, she felt like she had betrayed them both and her heart still sank when she saw the backdrop for the first time.

Her attention was drawn towards one of the exits, as she noticed a familiar-looking girl being escorted towards her by a technician. Pretty girl, black. Audrey recognised her from a number of meetings she'd had at the *Daily Ear* offices. She was a trainee or an intern or something. Audrey had been struck by how well spoken and polite the girl had been, and how she had gone out of her way to be helpful.

But Audrey couldn't remember her name, and so was relieved when the girl introduced herself.

"It's Felicity. Your son Sam sent me," she said, with a beaming smile.

"Yes of course, dear, I remember you. Of course I remember you. How could I forget such a sweet face?". Audrey nodded to the technician who then walked away. "And what brings you here?"

"Oh," Felicity replied, looking a little startled. "Did Sam not tell you I was coming?"

Audrey looked puzzled and shook her head. "No, no. I don't recall him mentioning it."

"Well, basically, I'm yours for the next seven days. He said the week before your live show can get very busy and thought you could do with a personal assistant to help out. So whatever you want me to do, I'll do it."

"Oh, how marvellous," Audrey said, thrilled that her son was still thinking of her even when he had so much to worry about himself. "But I hope I'm not dragging you away from anything important."

"Oh no, no," Felicity replied. "This will be amazing experience for me too. I hope that's OK."

Audrey gently patted Felicity on the shoulder. "Well, that's just lovely," she replied warmly. "I could certainly do with some help. And I'm glad he's keeping a nice young lady like you out of that snake pit for the time being."

Felicity didn't know how to respond. She wouldn't want Audrey to know that she had quite enjoyed being a fly-on-the-wall whilst Project Ear was in full swing and so she simply smiled and nodded as though she agreed. "It's an amazing studio," she said, swiftly changing the subject.

"Yes, and I know the team here really well," Audrey replied. "They always do a good job. They tell me it's their favourite show of the year. Especially when we honour a disabled child, or a soldier."

"It all looks like it's running to schedule."

Audrey sighed and took Felicity's arm. "Oh, my dear. It's been a very trying few days. Have you heard of something called Twitter?"

Felicity smiled.

"Oh, of course you have," Audrey said. "Well, we've had something of a hate campaign against the awards on Twitter."

"Why would anyone start a campaign against these awards?" Felicity asked.

Audrey shook her head sadly. "It's not really about us; it's about the *Daily Ear* and all this nasty business with Adam Jaymes. But some people went onto Twitter and starting harassing the celebrities who are presenting the awards. They started to get quite nasty, in fact, and unfortunately some of the celebs found the messages troubling and phoned me to say they wanted to withdraw from the event. But I couldn't afford to lose half my famous people so late in the day. Those awards aren't going to present themselves. So I had to personally visit every celebrity who was having second thoughts."

"And they're all back on board?" Felicity asked, not doubting for a moment that Audrey's gentle, elegant and persuasive manner would have won them all over.

"Just about," Audrey replied. "I was completely honest with them and told them I understood their concerns but they all agreed to put their doubts aside for one more year. And so here we are, back on track."

"It really is an exciting event. I always watch it with my mum and dad."

"Not this year, you won't," Audrey said. "You'll have to be here on the night, of course. You can sit at our table. I have a spare seat now Derek's not joining us."

Felicity grinned with excitement. "Oh, well, yes. Yes, of course. I'd love to," she gushed. "I hadn't really thought of that, but I'd love to."

Audrey became aware of Felicity's sombre attire and looked her up and down. They had met a number of times and she recalled that the girl had always looked somewhat plain, as if she didn't want to draw attention to herself. "The event is black tie. Do you have an evening gown?"

Felicity suddenly felt very awkward. No, she didn't own anything that could even remotely be called an evening gown. Why would she?

"Can you afford one?" Audrey asked, well aware that not everyone could pluck a few hundred pounds out of thin air.

Felicity didn't want to look as though she were angling for free clothes and so smiled and said, "I'm sure I'll be able to find something."

Audrey felt a pang of guilt. She had offered this nice young girl a glamorous night out which, in reality, she simply couldn't afford. "Nonsense," Audrey said. "This is a work event, so we'll need to buy you something new on the company account. Millions of people will be watching and you're going to be at the top table, representing the Harvey News Group and the *Daily Ear*." There was a chuckle to Audrey's voice as she took Felicity by the arm and started to lead her to the exit again. "Look, I was about to go to lunch anyway. We'll go to The Ivy. Does that sound good?"

"Oh. Oh yes," Felicity replied, getting a little wide-eyed with everything that was suddenly being offered to her.

"And on the way we'll stop at Vivienne's showroom near Hanover Square. Pick you up something to wear on the night. She's never been my cup of tea, to be honest, but perfect for a pretty young girl like you. I'm told her red carpet collection is exquisite."

19

THE POWERPOINT PRESENTATION took only 10 minutes but, like all PowerPoints, it felt much longer. The boardroom was filled with Harvey News Group's great and good and none understood why they had been called in for an emergency meeting, or why they were being given a guided tour of the company's finances. In particular, they couldn't understand why Sam had seconded a faceless junior accountant like Vincent Nash to do the research and front the numbers part of the presentation. Thirteen tired, distracted executives had been forced to sit through slide after slide of figures and line graphs, presented by a gangly, awkward young man with spiky hair and a Burton's suit that was too big for him. Vincent had been Oonagh's recommendation. He was newly qualified but exceptionally diligent and had been meticulous in his crawl through the bowels of the company's assets and expenses. Vincent also had an incredible capacity for idiot-proofing the most complex information, and had skilfully walked Sam through a seemingly endless collection of balance sheets and bank statements. No rock had remained unturned and his final conclusions were, at best, bleak. Harvey News Group was sinking but rather than trying to bail it out, the top team had been desperately grabbing for the silver.

None of the executives had really paid much attention to the presentation, assuming the whole meeting was simply an attempt by their new chief executive to impose his authority and air-grab for ideas. But these were not people who were used to being called on for answers. They were used to easy success during the decades when money poured in and there was little by way of personal consequence. They were aware the financial climate had changed outside but in their ivory towers they had hoped to sit out the double-dip recession and continue as if nothing was different. But things were different. As Sam stood to recap on Vincent's presentation, the final slide remained illuminated on the wall behind him: a line graph which started at a high top-left, and tumbled to a dramatic low bottom-right. "Thank you, Vincent," he said. "You've done a great job," and patted the young man on the back. It was a signal for Vincent to leave the boardroom. What was to follow was not for a junior member of staff to witness. And so the young accountant dutifully collected his papers and left, crossing with Oonagh as she entered the room. She smiled sweetly at him, thanked him and told him he could go. She then closed the door behind him and walked around the board table, carrying a small folder, and sat at Sam's side.

"When my father asked me to come to London to replace Gayesh, I had a look at some of our figures and I thought Harvey News Group was bucking the trend and actually doing OK," Sam started. "This isn't a good time for newspapers, particularly for a company like this which owns a big chunk of the regional press. But from the figures I was sent, it looked as though we were fine. We were riding out the storm and surviving where a lot of our competitors were failing. And, of course, it was made clear to me that this success was the result of having an executive team who had plenty of new and innovative ways of generating income and increasing sales."

A little bit of praise was all it took for the men around the board table to sit up and actually acknowledge what was being said. They were more than happy to take credit when things were going right.

"But then Vincent – young, recently qualified Vincent - ran me off these *new* figures," Sam continued, glancing at the graph behind him. "And these were very, very different to those which had been provided by our director of finance." He gestured to the portly, grey-haired man who was glaring at him from the end of the table: Uncle Tony. "So, I looked at how we'd managed to keep our head above water. I looked for these great ideas, these amazing innovations that such a coveted team of executives had generated. Was it a better use of digital, I asked myself. Were we building our web presence across our local papers and radio stations in the same way Oonagh has built the *Daily Ear*'s website into the success it is today?"

Oonagh smiled at Sam, happy to accept his only genuine praise.

"But what I found was nothing special at all. Just an over-reliance on cost cutting that has shaved this company to the bone." For effect, he banged his fist on the table. Although it seemed a little premeditated, it unsettled the assembled executives and made them begin to take note of what was happening. "So, you started with the small things," Sam said. "You told our staff across the whole of the UK that they were going to have to pay for their own tea and coffee. And we saved several thousand pounds a year doing that. So, come on, own up. Who came up with that amazing initiative?"

After an embarrassed pause, a hand went up in the corner of the room.

"Wow," Sam said. "No wonder you're paid a six-figure salary." He was trying to keep himself from sounding too smug but, just for once, was allowing himself the luxury of thinking he was actually smarter than the group of executives who had gathered in front of him. "And then you capped mileage claims. And then you brought in a non-replacement policy. But then you went hard-core and you closed offices, reduced print runs or shut papers entirely and made hundreds of staff redundant. You saved something in the region of seven million pounds. Well done all of you," he said. "But then you paid yourselves more than *eight* million in bonuses."

"Our bonuses are performance-related," Uncle Tony stated. "They are triggered automatically. We have no say over them."

"And I assume Gayesh set those targets?" Sam asked, rhetorically. "Or did you set your own targets and just ask Gayesh to sign them off?" Gayesh's name was forever soiled, intrinsically linked with greed, laziness and incompetence. If any decision could be traced back to Gayesh, it was automatically considered flawed. "Gentlemen, you failed to notice that this country is in the midst of a double dip recession, the likes of which we have never seen before. And whilst our competitors have developed new ways to generate income, you have relied on short-term measures such as cuts and closures. You have overseen the failure of a company whilst rewarding yourselves as though it had been a success."

Sam knew all of the men sitting in front of him. A few, like Uncle Tony, he had known since he was a boy. But it made no difference in the here and now. During the previous couple of days Vincent had shown him, in startling detail, just how much those 13 men cost Harvey News Group. He had shown the disproportionate amount of money that had been siphoned into their pension scheme, expense claims and salaries. And he had been shown all the little tricks they had used to create the impression of a company that was flourishing in order to trigger those *pesky* automatic bonuses. The end result was a deafening realisation that the top floor was filled to the brim with cheats and idiots and Sam had had enough. "Gentlemen, of course, you're all fired," he said, as though stating something obvious. "You have 10 minutes to say your goodbyes, and then you are to be out of the building."

Suddenly the room was alight with passion and anger and dispute as 13 heavy, middle-aged men started waving their fists and shouting at the unfairness of it all. Amidst the noise and protests, Sam continued to speak calmly. "The Harvey family would like to thank you for your service and wishes you all the best for the future." He then gestured towards the door.

"By God, Samuel, you've got a lot of nerve!" Uncle Tony shouted. "Where's your loyalty, boy?"

The room quietened down as everyone waited for Sam to respond. Only Sam was not prepared to be drawn into a debate about loyalty from a man he'd almost considered family, but who had been feathering his nest at the expense of the family business. "You are all to be out of the building within the next 10 minutes," Sam repeated. "I will issue a statement explaining this is due to a restructure within Harvey Media International. I've already prepared a fair severance package for each of you."

He gestured towards Oonagh who walked around the board table and handed each of the men an envelope. "We should explain," she said, as she made her way from one red-faced executive to the next, "that through the work Vincent did for us we found a large number of financial anomalies across each of your service areas and, indeed, in your own expense claims." She handed out the final envelope and returned to Sam's side. "I use the word 'anomalies' but there are other words I could use. Discrepancies. Irregularities. Transgressions. Crimes."

"But as an act of good will," Sam continued, seamlessly, "we won't be pressing charges. Instead, I have organised a generous severance package for each of you, the details of which you are holding in your hands now. It goes without saying, I am sure, that this package includes a confidentiality clause."

Uncle Tony had already slit open his envelope and was looking in horror at the company cheque he was holding in his hand. "One pound?" he said, barely able to gather enough breath to utter the words. "One fucking pound?" His colleagues immediately opened their envelopes and discovered the same.

"And coupled with our agreement not to press charges, a very fair severance package indeed," Oonagh said, smiling sweetly.

"Let me make it clear," Sam said, a finality in his tone that sent a clear signal the meeting was over. "This deal is all or nothing. If any one of you fails to accept this package, the deal's off the table for all of you. And I will have no choice but to report these matters to the police. Now, gentlemen, you have 10 minutes."

There was an awkward pause, as though time in the room was caught in a groove and unable to move on. Each of the men exchanged looks and seemed to be waiting for a colleague to speak up, or to raise a valid point of order or law. They didn't want to leave the room because, if they did, it would be as if they had accepted what was happening. But unless someone was able to put forward a decent challenge, there was nothing any of them could do.

"Get out!" Oonagh yelled. Time was suddenly jolted back on cue and the men furiously stumbled from the office. Once alone, Sam looked at Oonagh and raised his brow. "Well?" he asked.

She shrugged. "They all know what they've done," she said, "and the potential repercussions of a criminal investigation. I imagine they'll try to get hold of your father and, once they've failed to do that, they'll take their one pound severance pay and leave quietly."

"I hope you're right," Sam said, "because I don't want any of these old dinosaurs stomping around when the new team arrives from Los Angeles."

Tony Runwell remembered climbing out of bed that morning with nothing to worry about other than a nasty bout of heartburn and a number of missed calls from Leonard Twigg. He had planned to enjoy a quiet morning in his office, shoring-up the executive pension plan and booking a golfing holiday before heading off to meet his mistress for lunch. But that's not how his day had panned out. Instead, as he returned despondently to his office, he found that Oonagh and a team of security specialists had been busy during the 10-minute PowerPoint presentation. His shelves had been cleared, his filing cabinets vacuum-sealed and his computer no longer recognised his username or password. The rest of the executives found the same.

They weren't going to be given any opportunity to remove items or information which could be used against the Harveys in the future.

He sat silently at his desk staring at the company cheque for £1. After all his years, decades, in subservience to the Harvey family that little bit of paper was his recompense: a promise not to press charges and a spiteful quid. He knew he would have to cash the cheque, to make it clear he had accepted the offer. Sam Harvey might be green around the gills but he had them all by the balls, and with Howard still incommunicado there was nowhere for Tony or the others to go but down. With a grinding sense of betrayal rather than sorrow, he gently dropped a few keepsakes into his briefcase and clicked it shut.

"We need to talk!" came an unexpected voice, lifting the room out of silence and breaking Tony's concentration. He looked up and found Leonard Twigg standing at his door, arms folded. "And in future, I would prefer it if you were to return my fucking phone calls."

Tony was too weary for an argument, indeed he was almost too drained for any words at all. He wanted to leave the building quietly and with some modicum of dignity but knew that if he didn't give Twigg a few minutes to vent his spleen there was no way he'd be able to leave peacefully. "This could not be a worse moment," he said.

"There's never a good fucking moment," Twigg snapped back, and closed the door behind him. "Now, we need to talk."

"We have nothing to talk about, now please go away."

"You don't think Sam Harvey's ruination of the *Daily Ear* worth talking about?" Twigg demanded, assuming what was important to him would also be important to Tony.

"That may well be worth talking about," Tony replied, "but as of five minutes ago, it ceased to be any of my concern."

Twigg could sense something was up the moment he had stepped from the lift and saw so many members of the executive team in the office. But he had been so focused on the conversation he wanted to have with Tony that he hadn't paid it much attention. "Explain," he said.

"Sam's had a clear out."

"Who?"

"All of us."

"All?"

"Everyone. We're all going. Now."

Twigg's scheme to rid his world of Sam Harvey and Oonagh Boyle had hinged entirely on Tony Runwell's long-term friendship with Howard. That, it seemed, was another route now denied to him. "I'm shocked," Twigg said, and walked towards Tony's desk. "I hadn't anticipated this at all."

Tony sighed, a defeated man who simply wanted to go home and tell his wife the bad news. "If I were to be honest, I knew the writing was on the wall the moment Gayesh was pushed." He had a twinge to his voice that suggested he was trying not to cry. "Having a Harvey as chief executive was a ticking time-bomb."

"Let me guess," Twigg replied, his lack of empathy becoming clearer. "You thought or rather *hoped* that Adam Jaymes would keep Sam too busy to stick his nose in the company accounts?"

Those sanctimonious words reignited a small fire of defiance in Tony's gut, and so he looked Twigg in the eyes. "Leonard," he replied sternly, "I have never met anyone as ferocious as you when it comes to detail. I've seen you spot fraud or dishonesty from a hundred paces. It's like you can smell bullshit in the air before anyone's even spoken. Of all of your skills, and I will admit you have many, it is that ability to spot the tiniest of misdemeanours which is your greatest."

Twigg pursed his lips and glared. He could tell Tony's compliment was just the pre-amble into a criticism, and he was in no mood to be criticised.

"So tell me, Leonard, how it is that Gayesh Perera was able to spend years blundering through this company's finances in the most ham-fisted way imaginable without you once raising a concern?"

Twigg did not reply.

"I will tell you," Tony continued. "Because as long as he left you alone to run the *Daily Ear* without interference, you didn't care what he did. He could have bought a diamond-encrusted desk for his office, and you wouldn't have given two hoots as long as he never set foot in your precious newsroom. So don't stand there in judgement of me, because you've always known what was going on. And you benefitted just as much as anyone else by ignoring it."

With that, Tony lifted his briefcase from his desk and headed from the office. "Goodbye, Leonard," he said, as he opened the door. "And good luck old chap. We both know you're going to need it."

Twigg was left alone in the empty office, with its sealed filing cabinets and empty shelves. He had been so busy simply *dealing* with Project Ear that he hadn't had the chance to reflect on all the changes that were happening around him. There had been too much, too quickly and he could feel his grip on the *Daily Ear* quickly slipping away with each day that passed. For once in his busy, solitary life Leonard Twigg felt a curious urge for companionship.

It had been a quiet day at Valerie's Portman Square club but she had enjoyed having some time to herself. She had spent a leisurely afternoon on her own in the smallest of the gently lit drawing rooms with only her beloved Jasper for company. He was dozing on the floor next to her, his head gently rested on her foot. It was one of a handful of London clubs where dogs were welcome and one of the scarce few in the country which still had a dedicated smoking room, although technically smoking was overlooked rather than allowed. She had enjoyed having some time to herself, to quietly reflect on the events of the previous few weeks and speculate on what Adam Jaymes would do next. Although Derek had come as something of a surprise, everyone else on Jaymes' hitlist, from Valerie's perspective, had been quite predictable and she had no doubt that Twigg and Howard Harvey would be next. The question she had spent the afternoon pondering was: what did Jaymes have on them?

She had deduced that Howard's scandal would likely be something he had done in business, possibly a tax fiddle or an illegal payment to a politician or civil servant, although she hadn't yet ruled out the possibility that the rumours about Estelle were true. But Twigg was a closed book. Even after all the years she had known him, she could write what she knew about his private life on the back of a match box. She had a terrible feeling in her gut that Twigg would be next, and that his secret would make Jason's spy-cam scandal seem like an amusing mix-up in comparison. It was 7pm and she was onto her sixth glass of Merlot and second packet of cigarettes. She was waiting for Twigg to join her, and knew his obsession with punctuality meant he would doubtlessly arrive at any second. He had never accepted an invitation to her club before. He wasn't the sort of man who felt comfortable in venues that were restricted to members only, unless it was the bar at the Commons.

And so it had surprised her when he had replied promptly to her text - "Yes. I'll be there at seven". She liked to invite people to the club, if only to show it off. It had a famously opulent entrance hall with an enormous sweeping, grand staircase. This lead to drawing rooms, libraries and several bars and restaurants, a never-ending rabbit warren of lavish rooms and historic architecture. She had been a regular at the club for almost 30 years. Her membership was one of the many luxuries she had shared with her high-flying husband when he was alive, and something she had continued with long after his death. Every room in the building brought back fond memories of Jeremy and the many joyful, heady evenings they had spent with friends and colleagues or, sometimes, just with each other. Now the building and its staff and members were among the few constants in her life, and felt like a second home to her. As she sipped from her glass of wine, she could hear rain tapping against the outside of the window and a soft howl of wind circling the building. Jasper raised his head and let out a gentle growl, as he heard footsteps approaching. Twigg appeared at the door, looking damp and windswept, and as he was shown in Valerie stubbed out her cigarette and told Jasper to hush. She went to stand to greet him but Twigg gestured for her to stay where she was.

"Don't get up," he said, and he took off his jacket and kissed her on the forehead. It was an unexpected display of affection, and immediately made Valerie realise that something was badly wrong. Even when Jeremy had died, the most tactile gesture Twigg had managed was a one-armed hug ending in a pat on the back. It just wasn't something he did. She also caught a whiff of alcohol from his breath and realised he had been drinking. He rarely drank. He didn't really like the stuff.

"May I get you something, sir?" the elderly waiter asked.

Twigg slumped down into the armchair opposite Valerie. "Port please, whatever you have. I'm not fussy."

"Madam, the same again?"

"Please."

The waiter left and Valerie smiled at Twigg. "Well, either you're here to fire me or tell me that you've been fired," she said. "Either way, I can tell you are the harbinger of bad news."

Twigg sighed, nudged his glasses to the end of his nose and rubbed his tired eyes. "No, nothing so dramatic," he replied. "It was just a long, challenging day and I was surrounded by idiots and reprobates for all of it." He pushed his spectacles back up to his eyes, relaxed into the chair and stared Valerie in the face. "Anyway, what have you been up to for the past couple of days? Have you enjoyed the time off"

Valerie was disappointed Twigg hadn't commented on the club, but she could tell there were about a dozen conversations underway in his head and that he was struggling to concentrate on the one conversation he was actually having with her. "It's been lovely," she said. "I went down to Old Leigh yesterday and walked Jasper on the beach. I did a little shopping this morning and had lunch with friends. I've spent the rest of the day here."

Twigg nodded but with an absent-mindedness that made it obvious he hadn't taken in a word of what Valerie had just said. His mind was a chaotic jumble of conversations that had never happened, and arguments he wanted the chance to have. Oh, how he wished Howard had taken his call. He wanted Sam and Oonagh gone. The waiter brought another large red for Valerie and left Twigg with the decanter of port and a small glass that was already poured. Twigg downed it and then poured another.

"Leonard, darling, you're not on the verge of a breakdown, are you?" Valerie asked, matter-of-factly.

"Of course I'm fucking not," he replied.

"Well, you aren't yourself. You're very far from being yourself."

Twigg didn't reply. He didn't know how to. He didn't gossip or share feelings. He didn't confide in other people and he never, ever showed weakness. His entire character was anger and bluster and self-righteousness. He had no idea how to ask for help because he had never needed to.

"Leonard, you are an impossible human being," Valerie continued, softly. "I've never met anyone like you and I doubt I ever will again. But, just for once in your life, have a drink, relax and tell *me* about *your* day."

Valerie had kindly provided a structure to the conversation that Twigg was able to work with. But he didn't want to talk about his demotion, or Sam Harvey, or the fat Irish whore. He didn't want to tell her that Howard was refusing to take his calls, or describe the burning humiliation he'd felt when staff were told about Oonagh's new role. "Oh Valerie," he said. "I'm empty. I think I'm done."

"Oh, what nonsense," she replied. "You've survived worse than this. *We* both have. Adam Jaymes - "

"It's not Adam fucking Jaymes," Twigg said, a tone of defeat in his voice that Valerie had never heard before, not once. "I'm out of my time," he said. "This past year. The website, readers' comments. Twitter. This isn't what I signed up for."

"You think you're past it?" Valerie asked, somewhat taken aback that her invincible friend suddenly sounded so vulnerable.

"Look who we're competing against," Twigg said.

"Oh Leonard, even with Project Ear in full swing, we're still way ahead of our competitors."

"I'm not talking about other papers, Valerie," Leonard replied. "I'm talking about ordinary people. Ordinary people sat in their gloomy little kitchens, typing away on the budget laptop they got from Argos. They're looking out of their tiny windows at the rest of the world and they've all got a fucking blog to tell the rest of the world what they think. And you know what the rest of the world should say to those people? It should say, *'Piss off! Who cares what you think? You're no one!'*. But it doesn't. The world listens to them, and it agrees with them, and it repeats what they say like their stupid, poorly considered opinions actually matter."

Valerie shrugged. "That's the world we live in now, Leonard."

"But what does it mean for people like us, Valerie?" Twigg asked. "We're looking down at the world through a big window on the 100th floor. We *really* see what's going on, and we understand the power of words. That's the way it was. That's the way it's always been. *We* spoke and *they* listened. But now, all of those dreadful, boring kitchen people are holding us to account. Millions of stupid plebs without an education between them, they've been handed the internet and now they have a voice. And it's louder than ours."

20

THERE HAD BEEN a time, not so long ago, when all Leonard Twigg had to do was step from the lift into the *Daily Ear* newsroom and a moment of hush would greet him. No matter how hectic or how loud or full the newsroom, his presence was enough to create a moment of anxious delay. Heads would drop, conversations would pause and everyone would wait to see if it was their turn to be summoned into his office by the much dreaded finger of doom. But today was *phone call* day, and it was considered beyond any reasonable doubt that it was Twigg's turn to hear from Adam Jaymes. The expectation had stimulated the atmosphere in the newsroom into something that sat midway between mirth and panic. And so as Twigg stepped from the lift, his staff continued about their business with no interlude, leaving him with little doubt as to how diminished his great presence had become. Unhappy, he made his way to his office, closed the door and sat at his desk. He knew he wasn't focused enough to do his job efficiently that day. He was tired and his mind was hazy. He had made a half-hearted attempt to chair the morning news meeting, but had proven so distracted that Colin had gently taken over halfway through. He did it kindly, with little fuss, so as not to draw attention to Twigg's state of mind. But once the meeting was over, he told Twigg to go for walk and get some fresh air to clear his head. Twigg couldn't remember where he had walked to, but he knew he'd been gone for about an hour. He still couldn't quite focus on his job, and the day ahead seemed of little consequence. He couldn't visualise anything, not even the following day's front page. It was as if he was already a stranger in his own newsroom, an outsider who didn't really belong there anymore. His phone bleeped and he lifted the receiver to his ear. "Twigg," he said.

"I have Assistant Commissioner Lackie on the line for you, Mr Twigg."

It wasn't someone Twigg particularly wanted to speak with, just one of the many people who had let him down over the previous few weeks. But Lackie had been good company in the past and a good contact, and Twigg wondered if it was exactly the conversation he needed to snap him out of his haze. "Thank you, Jeanette. Please put him through."

"You're through to Mr Twigg," Jeanette said, and Lackie's voice came on the line.

"Twigg, how are you?" he asked, sounding genuinely concerned.

Twigg paused. He felt the briefest of stirrings in his chest, a fleeting sensation of warmth as a man he had always liked and respected enquired after his wellbeing. But he quickly drove it down, unable to tolerate a feeling that would likely make him share or gush. "I'm fine. You?"

"We didn't leave things on good terms, the last time we spoke. I wasn't happy to set you adrift like that, particularly taking into account your current ... troubles."

"I'm *fine*."

"Good. I wanted to give you some information that I hope will make things a little easier."

Twigg's mind was already drifting to an evening earlier that year, when he and Lackie had dined together at a gastro pub near Tower Bridge. It had been a simple evening and they'd enjoyed an easy, effortless conversation. Perhaps, Twigg wondered, they might share a few more evenings like that in the future, now that Lackie had extended an olive branch. "Go on," he said.

"We didn't find anything at your offices when we searched the other day," he said. "Everything we've got on Jason Spade is personal to his home computers. Apart from the spy-cam, he didn't use any *Daily Ear* facilities."

Twigg was grateful for the information. He knew it wouldn't make a great difference straight away, as Jason's exposé had already been extremely damaging. But at least the level of blame against the *Daily Ear* would lessen once the case was in court. "That is good news. Thank you. I appreciate the call." Twigg had intended to follow his comment with an olive branch of his own. Perhaps an invitation to drinks or dinner or, if Lackie was still shying away from a face-to-face meeting, a simple suggestion they keep in touch for the time-being.

But Lackie beat him to the punch. "I have to say goodbye now, Twigg. Obviously, we won't be speaking again," he said.

Twigg's blood ran cold as Lackie delivered the news with an off-hand quality that caught him completely by surprise.

"I'm retiring," he continued. "It's been fast-tracked, for reasons you can probably imagine. Tomorrow's my last day. It's all been kept quiet for now. Everyone thinks I'm just going on holiday. But there'll be a press release next month, long after I'm gone. Shirley's decided she's had enough of London, so we're going to stay with her sister and brother-in-law. They live in Portugal. Shirley says if we like it she wants us to buy an apartment nearby."

Twigg was overwhelmed by a profound sense of loss, a realisation that another constant in his life was about to vanish and it left him unable to speak.

"Whatever happens," Lackie continued, "we won't be coming back to the UK. And, like I said, you won't be hearing from me again. So I just wanted to have the opportunity to say thank you for everything. And I'm sorry for the way this has turned out. I don't think it's what either of us would have wanted."

Lackie paused just long enough for Twigg to offer a compliment or fond farewell, or to simply acknowledge his acceptance of this situation. But there was no sound from the other end of the line.

"I wish you all the best, Leonard," Lackie concluded and the line went dead.

Twigg sat for a few moments, with the phone pushed against his ear as though waiting for the conversation to resume. But with each second that ticked by, he became more aware of the emptiness at the other end of the line. He placed the receiver back in its cradle and wondered if he should ask Jeanette to call him back. Perhaps, he thought, if Lackie had received a less frosty reception it might have changed the outcome of the conversation. Perhaps he might not have been quite so clear-cut with Twigg, and left some scope for future conversations or drinks. Twigg picked up the receiver and called Jeanette, but had a last-minute change of heart and so quietly asked her to make sure he wasn't disturbed for the next hour. He then took himself off to his private bathroom and locked the door.

Colin sat alone in the snug at the Cock and Bull and was so distracted by the news coverage on the large, wall-mounted television that his pint of ale had sat in front of him, untouched, for almost an hour. He was engrossed in the countdown to Adam Jaymes' next exposé and had become increasingly unhappy with the tone of the reporting. The light-hearted banter and eager sense of anticipation seemed more fitting to a child on Christmas Eve than professional broadcast journalists. But then Colin had never liked TV reporters, and Project Ear had done little to change his mind.

Hopping from one rolling-news channel to the next, it became clear that Adam Jaymes had started a feeding frenzy which none of them could satiate. During the previous 60 minutes, Colin had watched a revolving door of talking heads, industry experts, commentators, ex-journalists, back bench MPs and former '*Ear* victims'. They'd all been interviewed countless times since Project Ear first started and no one had anything new to say. But Colin could tell they were all thrilled to have another opportunity to put the boot in, live on telly. And so he watched as they were each wheeled out and interviewed only to appear 15 minutes later on another news channel where they were asked the same questions. At least, he thought, the BBC had made an effort to find a couple of new people to add to the mix. There was a camp American business analyst who detailed, with great enjoyment, how the scandal had damaged Harvey Media International's reputation around the world. And there was a bright man in glasses from Ipsos MORI who explained how Project Ear had brought public trust in newspaper journalists to an all-time low. The pollster, much to Colin's annoyance, took great pains to distinguish between newspaper reporters and *other* journalists who rated far better. Colin took a mental note of both their names and filed them away at the back of his mind for future reference. As well as the guests, one other constant across all the channels was the choice of image used as a backdrop to the discussion. Leonard Twigg's face was no longer his own, it was public property and for the past week had become little more than a logo for Project Ear. Throughout all the coverage and discussion, it was clear everyone thought it a foregone conclusion that Twigg would get the next call. And, in reality, even Colin thought Twigg was the most likely candidate.

But he had been around long enough to know there were others whose behaviour might have caught Adam Jaymes' attention and, being conscientious, he had secretly prepared some background material on a number of his colleagues just in case. His *alternative* list was fairly short, but included the barely literate TV critic for whom no pun was too sexist, racist or homophobic, and the ever-smiling, name-dropping showbiz reporter who was every celebrity's best friend until he filed his copy. But top of Colin's alternative list was the *Ear*'s notorious fake Spanish prince who had carried out a number of high-profile stings the previous summer. One by one, he had lured kind-hearted celebrities to a posh London hotel suite so they could make a case for whichever charity they represented. Once there he plied each of them with charm and champagne and coaxed them into poking fun at Britain's own royal family.

One great dame of the British theatre had gotten particularly sloshed and cracked a famously misjudged joke about Prince Charles' penis which created such public uproar she'd had no choice but to renounce her dame-hood and leave the country. The name of the fake prince had never been released, but Colin had no doubt Adam Jaymes would have been able to identify him. His trail of thought concluded as a familiar voice purred, "Now, why did I think I would find you in here?" He swivelled on his stool and found Valerie standing in the doorway, a glass of red in her hand. "Hello stranger," he replied with a smile. "I've been let out of the madhouse for a couple of hours. Oonagh wants me ready for action at nine."

Valerie joined him at his table and grimaced. "And I hope by 'action' you mean 'work'."

"Of course," he replied. "I think she's aiming a little higher than a newsroom grunt like me. Anyway, you look well. Enjoy your time off?"

Immediately, Valerie felt troubled by Colin's comment as she realised she was not the only person who could see Oonagh was closing in on Sam Harvey. But she decided that was a conversation for another time. "Yes, very nice," she said. "I caught up with my friends who were all marvellously supportive and kind. It really helped put all of this Project Ear nonsense into perspective." She noticed a mobile phone lying on the table, and recognised it was Colin's personal iPhone rather than his work Blackberry. "Are you expecting a call?" she asked.

He sipped his ale and, with a degree of melancholy, shook his head. "Nah," he replied. "I've sent her dozens of texts and she hasn't replied to any of them. She was due today. Regardless of what I've done, I still think I have a right to know what's going on. I could be a dad. I could have a son or daughter and not even know."

"Darling, I realise the timing couldn't be worse and I understand you want to speak to her. But it's been less than a fortnight. She's going to need some space."

"She's got space," he replied, glumly. "400 bloody miles of it."

"She'll be back," Valerie said, attempting to sound reassuring.

"No. No she won't. She hasn't just gone to stay with her family in Edinburgh. She's moved back. It's permanent."

"You can't know that."

"I spoke to her dad yesterday. It's permanent."

Valerie wasn't sure what to say. She wanted to offer Colin some hope but hadn't really been left with anywhere to go. "How was Fiona's father with you?" she asked.

"Oh, he's great. Funny old boy. We're basically the same age but he always plays the role of father-in-law. He's always ready with the wise words and common sense. And in spite of everything that happened, he didn't judge me or blame me. But he did tell me that Fiona wasn't coming back and said, maybe, it had all been for the best."

"What, that Adam Jaymes has done you a favour?"

"Well, I know it sounds a bit odd but I take his point."

"I don't," Valerie snapped. "What a ridiculous thing to say."

Colin sighed and glanced back to the TV. He knew Valerie would never allow a good word to be said about Adam Jaymes but perhaps, just perhaps, Fiona's dad was right and it had all for the best. Perhaps, bizarrely, Adam Jaymes had done them all a favour. Fiona, clever sparkling Fiona, would have the baby she craved and the freedom to find a good man to love and care for her. Colin knew he could never be that man and not because he was twice her age. Their short relationship had been happy enough, but it was clear Fiona wanted to create a vanilla, middle-class home that would have been more of a prison than a life for Colin. She wanted play dates and John Lewis and theatre evenings, and highbrow holidays to grim-sounding destinations like Vietnam and Berlin. Colin wanted a wife and kids but with none of the trappings. His work would always come first, and he could never be loyal in the way a wife would expect. Indeed, since Fiona had moved back to Scotland it had become clear that his casual approach to sex hadn't been tempered by marriage.

Without Fiona, his world had quickly jigsawed back into place and returned him to the familiar routines of single life. Once again his days were a rush of work, sandwiches, phone calls, coffee, trains and pints. He had enjoyed the company of a couple of random women during two particularly dark and boozy nights. They weren't anyone he knew: a businesswoman in a hotel bar who said he looked sad, and an American who'd spent an entire tube journey staring at his crotch before offering to buy him a drink. The sex had been good, a welcome relief from masturbation, and he hadn't felt any guilt afterwards. But then the only time he'd ever felt guilt was when he had been with Laura. For Colin, a one night stand was easily forgotten, but Laura had been much more than that. For more than 30 years they had skirted around their attraction for each other, kept at arm's length by their mutual bond with Terry. But just a few weeks after Colin and Fiona's wedding, there had been a chance meeting at a conference in Leeds and a few too many glasses of complimentary wine. Colin wanted to be faithful to his new wife, but the chance to finally be with Laura was a schoolboy's dream come true. The next morning he and Laura awoke with hangovers and regrets and agreed it would never ever happen again, but neither really believed it. And as a few more trysts blossomed into an affair, Colin realised it had spiralled out of his control and he had felt powerless to stop it. If it hadn't been for Adam Jaymes, he and Laura would probably still be seeing each other. "Laura and Terry are back together," he said, with some small measure of happiness in his voice.

"Ah, the collateral damage," Valerie said softly. "Every scandal has its Laura and Terry."

"Terry's been in touch. He sent me a long letter a few days ago," Colin continued.

"A letter?" Valerie enquired, surprised. "How sweet. I didn't know people still sent letters."

"Terry's a complete technophobe. No email, no Twitter. He still doesn't have a mobile. Even his letters are handwritten."

"A handwritten letter," Valerie said and then sighed as though mourning a good friend who had been inexplicably lost to the past. "Good letter or bad letter?"

Colin shrugged, pretending it was much of a muchness and didn't really matter but Valerie knew it mattered to him a lot. "Bit of both," he said. "But I know Terry. Give him a few months and we'll be mates again." He checked his watch and realised it was time to head back to the office, and so downed his pint. "You coming then?" he asked.

Valerie shook her head. "Not this time," she replied, as though Project Ear was a terrible palaver she had grown weary of. "I only popped in to see you. I'm going to finish this and then watch from the safety of my own home. I'm sure it will all be fine, but call me if you need any help."

Colin kissed her on the cheek and headed off. "I will," he said, and then hurried out of the snug. Valerie sipped her wine and watched as the countdown continued on *Sky News*. "And if there's a God in heaven, Oonagh Boyle, you will be next," she muttered to herself.

"It feels different this time," Sam remarked, as the usual suspects gathered in Twigg's office in preparation for the call. No one needed him to elaborate because they each felt the same way. Adam Jaymes' first two exposés had been as ridiculous as they were dramatic, hitting Colin and Valerie on a very personal level but with little impact on the *Daily Ear* itself. In retrospect, they seemed little more than flirtation compared to what had followed. The stories about Derek and Jason had brought genuine disgrace on the *Daily Ear* and left a massive dent in the company's advertising income. Those two exposés had forced dozens of councillors across the country to resign their seats, given opposition MPs the chance to score heavy political points during Prime Minister's questions and forced the Met to launch a criminal investigation that would doubtlessly land Jason in prison. Adam Jaymes had proven he could up his game anytime and without warning, and so it did feel different because everyone realised his next exposé could bring Harvey News Group crashing to the ground. Sam stared at his phone, his mind whirling through all the possible targets and outcomes of the next call. He had spent hours poring over the reputation management documents with Oonagh and the lawyers but, through experience, he doubted their preparation would prove to be of any use. Adam Jaymes had the most amazing ability to reveal secrets about the *Daily Ear* that even the *Daily Ear* didn't seem to know.

Sam sat with Oonagh and Colin at the meeting table with their mobile phones in front of them. Twigg chose not to join them. Instead he sat at his desk with his mobile phone, a little 10-year-old Nokia, tucked away in his jacket pocket and continued rattling away merrily on his keyboard as though he had little interest in what was happening around him. As 9pm approached, Sam could feel a heaviness in the air that hadn't been there for the previous calls. The second hand on the wall clock seemed to tick with an unpleasant haste towards deadline, and as it did Sam could feel every iota of control slip from his hands. "He means business," he eventually said, his mind racing through every file in his internet porn collection. "This is going to be a bad one."

"Sam, we don't know that," Oonagh said. "Let's just keep hoping. He might want to calm things down with something a little more - "

"Be quiet!" Colin said suddenly and raised his hands slightly off the table. "What was that?"

They all listened for a noise, and amidst the muffled hum from the newsroom outside they could hear something quietly buzzing inside Twigg's office.

"It's a phone," Oonagh said. "It's on vibrate. Which one?"

They looked down at the table. None of the phones were lit or moving.

"Well, it must be one of them," Sam said. "Where's that buzzing coming from?"

The noise continued unabated and gradually Sam, Oonagh and Colin realised it was coming from the other side of Twigg's desk. One by one they each turned to face him, but he continued to type as though nothing was happening.

"Twigg, where's your phone?" Sam asked.

Twigg didn't reply.

"Leonard!" Oonagh snapped. "Answer your phone."

"No," Twigg said. "I refuse to participate in his childish game."

"Leonard, answer your phone," Oonagh said again, this time with a firmness which made clear that she was his boss. But Twigg continued to ignore her and so she marched around the desk and pulled his phone from his jacket pocket. She looked at it for a moment, slightly puzzled by its antiquated design, but then she realised it still had the basic controls of a modern phone and hit the answer key twice. The phone stopped buzzing, the call had been answered. Oonagh held the phone towards Twigg's mouth for him to say hello and start the conversation, but he pursed his lips and looked away like a toddler refusing a spoonful of medicine.

"Twigg, say hello," Sam whispered angrily at him. "Say. Hello."

Twigg stopped typing. He took a deep, irritated breath and turned towards Oonagh's outstretched hand. He stared at his phone, its little square screen lit up with only the word 'Unknown' to indicate someone was on the line. Before he spoke, he glanced over to his glass wall and could see every journalist in the newsroom on their feet, staring intently back at him. "Twigg!" he snapped.

"Hello Leonard Twigg. This is Adam Jaymes. I just called to let you know it's your turn." And with that, the little screen on the phone went dark.

Oonagh gently placed the mobile onto Twigg's desk and with an unexpected kindness in her voice said, "No surprises then, Leonard.

We knew he would pick on you next. Whatever it is, we'll deal with it together. All of us. You're not on your own."

Twigg scowled at her, rejecting her pity, and then looked back to his monitor and continued typing.

"We need to face this one head-on, see what it's about," Sam said, trying his hardest to sound commanding and in control, and not let slip any measure of his own personal relief. He knew, once again, that all the planning and guessing and preparing would be for nothing. He had a list of possible scandals next to Twigg's name and most of them involved illegal payments to officials, blackmail or phone hacking. Any one of them could prove to be the final nail in the *Ear*'s coffin.

But Sam no longer believed that would be enough for Adam Jaymes. He feared Project Ear was about to reveal a terrible truth about Leonard Twigg so great and so scandalous that Harvey News Group itself would be lost. After all, Twigg was an unmarried middle-aged man who still lived at home with his mother. On some estates in the UK, that alone would have been enough for a lighted rag through the letterbox.

"Are you coming?" Colin quietly asked Twigg, as Sam and Oonagh headed out to the main office to look at the giant screen. Twigg stopped what he was doing for a moment and politely said, "I'm writing my handovers. I really don't have time," and then waved Colin out of his office, too. Colin knew Twigg wasn't sentimental and wouldn't react well to kind words or a reassuring shoulder pat. And so he did as he was asked and left him alone, following Oonagh and Sam into the newsroom and through the maze of desks to get a clear view of the Project Ear website. But as he arrived at their side he became aware of a most unexpected noise, a sound so surprising that it took a moment for him to recognise it. All around him, he could hear an entire newsroom quietly giggling.

The reporters were all standing with their hands covering their mouths trying to suppress a wave of laughter from erupting across the whole office. Everyone was gazing upwards at the Project Ear website and as Colin attempted to assess the mood of his colleagues he noticed Oonagh was standing with her hand on her chest, looking relieved. "Is that it? Oh, thank goodness. That's nothing at all," he heard her say quietly to Sam.

Colin looked upward to the giant screen that was streaming the Project Ear front page and his gaze was met by a curious sight: a head and shoulders shot of his editor, Leonard Twigg, but looking quite different to the man he had known for the past 30 years. The image that met his gaze was of a man who was entirely bald. Next to the photograph were the words *"World Exclusive: T-wigg's hair-raising secret"*.

"You're joking," Colin said. "Twigg's got a rug? Rubbish. I'd have known. I would have been able to tell. Rubbish. This is bullshit."

"Ok, ok," Sam said, "keep your hair on Colin," and then he sniggered. It was just enough to tip Oonagh over the edge who then starting giggling herself. Colin looked at them both in disgust and thought of the terrible example they were setting the rest of the team. And then he burst out laughing. And everyone took that to be a sign that it was OK to find it funny and a roar of amusement filled the room.

At his desk, Twigg's attention was drawn briefly from his work by the noise from outside his office. For a man who shared so little of himself with others, he realised there was only one of his many secrets that could leave an entire newsroom of journalists laughing their socks off. It was the secret he had guarded most obsessively, the one he had been least willing to surrender. He flicked briefly to the Project Ear front page and there, as expected, he found a photograph of himself with no hair. He knew there was only one place it could have been taken, the one hour every couple of months when he was without his hair, a standing appointment at a clinic near Oxford Circus. He would be taken to a private cubicle where a technician would completely remove his hair system, and then take it to another room to clean it and weave new hair into any sections that were becoming thin. Once completed, the technician would return and fasten it tightly back onto his head by tying it to his own hair and sticking the front to his skin with glue and double-sided adhesive tape. Twigg would then have it cut and styled as though it was a genuine head of hair. As he continued to study the image, he realised he had never seen his own bald head before. At the clinic, he always insisted on a cubicle with no mirror and thanks to Adam Jaymes he was seeing his true self for the first time. But, for Leonard Twigg, Project Ear was a triviality he no longer cared about. He knew his mother was waiting for him. She had promised him pork chops and mash in gravy with buttered peas, his favourite meal. As soon as he had finished his emails, he would go.

"Alright, alright," Colin bellowed, clapping his hands at the howling mob around him. "Back to work, all of you. Start answering those phones. We'll have a statement ready in 30 minutes. No interviews. And I don't want to see any nonsense on your Twitter or Facebook accounts, either." The laughter quickly subsided and the reporters returned to work. Sam's heart began to slow back to its normal pace and he felt the tension in the air quickly evaporate. The great pressure that had been pushing down on them all for the whole day had been swept away by a story as silly as it was insignificant. The *Daily Ear* would live to fight another day.

"Oh for goodness sake, this is ridiculous," Oonagh said, wiping tears from her eyes whilst trying to keep a modicum of composure in front of the staff. "Is this really the best Adam Jaymes has left? A member of staff wears a wig? Who cares?"

"Leonard's going to be very embarrassed," Sam said. "We need to go and speak with him and work out what statement to make."

They returned to Twigg's office and closed the door. Oonagh went to explain what had happened but he cut her off before she could speak. "I know. I've seen it. It's fine."

"It's not that big a deal, Leonard," Oonagh said. "I think he's let us off lightly this time. So you wear a wig. So what?"

Leonard said something in response, something muttered under his breath that no one in the room could quite distinguish.

"What was that, Leonard?" Oonagh enquired.

"No, I don't," he replied, quietly.

"You don't what?"

"I do not wear a wig."

"But ... Adam Jaymes' story?"

"It is not a wig. It is a natural hair system."

Oonagh rolled her lips together to prevent a gasp of laughter escaping from her mouth, relieved that Twigg had continued to focus on his monitor and not her face. When she knew she was in control again, and it was safe to speak, she nodded and said, "Of course. It's a *system*."

"What's our line on this one?" Sam asked. "It's times like this I do actually miss Derek. He might not have been up to much but he could encapsulate a response very efficiently."

"What did we say for Valerie?" Oonagh asked. "I seem to remember that was a good one. It was angry. Something about a regrettable personal matter."

"No, we wouldn't get away with that one," Colin said. "We did a feature a couple of years back. The top ten celebrity wig wearers. Might make us look a bit hypocritical."

Oonagh raised an eye brow and looked unimpressed. "You *outed* 10 celebrities for wearing a wig?"

"Yes. But in a good way. We were trying to raise the profile of ... "

Oonagh raised her hand and Colin stopped speaking. "I'm sure it was for a very just cause," she said. "So in reality, the best thing we can do is just take this one on the chin. We don't mention it at all. Our statement will be something about how we remain committed to producing the nation's best-selling daily paper."

"Perfect," Sam said. He turned to Twigg, who continued typing with only a moderate awareness of the conversation that was taking place in front of him. "I know this is embarrassing, Twigg. But it's a light touch compared with the others. I hope you can see that, and believe me when I say that no one will think any differently of you."

"Thanks," Twigg replied, not looking up.

"How long will you be?" Sam enquired. "We have a decoy ready to draw the photographers from the front of the building so you can get out quietly."

"Ten minutes and I'll be done," Twigg replied.

"Ten minutes," Sam said, and although he would rather Twigg had agreed to leave straight away, he assumed he was working on something important and so left him to it. "That's fine. I'll let them know." He then exchanged glances with Oonagh and Colin as they all realised they had outstayed their welcome. "We'll leave you to it," he concluded and they quietly left Leonard Twigg to continue with his work.

"He is going to have to get over himself," Oonagh said as she and Sam made their way to the lift. "He's had things his own way for too long and he's going to have to accept the fact that he works for me now."

"Give him a few days," Sam said. "Once this wig ... um, *system* ... business has settled down I'll have a chat with him."

At 9.15pm, Leonard Twigg sent his final email and shut down his computer. He made a neat pile of documents and papers in his in-tray, in order of priority, and left his little Nokia on top. He then walked over to the meeting table and pushed all of the chairs back into place. He surveyed his office to ensure everything was at it should be and then put on his coat, picked up his briefcase and left. It was an orderly routine that he had stuck to throughout his 30 years as editor of the *Daily Ear*. He always left his office in exactly the same condition as he found it. Tidy.

As he made his way through the newsroom there was a gentle undercurrent of laughter amid the noise of shouted phone calls and rattling keyboards. But Twigg was lost in thought and so didn't notice. His mind was distracted by an image of his elderly mother. She was sitting in her armchair with a cup of tea in her hand, watching *Coronation Street* whilst giving a running commentary on what was going on. It made him smile. He quietly entered the lift and travelled alone to the ground floor where he waited patiently with the guard in the security office. He watched on the colour monitors as the bogus car left the underground car park. Word quickly spread through the pack of photographers and film crews and en masse they rushed from the front of the building to try to capture a glimpse of the humiliated newspaper editor as he was driven away.

"Good night, Bryan," Twigg said politely and then walked through the exit and onto the busy pavement outside. He lost himself in the bustle of late night shoppers on the cold London street and became just another anonymous face as he made the familiar short journey to the local tube. Unless a major story was breaking, Twigg always travelled at about the same time; well after rush hour but before the pubs, bars and restaurants emptied for the night. The station was usually quiet and often he would be alone, a sole passenger waiting for his train home.

At 9.25pm he arrived at his platform and, as usual, there was nobody else there. Twigg sat on a bench and waited, oblivious to the emptiness around him. He was lost in happier thoughts, of his mother dishing up dinner. They never ate on their laps. She always laid the table properly with a cloth and napkins. She would ask about his day at work, and then suggest plans for the weekend. Perhaps a visit to his aunt in Chelmsford.

Across the track, immediately opposite Twigg, was a huge digital billboard streaming an advert for shampoo. It was a short, silent film that showed Adam Jaymes stepping from the shower, his toned and muscular torso glistening with moisture. He then stared directly at the camera and smiled, brushing his hand through his thick, glossy, dark hair. The screen then faded to black, briefly, before lighting up again and repeating the advert.

Twigg stared at the hoarding but his mind was adrift, somewhere else. The advert repeated over and over in front of his eyes but he simply wasn't able to recognise or acknowledge any aspect of it. In his mind he was already at home, sitting at the table eating pork chops with his mum. And so, as Leonard Twigg threw himself under the 9.33 train to Wimbledon, he had no idea that Adam Jaymes' smiling face was beaming down on him from above.

21

@Realadamjaymes You May as well have pushed him under the train yourself

"**HAVE CONFIRMED THAT** a man who died after falling under a moving tube train in London last night was Leonard Twigg, the editor of the *Daily Ear* newspaper and the most recent victim of Adam Jaymes' 'Project Ear' campaign"

Rot in hell #LeonardTwigg #WellDoneAdamjaymes #ProjectEar

at the centre of the most recent Project Ear exposé had died in a suspected suicide. *Daily Ear* editor Leonard Twigg, a 55-year-old bachelor, is believed to have thrown himself under a train less than an hour after the actor Adam Jaymes published photographs which revealed he wore a wig. The chief executive of Harvey News Group, Sam Harvey, said staff at the newspaper were *"completely shattered"* and had been offered counselling. In a statement released this morning, Harvey said: *"Management offered Leonard our full support and told him we considered him the victim of a cruel prank. We will be working with the police as they investigate this terrible tragedy, and call on Adam Jaymes to accept full responsibility for Leonard's tragic death.*

Please remember that #LeonardTwigg make a living out of exposing other people's private lives #ProjectEar

"one of the most bankable stars in America. This morning, however, his career is in tatters. And even his super rich husband won't be able to"

"as to whether the former *Doctor Who* star will be facing any criminal charges. It's been confirmed that Adam Jaymes is currently in California, preparing to film the new season of *True Blood* although other reports suggest the actor has gone into hiding. So far, Jaymes has declined to comment on Leonard Twigg's death although it is believed the American cable channel HBO is under increasing pressure to suspend him, pending"

in life was a bully and a ruthless merchant of secrets and private moments. In death, he has proven himself to be a hypocrite and a coward, unable to tolerate the smallest aspect of his own life being exposed to public scrutiny in the way he exposed the secrets of some many others

when pranks go wrong #LeonardTwigg #ProjectEar

"agent has described the suspected suicide of *Daily Ear* editor Leonard Twigg as *"tragic"*, but said he is satisfied the actor had broken no laws. Chris Subrt, of London-based Eric V. William Associates, said the actor could not have *"reasonably foreseen"* the events which unfolded. *"We are very confident Adam hasn't done anything illegal,"* he said" "no, no, what I'm saying John ... if I can just finish what I'm saying ... what I am saying, and I'm saying this with the greatest respect to Leonard Twigg's family and friends. But what I am saying is that after a time of mourning and reflection, I hope the *Daily Ear* management team will see this as an opportunity to reconsider its methods. Because tragic though this is, Adam Jaymes has simply reflected back onto the *Daily Ear* its own actions. The very practices it has used against hundreds of celebrities, politicians and private individuals over the years. And I have no doubt that Pearl Martin's family must be feeling some sense of justice"

If you live by the sword, you die by the sword #LeonardTwigg#ProjectEar

had a private meeting with the actor where he had pleaded with him to stop his hate campaign against the *Daily Ear*. Insiders say Harvey, the recently appointed chief executive of Harvey News Group, used the meeting to warn Jaymes that 'Project Ear' could end in tragedy if he did not reconsider

"was simply giving the *Daily Ear* staff a taste of their own medicine. But he wakes up this morning with blood, real human blood, on his hands and I imagine he is asking himself"

frail mother Doris, 81, was being comforted by friends and family last night after police broke the news about her son's death. A neighbour told the *Ear*: "Leonard was everything to her. He was her carer, her son and her best friend. She's been crying, saying she has nothing left worth living for. Adam Jaymes should be strung up for what he's done to

Why is everyone having a go at @RealAdamJaymes ? It's not his fault Twigg could dish it out but not take it

"The actor now faces being questioned by detectives following the death of *Daily Ear* editor Leonard Twigg. Scotland Yard is understood to have been in contact with police in California as it emerged Adam Jaymes had gone into hiding. The latest episode in Jaymes' 'Project Ear' campaign caused public outcry when Twigg was found dead Monday night after police were called to"

22

VALERIE SAT QUIETLY in her car which was parked slightly on the kerb outside Leonard Twigg's house, a bouquet of tulips for his mother on the passenger seat next to her. She was dressed in a black suit and was smoking another cigarette, her third since she had arrived. She was suffering an uncharacteristic attack of doubt, unable to bring herself to leave the car and knock at the front door. She knew the house would be bustling with family and friends, all of Twigg's aunts and uncles rallying round to help his mother Doris through the dark days ahead. And although Valerie was visiting his mother with honest and true intentions, she knew Twigg would have still considered it a gross intrusion. Valerie had never been to Twigg's house before, not once in all the years she had known him. Twigg had been a dear friend but always maintained a clear line between his friendships and his home life. His house was private and his mother was not shared with people from work.

The few times Valerie had met Doris had been mostly accidental. On one occasion she had bumped into the two of them having dinner at the Oxo Tower restaurant; on another it was during high tea at Grosvenor House. Twigg had enjoyed treating his mum to dinner at fancy places; he wanted to make sure she enjoyed the financial rewards of having raised a successful son.

The one and only time Twigg had deliberately organised for Valerie to spend time with Doris was shortly after Jeremy died. He had invited Valerie out for dinner and surprised her by arriving at the restaurant with his mother in tow. And as the evening had progressed, Valerie had understood why Twigg had brought her along. He lived his adult life amid the great, the powerful and the wealthy and stood on equal ground with all them. But the smaller parts of life, the quieter more intimate moments that forged friendships and love, those were mostly beyond him. That evening Valerie had needed a shoulder to cry on but that was well outside of Twigg's expertise and so he had brought his mother along to do it for him.

Doris had left an indelible impression on Valerie, largely because she proven herself to be the exact opposite of her son. She was gregarious and welcoming and warm, and could natter for ages about the most inane topics but with such enthusiasm and interest as to make the conversation seem riveting. And whilst Twigg was obsessively private, his down-to-earth mother over-shared on every topic imaginable. Valerie remembered Doris telling with great pride how she and Twigg's father, Jack, had come from the grit and noise of the East End. Jack had left school at 12 to train as a plumber while Doris came from a big, loud family and spent most of her early years cleaning, cooking and caring for younger siblings. But together they had been the perfect combination of ambition and hard work. Jack built his plumbing business into something just short of a success while Doris squirrelled away money for a down payment on a house in a better part of the city. She had decided at a young age that she wasn't going to spend her life beholden to any landlord and so she and Jack had become the first members of their respective families to own their own home.

And there in front of Valerie's parked car was that very house, an unremarkable small terrace on a busy main road. But it was everything Doris had wanted and she had proudly lived there for almost 60 years. Her son was born there and her husband had died there.

Doris would likely spend the rest of her life in the house alone and for Valerie that was the most unforgivable part of Twigg's suicide. She found it hard to believe he would abandon his own mother, no matter how desperate he had felt, and the thought of poor old Doris all alone in that house left Valerie with as much of a sense of anger as loss. Even her natural desire to blame Adam Jaymes had been lessened by her anger at Twigg. She tossed her cigarette onto the road and then took the bouquet from the car and headed up the short path to the front door step. The news of Twigg's death had come too late for the print edition of the *Ear*, but the website had been updated with the full story and lots of reaction from shocked staff, politicians and industry peers. Valerie had read the section about Doris being cared for by friends and family and had expected to find the house buzzing with activity, with half a dozen cars parked up on the kerb outside, and the front door ajar to reveal a line of old women in cardigans making tea and sandwiches in the kitchen. But there were no other cars outside, and as she stood at the door, she realised that the house seemed strangely quiet and shut-up.

She rang the doorbell a number of times, but the noise from the road made it difficult to tell if it was working. After a few more attempts she leant across to the bay window and tapped on the glass, trying to peer through the quaint lace curtains for any signs of movement. But no one answered the door and there was no sign of life from inside.

"Can I help you, love?" a rasping voice enquired from the other side of Doris's neatly trimmed privet hedge. Valerie turned and found a thin, elderly woman leaning out of the front door of the neighbouring property. She was wearing a floral housecoat and had a grim and unwelcoming scowl on her lined face. "There's no one there, you know."

"I'm here to see Doris. I just want to see how she is," Valerie said, lifting her bouquet into view as though it were proof of her credentials. "I thought she would be at home."

"And you are?"

"Valerie. I'm a friend of the family."

The woman looked her up and down and seemed magnificently unimpressed with her. "Oh, a friend of the family, are you?"

"Yes."

"Are you now?"

"Yes, I am."

The woman stepped from her door, hands pressed into the small of her back, and leaned over the hedge to stare Valerie in the face, as though trying to get a measure of her. After a moment, where it seemed as though she were readjusting her dentures with her tongue, the woman asked, "If you're such a fucking good friend of the family, how come you didn't know that Doris is dead?"

The woman's comment made absolutely no sense to Valerie. She stared in complete disbelief and, as her mind tried to process the information, she suddenly found herself at a loss for words. The neighbour straightened her back and allowed her scowl to lessen, replaced with a delicate smile that suggested she had won an argument or proven a point. After a few moments Valerie managed to gasp, "Oh no," but was so weakened by the shock her arm dropped and the tulips slipped from her grasp and landed on the doorstep. "No, no," she continued. "Oh, it must have been too much for her. Oh goodness, poor Doris. Who found her? Was it you?"

The neighbour's smiled vanished and was replaced with a look of confusion. "What are you talking about?" she grumbled. "Found who? Doris? Was it *me* that found *Doris*? Is that what you're saying?"

Valerie didn't understand why the neighbour was being so obtuse. Surely it had been a perfectly reasonable question? And so she took a deep, replenishing breath and fixed the neighbour with her famous glare. "Clearly, I did not know that Doris had died. I am now – also clearly, I thought – asking you what happened to her. Is that really so very confusing for you?"

Her adversary didn't budge. She continued to look at Valerie with an air of indignation. "I don't want to say anything to any bloody reporters," she said, her words laced with anger. "They've already made me look an idiot. Or a liar. I've seen what they've written. That a 'neighbour' said all the family was round taking care of Doris. Well, I didn't say that. No one round here did. I know, because I've been banging on doors all morning trying to find the idiot that spoke to them."

"I'm not a reporter," Valerie replied. "I was a good friend of Leonard's. Now please tell me what happened to Doris."

"Cancer," the neighbour replied, abruptly.

"Cancer?"

"That's what I said."

Valerie simply couldn't join the dots between what she knew of Twigg's mother and what the neighbour was telling her. Was it actually possible that the shock of Leonard's death had caused such a virulent form of cancer that it had killed poor Doris within just hours? Can grief cause cancer? And if so, why hadn't the *Ear*'s health team written about it? They wrote endlessly about anything else that was even vaguely connected with cancer. Once, famously, they'd even linked breast cancer to blinking. "Are you saying that the shock of Leonard's death gave Doris cancer? And that she died?" Valerie asked, realising as she spoke how ridiculous her question was.

The neighbour groaned. "Of course not, you silly cow!" she replied. And then the harshness in her voice ebbed away and with a twinge of genuine sadness she explained. "Doris died last year. She had been right as rain. Then she went to see her doctor for a routine check-up and suddenly she's got cancer. They ran a few tests and gave her six months, but she only lasted two. I've never seen anyone go downhill so quickly. Poor Lenny was beside himself. You should have seen the state of him on the day of the funeral. We all tried to support him, but you know what he's like. What he *was* like. He was too proud to ask for help."

As her shock subsided Valerie suddenly felt very foolish, standing outside Twigg's empty house hoping to offer a few words of love and support to a woman who had been dead for months.

"I've known Lenny since he was a baby," the neighbour continued. "We moved in when he was just a couple of months old. He was always a funny little lad. Always serious, putting the world to rights, telling people off. Even the adults. I remember when he was about seven he was stood right where you are now, telling off a policeman for riding his bike on the pavement outside his house. One of the funniest things I've ever seen. This scrawny little boy in shorts and glasses, waggling his finger at this great big policeman." The woman's tone suddenly dipped, as her anger and frustration gave way to grief. "I'm sorry," she said, heading back to her own front door. "It's hard to believe all three of them have gone. I guess losing his mum finally got the better of him."

Alone on the doorstep again Valerie found herself dipping from one sad thought to the next, the roar of the busy road little more than a murmur in the background. Twigg had kept it all secret from them, even his own mother's death. She remembered something from the past year, a few days when Twigg had called in sick with flu or taken leave unexpectedly. She didn't remember the exact details because it had seemed so trivial at the time. Had that been the time when Doris had passed away? Twigg hadn't seemed any different, perhaps a little more short-tempered but then he had phases like that. Valerie returned to her car and sat at the wheel, trying to make sense of it all. Twigg's mother – his beloved mother - had died and he hadn't shared an ounce of his pain. He hadn't even shared the news, just quietly taken some time off for the funeral and then returned as though nothing had happened. And then it occurred to her how ridiculous the *Ear* was going to look when word got out that Twigg's mother was dead and not being cared for by relatives. It was a small mercy the copy was only online and it could be easily deleted. And so she called Colin to tell him the news.

If Twigg's suicide had happened a month earlier, the news would likely have knocked Howard for six. But his trip to New York had been an unmitigated disaster and after ten tense and frustrating days he had returned home without a deal and, worse still, without his wife. For the first time in their eight-year marriage, Howard and Estelle had spent the night apart. And not only apart, but in different countries. With so much going on, Howard couldn't even remember the last time he had spoken to Twigg. It seemed a lifetime ago, especially after his decision to cut all his ties with the *Daily Ear* and hand it entirely to Sam. It felt as though he wasn't really a part of those events anymore, like he was watching from a comfortable distance. He had spent a peaceful morning on his terrace, drinking coffee in his bathrobe and trying to glean some enjoyment from his view of Hyde Park. Occasionally, he returned to the sitting room to review some of the television coverage of Twigg's death or to send Sam a reassuring text. But by midday the coffee had become a brandy and Howard's mood had become despondent.

The events in New York were playing over and over in his head and he knew in his heart there was nothing he could have done to change the outcome. The trip should have been routine, the sort of deal Howard would usually have sown up before breakfast, but he had underestimated the impact and reach of Project Ear. He and Estelle had arrived in New York to a hostile reception, with his plans to buy a popular American newspaper chain facing fierce public, political and commercial opposition. It was clear that even his longest and most trusted contacts were keen to keep him at arm's length, at least for the time being. But Howard knew he had to return to London with a win under his belt, to prove to everybody that he was still in the game. He and his team had worked every angle imaginable to try to salvage something from what appeared a hopeless situation. But, in the end he had returned home empty-handed. Now, alone with a brandy and a view, he realised he had a mountain to climb, the size of which he thought he'd never have to scale again. He had his reputation to rebuild, usurpers to crush, contracts to salvage and a marriage to reassess.

"Oh Howard, you could at least have put a pair of trousers on for me," Audrey said as she appeared on the terrace, sounding like a disapproving school mistress. She was dressed in a plain, sombre suit out of respect for Twigg and was carrying a small box of Turkish Delight for Howard as a welcome home present. "I thought you could do with a little cheering up," she said, and presented him with the box. She then kissed him on the forehead and sat opposite him.

"Thanks for coming," he said. "Tea?"

She shook her head. "I'm just popping in," she replied. "I've left Felicity in the car downstairs. We've got lots to do. Besides, she's been in tears for most of the morning over poor Leonard. Funny, really, to see someone actually crying over him. Particularly a young girl."

Howard popped a powdered cube of Turkish Delight into his mouth and shrugged as though not understanding the youth of today. He swallowed and said, "It takes all sorts," before popping another cube into his mouth. Audrey knew she hadn't been invited to the apartment to talk about Twigg. As sad as his passing was, she knew Howard had another priority. Several of her New York friends had been quick to pass on the news that Estelle could still be heard clunking around in their Upper East Side penthouse on her own. Howard needed marital advice and wanted to ask his oldest friend what he should do. The fact his oldest friend was also his ex-wife didn't appear to be an issue for him.

"So," Howard eventually said, "I imagine Gunilla or Joan have already told you I left Estelle behind in New York."

Audrey smiled sweetly at Howard. She liked that there was no pretence in their relationship and that he could get straight to the point without feeling the need to mollycoddle or explain. "It's been a difficult couple of weeks, Howard. I'm sure it's all going to fall back into place."

"No, it won't," Howard replied, categorically. "I cannot tell you how badly behaved Estelle was. She just didn't get it. She didn't understand how important that deal was to me. I spent the whole bloody trip pleading with her to go out and find something to do. She had the whole of New York, thousands of shops and restaurants, art galleries or theatres – but she just refused to go. She said she felt side-lined. So she spent the whole trip huffing and tutting around the penthouse. She interrupted meetings, complained every time she found me working on the laptop and was rude to my team when they phoned in the evening. She ruined everything."

Audrey had seen Howard like this many times over the past 40 years, throwing all of his toys out of the pram when he couldn't get his own way. Even now they were divorced she was still his shoulder to cry on and the person he would seek out to complain about his second wife. But Audrey was wise enough to know she should never take sides or criticise Estelle, because she knew Howard's marital problems were always short-lived. She would not allow herself to be seduced into criticising his wife, knowing he would remember those criticisms once he and Estelle were reconciled. "Howard, darling, you know Estelle wasn't to blame for that deal falling through don't you?" she asked, gently, the question clearly rhetorical.

Howard knew. Of course he knew. But he had been so angry that he had made Estelle think she was partly responsible. In a heated moment of frustration and disappointment, he packed a suitcase and told her to stay behind. Such was his unbridled fury that, just for once, she did as she was told and let him leave alone. "That's not the point," he eventually replied.

"You two have been married for, what, eight years? And for eight years Estelle has faithfully, although some have suggested *obsessively*, stayed at your side. She's travelled with you on every trip. And be honest, Howard, that's something you used to encourage. I think you got a buzz from turning up at those boring old business events with a pretty young wife hanging on your arm."

Howard continued to consume his Turkish Delight without commenting.

"Darling, business trips are boring when you're the wife. That's why I never went. But you and Estelle live your life together every day. And that is as much your choice as it is hers. It's not fair that you're blaming her now for wanting to spend time with you."

"It's more than that," Howard said. "It's suffocating. Not just the business trips but all the time. I get no peace or privacy. I have a glass of wine and she pulls a face. I sit down to watch a TV show and I have to justify it to her first. I can't even get dressed on my own. She has to be there, giving me her opinion on whatever suit I'm putting on or whether she thinks I've gained weight. It is beyond a fucking joke. And the way she acted in New York was the final straw. Enough is enough."

Audrey began to realise there was more to this marital row than she had originally appreciated. It had been a catalyst, an opportunity for all of Howard's anger with Estelle to bubble to the surface and for him to reflect on whether she was really able to fulfil the role of Mrs Howard Harvey.

"You never let me down, not once," he said, unexpectedly. His eyes were suddenly wide open, glistening, as though pleading for Audrey to reciprocate with an equally affectionate comment. "You were always supportive, always appropriate. You gave me all the time and freedom I needed to chase deals and dreams and ambitions around the world. You understand business and the value of money. When I think of all of those stupid expensive advisers I've had over the years, and when push came to shove it was always you I would go to for advice. How could I have ever been so stupid as to let you go?"

Audrey's flawless demeanour dissolved and her mouth dropped open with surprise. There was a part of her that hated Howard for what he had just said, for putting her in such a compromising position. As he sat gazing at her with his big sad eyes, Audrey felt a little ashamed of herself. For the first time, Howard had made her feel like *the other woman* stealing a private moment with someone else's husband. For the better part of a decade, she had carefully managed a perfect and proper relationship with him and shown great respect for his marriage to Estelle. It had often been hard because even now, in her heart, she still considered Howard to be hers. There were parts of him, of his life, that he still shared only with Audrey. Their history was too great and important to be swept away by something as trivial as a divorce and a second marriage. In many ways for Audrey, the Harvey family had stayed the same. There was Howard, Audrey and Sam. And then there was Estelle, on the outside looking in. Always, always on the outside. But Audrey wasn't about to use the first sign of trouble to recklessly grab at a chance for a reconciliation. She had no doubt the storm would pass and Howard and Estelle would be together again. And she had no intention of leaving Howard with the impression that she had any other than complete respect for his second wife.

"Well, you did let me go," she replied tersely. Her warmth and concern were suddenly gone and she quickly stood and made her way from the terrace. "I'll see you and Estelle at the awards on Thursday," she said. She could feel her heart pounding in her chest and had a terrible urge to turn back, to rush to Howard and embrace him as if they were still married. But her mind was telling her to keep walking, to not let herself be fooled into thinking there was anything more to the exchange than an irritated husband moaning about his wife. And with that she was gone.

Alone again with his brandy and his view, Howard Harvey polished off his Turkish Delight and wondered if anything was going to go right for him that week.

Valerie returned to the newsroom and quietly made her way to her desk. No one attended to her or asked how she was. The rest of the news team gave her a wide berth at the best of times and it seemed, in grief, little had changed. From the side-lines, watching from the shadows of her dimly lit office, Valerie found it difficult to reconcile her own dark thoughts with the almost joyous atmosphere on the other side of her wall of glass. Colin was rushing around the newsroom with the look of a football star who'd just scored the winning goal in the FA cup, the other reporters virtually high-fiving him at the end of each conversation. He had always been Twigg's heir apparent even though there had never been any succession planning. Twigg hadn't allowed for it. But with Twigg out of the way, everyone gravitated to Colin as though it were a foregone conclusion that he would be the *Ear*'s new editor. He looked like an excited boy again, the young lad who'd come to the *Ear* for a couple of weeks of work experience and stayed.

Valerie remembered the desperate 3am call from Colin. She remembered the shock and sadness in his words, the moment when he stopped to catch his breath and how his voice cracked, as though he were about to cry. He had described every horrific detail of Twigg's death in the way that a reporter would need to over-share, and finished the call by saying, "God bless him, he's handed us Jaymes on a plate." Just six hours had passed since that awful call but it might as well have been six months. Valerie could see that no one was mourning Leonard Twigg because everyone knew that his death was the best thing to happen to the *Daily Ear* in a long time. *Sky News* and the BBC News channel were streaming across the giant screens. Adam Jaymes was the story of the day. Not Leonard Twigg, but Adam Jaymes. Had he gone too far? Was it his fault? Was his career over? Was he in hiding? Are the police looking for him? "We finally nailed him," Valerie said quietly to herself. "And all it cost was dear Leonard's life."

Just outside Twigg's office were Sam and Oonagh. Not quite hand-in-hand, Valerie thought, but not far off it she suspected. They were managing, overseeing, and their smiles reflected the jubilant mood across the whole office. With them were a camera operator and reporter from *Sky News*, setting up to interview one of the senior team (Valerie assumed it would be Colin) with the bustling newsroom as a backdrop. Sitting alone with her door closed and her lights off, occasionally sipping from her coffee mug and drawing on yet another cigarette, Valerie knew she was expected to hammer out 500 angry words for the next edition. Colin had made it clear he didn't want anything sad or reflective. It had to be ferocious, the most angry she had ever been, an Exocet missile aimed right at Adam Jaymes. When it came to the actor's career, everyone was now waiting for Valerie to deliver the killing blow. As she fired up her laptop, she gently caressed the silver crucifix hanging from her neck as though trying to take some genuine comfort and inspiration from it. For so many years she had used the Christian faith as little more than a weapon, her first retort against the politically correct or the unrelenting march of equality. But for the first time since her husband had died, she found an emptiness within herself and yearned for a sign from above to show her what to do next.

Her computer screen lit up and her inbox appeared filled with goodwill messages from the usual sycophants mixed with the same old toot she got every day. She scrolled past dozens of messages and then paused as she came across an email from Twigg. He'd sent it at 5.07pm the previous day, just a few short hours before he had taken his own life. There, tucked quietly between an invitation to a conference on Alzheimer's and a spam message about a balance transfer, were the final thoughts of Leonard Twigg in an email titled *'Handover'*. As Valerie clicked it open she could feel her heart pounding in her chest. She scanned the text hoping for something more than a simple handover note, perhaps a goodbye or best wishes for the future. She wanted something that felt a part of him, rather than something that was little more than part of a process. But the email was short and to the point, bullets listing her upcoming deadlines, features and speaking opportunities. There was little to glean from it other than Twigg's remarkably organised nature. The only thing she felt was out of the ordinary was the salutation *'Dear Valerie'*, a greeting Twigg never used in an email. An email from Twigg would, at best, begin with *'Valerie'* but usually there would be no salutation at all. Indeed he had reprimanded many staff at the *Ear* for lacking professionalism, simply because they had started an email with the word *'Dear'*. A little further down she found an email from Sam, a confidential note sent to senior staff only, in which he thanked Harvey News Group's executive team for their years of service and then disclosed that they had all now left the company. He also revealed a change in the *Daily Ear*'s editorial management, with Oonagh taking the new role of executive editor for both the paper and the website.

"Dear God, Leonard," Valerie said, "No wonder you threw yourself under a train." She chuckled to herself as though sharing a private joke with Twigg, but then her own words repeated in her mind and an awful idea presented itself to her. She remembered the unpleasant evening she had spent with Twigg at her club a couple of days earlier, where he had been so painfully agitated and distracted. And she began to appreciate how enormous those other events would have seemed to Twigg, the removal of his allies on the top floor and his own humiliating demotion at the hands of Sam and Oonagh. The *Daily Ear* had been Leonard Twigg's everything. After the death of his beloved mother, it would have been the one and only thing that give him a sense of purpose, of significance. And Valerie began to weep as she realised her friend's final days would have been spent watching powerlessly as it was all stolen away from him.

"You OK?" a voice asked her softly, as the sound of the newsroom suddenly grew louder. She wiped her tears before she turned, and then looked across to find Colin leaning half into her office. "Sorry, Valerie," he said. "I've been busy. I saw you come in and wanted to see how you are. Are you crying?"

Valerie shrugged and, just for moment, realised she couldn't say anything without bursting into tears again. And so she quickly placed her cigarette to her lips and waited for the moment to pass. Colin stepped inside and then leaned back against the door, clicking it shut. He looked scruffy and tired. He wasn't wearing a tie and the top buttons of his white shirt were undone with the sleeves rolled up to his elbows. He had the drained look of a man who'd been running on empty all night. "I know how it looks, Valerie. I honestly do. But we just don't have time to grieve. Not right now."

Valerie shrugged again, still unable to speak.

"You've been talking about this as a war, haven't you? A battle," Colin continued, trying to win Valerie over with her own words. "Well, that's exactly what this is today. We don't have the luxury to mourn a fallen comrade. If we stop to catch our breath, we'll lose this advantage and then the battle will be lost and everything Twigg fought for will have been for nothing."

Valerie took a deep breath. It felt OK now, she thought. It would be OK to speak. "If we don't mourn him now, we never will," she said, her usually sharp voice suddenly gentle and soft, controlled. "Have you sorted out the website?"

"Yes, all done. No one seems to have noticed. We might have gotten away with it."

"Who wrote it?"

Colin looked shifty, a schoolboy being asked why the sweet jar was empty. "There was a miscommunication," he said.

Valerie shrugged. "Just blame the subs. That's what we normally do," she replied. "Besides, you weren't to know. No one was, it seems. You're friends with a man for three decades. You'd expect him to tell you that his mother has died."

Colin perched on the edge of her desk. "Valerie, let's be honest. Twigg didn't have friends."

"Of course he did."

"No, he didn't. Not really. Not in any way a normal person would have friends. He had contacts, colleagues and acquaintances. In that order. But not friends, not really." He then leaned forward and kissed her firmly on the forehead, before returning to the door.

Valerie picked up her phone and went to dial. "I think I should give Howard a call, see how he is" she said, with an everyday tone to her voice.

"Why?" asked Colin.

Valerie shrugged. "Just for a chat. He knew Leonard longer than any of us. I thought he might appreciate one of us showing some empathy."

"He won't take your call," Colin said.

"Of course he will," Valerie replied, and continued dialling.

Colin returned to her side, gently removed the receiver from her hand and returned it to its base. "No, he won't Valerie," he said again. "He won't take your call, or your texts or your emails. He's cut himself off from the *Ear*. All communication with Howard Harvey is now done via Sam, and that's without exception. Even Twigg was told the same."

The final piece of the jigsaw fell into place as Valerie realised Twigg's humiliation had been complete. Deserted by the top floor, degraded by Sam and Oonagh and forsaken by Howard too. His fall from power had been absolute. And with that she realised the awful truth that Adam Jaymes was not to blame for her friend's suicide because the *Daily Ear* had killed Leonard Twigg. "He sent me a handover note." she said. "Leonard did, before he died."

Colin nodded. "Yes, he sent me one too. Actually, he sent quite a few. Oonagh and Sam both got one."

"A *handover*, Colin. Why on earth would he do that?"

Colin shrugged, appearing uninterested and increasingly impatient.

"Oh for God's sake, stop being so obstructive," Valerie snapped, and was so uptight she stubbed out her cigarette even though it was less than half gone. "This isn't a handover note, it's a suicide note. Or the closest we'd ever get to one from Leonard. And he sent it hours before Adam Jaymes' ridiculous story about his bloody wig."

Colin raised his hand and stepped back towards Valerie. "Hey, hey, hey, none of that," he said, firmly. "Not another word like that."

The door opened and Oonagh appeared, respectfully dressed in black from head to toe. "Colin, I'm sorry to interrupt," she said with a solemn and sympathetic tone, "but the *Sky News* team is ready for you."

Colin nodded. "I'll be straight there," he said, and then he looked back at Valerie. "Not. Another. Word," he repeated. With that, he and Oonagh left Valerie's office and returned to the thunderous excitement of the newsroom.

Valerie felt as though she had been chastised, or perhaps censored, but she understood why Colin was keen to keep her quiet. Clearly he had an angle for the story and would not tolerate any deviation from it. Adam Jaymes was entirely responsible for the tragic suicide of Leonard Twigg and that was all the public needed to know. Colin was Head Boy now, desperate to keep Sam and Oonagh happy. He wanted to be seen as the man who could do what Twigg couldn't and turn the tide of public opinion against Adam Jaymes. It wouldn't be hard to do either, Valerie thought. Across the board the media was already blaming the actor and she could tell there would be little sympathy at the *Daily Ear* for anyone who wanted to suggest anything else. But if the public had all the facts about Twigg's desperate final days, Valerie knew they would think twice about blaming Adam Jaymes. They would realise a silly story about a toupee wouldn't have been nearly enough to make Twigg throw himself under a train. His suicide was the final act of a grieving man whose years of loyal service to the Harvey family had just been spat back into his face.

She watched as Colin and Oonagh joined Sam by the Sky team and with a cold curiosity studied Oonagh's mannerisms. She noted how managerial she had become, fussing around the men like Queen Bee to the point that she had Sam remove his dark jacket and black tie and then used them to dress Colin for his interview. She looked like a bossy Irish mother getting her two boys ready for church. For a few more silent moments, Valerie watched the interactions of the reporters, editors and managers across the newsroom. It was a noisy, chaotic mess of shouting and rushing and back-slapping that would never have been allowed under Twigg. Even when the Twin Towers were falling, he had brought a sense of quiet order to the proceedings. The commotion playing out in front of her eyes was the clearest signal that things had already changed and that everyone had already moved on.

And in that moment Valerie found her comfort and inspiration because, no matter what Colin said, she *knew* she had been Twigg's friend and that he had tried his very best to be a good friend in return. And she would be damned before she conspired with the likes of Sam Harvey and Oonagh Boyle or suffered in obedient silence to conceal their appalling treatment of a man she had cherished. Colin would never forgive her, of course, but she could already see how they were set on two very different paths, with Colin heading for the new inner sanctum and Valerie left very much on the outside, glaring in. With sudden clarity, her mood immediately lifted and she knew what she was going to do. There would be no fond farewells or histrionics, no speech or bitter 'all staff' email. She would quietly leave on her own terms and never again return to the *Daily Ear* newsroom. She spent a few moments printing up emails and collecting the personal possessions she was keen to take with her. And then she slipped her black jacket on again, threw her handbag strap over her shoulder and reviewed her office one final time. It was neat and tidy, everything in its place. Leonard Twigg would have been proud.

To her annoyance, her discreet exit was spoiled when Oonagh unexpectedly re-entered the room. "I thought you were looking after Colin," Valerie said, attempting to make it clear she had no time for the likes of Oonagh Boyle that day.

"We've been pushed back by a few minutes," Oonagh replied, "and I just wanted to say how sorry I am. I know we've never seen eye-to-eye, Valerie, but Leonard's death is a terrible tragedy and I know you were close. If you need any time off you only need to ask."

Valerie faked a smile and nodded with pretend appreciation. At that very moment, she couldn't remember the last time she had hated anyone as much as she hated Oonagh Boyle. But she wanted to slip away quietly, without incident, and so tried her hardest to remain civil. "Thank you," she said.

"I really mean it, Valerie," Oonagh said. "Take a few days off. And when you get back you and I can sit down and talk about how you're feeling, and perhaps we could talk about what sort of role you will have at the *Ear*, once we've re-launched."

"Re-launched?" Valerie said, curiously. "Goodness. And to think poor Leonard's only been dead a few hours."

"No, no, it's not like that," Oonagh replied. "Honestly, Valerie, please don't think we are in any way taking advantage of this awful situation. Sam and I are very clear that we need to take the *Ear* in a new direction and were planning to have Leonard lead that process of change."

Try as she might, Valerie knew Oonagh was going to bring out the very worst in her. She had no doubt Oonagh's sympathy was insincere, her visit little more than an opportunity to remind Valerie who was boss now. And her suggestion of a comforting conversation at some point in the future was a veiled threat, a signal that Valerie Pierce might not have a place in the *new Daily Ear*. But most unbearable of all, for Valerie, was the simple fact that while Leonard Twigg's shredded corpse was being sown back together in some grotty NHS morgue, Oonagh was standing in front of her, happy and healthy and alive. "It's funny, Oonagh," she said, with a clipped, pointed tone to her voice, "but the last time I checked, the *Daily Ear* was the biggest selling daily paper in the UK. And its sales are going up, not down. Strange, really, that you should look at that success and think we need a change of direction."

"Valerie, our success is unsustainable given the current climate," Oonagh replied. "We have to respond to changing public attitudes and pressure from our own peers within the industry."

"Our 'peers'," Valerie replied, mocking. "Our peers?" she laughed. "Do you honestly think there is a single newspaper out there which could be considered our equal? Absolute poppycock."

Oonagh sighed as she realised it had clearly been an error of judgement, on her part, to attempt a few kind words with Valerie. "The world has changed, Valerie, but the *Daily Ear* hasn't. It's time to look at our practices and see how we can move forward." Oonagh considered her solemn words to be a suitable way to end the conversation, but Valerie wasn't done with her yet.

"Under Leonard Twigg, this paper had no equals," Valerie stated. "He took a tatty tabloid that was about to go bust and he made it the best-selling daily in the UK. The only reason you have a job – the only reason any of those morons out in that office have a job - is because Leonard Twigg turned this ship around and made it the success it is today. He was willing to do the things our 'peers' didn't have the balls to do. Oh yes, I know all of the accusations that are made against us. All the criticisms and complaints. Half of them are aimed at me. But like it or not, Oonagh, our 'peers' *need* us to be the bad guy, to be the *nasty* newspaper. They need someone to pick on people and hound people, to defend traditional values and challenge the oppressive march of political correctness. We run a story, Oonagh, and the next day you'll see it in all the other tabloids. They might pretend to be outraged by what we've done, but every week their pages are filled with second-hand stories from the *Daily Ear*. And the broadsheets are even more hypocritical. They snipe at us for our morals and our practices. They blame us for the public's poor opinion of the press. But every time we have a big exclusive, they're all over it like a rash. Oh, they pretend to report our stories in a different way. They think their coverage is academic rather than salacious. They claim it's their job to *comment* and *examine* and *dissect*. They pretend to be looking at the *broader issues* or at the *repercussions* of what we've done. But when you get past the arty-farty rhetoric all they're really doing is reprinting our stories. And you know why, Oonagh? It's because we don't report the news. We *create* it. Every day this country's news agenda is set by the *Daily Ear*. That's how great Leonard Twigg made this paper. When we shout, everyone listens. Even the Prime Minister listens. And Leonard Twigg did that."

Valerie buttoned her jacket, ready to leave. She then stepped towards her door, turned, drew on her cigarette and blew smoke back in Oonagh's direction. "You may think you've earned your page on Wikipedia with your little website, Oonagh. But you mess with this newspaper and the one and only thing you will be remembered as is the woman who destroyed the *Daily Ear*. You might want to consider that."

Oonagh allowed Valerie the final word, if only to ensure the conversation was over. Valerie was satisfied she had said her piece and marched through the *Daily Ear* newsroom triumphant. As the lift doors slid closed in front of her, and the *Daily Ear* vanished from her life, she found herself smiling. She knew she would never return. She was about to burn all her bridges, but she didn't care.

The world was about to learn the truth about Leonard Twigg's death and Valerie Pierce had the exclusive.

23

"MURDERER!" **SCREAMED THE** front page of the *Daily Ear*, a dramatic headline straddling a strangely sinister picture of Adam Jaymes' face that Felicity guessed must have been photoshopped. It was 5am, and she was once again standing on the pavement outside the little newsagents just up the road from the *Daily Ear* office. She watched quietly as the owner placed that day's papers out on display.

"*Bitter Jaymes' revenge blamed for tragic tube suicide: Full story on pages 4, 5, 6, 7, 8, 9 and 10*". It was a dramatic and daring attempt by the *Daily Ear* to finally place a stranglehold on Project Ear, in the hope the coverage would be a death blow to whatever was left of Adam Jaymes' career. The day before, Felicity had seen the star's name and reputation go into a free fall as his staunchest fans in the media struggled to support him. Even the most outspoken broadcasters hadn't felt they could suggest (on air at least) that Twigg had simply reaped what he had sown.

On social media things had been somewhat different. There had been a huge, angry wave of support for the actor underpinned by a core of people who thought, very simply, that the world was well rid of Leonard Twigg. Adam Jaymes' fans had taken to Twitter and Facebook in their thousands and demanded that their voices were heard. But their comments went unreported because *that* wasn't the story, at least for that day. For 24 hours, Adam Jaymes had been solely responsible for the tragic death of a newspaper editor and Colin Merroney had confidently put Wednesday's paper to bed expecting the rest of the printed press to follow suit.

But no one, and particularly not the staff at the *Daily Ear*, could have foreseen Adam Jaymes gaining the most unexpected ally. Valerie Pierce was supposed to have written a blazing criticism of the actor, but she had taken herself to the Press Association and dropped a bomb on the *Daily Ear* instead. She had handed over confidential emails and provided a devastating first-hand account of what had really happened behind the scenes in the days before Twigg's suicide. *"Bereaved, Blamed and Belittled; The truth behind Leonard Twigg's death"* was the *Mail*'s take on the story while the *Daily Mirror* revealed *"Twigg 'suicide note' sent hours before wig exposé"*. *"Billionaire Harvey 'killed' Leonard Twigg"* said the *Sun*, whilst the *Guardian* teased with *"Valerie Pierce reveals how the powerful Harvey family turned on their most loyal servant in the days before his suicide"*. All the papers had taken the story from PA, and the television and radio news reports had followed suit. The *Daily Ear* front page now looked as ridiculous as it did anomalous, reporting a version of a story that the rest of the world's media had already decided was entirely discredited.

For Felicity, it had been a fascinating turn of events. Unable to sleep, she had quietly left her flat and made her way to the newsagents to see how the story was playing out. She had checked her Twitter account on the way and realised Valerie had done something big, but hadn't realised the full repercussions until she was standing with all the front pages in front of her. In a single day the story had totally flipped. Adam Jaymes was completely exonerated and the blame now sat entirely with the Harveys.

"Have you come for the papers?" the shop owner asked. "Only no one's been to collect them for a couple of days so I didn't think you were still taking them. Won't take me a moment to put them together, though."

Felicity shook her head. "No, sorry, I just came to look," she replied. "I couldn't sleep, so I thought I'd take a walk and come and see what the papers were saying this morning."

The shop owner stepped back and looked at all the papers he had just placed out on display. "I can't see the *Daily Ear* lasting another week, not like this," he said and then suddenly looked at Felicity, worried he had offended her. "Sorry," he said, "I don't mean to worry you. I'm sure your job is fine."

She smiled at him. "Oh, I don't work there. I'm just a student getting some work experience."

The man was relieved, and then looked back at the papers again. "It's quite something though, isn't it?" he said. "They're like a pack of wolves, aren't they, these newspapers? It's like they've spotted a weak one and have all turned on it."

"Did you mean what you said?" Felicity asked. "About the *Ear* not staying open? Do you think that could really happen?"

The man shrugged. "If you'd asked me that a few years ago, I would have said no. No chance," he replied. "But a few years ago, no one could ever have guessed that the *News of the World* would close. Or that newspaper reporters would be going to prison for phone hacking." He collected together the plastic ties and paper wraps from the piles of newspapers he had just put out and then sighed, suddenly sounding like an old man. "Nothing lasts forever, anymore," he said. "If there is one thing I do understand about this modern age, it's that. Nothing lasts forever."

"I thought we had him," Sam said solemnly, as he studied the front pages that were sprawled across his desk. "I just don't understand how this could have happened. I don't understand how she could have done this. Of all the people to help Adam Jaymes. It just doesn't make sense."

As the morning had progressed, it had become painfully clear to the *Daily Ear*'s senior team how fleeting their victory had been as they plunged back into another reputational crisis. Leonard Twigg's death had offered them little more than a short respite which Valerie Pierce had snatched away. Colin stood looking out of Sam's window, his hands jammed into his pockets and his shoulders hunched forward, defeated. Although Sam, as usual, was failing to address the issue directly, Colin knew what he was after. Sam wanted Colin to offer some words, some explanation, for Valerie's betrayal. And there was a tone in Sam's voice that implied blame, as though Colin should have guessed what Valerie was going to do and prevented it.

Oonagh sat in front of Sam, staring intently at her iPad as she silently scanned Twitter and news websites in other parts of the world. "Sam, it's too late for 'what ifs'," she said bluntly, and rested the tablet onto her lap. She rubbed her tired eyes and arched her aching back, wondering if it was time for yet another coffee. "It's done. Your new PR director is getting our lines sorted and she clearly knows what she's doing. But this isn't going to be an easy few days. Valerie's looking for a new job and I imagine she'll be doing the rounds to promote herself. Radio, television, *Loose Women*, *This Morning*. You name it, I've no doubt she'll be on it. In a very real way, she's just become a bigger liability than Adam Jaymes himself."

Colin turned his head, ever so slightly, at Oonagh's words. A small part of him was still protective over Valerie and he felt an urge to jump to her defence. But he knew that Oonagh was making a fair and valid point. With her column at the *Daily Ear* now history, Valerie would be scouting around for a new role. She didn't need to work, of course. Colin knew she had earned a small fortune at the *Ear* and been very well provided for by her late husband too. But he also knew how much Valerie enjoyed having a public profile and a sense that her opinion mattered. She liked feeling that she could influence anything from government policy to the career of a reality TV star. That sense of power would be difficult to give up. And as much as he hated to admit it, even to himself, Colin had been a little heartbroken by her actions. That day's paper had been his first as acting editor and he had signed it off with pride and excitement. It had felt, to Colin at least, like a truly momentous occasion; the former work experience boy finally being handed the top job. But what should have proven an historic day had left him feeling humiliated and inept. Across the industry, and possibly within his own newsroom, Colin feared he was now a laughing stock. And Valerie had done that to him.

"Colin, what are you going to do about her?" Oonagh asked, determined that her acting editor should express some opinion on their former colleague. "You know her better than anyone, what have we got on her?"

Colin turned and found Sam and Oonagh both staring at him. They were waiting for him to share some gem of information with them, something they could use to rubbish Valerie's version of events. And he knew they could only do that by ruining Valerie herself. He realised that was what Sam and Oonagh had already decided they were going to do, destroy Valerie Pierce's reputation so no one would consider her version of events reliable. But as upset as Colin was, the situation still wasn't so cut and dry. For the first time in a very long time he was facing a genuine moral dilemma: his friend or his career. He owed Valerie a lot, and not just because of how she had looked after him when Fiona left. She had been looking after him for his entire adult life, since he had first arrived at the *Daily Ear* as a sweaty and nervous 16-year-old on work experience. Valerie had been the only member of staff to treat him with respect from day one. She had kept an eye on him, made sure he got credit for his work and put his name forward when promotion opportunities came up. And over the years, she had also been pretty much the only woman in the whole building who had never tried to sleep with him. And when all was said and done, Colin knew there was a lot of truth to Valerie's story. He understood how angry she must have been when she became aware of all the events leading to Leonard Twigg's suicide. She may well have acted out of malice, but at least she'd had a legitimate reason to be so angry. "We're going to look reckless if we attack Valerie," he said, trying to sound confident and informed. "We need to take this one on the chin. She has confidential emails that can prove - "

"Not an option," Oonagh interrupted, sternly. "All Valerie has is an email proving we had a management restructure, and another showing that Leonard wrote handover notes. That is all. Everything else is just her opinion, pure conjecture."

"But - "

"It was her decision to leave. And it was her decision to make the *Daily Ear* an enemy," Oonagh continued.

"I think 'enemy' is a bit - "

"Enemy is exactly the right word, Colin," Oonagh stated. "Valerie's a big girl and she knew what she was doing, what she was getting herself into. She knew what we would *have* to do in response to her story." In the absence of any ideas from Colin, Oonagh shrugged and said, "I suppose we could always use the drink-drive story. What do you think?"

Colin could see the irony in that suggestion, even if Oonagh and Sam couldn't. It hadn't been so long ago they thought it was something Adam Jaymes would throw at them. Now it was something the *Daily Ear* might use itself. "That's no good," he said. "Valerie's got a cancer sob-story attached to it, and she also knows the *Ear* covered it up. It would do more harm than good."

"In which case you need to tell us what you're going to do," Oonagh snapped, impatiently.

"Colin, we both understand that this is a difficult situation for you," Sam said, finally chipping in and offering a gentler, more persuasive tone. "You've know Valerie for a long time and this is tough. But you must realise that this isn't just business anymore. Valerie's made this personal. This is my family she's attacked. She's blamed us for Twigg's suicide and we need to respond to that as strongly as we can. And if that means we have to take Valerie down, that's what we shall do."

Colin fell silent, feeling a gnawing resentment at what Sam had just said. The Harvey family hadn't considered it 'personal' when Adam Jaymes had revealed Colin's affair live on *Newsnight*, or exposed Valerie's secret first marriage. Or even when Twigg had thrown himself under a train. That, it would appear, was just business. But criticise the Harvey family and suddenly everyone has to take it personally, even the staff.

"We could issue a statement confirming Valerie was about to be released from her contract," Oonagh suggested, clearly tired of waiting for any constructive ideas from Colin. "She and I had a conversation shortly before she walked out, and I think I made it clear that was a possibility."

"Interesting idea," Sam said, thoughtfully. "So, rather than looking like an honourable whistle-blower, she'd look like little more than a bitter former employee with an axe to grind."

As Colin stood and listened, he realised he had no idea what to do. Over the years, whenever he had faced a difficult decision, he had always been able to seek out Twigg's advice. Colin could explain the most complex situation, any ethical minefield, and within moments Twigg would have analysed the information, weighed the pros and cons and delivered a clear and precise action. And even though he was gone, Colin felt he knew what Twigg would have told him to do. With a heavy heart, he suspected Twigg would have agreed with Oonagh and Sam and told him to go after Valerie.

"Well?" Oonagh asked again. "Colin? We're not getting much from you this morning. What are you going to do about Valerie Pierce?"

Just as Colin was about to reply, his mobile phone started purring in his jacket pocket. At first he was going to ignore it, but then he realised which mobile phone it was. It was a new phone he had bought and given the number only to Fiona's dad to call him with any news. "I'm sorry," he said, and reached to his inside pocket and pulled it out. "It's about Fiona. I have to take this."

Sam rolled his eyes as he sat back in his chair and looked at Oonagh, who gently shook her head, as though indicating that Colin was a lost cause. They listened to one half of the conversation, which was mostly a series of short responses to whatever information Fiona's dad was relaying. "OK ... right ... ahah ... right ... I see." When the call ended, Colin gently slipped the phone back into his pocket and said nothing. Oonagh noticed that he appeared to be shaking and his eyes were glistening as though he were on the verge of tears. "Colin, what's happened?" she asked.

Colin spoke slowly, his face drained of all colour and his voice reduced to little more than a whisper. "Fiona's been in a car accident," he said. "She's in hospital. It's serious."

"Oh dear Lord," Oonagh said, and immediately stood and clutched his hand to show her support. "The baby?" she enquired. "How is the baby?"

"She's having an emergency caesarean but it's too early to tell," he replied. "I'm sorry, but I have to be there. She's still my wife. That's my child. I need to get to the airport."

Sam stood and patted Colin on the back. "Of course," he said. "We'll sort everything out here. You just go. Just go. We'll all be praying for you."

Distracted and alarmed and without a second thought for the *Daily Ear*, Colin hurried from the office and headed into the lift. In spite of the terrible circumstances, Fiona's dad had been typically level-headed on the phone and delivered the awful news clearly and calmly so there was no misunderstanding about what had happened or the seriousness of the situation. Fiona's brother Alastair had taken her out for breakfast when they had been approached by a reporter and photographer from a rival paper who demanded an interview and some pictures. Fiona had declined but the photographer had started taking pictures while the reporter threw insulting questions at her which had made her cry. Alastair then lost his temper and pushed the reporter to the ground, before helping Fiona into his car and driving away. But the journalists followed and the resulting car chase through country lanes had ended dramatically when Alastair lost control on a sharp bend and the car left the road and overturned in a ditch. Fiona's father had taken time to warn Colin that photographs of Fiona and Alastair being rescued from the wreck of the car by emergency services were already online. The rival paper, it seemed, hadn't disclosed that its own staff had been involved in the crash but was gladly reporting that Alastair had been charged with both assault and dangerous driving.

As the lift doors closed, an unexpected tear trickled down Colin's cheek. The thought of Fiona, his Fiona, battered and broken and undergoing an emergency caesarean section was almost too much for him to bear, and he blamed himself for every aspect of her predicament. He blamed himself for the pregnancy, for rushing her into a marriage, for breaking her heart with his affair and for leaving her as little more than fodder for a rival tabloid. For the first time in his life, Colin had been responsible for someone else's life and happiness and he knew he had completely failed. His young wife and unborn child were both in terrible danger and as he headed to the airport, he knew that if either one of them died he would never be able to forgive himself.

The moment Audrey heard the clunking of Estelle's platform shoes along the passageway toward the kitchen, her heart sank. Quietly, somewhere at the back of her mind, she had allowed herself the luxury of thinking she would have Howard to herself for just one more evening. But Estelle and Howard had obviously reunited, either happily or unhappily, and Audrey sadly realised she would once again be relegated to the role of ex-wife. She tried not to let it distract her or change her demeanour in any way, and instead popped open a bottle of vintage Dom Perignon and started to pour them each a champagne flute. She assumed Howard hadn't told Estelle about their conversation, and chose to act as though in complete ignorance of their recent estrangement. And as Howard loomed into view, Audrey carried herself with a breeziness that belied her true feelings. "Good evening," she said warmly, as though she had fully expected them both. Howard entered the kitchen first and left his wife standing awkwardly behind him in the passage. He kissed Audrey on the cheek and took a glass of champagne. "Something smells good," he noted and walked around the table and sat down. Audrey held up a glass to coax Estelle through the doorway. "And one for you, Estelle?" she asked, smiling sweetly. Estelle stepped forward and kissed Audrey on both cheeks. "Thank you Audrey," she said, immediately looking more relaxed. She then took her glass and sat down at the table opposite her husband.

At some point it had become a Harvey family tradition to get together the night before the *Amazing People Awards*. Howard had always factored it into his plans and made sure he was able to fly back to London regardless of where he was or what he was doing. And when Sam had relocated to LA, he always set aside a few days each year to fly home for the awards, ensuring he arrived a day early so he could attend his mother's pre-event supper. It even continued when Howard married Estelle, with his young wife simply becoming part of the tradition too. And although Audrey hadn't spoken to either her son or ex-husband that day, she had prepared the usual supper without a hint of doubt that both of them would make an appearance. "There are going to be hot and cold canapés, and different cheeses," she said, trying to prevent the room from falling into a hate-filled silence. But Howard was staring into the distance, ignoring Estelle to the very best of his ability within such a confined space. Estelle, meanwhile, was staring directly at him with an exaggerated look of loathing on her face.

"And I've made some mini puddings, as well, just for tonight. Thought it might be fun," Audrey concluded, embellishing the sentence with a little chuckle at the end. But neither of her guests laughed, smiled or even acknowledged what she had said. "There's a New York cheesecake you can fit onto a single dessert spoon. Just pop it straight into your mouth."

Howard continued staring into the distance and Estelle continued to glare at him.

"I think they're Nigella's recipes but they might be Delia's. I can't remember. But they're all delightful."

Estelle sipped her champagne, her top lip curled as though it was vinegar, and then she turned in her seat to look towards Audrey. "Sounds lovely," she said. "I do like *New York* cheesecake. And I've certainly had plenty of time to enjoy *New York* cheesecake over the past few days. Haven't I, Howard?"

"Estelle, not here!" Howard barked.

Audrey pulled out a chair and sat down, gently drawing one of the champagne flutes towards her. "Well. I'm very glad you are both here tonight," she said. "Now all of that nastiness with Adam Jaymes is over, I'm glad we can still get together as a family."

"Oh, but that's not really the case, Audrey," Estelle replied with a tone that was deep and sarcastic, having completely lost her tolerance of Howard for that day.

"Estelle. Behave!" he ordered sternly, looking directly at her for the first time since they had arrived.

"No, apparently my attendance here this evening is a test, Audrey," Estelle continued. "A test! You see, apparently, I'm on very thin ice. According to my husband. Very, very thin ice."

"Estelle!"

"The final straw," she continued, louder, ignoring her husband's protests.

"Estelle!"

"Drinking at the last chance saloon!" she yelled and then downed her champagne.

The room fell silent. Howard glared at his wife, gently shaking his head to indicate his disgust at her behaviour. "My apologies, Audrey," he said. "Apparently Estelle's appalling behaviour in New York wasn't enough. We're going to get a repeat performance here this evening for anyone who missed it."

Estelle leaned forward towards Howard, ready for a fight, but Audrey piped up before either could get another word out. "Enough!" she said loudly, with a harshness to her voice that caught Estelle by surprise. Audrey looked at each of them in turn with a severe, disapproving scowl on her face. "Let me make it perfectly clear to both of you," she said crossly, "that we are going to have a perfectly pleasant evening. We will drink champagne and eat canapés, and chat about nice things, pleasant things. And we will use our indoor voices at all times. Because in spite of an awful, awful couple of weeks we are still here, as a family. And the *Amazing People Awards* are going ahead, as planned. And tomorrow night, when we are sitting at those awards and the cameras are on us, and we are live on national television – and, mark my words, we *will* be live on national television – all the viewers will see is a completely happy, unchanged, united family. Is that clear?"

Howard and Estelle both lowered their faces slightly, like scolded children. Audrey had laid down firm ground rules for the following 24 hours and left them in no doubt that their marital problems, no matter how severe, were not to be discussed or even referenced until the awards were over.

"Sorry Audrey, honey" Estelle said quietly, a gentle hint of warmth seeping back into her tone as she realised someone other than Howard was suffering by her actions.

"Yes, sorry Audrey," Howard echoed. "And you're right. If we keep acting like this, it's like Adam Jaymes beat us."

Audrey was pleased to have made her point but no longer had the patience to be the sole source of conversation and so she busied herself with her canapés. After a few moments, the stony silence gently eased into an uncomfortable conversation. Estelle began to detail her quest to find a gown for the awards during her stay in New York. And then Howard talked about his plans to make a sizeable donation to the NCTJ's training programme in Leonard Twigg's honour. Both directed their words at Audrey rather than each other but Audrey was content that at least a conversation of some description was underway. Before long Sam arrived, appearing at the kitchen door with a bouquet of flowers for his mum. "Oh, they're lovely," Audrey said and embraced him. She took the flowers and then proudly paraded them across the kitchen before popping them into a clay vase that she had filled with water earlier, just in case. "I'll sort them out later," she said, and then kissed Sam on the cheek. "Thank you."

To her surprise, Audrey then noticed another figure entering the kitchen from behind Sam. She almost asked "May I help you?" but caught herself just in time as she recognised the unexpected guest as Oonagh Boyle from the *Daily Ear*. Decades of good hosting quickly kicked into gear and she greeted Oonagh with the same warmth and familiarity that she had the others. "Oh, I'm so delighted you were able to make it," she said, pretending she had known all along that Oonagh might attend. Audrey embraced her and then poured two more glasses of champagne. "You must have had an absolutely horrendous day," she said.

"Nothing she couldn't handle, I'll bet," Howard said, and then raised his glass at Oonagh as a greeting. "Come on you two, grab some champagne and sit down. Tell us everything. Is the *Ear* still in business or has Valerie Pierce finished you off?"

"It's been quite something," Oonagh said with a sigh. Sam pulled out a chair for her and once she was seated he sat next to her and handed her a glass, his arm rested across the back of her chair.

"Are you still in business?" Howard asked again, less jovially this time.

"We are still in business, Howard, yes," Oonagh replied. "We've got a tough few days ahead of us, but Sam's people from LA have hit the ground running. I have to be honest, though, we're getting a lot of mixed messages about what Valerie will do next and that's currently our greatest concern."

"It's great isn't it?" Estelle said, unexpectedly wading into a conversation about the family business. "You survive everything that Adam Jaymes throws at you, and then it's one of your own who tries to finish you off. Bloody Valerie Pierce, I never liked her. And it's not because she never met me for lunch. But purple, always in bloody purple. OK, OK, we get it. You have a signature colour but you don't have to live in it. I half expected her to paint herself bloody purple. Any every time I saw her, she had a glass of red wine in her hand. How she ever got any work done, God only knows. It's like she had it on a drip."

Audrey laid plates of food on the table and then sat down and joined the others. "I was going to give her a call," she said. "But I was so cross with her, I realised I would probably only make matters worse. After everything we've done for her, the way we protected her through all those dramas, Pearl Martin and all the others. It just beggars belief that she would do something so treacherous."

"It is what it is, Audrey," Howard said, glumly. "But I don't think Valerie wanted to ruin the paper. She just wanted to give us a bloody nose."

"And now Adam Jaymes has finished with his stupid project, we think we're on the home run," Sam concluded. He and Oonagh smiled at each other and then clinked their glasses together. For a moment everyone else in the room paused, expecting them to kiss, but they just sipped their champagne. Audrey glanced over to Howard and noticed a hint of a smile on his face. She knew he would approve of a relationship between Sam and Oonagh. He had always spoken proudly of her, of how he had discovered her in the Dublin coffee shop. And it hadn't been so very long ago that he had told Audrey he was thinking of moving Oonagh into a new strategic role within Harvey Media International. But then Adam Jaymes had launched Project Ear and the moment Sam returned from LA, Oonagh's planned promotion had evaporated. Howard knew Sam would need someone like Oonagh at his side if he had any chance of surviving not only Project Ear but the *Daily Ear* itself. Audrey had no doubt that

Howard was proud of their son. She knew that he didn't think of Sam as a disappointment, that he considered him to be much closer to a success than a failure. But she also knew he had always given Sam his most talented people to work with. He believed their son would only truly thrive when surrounded by excellence and that's why he had kept Oonagh where she was, to help their son save the company and the family name.

"Well, now we're all here, perhaps I can make a toast," Howard said. Audrey quickly topped up everyone's glass and then raised hers aloft. Everyone did the same.

"To the Harveys," Howard said. "We're still bloody well here."

They all laughed and sipped their champagne.

"We certainly bloody well are," Audrey agreed. Howard then smiled at his ex-wife with such obvious affection as to catch the eye of his current wife, who began to wonder what had gone on during her extended stay in New York.

Oonagh put down her glass and dipped into her handbag. "I think that's me," she said, as everyone else became aware of a buzzing noise. She drew out her Blackberry and then operated a few keys before uttering a quiet "It's from Felicity ... oh no," and then she tapped the screen a few more times and showed it to Sam.

"Oh shit!" Sam cried. "Shit, shit, shit!"

"Oh God, its Valerie Pierce isn't it?" Estelle said. "What's the silly cow done now?"

"No, no, it's not Valerie," Oonagh said. "I wish it was, but it's not."

"Well?" Howard demanded. "What is it?"

Oonagh handed him her phone and he stared at the little glowing screen that was showing Oonagh's Twitter feed. There, right in front of his eyes, was an update he most certainly did not want to see and, more than that, did not want to show Audrey.

Adam Jaymes @RealAdamJaymes - 3m
    #ProjectEar concludes tomorrow night, live on @channel5_tv

24

We're throwing a #ProjectEar party tonight. Can't wait! Go get 'em @RealAdamJaymes

"**THE AWARDS HAVE** suffered dwindling viewing figures over the past few years, culminating in the event being dropped by ITV. But a single tweet last night from the actor Adam Jaymes and they've unexpectedly become the country's 'must see' television event of the year, if not the decade"

quickly became a national obsession, with Project Ear dominating newspaper coverage for the past fortnight and being the topic everyone in the country has an opinion on. But with recent events casting a dark shadow over the whole affair, one has to question the recklessness of the man behind Project Ear, Adam Jaymes

I went to put £50 on Estelle Harvey being a man but none of the bookies are taking bets anymore because of bloody #LeonardTwigg

"and like a ruthless murderer in an Agatha Christie novel, Adam Jaymes has announced his final act of vengeance in advance. We've all been sent an invitation to the party and can watch from the side-lines with unbridled glee as he takes down another member of the *Daily Ear* family. So, we know all know Whodunit. The question is, who is going to be his final victim?"

25

LEONARD TWIGG'S GREATEST ambition had been to destroy the NHS. If he had lived long enough to see it dismantled and abolished he would have died a much happier man. During 30 years as editor of the *Daily Ear,* he had done his upmost to carefully and methodically fashion its public image into that of a lumbering, archaic money pit riddled with corruption, cover-ups and soaring death rates. He had printed a seemingly endless procession of shame-filled stories about slipshod doctors, uncaring nurses, greedy executives and dirty wards. As a result, NHS employees tended not to like the *Daily Ear*.

Colin had never really been involved in the NHS stories, not that it made a difference to the staff at Edinburgh's Royal Infirmary. Any *Daily Ear* reporter was considered to be little more than a scabby, immoral, lying bawbag. But despite this he'd been treated with an incredible amount of care and compassion. The hospital's press team had organised for him to be secreted into the building in the back of an ambulance to avoid the crowing group of rival journalists at the entrance. They had then dressed him as an orderly, complete with surgeon's mask, and a small team of student nurses escorted him through the corridors of the hospital to a private waiting area not far from Fiona's guarded room. Although the student nurses hadn't really said anything to him, their expressions and whispered exchanges made it clear they didn't approve of him. Clearly, they knew he was the '*Newsnight* man' and that his young wife's life had been ruined and nearly ended because of his indiscretions.

As the hours of waiting and thinking and bizarrely hot coffee in foam cups drifted by, Colin found he had an unfortunate amount of time to consider the irony of his situation; his pregnant wife had been dragged from a wrecked car after being pursued by the press. And now here he was, the *Daily Ear* reporter, sitting in a clean, modern £200m NHS hospital where the staff had performed little short of a miracle and saved not only Fiona's life but that of his new baby son, too. The charge nurse visited at regular intervals and offered reassuring updates about his wife and baby. She was a thickset, sturdy Scot who was clearly too proficient to waste any time on unnecessary pleasantries or humour. But far from disliking her, he quickly grew to appreciate her bossy and no-nonsense attitude. She was always very serious and seemed to have a permanently furrowed brow, but it gave her a distinct air of confidence that made Colin feel Fiona and his son were in safe hands. And the news she delivered with each visit became increasingly more positive. His wife and baby were doing well. In spite of everything, both were doing well. She took Colin to the maternity ward to meet his son, a little bundle of miracle with a wisp of Fiona's red hair. For the past few months, Colin had been dreading that moment, when he would have to hold his baby in his arms for the first time. He was paranoid about dropping it. But the nurse introduced them in a very matter-of-fact manner as she passed him his baby boy. "This is your son, and he is *very* pleased to meet his daddy." And somehow having that nurse there, with her indisputable air of authority, made it less alarming because he knew she would never hand a baby to anyone she thought would drop it.

In spite of everything Colin had said to himself during the previous 24 hours, the blame he had laid at the feet of Adam Jaymes and the curses he had muttered under his breath, the first thing he said to his tiny baby son was an apology. "Sorry. I'm so, so sorry. It shouldn't have been like this. I'll make it up to you, I promise. You and your mum. I promise." Colin was then returned to his private waiting room, solemn rather than euphoric, and sat quietly with his head in his hands while the nurse went to see if he could visit Fiona too. She returned quickly, and gestured with her hand for Colin to stand. "You can see her now," she said, "but she needs her rest so only 10 minutes. Is that clear?"

Colin nodded. "Yes of course," he said. "And thank you. For everything. All of you. You're all amazing."

"Yes, we are," the nurse replied. "And perhaps you'd be so kind as to remember that when you're back at that disgusting arse-wipe of a newspaper." She then gently nudged Colin out of the waiting area.

As Felicity gazed at herself in the full-length mirror fixed to the inside of her bedroom door she felt cold inside, as if there was very little of herself left. The girl staring back at her could not have looked more out of place in the small untidy bedroom surrounded by piles of un-ironed clothes, half-read magazines and empty coffee mugs. The plain, studious intern was nowhere to be seen. Audrey's people had swathed her in a glamorous façade for the award ceremony, a bright sparkling disguise that would allow her to mingle with the great and the good, the famous and the infamous without anyone questioning whether she should be there. She was wearing a short dress made from tumbling folds of grey silk. Around her neck was a silver chain with a crystal encrusted orb pendant, and her shoes were a pair of croc-printed leather platform pumps. For once she had agreed to wear her long black hair down, sweeping across one side of her face and onto her shoulders.

She had no idea how much any of it had cost Audrey, but guessed it was thousands. Felicity had spent the previous few hours at a private salon where she had been complimented and pampered and offered champagne while her hair and make-up were all done for her. Audrey had an account there and so there was no discussion about payment.

And the exclusive fashion studio in Battersea wasn't the sort of place to have price tags on the clothes or jewellery. Felicity wondered if this was what life was like for a celebrity. The process she had been through had seemed ridiculously complicated and extravagant, but as she waited for the car to arrive she realised she would have felt ill-prepared for the evening ahead if she had simply bought a dress from a shop and then gotten ready at home by herself. The only thing that was her own that evening was her perfume, Rive Gauche. It wasn't a scent she wore very often, just when she was nervous and needed something familiar to make her feel that she wasn't completely alone. It had been her mum's favourite perfume when Felicity was a little girl, a fragrance that reminded her of cuddles before bedtime or sitting on her mum's lap if a TV show was a bit frightening.

But with those comfortable memories came a gnawing feeling of guilt. She knew that she owed her mum a letter, something she had been putting off for a long time. She would have to confess the truth about her time at the *Daily Ear* and some of the unscrupulous individuals she had associated with during that time. Her parents still believed she was working at the *Guardian* and she had explained her attendance at the awards that evening by claiming she was writing an article for one of its supplements. But she knew they would see her on TV, sitting side by side with the great and powerful Harvey family, and they would quickly realise she had not been telling them the truth. Felicity felt as though she had spent most of the past six months doing little else but telling lies. Deceit didn't sit comfortably with her and as she prepared for what could be the most important night of her life, she was relieved that the clock was ticking and it would soon all be over.

The car slowed for the final approach to the event and as Sam fiddled with his bow tie he suffered another wave of cold panic as he again remembered what was about to happen. Hundreds of people were lining the street outside the venue, held back by crash barriers and security. They were pushing forward, and cheering, and screaming, and holding out iPhones and taking pictures as famous people arrived, waved and then set sail in the opposite direction, up the red carpet and into TV land. Sam watched them, the people, reaching out to the celebrities with grasping hands and pleading faces. They all seemed desperate to entice at least one of the personalities over, perhaps someone from *TOWIE*, so they could snap a selfie and upload it. It was as though they believed Facebook, Twitter and Instagram would not survive another second unless graced by a photograph of Mark from Ilford wedged awkwardly against one of the judges from *Strictly Come Dancing*.

At first sight it could have been any TV event or film premiere, but Sam knew it wasn't. Beyond the excited crowd outside, flashing cameras and the red carpet, he knew no one was going to be tuning in at home to see who won which award. The whole evening was now little more than a vehicle for the grand finale of Project Ear. His poor mother had worked her socks off for months on end to make sure this was the perfect event, but it had been twisted and corrupted and now offered the most unfair opportunity for the Harveys to be destroyed in public once and for all. It wasn't an award show anymore, not for Sam. It was the reign of terror, with the wealthy and powerful being led to a dirty, brutal and public end in front of a screaming crowd of the great unwashed.

"Stop, Sam, please," Audrey said quietly, staring at him from the opposite seat. "Leave your bow tie alone."

"It will all be fine," Oonagh said, and gently squeezed Sam by the hand. "We're walking in with our heads held high and that's exactly how we'll walk out."

Sam attempted a brave face but he had spent the journey in various degrees of fear and dread, terrified by very real prospect that Adam Jaymes had his most shameful secret and was about to unzip it in public for all to see. He knew it wouldn't be done vaguely or kindly or with anything remotely resembling balance. It would be all detail and pictures, and shocked reactions and outraged women's charities and anti-porn campaigners. And he knew that the most awful part, the most terrible part of all, would be the shame he would bring on his mother and the look on her face when his porn addiction was made public. But with Adam Jaymes' propensity for surprises, he knew there was still a chance it might be something else or, indeed, someone else. Maybe it would be Estelle and her enormous hands or a dodgy deal of his dad's.

"I think we're here," Oonagh said, and began to gather her floor-length emerald gown ready to exit the car. Audrey was in a sparkling brown trouser suit, something a little less fussy she had chosen mainly for its practical quality, so she could rush around with the event team should she need to. "Remember what Oonagh said," Audrey reminded them with a smile. "We walk in with our heads held high and, whatever happens, we walk out the same way." She held his hand tightly and then, as an unexpected show of appreciation and acceptance, she reached over and squeezed Oonagh's hand too. "We're the Harvey family," Audrey said. "Adam Jaymes will not defeat us."

But as they stepped from the car, Sam discovered his much-treasured public anonymity had been stripped from him. He was immediately recognised and the crowd erupted with the most extraordinary roar, a wall of noise that overwhelmed all his senses and stopped him dead in his tracks. Most of the crowd howled and booed their disapproval, while others screamed with the sheer excitement of being so close to one of the main players of Project Ear. Oonagh had been expecting Sam to reach back into the car to help her and his mother onto the red carpet but she realised he was frozen to the spot. Fearful that the sudden barrage of camera flashes would expose his bewilderment, she quickly climbed from her seat and took her place at his side. This was not time to be a deer in the headlights, a weakling son publicly failing his juggernaut father. And so she gazed lovingly into his empty eyes and pretended they were quietly speaking. She laughed as though he had said something witty, and then caressed his cheek and kissed him on the lips. The kiss stole the show. If possible, the photographic frenzy increased even more as the Harvey heir stood publicly with his new love for the first time. Oonagh gently coaxed Sam back from his frightened place and as she withdrew from their kiss, he smiled at her.

"Thank you," he said.

"You're welcome," she replied.

Audrey, an old pro, appeared in front of them and simply smiled and waved and shouted, "Thank you so much for coming to support this wonderful event!" although no one could hear her. She then gently guided Sam and Oonagh towards the red carpet, confident they could make it to the lobby without any further incident. But just as they seemed to be on the home stretch, Audrey was met with such an unexpected sight that she almost tripped over her own feet. There right in front of her, larger than life and loving every second of the attention she was getting, was one of Audrey's oldest acquaintances, reporting live from the red carpet for *Sky News* wearing a sparkling gown in her signature purple.

Valerie Pierce was talking directly into the camera, holding her own microphone and doubtlessly using every ounce of her inside knowledge about both the event and the Harvey family. And in that moment everything Audrey had ever secretly thought about Valerie bubbled to the service – treacherous, hypocritical and self-serving Valerie Pierce. She was building a new career and life for herself by helping the media bury the Harveys.

"You absolute fucking bitch," Audrey hissed, and then tugged Sam and Oonagh by their wrists up the red carpet like an angry mum dragging two screaming toddlers to the dentist.

Valerie caught sight of them just too late, and as she called to them – hoping against hope they would stop for a quick chat – Audrey rushed by with Sam and Oonagh in tow and vanished into the building.

"It doesn't look like they were keen to speak with you Valerie. What do you think the Harveys are thinking right now?"

"This, Jeremy, this is exactly what I would have expected of the Harveys. This is the family at its most bold. Standing proudly together, in public, on the very night Adam Jaymes is due to make his final phone call. This is not a family that runs and hides. These people are ruthless and resolute. They will not be bullied into the shadows. This is a very public fight back. Jeremy, fasten your seatbelt. It's going to be a bumpy night."

"Oh good God, she's quoting Bette Davis now," Colin groaned, as his former colleague smiled from the TV fixed to the wall of Fiona's private hospital room. As hurt as he had been by Valerie's actions he was, on some level, pleased she had escaped Project Ear virtually unscathed and was now building a new life for herself.

"Bizarre it took her this long to realise who her natural fan base is," Fiona said, her voice weak and uneven, her blackened eyes barely open. "The number of drag queens I've seen dressed as Valerie Pierce ... "

Colin smiled at his wife. "I think the gay community's going to need a bit more convincing than a single line from *All About Eve*," he said.

"Oh, you haven't seen her article in the *Guardian* then?" Fiona asked, and then chuckled to herself as much as her dry throat would allow. "Dad read it to me earlier. It's all about how her views are softening, how she's been on a journey, the usual shit."

Colin was genuinely surprised. He had always considered Valerie's opinions to be a fixed point in time. They never changed and she was never wrong. But perhaps, he wondered, after stumbling from the *Daily Ear* cocoon she was now genuinely trying to join a modern society that she had only ever screamed at from the safety of the past. "I'll be interested to see how that one plays out," he said.

"Oh, you know these newspaper columnists," Fiona replied, disapprovingly, "expressing whatever opinion they're paid to have."

Colin did not really agree with what Fiona had said but he chose not to start a debate with her and instead just smiled and then clicked the TV off.

"I was watching that," Fiona said, sounding cross. "I want to see Howard Harvey arrive with his man-wife." Although she was all bandaged, shiny and swabbed and could barely move, her spirit was unbroken. She was determined to say goodbye to the dreary and quiet person she had become in London and prove she could still be the smartest, funniest person in any room. "Have you seen him, yet?" she asked.

"Yes, the nurse took me earlier. Looks just like his mum."

"Oh, he's got my hair and complexion. But, take my word for it, from the waist down he's every inch his father," she said and then laughed. It was a deep, dirty laugh that reminded Colin of their first encounter and the flirty conversation that had led so quickly to their sexual encounter in a laundry closet. He couldn't believe how quickly those nine months had passed, and how quickly he had cocked everything up. He put the remote control back onto the cabinet by Fiona's bed and then kissed her gently on the forehead, but she groaned with disapproval and tried to move her head to one side, away from him. "Don't!" she said sternly.

"I'm sorry," Colin said. At first he was surprised by her rejection but then realised he'd allowed his emotions to get the better of him and had momentarily misjudged the situation. "I know you're angry with me," he said and Fiona chuckled, but it was an unfriendly sound laced with sarcasm.

"Colin, please do not even think of making some stupid plea for us to work through our issues," she said, quietly. "And don't you dare say we owe it to our baby."

"Please, just hear me out," he replied. He was positive he could persuade her, if he could just get the words out. Because that's what he did for a living, persuade people; coax them into doing what he wanted. And he knew, absolutely knew, that if he could just talk at Fiona for a few moments she would agree to take him back and return home to London.

"Colin, look," Fiona said. The sternness in her voice had waned and was replaced with a troubling tone of pity and sadness. "Our marriage is over. It was over the second Adam Jaymes pulled out those photographs on *Newsnight*. There is no going back, I promise you. But there is a way forward. A really sensible, practical way forward."

"No, no, just hear me out."

"Our marriage is over," Fiona repeated, more loudly, and then moved her head as much as she could to stare at him directly in the eyes. "I am not going back to London. I've moved home and I'm staying here. It's the best place to raise my baby. I'll have lots of support, family and friends. People I can trust and rely on."

It was not a pleasant truth to hear but the moment the words were spoken Colin knew she was right. He knew how miserable her life would be if she returned to London with him. The distress he had caused Fiona by his affair would be nothing compared with a marriage of last-minute cancellations, apologetic texts and half-hearted promises. Colin's work would always come first. The *Daily Ear* would always come first. And if Fiona moved back to London with him she would face little more than the lonely reality of raising a child virtually single-handed in a city 400 miles from home. Without a shadow of a doubt the best place for Fiona and their baby was in Edinburgh supported and loved by all of her relatives and friends.

Colin knew what Fiona was offering him; a free pass. She was releasing him from their marriage and letting him off the hook when it came to the day-to-day responsibilities of fatherhood. She was given him exactly what he had always wanted, a son but with none of the strings. And in that moment he allowed his guilt and anxiety to ebb away, replaced with the happy realisation that his life would return to what it had been, before the linen closet. His beautiful wife was handing him back to the *Daily Ear*, and they would both be better off for it. "You're right," he said. "I'm not going to argue with you. Of course you're right."

"Good," she said.

"I just wanted to ask one thing. Well, not ask exactly. Suggest. I wanted to suggest a name."

"We decided his name months ago," Fiona responded.

"But things have happened, and I lost someone that meant a lot to me. So I wondered if we might call him Lenny."

Fiona closed her eyes completely as though unable to bear the sight of her husband, and a slight frown appeared on her brow. "Are you having a fucking laugh? Are you seriously asking me to name my son after Leonard fucking Twigg?"

"It's just that, well, I thought it would be a nice way to remember him. How important he was to me. He was a great man. I want our son to be a great man."

Fiona's lip curled ever so slightly and her disapproval became more pronounced. "You have no idea how much I want to get out of this bed and punch you in the face right now," she said.

"It was just a suggestion."

"Seriously. I would get that fucking chair you're sitting on and use it to beat the fucking shit out of you."

"OK, OK. Not a good suggestion," Colin replied, surprised at his wife's colourful language and wondering if it was a result of the morphine or if she'd just gone native.

She turned away and groaned. "I'm in this bed because of him and that stupid newspaper. I was almost killed because of them. So were my baby and my brother but you're so busy idolising him you can't even begin to see what an absolute monster he was."

"Fiona, the man's dead. And everything that happened is because of Adam Jaymes," Colin replied.

"I'm here because of you and Leonard Twigg and all of your awful colleagues at the *Daily Ear*. That reporter, the one who found me in the coffee shop. The one who chased us and made us crash the car.

That might as well have been you. That's what you do for a living, isn't it?"

Colin didn't respond.

"So this is what you are going to do. You're going to buy me a house, near my parents," Fiona stated.

"Yes," Colin replied.

"You will use your contacts to get all charges against my brother dropped."

"Yes."

"And when you make arrangements to see our son, you will stick to them. You will never cancel, not even once. Is that clear?"

"Yes."

Fiona was drifting back to sleep but Colin was grateful for her brief moment of lucidity. Everything was fine. They had a plan, a great plan in fact. He and Fiona had been saved from years of unhappiness and could now continue with the lives they were supposed to lead and possibly even become friends.

"He's David Timothy," Fiona whispered, "and he's going to be a better man than Leonard fucking Twigg." And then she was asleep.

Colin sat for a while and just stared at her. Beyond the bruises and the bandages he could still recognise the sexy, vivacious and clever woman he had married. But for the first time, she looked like a girl rather than a woman. Her pale, freckled skin seemed to glow under the gentle light from above and her tumbling red hair had been washed and brushed back from her face. The age gap between them had never seemed more pronounced. "David Timothy," he said, quietly. "Yes, good name."

A downcast Audrey was sitting at the Harvey table feeling as though her evening had already been ruined. Her fury at seeing Valerie on the red carpet had turned into exasperation as she had failed to track down the producer that she absolutely blamed for the debacle. And now as the lights dipped and the awards ceremony was about to begin, all she could see around her was a thousand people sitting at a hundred other tables, all peering back at her with knowing smiles and eager expressions. Audrey's bark and bluster was gone and she realised her son was right. The awards were secondary to the main event. "That producer, the stupid woman with the frizzy hair, where is she?" Audrey asked.

"Audrey, leave it! You're going to make yourself ill," Howard replied. "Now just enjoy your evening." Smartly dressed in a black tux with a red dicky bow, he reached across the table and patted his ex-wife on the hand. He wanted to show her more affection, but Estelle was seated at his side watching everything he did, listening to every word and judging the tiniest inflection in his voice. And he wasn't in the mood for another fight.

Audrey sighed and sat back in her chair. She looked around the packed venue, garlanded with overhead lights and speakers and cameras, and realised she was obsessing about something that simply couldn't be changed. "Yes, yes," she said. "I'm sorry. I hoped this evening would be better for us. For all of us. I just cannot believe Valerie would do that."

"Audrey, it's all fine," Oonagh said. "The security coming into this place was first class. There's not a camera or mobile phone anywhere. Adam Jaymes is going to be very disappointed when he realises he can't make his final phone call. And it's a big let-down for all those idiots who thought they'd spend the evening taking pictures of us. Now, the show's going to start any minute, and we'll have two hours of fantastic telly. All those wonderful children and soldiers and people with their amazing stories. There won't be a dry eye in the house."

Audrey smiled and nodded a gracious 'thank you' at Oonagh but couldn't move past her feeling of how conspicuous they were. Every other table seated at least 10 people, but even with Howard, Estelle and Felicity, the Harvey table only sat six. "It does feel strange," Audrey said, quietly, "being here without the others. No Leonard or Colin, Valerie out there with the news and everyone else watching.

All those eyes peering across the tables at us, waiting for us to fall down."

"Whatever," Howard said, clearly in no mood to pander to Adam Jaymes' drama. "This will all be over before you know it and then, I promise you, I'll personally bury Adam Jaymes once and for all."

Estelle sat next to Howard in a dramatic black gown of feathers and sequins. Her hair was tightly weaved into an oversized top knot and her ears and neck were adorned with dazzling jewels and silver. She could not have looked more like a drag queen if she'd tried, but Howard was still so filled with contempt for her that he decided to say nothing and instead let her be further ridiculed by the media. "Perhaps you should just admit when you're beat, darling," she said, a flute of champagne in her hand and clearly irritated by his continued intimacy with his ex-wife. "Adam Jaymes' husband is a lot richer than you. And more powerful. I've heard he's thinking of buying you out and shutting down the *Daily Ear* for good. Mind you, the way things are going he probably won't need to."

Howard sneered at Estelle and Audrey could tell he was spoiling for a fight, so tapped his hand and shook her head. "Oonagh's right. Let's try to enjoy the show," she said.

The *Amazing People Awards* theme tune exploded from the speakers, and the audience hum swelled into an enormous applause as the host took to the stage. She was one of the TV blondes, but Audrey couldn't remember which one. There was a grand opening monologue, something about British values and the recession, and then the awards began. Everything progressed normally as it had every year before. And Audrey relaxed and began to think that perhaps – just perhaps – this year would be as successful as any other. She allowed herself a moment of hope, that Adam Jaymes had changed his mind and nothing would happen.

She looked across the table at the beautiful girl she had brought as her personal guest, someone she hoped would say nice things about the Harveys when no one else did. Felicity had attempted to arrive quietly, without a fuss. But she looked so exquisite that she had drawn the attention of almost everyone in the room, and Audrey knew her place at the Harvey table had created something of a buzz around the event. Everyone wanted to know who she was.

Audrey then looked to her son who was sitting hand in hand with his new love, suddenly relaxed and enjoying the evening along with everyone else. In comparison, her ex-husband and his new wife remained stern and distant with each other. Howard turned and smiled at her reassuringly before turning back to the stage. It was a fleeting private moment between a man and his ex-wife, a show of warmth and familiarity that suggested they had unfinished business. It was smile that still somehow left Audrey a little weak at the knees.

It was another dark, dismal night in another generic hotel bar. Colin stared glumly at his third glass of pinot and tried to find some solace in the fact that, just for once, he wasn't working. He didn't have to file any copy by some impossible deadline or spend the evening making endless phone calls to keep tabs on his prey. For once he could just sit, and drink, and relax, and wallow. He occasionally glanced over to the widescreen TV, where the settees and armchairs had been claimed by a dozen or so excited business travellers all merrily tanked-up and anxiously waiting for Adam Jaymes' final exposé. The barman had been nice to Colin. A young blonde guy from Australia or New Zealand, who'd kept his glass filled and shown great patience when Colin had spoken at length about his awful day. It was only when the barman had slipped him his phone number that Colin realised he was being cruised, but by that stage he didn't care. A gay shoulder to cry on was as good as any other.

"It's Colin Merroney, isn't it?" a woman asked, leaning against the bar. She was about the same age as Colin, and the wide-eyed expression on her pretty face showed how surprised she was to have run into him. Her blonde hair was cut short and she wore a thick jumper and boot-cut jeans. He couldn't work out if she was staff or a guest and where she knew him from, but he could tell by her voice that she was English.

"Sorry?" he asked.

"Oh, you must remember me. Dee? Dee Hughes?"

Colin hated situations like this. His life was different to other people. His world was big and busy and filled with thousands of fleeting encounters and short conversations. Everyone remembered meeting Colin Merroney but he always struggled with the faces and names of the ordinary people whose lives he had touched. And so he shrugged and raised his hands, an honest gesture to show he had no idea who Dee Hughes was.

"Well, you've ruined so many lives over the years I can't say I'm surprised you don't remember me."

"Oh!" Colin thought. "It's going to be one of *those* conversations."

"Let me refresh your memory. I'm the girl who dumped her fiancée and ran off with the bridesmaid. You remember? About 30 years ago, you stood on my doorstep and demanded an exclusive interview and when I had the audacity to decline you decided to ruin my life. You must remember, surely?"

Colin remembered the story, of course. Dee had jilted her fiancée a few days before their wedding and run off with her best friend. The humiliated groom had been a champion body builder and was considered something of an Adonis. The picture opportunities had been endless.

"We moved after you printed that revolting story," Dee said. "We had to move hundreds of miles away because you made it impossible for me and Tina to stay in our home town. It wasn't enough to just prostitute my private life to sell your fucking newspaper, was it? You had to print all those lies other people told you. People who didn't even know us. But you know what, all these years later, we're still together. And despite your best efforts we're very happy. This is our hotel."

"It was booked for me. I had no idea," Colin replied, feeling he had to explain the coincidence so she didn't think he was stalking her. "And, to be fair, the reason I came to see you was to give you the chance to respond to those accusations."

Dee moved forward and for a moment it looked as though she was about to strike Colin around the face, but she didn't. "I shouldn't have had to respond to anything," she yelled angrily. "This was a private matter, a very painful, private matter. What business was it of yours, of anyone outside of my family? But you went and found all the local busybodies, people who didn't even know us but who wanted to have their say on my private life. They accused me and Tina of everything from financial fraud to all kinds of sexual deviance and you printed it, every last word of it. How dare you! How fucking dare you!"

Colin knew he was onto a losing battle. There, in front of him, was 30 years of anger and resentment. Dee had probably rehearsed this conversation a thousand times in her head and there was no way he could compete with that. All he had in his defence was a seriously injured wife and a new baby son. He hoped that would be enough. "Dee," he said, sadly, "the story was out there. If I hadn't knocked on your door, someone else would have done. Now, if you don't mind, I'm just trying to have a quiet drink in your lovely hotel. My wife's in hospital and - " and suddenly his pinot was all over his face. The bar went quiet. Even the barman failed to rush to his aid.

"I know all about your wife and I am *thrilled* that you are having such a fucking horrible day," Dee said. "I hope every shade of shit under the sun rains down on you from a great height. Because however horrible your day, no matter how bad your life becomes, just know ... just KNOW ... that you deserve every vile, horrible, disgusting second of it." She picked up some paper napkins from the bar and threw them at him. "Have that one on the house," she snapped and then walked out.

Once Dee was gone, the barman hurried over with a cloth napkin and the awkward silence quickly turned into a hum of excited, whispered conversations.

"Well, you can take the girl out of Essex ..." Colin said, drying his face and chuckling a little to show he had kept his sense of humour.

"She's OK. They both are, actually. They're really good people. I'm not sure what all that was about," the barman replied looking a little mystified, and then he refilled the empty wine glass.

Colin had a special reason for remembering Dee. He had only just turned 18 and it was the first time he'd been sent on his own to doorstep anyone. He remembered the bright, sunny cul-de-sac that was so ordinary and so silent in the middle of the day. He remembered marching up to her semi-detached house with a fake bravado that all but vanished when she coyly answered the door and peeked through the crack, a gold security chain hanging down in front of her pale face. He remembered her nervous, frail voice as she asked if she could help and the tiny gasp of genuine horror as he introduced himself and explained he was from the *Daily Ear*. He remembered the timid, polite way she had told him she didn't want to speak to him and then closed the door again, hoping that would be the end of the matter. And finally he remembered ambling back to the train station with his hands in his pockets, feeling very much at odds with what he had just tried to do.

But his news editor was furious when he returned without an interview and immediately sent him back with a clear instruction – get *something*. And so Colin returned to the sunny little town and unexpectedly found a multitude of local people willing to give back stories and make accusations and offer disapproving comments. He quickly learnt there was little room for sentiment or empathy if he wanted to get on. And with each job, with every successive doorstep or phone call, his conscience was less troubled. Eventually his guilt faded entirely and he grew increasingly angry and frustrated if anyone refused his request for an interview. He pursued those who ran and hid, and discovered the most remarkable ability to track down the most elusive of stars. His boyish charm – that smile and those dimples – helped him draw information from the most trusted of friends. His reputation as the 'Kiss-and-Tell King' was well earned. But as he sipped from his glass of wine he could sense for a moment, just a brief moment, the young man he used to be, staring at him from that sunny cul-de-sac all those years ago. And he doubted that young man would like what he had become.

"Ladies and gentlemen," the host boomed, her empty eyes staring at the autocue and her voice loud and flat, "a big hand for Kyle and his amazing, courageous mum Shirley." The audience cheered and applauded as a little scrap of a lad in a boy's tuxedo took his mum's hand and escorted her from the stage. Shirley, in a new dress she'd starved herself for three months to fit into, proudly held her Amazing People Award aloft as they disappeared from sight.

"And when we come back we'll have another amazing surprise for a very special someone, right here in the audience. Believe me, you will not want to miss this!" The theme tune played, the host beamed at the camera and the audience applauded as the channel clicked to the adverts. As the applause subsided, the venue filled with the hum of excited conversation.

Audrey was thrilled. Everything had gone perfectly. Every entrance, dress change, surprise appearance and video-taped sob-story had gone exactly to plan. There was a real buzz at the venue, and it seemed as though everyone had forgotten all about Adam Jaymes. "One more surprise and we're done for another year," she said to Howard and then quietly enquired, "Are you and Estelle both coming back to the house for drinks?"

Howard leaned towards her ever so slightly but kept his eyes to the stage so as not to draw Estelle's attention. "One of us will be," he replied and then sat back into his original position. It was suddenly as if he and Audrey had a little secret, something only the pair of them knew but no one else not even his wife.

Audrey had quietly accepted her own truth, that she would take Howard back in a heartbeat. She wasn't proud of that and certainly wasn't looking forward to the melodramas that would come hand in hand with a potential reunion. But she had finally forgiven Howard for the morning he'd left and for that awful conversation, for the moment he had rolled over in bed and stared at her like she was a stranger and asked, "Why am I in bed with an old woman?" Within 10 minutes he had washed, dressed, packed his bags and left. Audrey had simply sat on the side of the bed, quietly watching as her marriage vanished right in front of her. She had remained silent because she knew it would have been undignified to plead. And now so many lost years later, Howard finally seemed ready to call it a day with Estelle and Audrey was ready and willing to take him back. "Nearly done," she said.

Sam watched from the other side of the table, a little perplexed by the body language between his parents and wondering if a reunion had somehow become a genuine possibility. And then he pondered the implications for Estelle if she were to become Howard's childless ex-wife. Estelle had sat with her back to the table for most of the evening, only occasionally turning back to criticise something Howard had said. Sam wondered if on some level she knew what was going on, that this wasn't just another marital row and that her husband's affections had already been restored to his first wife. He wondered if Estelle herself was equally bored of it all, and that her marriage to a man so much older than she (albeit one of the wealthiest men in the country) was a novelty that had finally worn thin. Perhaps, he thought, she would go quietly, take the money and run off into the sunset with the manager of some premiership football team.

"We're uploading all of this to the website as we go along," Oonagh said, affectionately squeezing Sam's hand. "And I must give Valerie some credit. She did a great job getting all of these stories written up. It's a terrible shame, really, because she is a truly great writer. Her interviews are just superb, full of emotion. So much clout."

"She needs a new vocation. Perhaps she'll find something where she can put her skills to better use," Sam replied. "Perhaps she'll get a column in *Attitude* magazine."

Oonagh chuckled but then noticed that Felicity, sitting next to her, was quietly looking to the empty stage, her arms folded and with no one to talk to. She reached over and touched the girl's shoulder, and Felicity looked at her and immediately smiled politely. "Sorry, my mind was wandering," she said.

"I just wanted to say how lovely you look this evening," Oonagh said.

"Oh, this is all Audrey," Felicity said, refusing to take any credit for the way she looked. "She really spoilt me."

"Oh no, you're a beautiful girl," Oonagh replied. "I hope you're getting some photographs taken to show your parents."

Felicity smiled and nodded.

"Listen," Oonagh said, a more business-like tone to her voice. "I've had a lot of really positive feedback about you, Felicity. Everyone is singing your praises. Sam has really appreciated your help and support since he first arrived. I know you have to go back to college to complete your course, but I wanted to talk to you about an opportunity I could offer you once that's done. Let's have a conversation early next week. I think the team at *dailyear.com* could do with someone like you. It would be a really good fit. We'd start with a support role but, you know how these things go, there would be plenty of development opportunities. Travel, events, training. Promise me you'll think about it. I'd love to have you on board."

For Felicity the opportunity to stay with the *Daily Ear* came completely out of the blue. Whilst it was flattering to hear she had made a good impression, she was ready to leave the newspaper and get on with the rest of her life. All she could manage in reply to Oonagh's offer was a polite smile and a nod.

"This has been a great event," Sam said, smiling proudly at his mother. "I think we'll be back on ITV next year."

"Oh, we'll see," Audrey said. "Apart from that silly mishap on the red carpet with Valerie, I think the production company's done a great job. We've got a mop-up with them in a couple of days. I'll give them your feedback."

"It's Indigo, isn't it?" Oonagh asked.

"No, not this year. One of the big changes. We lost Indigo," Audrey replied. "We went with Trojan Horse. Have you heard of them? They're American but they've just starting to work in the UK, too. They're very successful."

Oonagh's friendly expression immediately changed. Her smile disappeared and a deep, concerned frown replaced it. "Trojan Horse?" she asked. "Trojan Horse is producing this programme?"

"Yes," Audrey replied, slightly disconcerted by Oonagh's sudden change of demeanour. "Is there a problem?"

The tone of Oonagh's concerned question had attracted even Estelle's attention. She, Sam, Howard and Felicity all turned to listen to the conversation.

"Audrey," Oonagh replied, desperately trying to look in complete control in case any of the other thousand people in the room were looking at her, "Trojan Horse is owned by Adam Jaymes' husband."

It was too late to change anything. The commercial break was over. The audience was told to applaud and the host, in her fifth dress of the evening, trotted back to centre stage and found her camera. "Welcome back to this year's *Amazing People Awards*," she said, beaming. "And I have someone truly amazing for you all to meet right now."

26

Oh come on #ProjectEar – last victim please!

Welcome to Twitter, @RealValeriePierce sweetheart. Now fuck off back to the 1980s where you belong

"**SECURITY MEANS NONE** of the guests, including the Harveys, have been able to take their mobile phones into the awards. It looks like Adam Jaymes is going to be sorely disappointed"

@RealAdamJaymes Hurry up. I can't watch anymore of this rubbish

@RealAdamJaymes All those brave kids and courageous soldiers. This is THEIR night not yours. Don't be a prick and ruin it!

8.47pm BST
I bet she has another dress change during the commercial break. Clever distraction from the inevitable realisation that she's a bit shit at this.

8.49pm BST
Several texts from friends asking if I know what the big surprise is. I've suggested Leonard Twigg's hairpiece has been encased in plastic resin and is being handed out as the final award of the evening. Probably to a small child suffering from alopecia.

8.51pm BST
Oh thank God, my Chinese is here. I can finally pop open the Prosecco without feeling like an alky.

8.52pm BST
"And welcome back. During the commercial break I changed my dress and had a poop." Silly cow.

> #AmazingPeopleAwards Some truly inspiring stories. Well done. Now hurry up and get to the #ProjectEar bit.

> I guess it makes sense that @RealValeriePierce would end up presenting on Sky News. Who the hell else would have her?

"truly has become event telly. We've got Project Ear, Adam Jaymes, Valerie Pierce and *Amazing People Awards* all trending on Twitter right now, and not just here but in other parts the globe. This is a defining moment for British broadcasting and the British media more broadly. And in just a few moments time we are likely to have an answer to the question that is on everyone's lips: who will be the final victim of Project Ear?"

27

"I HAVE SOMEONE *truly* amazing for you all to meet right now. He's an actor, a singer and an amazing dancer too. He's won countless awards for his work in television and on the stage but tonight he's here not to collect an award, he's here to give one."

"They wouldn't dare," Audrey cried. "Oh please, dear God, they wouldn't!"

"More recently you'll know him from *Glee* or *True Blood*, but for millions of us he'll always be Doctor Who's companion Joe!"

There was a gasp from the audience, followed by several squeals of excitement and a premature ripple of applause.

"You have got to be fucking kidding," Howard hissed.

"Oh dear Lord," Oonagh whispered, before burying her face in her hands.

Sam, who'd allowed himself to think he'd found shelter at the awards and its strictly enforced phone ban, felt his blood run cold as all his fear and anxiety rushed back and the walls of his safe haven collapsed around him. "Oh shit!" he gasped.

"He's been in the news quite a bit himself recently, but he's here tonight to set the record straight."

"That silly bitch hasn't a clue what she's saying," Howard snarled. "She could be reading out the instructions for haemorrhoid cream and she wouldn't know."

"Please will you give a fantastic welcome for the amazing - Adam! Jaymes!"

And there it was. His name said out loud for all to hear. There was no going back. The Harveys – each and every one of them – realised they had been duped. Far from cleverly eluding his final phone call, they had delivered themselves to his grand finale in front of a thousand delighted audience members and millions of viewers watching live at home. Before Adam Jaymes had even appeared on stage the audience were on their feet screaming and applauding, almost hysterical with the intoxicating anticipation of what was about to happen. The Harveys, conspicuous by being the only table to remain seated, could only hope that the cameras were not on them. Sam's heart was beating so hard he thought it was going to burst. He tried to detect some small sound amid the roar to suggest the audience was not applauding as one, that there was some discord and some disapproval of the actor's involvement in the evening. But there was nothing, not a single boo or shouted insult. Adam Jaymes was returning to the public stage triumphant, a hero in fact. Everyone was on his side. No one was backing the Harveys.

He appeared with a dazzling smile, and the roar from the audience grew even louder. He was dressed in a neatly tailored navy suit with his thick, glistening hair brushed back from his face. The host greeted him with a delicate embrace and then quietly disappeared into the wings. This was no longer her show. Adam approached the centre of the stage and, in a perfectly choreographed motion, a metal lectern rose from the floor to meet him. He leaned onto it and said "Good evening" into the microphone, but the audience got a second wind and the cheering and applauding grew louder. And then there was a chorus of foot stamping too.

"For fuck's sake," Howard said, just loud enough for Audrey to hear. "That's the man who put Leonard Twigg in the ground and they're treating him like he's a fucking hero."

Estelle leaned back, and turned her face ever so slightly towards her husband. "Haven't you realised yet, you old fool? They blame you lot for what happened to Leonard. You don't have a single friend in this entire hall." And then, with a smile, she turned her back on the whole family and looked to the stage.

"Can I just say … " Adam Jaymes started, his calm voice gradually bringing the audience back to their seats, "can I just say, to begin with, what an honour it is to be here this evening."

"We love you!" a woman screamed from the audience, and there was a roar of laughter followed by a small round of applause.

"Thank you," Adam replied, with a friendly chuckle. "But this really is an honour. I've spent the past few hours backstage, listening to your amazing stories, so many tales of courage and bravery from the battlefield or at home. From the soldier who risked her life to protect a fallen comrade, to the teenage boy who became a full-time carer when his mother was diagnosed with terminal cancer. Listening to these astonishing stories, I'm sure we're all humbled."

The audience clapped to show they were agreeing with everything Adam said.

Sam sat quietly, enthralled by the way Adam Jaymes had so effortlessly won the support of the entire audience and had them eating from the palm of his hand. He could sense the excitement in the air around him, the way everyone was watching the stage but keeping half an eye on the Harvey table. Without their phones and cameras, the guests would all have to rely in their memories for once and were clearly keen to capture every detail of the Harvey family's public humiliation. Estelle was right, 100% right. They did not have a single friend in the entire venue.

"What we have seen here this evening, so very clearly, is that courage comes in many different forms," Adam continued. "I was particularly taken by Danny's story, the young boy who stood up to a gang of bullies at his school."

The audience applauded and a camera zoomed in on Danny and his parents, sitting proudly in the audience with his award on the table in front of them.

"Oh, this bullying bullshit again," Howard groaned. "I might have known."

"What Danny showed us all, I hope, is that sometimes it can take just one person to say 'enough' and things really can change for the better." Adam paused, a silent segue into the rest of his speech. For a moment, there was complete silence in the auditorium. The actor was about to move onto a different topic and the audience was ready and waiting to go with him, for him to deliver the final shock of the evening.

"Many of you will remember a friend of mine, Pearl Martin." At the mention of Pearl's name, the audience applauded respectfully. Some of the younger guests did not know who she was, but everyone else did. Even though she had died so many years earlier, her name could still evoke a powerful, collective sense of an injustice that had never been redressed. "Sadly, many people see Pearl as a tragic figure. They remember how she died, that awful morning she was found at the foot of Beachy Head. But I was lucky enough to know Pearl very well and I like to remember her for how she lived."

Her face appeared on the enormous screen behind Adam, but not the ghostly pale image so often used. This was a new image, one of her in a summer garden, surrounded by colourful flowers and laughing at the camera. It was an image no one had seen before, a picture from Adam's personal album. It showed a young woman radiating happiness, who had her whole life ahead of her. But for the Harveys it simply reinforced the knowledge that they had been set up by the production company. Sam glanced across the table at his father and gestured with his hand that perhaps they should leave. But Howard shook his head and placed his hands firmly on the table top. The Harveys were not going to run and hide. They would sit proudly and see this through to the end.

"She played my big sister on *Eastenders* and that was a relationship we continued off screen too. We were very close and gradually, over the years, I became painfully aware that she was struggling with depression. You all know her story, of course. How she had to leave *Eastenders* and the role she loved so much. How her young child was taken into foster care. And how she eventually found life just too much, and so ended it all. And throughout all of her troubles and her darkest days, she was pursued ruthlessly and relentlessly by the media and by the staff at one newspaper in particular."

Without even hearing the name *'Daily Ear'* there was a grumble from the audience and heads turned towards the Harvey table. But then there was laughter too. As sad as they doubtlessly found Pearl's story, and although they were clearly disapproving of the *Daily Ear*, the thousand people in the audience were mostly just excited about the inevitability of Adam Jaymes' final exposé. The Harveys' private lives, their reputations and careers were now little more than fodder for the masses. Adam Jaymes was closing in for his final kill, and everyone seemed to think it was hilarious.

"Many of us thought that Pearl's tragic death would change things, that those in the media would appreciate the magnitude of what had happened and acknowledge the depth of the public's anger and disgust. I think we all believed things would change for the better. Certainly, we were promised change. We were promised stricter self-regulation and a tightening of rules governing press intrusion into a person's private life. But let me ask you, is this what we got?"

There was a pause, and then a few people in the audience started shouting back at the stage. "No", "Disgrace", "Liars".

"If anything, things have gotten worse. Indeed, I would suggest they have spiralled out of control. And this is why I made the decision to take a stand. On this occasion, I was Danny, the one person who was willing to say 'enough'. I launched Project Ear a few weeks ago and my aim was very simply to show the staff at the *Daily Ear* what it was like to be on the receiving end of an intrusive press. I wanted them to know how it felt to be ridiculed in public, or to have an embarrassing secret exposed for all to see. Certainly, where I uncovered illegal activity or unethical practices, those were exposed as well. It was never a vengeful campaign but a deliberate attempt to force a fundamental change in the working practices of the UK's newspaper industry. A change that neither the industry itself nor the government was willing to implement. I certainly did not set out to hurt anyone and whilst I do not accept any responsibility for Leonard Twigg's death I would like to express, publicly, my condolences to his friends and colleagues."

Howard's anger began to swell as he heard Adam Jaymes so casually brush over the death of Leonard Twigg, as though it was an annoying footnote the actor felt he needed to acknowledge, albeit briefly. And then the audience applauded and Howard could tell it wasn't out of respect for Twigg but to show their support for Adam Jaymes, to let him know they did not find him in any way culpable. "That's our headline," he said, leaning towards Oonagh and Sam. "'*I'm Not Sorry*'. That's our headline."

"Let's see how this plays out, Howard", Oonagh replied and then turned back to the stage.

Howard wasn't used to being dismissed and was so furious with how the evening was playing out he almost exploded at Oonagh, right then and there. But then Audrey took his hand to reassure him. "Oonagh's right, dear. Let's wait and see," she said. And Howard's fury waned just enough for him to return his attention to the stage as well.

"Over the past few weeks, through Project Ear, I've published five exposés. These were the sort of stories the *Daily Ear* publishes every day. The only difference is that these stories were about the

Daily Ear's own staff. This has been everything from the Kiss-and-Tell King who was cheating on his own wife" – there was a chorus of boos and laughter from the audience – "to the photographer whose seedy paparazzi pictures masked an even seedier photographic agenda in his private life." There were more boos and more heads turned to the Harvey table. "I was even invited in to discuss an early end to Project Ear. But those talks broke down almost immediately, because the team at the Harvey News Group simply wanted to protect their own privacy. They had no intention of showing any measure of respect for anyone else's. And throughout the past few weeks there has not been any sign from that company that made me think they were getting the message. Instead they have continued in the same despicable manner. They have attacked me and my husband, printed revolting stories about the private lives of actors and sports stars and made it quite clear that they're happy to continue making money by exploiting anyone and everyone. And let me make it clear to you all here today, every single one of you sat in this audience or at home." Adam Jaymes pointed into the audience directly at the Harvey table and a spotlight lit up from above and exposed them clearly for all to see. "The Harvey family would happily ruin the lives of any single person here tonight." He lowered his hand and looked out across the audience, somehow making each and every person feel he was talking directly at them. "You think you're safe because you're not famous or in the public eye, that what happened to Pearl Martin and a thousand other people could not possibly happen to you. Think again. You don't have to be a celebrity, you just need to be in the wrong place at the wrong time. Perhaps you tweeted something years ago, before you were old enough to understand the impact your words can have on other people. Or you sent a disparaging email to a future in-law, not realising it would be shared with their friends. Perhaps you dared to ask your local authority for a bigger council house. Or maybe, just maybe, you become the *Daily Ear*'s prime suspect in a murder case, simply because you lived next door to the victim and a reporter decided you were a little eccentric. From the most routine to the most unfortunate of situations, any one of you could end up splashed all over the *Daily Ear* and its website, portrayed as a villain for the whole nation to despise. Your life and reputation would be ruined. But, hey, at least you know your misery had benefitted someone. Howard Harvey would have the down-payment on another yacht."

"What's he talking about?" Howard grumbled. "I don't have a fucking yacht."

"I'm very proud of Project Ear because it has, at least, created a discussion. It has exposed those in government who are too weak to take action and those in the newspaper industry too greedy to change their ways. It has allowed journalists in other parts of the media to reflect upon their own behaviour and shone a light into the darkest corners of our own society. Because we should never forget that the only reason the *Daily Ear* has been able to continue down this sordid path is because four million people buy it every day. However, Project Ear has run its course and it is time to draw a line under it and move on."

Adam removed a mobile phone from his top pocket and dramatically flipped it open. "I just have one final phone call to make." There were squeals of delight from across the venue, as well as laughter and some applause.

"They think it's a fucking pantomime," Howard whispered to Audrey, who then gently clutched his arm.

"Whatever it is, we'll deal with it," she said and offered him a reassuring smile.

Oonagh held Sam's hand and squeezed it tightly, but he was lost to his panic again and could barely notice. Adam pressed a single button on his phone and without a hint of expression on his face to suggest his mood, he lifted it to his ear. Almost immediately, down in the audience, a ringtone started to play: The Police, *Every Breath You Take*. It was slightly muffled, coming from inside a handbag or a jacket pocket, but it was immediately recognisable and without a doubt coming from the Harveys' table. There were shrieks of excitement, and gasps, and people began to stand up to get a better look. Some stood on their chairs, peering over the heads of the hundreds of other guests, determined to see which of the Harveys would get the call. But then the screen behind Adam Jaymes shimmered and changed and the still image of Pearl Martin was replaced with a camera shot from inside the venue, a live feed of Audrey, Howard, Estelle, Sam and Oonagh. For a moment no one at the table moved, but then Howard uttered an exasperated, "Oh for fuck's sake!" and started patting his jacket pockets, his comment somehow picked up by a microphone and fed back through the speakers for all to hear.

"Dad, we weren't supposed to bring our phones," Sam said, gasping the words through a breathless panic.

"I didn't bring a phone. That wanker has obviously planted one at the table. Now see where it's coming from!"

Aware that everyone could now see and hear them, Sam and Oonagh began to check the area around them. Sam rummaged through his jacket pockets, his fear getting the better of him and he found himself wishing the phone call on Estelle. He wished and wished and wished that all those stories about her were true and that his father had either knowingly or unknowingly married a transsexual. Pre-op, post-op or in-between, Sam didn't care. At that moment in time, he just didn't want his own secret to be splashed all over the news. "Please make it Estelle, please make it Estelle" he thought to himself. And then he looked up, and realised everyone at the table was glaring at him, especially Estelle.

"You were saying that out loud, Sam," Oonagh whispered to him, a crossness in her voice he hadn't heard before.

"Oh," he said, sheepishly. And then he smiled at his stepmother. "Sorry."

"Estelle, you need to check your bag too," Oonagh said, trying to remain practical and in control amid the insanity that was playing out around her.

Estelle rolled her eyes as though she no longer expected anything from any of the Harvey family, not even a small measure of loyalty or support, and dumped her handbag onto the table.

"Please please please let it be her," Sam thought to himself, keeping his lips tightly closed so as not to repeat his unfortunate faux pas. And for a moment time seemed to slow down around him. Everyone at the table paused, and there was a sudden hush across the auditorium as Estelle gently slipped her long fingers and bejewelled nails over the gold clasp and clicked her bag open. Sam waited, heart pounding, for the sound of the ringtone to get louder. He waited for Estelle to reach into her bag, for the sullen expression on her face to change to one of shock as she found the planted mobile phone and realised the final call was, indeed, for her. But the sound of the ringtone remained muffled. Estelle briefly looked through her bag but quickly clicked it closed again. "It's not me," she said, smugly. She then sat back with folded arms and watched with an air of amusement to see how things would now play out.

There were gasps from the audience and a few disappointed groans. Sam glanced across the table, bewildered by what had just happened. "How the hell could it not be Estelle?" he thought to himself, lips still tightly sealed. "There's no one else."

"Howard?" Oonagh asked.

"Nothing."

"Sam?"

He checked and then checked again. There was nothing. The phone wasn't on him. The call wasn't for him. He immediately felt his panic begin to subside as he realised someone else's secret was about to be revealed. "No, not me. Oh God, it's not on me."

"And it's not Estelle," Oonagh said. "And it's not me."

There were only two other people at the table, Felicity and Audrey, but Felicity had already stepped away from the group and was keeping herself out of sight of the cameras, trying to merge into the crowd around them. Oonagh didn't think badly of the girl for that. This wasn't her drama and it wasn't fair for her to be involved. Besides, the sound of the ringtone was clearly coming from the other side of the table. From the general whereabouts of Audrey, the one person Oonagh had discounted from the outset. If truth be told, no one had considered the possibility that Audrey would get the final call, not even Audrey herself. Oonagh leaned onto the table and smiled kindly at her. "Audrey, dear, can you please check your handbag?"

Audrey's face dropped, not only because she was shocked at Oonagh's request but because she hadn't expected to be involved in the conversation at all. "I beg your pardon?" she asked, curtly. "Don't be ridiculous."

"Audrey, there's only you left. Please, check your handbag," Oonagh said again.

Audrey looked around her at her family and, beyond them, a thousand strangers all staring at her, suddenly the most famous person in the country. Beyond them, on the stage, was Adam Jaymes silently and patiently waiting with his mobile phone still held to his ear. And on the screen behind him she saw herself, the camera now isolating her from the rest of the family. Nervously and gently, Audrey reached to the floor and collected her clutch bag. She rested it onto her lap and could immediately feel the hateful vibration of a mobile phone pulsating through the sparkling brown fabric. "Oh dear Lord," she gasped quietly, keeping her eyes down so as not to have to look at all of those enthralled and delighted expressions, a thousand people captivated by her public humiliation. As she opened her bag the phone was the first thing she could see, an alien object in her perfectly organised world. It was lit up with Adam Jaymes' name on the screen, the incoming call. "I don't understand," she said. "I haven't done a thing. Not a single thing."

And then, without a hint of shame, Howard took Audrey's hand and kissed her firmly on the cheek. "Whatever," he said, "just answer the bloody thing. We'll deal with it, whatever it is."

"Mum, Mum, it's fine," Sam said, filled with grief and shame that he had somehow wished this away from himself and onto his beloved mother. "We're all here. It's fine."

Audrey took a deep breath, looked Adam Jaymes directly in the face and answered the phone. "This is Audrey," she said, solemnly.

"Hello Audrey Harvey, this is Adam Jaymes. I just called to let you know it's your turn."

As his perfect diction boomed throughout the venue, there were a few more gasps from the audience at the unexpected turn of events. Audrey's public profile had always been slight, certainly nothing compared with the juggernaut of publicity that heralded the arrival of Estelle into Howard's life all those years earlier. If anything, the crowd seemed a little deflated.

With that Adam ended the call, turned to his left and walked into the wings. There was a brief hiatus as everyone waited for something to happen next – a burst of theme tune or perhaps for the host to return. But there was no one. The show wasn't on the stage anymore; it was in the audience, at the Harvey table.

"Mum, what was it?" Sam asked, trying his best to keep his voice down. "Anything?"

Audrey placed the mobile phone onto the table and glanced up, staring her son in the face. "There's nothing," she said, honestly. "What can there be? I've done nothing."

"Anything, Audrey. Think. Anything at all?" Oonagh demanded.

But Audrey was at a loss. Her mind was racing through what she considered to have been a blameless life, and she could not think of a single misdemeanour that would justify Adam's final call.

"Don't worry," Estelle said, and leaned back towards the table. "It looks like your questions are going to be answered for you." She nodded towards the giant screen, the backdrop to the entire event, which had begun to shimmer and change. There were whoops of excitement and laughter from the audience as a giant line of animated sparkles swept across the screen, replacing the close-up of Audrey with the Project Ear website. All heads turned to the stage, as the front page headline flashed into view.

DNA Exclusive: Heir Apparent-ly Not!

Under the headline, in a row, were individual pictures. Head-and-shoulder shots of Audrey, Howard and Sam. But there was also a fourth picture, a silhouette of a man's profile with a big red question mark superimposed over the image. At first, the headline didn't make sense to anyone at the Harvey table, a glib play on words that didn't appear to have any connection to them. And the pictures below, of the Harveys and their son with the mystery fourth person, made even less sense. There was a quiet rumble of conversation from across the venue, a few gasps and more laughter. It seemed other guests had started to cotton on, but the Harveys themselves remained in the dark.

"What the fuck?" Howard bellowed, no longer able to control his frustration and caring little for how he might be perceived by the giggling, pointing masses around him. "What the hell does that mean? Audrey, tell me what the fuck that means!"

"I ... I just don't know," she cried back at him and then glanced across the table at her son, hoping he would offer a reassuring smile or supportive comment. But instead he just looked at her with an expression of horror as though she had committed the most treacherous act a mother could possibly commit.

"Mum," he said, his eyes wide with fright as he began to consider what the exposé might be about. "Mum?"

"I don't know what I'm being accused of. Of course it's not true. I don't know what I'm supposed to have done. What am I supposed to have done?"

Sam took a deep breath and as the thousand people around him suddenly fell silent, he asked, "Is Howard not my father?"

Confused and humiliated, Audrey stared at Sam and tried to understand what he was asking her. There had never been any shadow of a doubt that Sam was a Harvey, that Howard was his father. She couldn't even begin to comprehend why he was asking such a disgraceful question, why there were suddenly any misgivings. But amid the awful and oppressive silence that filled the enormous hall, Audrey's shock and panic subsided and the final piece of the puzzle slotted into place. A memory long and shamefully forgotten, a momentary lapse of judgement that flashed before her eyes, the most terrible of betrayals suddenly exposed for the world to see. "Oh my God," she whispered.

Her 30th birthday. A sunny afternoon in the garden, reading a book. Lonely, too many glasses of Chardonnay. An unexpected visit from a handsome boy, delivering apologetic presents from her absent husband. The boy, polite and eager to please; one of Howard's chosen few, someone he has plans for. He stays for a glass of wine. Talking, jokes, unexpectedly clever and witty. Compliments and then flirting. He sunbathes, his shirt off. She offers him sun cream, smoothes it onto his muscular back. He turns to face her. "Can you do my front?" Amazing chest, muscles on his arms. Not a boy. A handsome young man. Dimples and a square jaw. Bright blue eyes. A deep voice, a man's laugh. Thick wavy hair. He walks Audrey to the kitchen, lays her on the table. Kissing, pushing. He's naked. Surprise at the sight of him, of his size. He removes her clothes. Kissing, panting. She takes him upstairs and pulls him onto the bed, on top of her. She holds him, feels him inside. His energy, stamina. His passion. How lovely that he wants her.

"It never occurred to me, not once," she said softly, looking at the floor in shame. "I never thought for a moment you were anyone but Howard's. I would never have lied to you. To either of you."

A thousand people vanished into thin air. The TV cameras and studio staff faded into the background. In that moment, none of it mattered. Audrey's entire life fell to pieces, right there and then, in front of her son and her ex-husband. "Audrey," Howard growled, in no mood for kindness or sympathy. "Who the fuck is he?"

"Howard!" Oonagh snapped, still very much aware of what was going on around them. "None of that here. We need to leave."

"WHO THE FUCK IS HE?" Howard shouted, half through anger and half through a need to show Oonagh he wouldn't be told what to do.

Audrey couldn't answer, too ashamed to look up and too frightened to speak.

Estelle stood up, a glass of champagne in her hand, and nodded towards the screen. "I think we're about to find out, sweetheart," she said, smugly, as the graphics shimmered once more and the mystery silhouette was replaced with a photograph of a man's face.

Four hundred miles north in a hotel lounge in Edinburgh, a crowd of business travellers watched in a shocked silence as a familiar face appeared on the large wall-mounted TV. It was the man sitting behind them at the bar, the man who'd recently had a glass of wine thrown over him. "Oh my God, that's you," the barman said. But Colin Merroney didn't reply. He was frozen with his eyes wide and his mouth open. He sat oblivious to the excited crowd around him, because in his mind he was reliving a moment from his youth; an eager 17-year-old charming an attractive, lonely rich woman into bed. It was an exciting memory that had always existed in perfect isolation, never shared or set into any other context beyond what it had meant to him: the moment he had lost his virginity. But Adam Jaymes had somehow, impossibly, set that happy memory into an entirely new context. Suddenly there were repercussions and Colin realised that, in a single day, he had become a father twice over.

Soon the phones were out, two dozen mobile devices taking pictures and videos and tweeting and texting. And unbeknown to Colin and everyone else in the room, one of those swiftly taken photographs would soon become world famous; a man sitting at a bar with a glass of white wine in his hand, his face frozen with an expression of absolute panic and shock. At some point the following day, some clever dick would add the caption 'What do you mean I'm the father?' and for years afterwards the image was reused and recycled whenever there was unexpected news that needed to be ridiculed. Colin would lose his label as the 'Kiss-and-Tell King' and be forever recognised as the 'What do you mean?' guy instead.

"Are you having a laugh?" Sam gasped, looking at Colin's image on the big screen. He turned to his mother, who had managed to lift her head and was staring at him with tears streaming down her face.

"Please, please, I'm so sorry. I had no idea." She turned to Howard, trying to find someone who would embrace her, let her hide her face in their shoulder. But Howard had already stepped away from her and was back next to Estelle, who had decided to show her husband some support in his moment of need and had linked his arm through her muscular own.

"All these years, all these fucking years you let me think he was my son," he said, spitting through gritted teeth and angrily jabbing his finger through the air in Sam's direction.

"He is your son," Audrey replied, yelling the words by accident.

"No, he is not. I don't have a son," he said.

"Dad!" Sam wailed, a lost and frightened little boy. "Dad, don't say that."

But Howard just looked at him as though he were a stranger. Then he muttered, "Come on," to Estelle and turned his back on the table. The two walked away, Howard pushing angrily through the crowd and swearing at anyone who didn't move out of his way quickly enough.

"Howard, no!" Audrey begged, but he carried on walking. "Howard!" she wailed, an appeal for one last chance to speak with him, to convince him not to turn his back on their son or on her. But Howard marched away with no interest in the people he was leaving behind at the table. Just before they disappeared from view, Estelle glanced back, but her expression was one of despair, not victory: a wife who knew her husband's sudden need for an heir was greater than his need for her.

Audrey was left alone, quietly sobbing with a thousand people watching as her bewildered son failed to console her, too lost to know what he should do next. Oonagh took his hand and whispered into his ear. "Go to your mother," she said. "Whatever else has happened, she's your mum and she's just lost everything. She needs you now more than ever." She nudged him forward and as he automatically opened his arms, Audrey fell into his embrace and cried. Around them, there was a chorus of "aaahhh!" and the audience applauded as though satisfied by the conclusion of a short play.

Many were frustrated that beyond their memories they would have no personal record of these events. They would have no photobomb for Facebook and no selfie for Instagram. All they would have is an after-dinner story, a tale of how they stood just metres away from the great Harvey family as Adam Jaymes finally and completely destroyed them.

But amid the thousand different versions of the story, there would be one detail that would be missing from them all. A relatively small detail but one that, if noticed, could have revealed a great truth: a young black girl in a grey silk dress, standing just to the edge of the Harvey table with her arms folded. And the slightest hint of a smile on her beautiful face.

Epilogue

I KNEW I would have to write you this letter sooner or later. I've been putting it off, to be honest. Sorry. But I've a lot to tell you and I know you really won't approve. I guess that's why this letter feels more like a confession. I've done so many things that are the exact opposite of what you would want me to do. I put everything on the line. I risked my privacy, my secret life away from the glare of publicity. The one thing you fought so hard to ensure I had. And worse than that, I let Uncle Adam risk his whole career, everything he's worked so hard to achieve. He did that just to protect me and keep me safe, because he knew he couldn't stop me or talk me out of it. He knew this was something I had to do, that it's been eating me up since I was a girl, since the day you died.

I was eight-years-old when I was taken into foster care. You told me it wasn't going to be for long, that you just needed some time to get better and then I could come home. And I believed that, completely. That promise was all I had because I wasn't allowed to see you or even speak to you on the phone. The one thing I had to cling to was the knowledge that I'd be home soon. But then my social worker kept making decisions about my life that seemed permanent, and I got so angry with her because I knew I should only be in foster care for a few weeks.

She moved me so far away that I had to change schools, and I kept telling her it wasn't fair as I would have loads of lessons to catch up on when I went back to my proper school. Then she told me I needed to make new friends, but I told her I didn't want to because I had plenty of friends at home. And then she told me I needed to decorate my bedroom, to make it feel like it was mine. But I told her it wasn't my bedroom. My bedroom was at home. I didn't care what colour the walls of this other stupid room were painted because I wouldn't be there for long. And every day I'd skip home from school expecting my social worker to greet me, with my bags already packed and her car parked outside, engine running. In my heart, I was only ever a day away from coming home. But then two years went by. That's a lifetime for a little girl. Two whole years went by and I hadn't seen you or spoken to you but I still absolutely expected to come home.

On my tenth birthday, when I was blowing out my candles, I wished I could go home. I squeezed my eyes together and wished so hard, because it was all I wanted. The next day, after school, my social worker was waiting in the front room and said she wanted to talk to me about something important. And I sat there with a huge smile on my face, trying not to giggle, waiting for the good news. My wish had come true. But she started saying something else. She said she had some sad news, and that you had been very ill and the doctors had tried to help you but they couldn't. And that you had died. I didn't believe her. I kept saying she was wrong, that you had told me I would only be in care for a while and that I could go home eventually. And then I started crying and screaming at her for lying to me. It just didn't make any sense. How could it? We had our whole lives ahead of us. I was only 10. How could my mum be dead when I was only 10? You said I would be home soon. I was supposed to be coming home.

I knew I was different after that. I could feel it. Even though I was still only little, I knew I wasn't the same. It was more than just grief. There was something inside me that had changed, it was an emptiness, like I was hollow and to be honest that horrible feeling has never really left me. Of course, I needed someone to blame it all on and so I put my foster carers through absolute hell for the next few years. But they stuck with me and cared for me, even when I was smashing up their home or spitting in their face or arriving back at midnight with the police in tow. They just seemed to love me whatever I did or however horrible I was. I'm so ashamed of that now because they deserved so much better. I always knew my foster carers weren't really to blame for anything. They were just an easy target and I did eventually begin to realise that.

But then I started to hear things, snippets of conversation on TV (before the channel was quickly changed) or adult discussions which ended abruptly when I entered the room. I began to get the impression that there were other people out there in the world, somewhere, people who really were to blame for what had happened to you. There's a picture of you, the one you had taken for the cover of *Attitude* magazine a few months before you died. It's such a famous picture now, your pale face and big eyes, and there's something very sad about your expression. After you died it sort of went viral, I saw it everywhere almost every day. It was on posters and trendy t-shirts. I knew that it meant something and that you were important for another reason, not just because you'd been on a soap. I decided that somehow I would find out the truth, and if there were other people who really were responsible for your death then I would make them pay.

But I didn't let it take me over. Actually, once I had calmed down I started to do a lot better, at everything. I finally accepted that I wasn't going home, and that I needed to commit to this life I had with my foster carers. I started to pay attention at school and it turned out I was quite academic. Who knew? And I started making friends, too. I joined clubs and got a paper round and even learnt to bake. My life finally became bearable. No, not bearable. Enjoyable. I actually started to enjoy my life, just for what it was. I was having fun and *normal* fun, too, rather than something that ends up with a ride home in a police car. None of my friends ever knew the truth about me, of course. It's difficult keeping secrets at that age, but I knew it was important. It was about this time that I had a talk with my foster carers and social worker, too. After all those years, and everything we'd been through, it didn't feel right calling my foster carers by their names anymore. So I asked if I could call them Mum and Dad, and they said I could. I hope you don't mind, but it just felt really right, for all of us. You would like them, though, I promise. You really would.

With the placement happy and stable again, social services started to let other people write to me. I started to get letters, photographs and presents from Auntie Pat and Uncle Adam. It was strange after all those years, like I was getting messages from another world that didn't exist anymore. And then we were allowed to visit. It was hard seeing Auntie Pat that first time, because I'd forgotten how much she looks like you. She talks like you too. We were very awkward with each other at first, but Mum and Dad gave us plenty of space and before long we were chatting and catching up, and then crying and hugging, and then laughing and crying. But it was happy crying.

And a few months after that I was allowed to see Uncle Adam too. He'd only just left *Eastenders* and was about to move to Cardiff to work on *Doctor Who*. It was strange seeing him again because he'd been the only constant in my life. Even though he'd only been on TV and he was playing a character, I'd been able to see him every week. And it felt like I was keeping in touch with him all along. And then I was taken to visit him at his house and I was suddenly star struck. Here I was with this man I'd known since I was a baby but he was also this big star off the telly, and he'd made me lunch and had photographs for us to look through. Pictures of you I'd not seen before. You were so beautiful. And after a while he began to feel familiar again, like the Uncle Adam I had grown up with. But I was still a little star-struck. I still am, to be honest. He's amazing. You would be so proud of him, of everything he's achieved and the way he handles life. He still talks about you like you really were his big sister and I can tell how much he loved you, how much it still hurts him that you're gone. He doesn't give much away, not about how he's feeling. I know other people think he's a bit of a cold fish, but I can tell when he's sad. There's something in his eyes, something that changes.

I was 15 when I finally found out the truth about how you had died, about what the *Daily Ear* had done to you. I had internet access at school and my curiosity finally got the better of me. I began to look you up during class. Wikipedia can be very useful for revision, but it can also be the worst thing in the world when you're reading about someone you know, someone you love. It was harder than I thought it was going to be, reading your entire life stripped down to bare facts. But then I read the sub-section about press intrusion and your final moments at Beachy Head and I realised I hadn't been told the whole story. I left school that afternoon and rather than walking home I got on the tube and went straight to see Uncle Adam. Luckily he was at home and he took me in and phoned Mum and Dad and they came to the house. They called Auntie Pat, too. And they all sat me down and talked me through everything, the whole story. I asked question after question, and they answered everything. For the first time, they were all really honest with me. I guess they thought I was old enough to know the truth. Or maybe they realised I would find out anyway, and they would rather tell me themselves then have me stumble upon some awful website where I'd get the wrong version of the story.

So they told me about Jason stalking you, screaming abuse at you in the streets to get the pictures he wanted. They told me about Colin's obsession with your private life, printing every detail of every man you as much as looked at. They told me about your depression, the accusations of drug use and Valerie's claim that you often left me home alone to go out drinking and partying. None of it was true, of course, but it was repeated over and over and was eventually considered an accepted truth. It ruined your reputation and then your career. Your life, or at least the *Daily Ear*'s version of your life, became a public obsession and the *Ear*'s readers just wanted more and more. I doubt they even cared that most of it was made up. They told me how Leonard Twigg had overseen it all, knowing each 'Pearl Martin exclusive' pushed his sales through the roof. The public would scream their disapproval at how you were being treated, but the next day they'd see your face on the front page and buy the *Daily Ear* all over again. After you died the country was in uproar and it would have been easy to put the *Daily Ear* out of business. People just had to stop buying it. But they chose not to. It seems the public can lie just as much as a newspaper.

    Auntie Pat told me other things too, like everything you'd done to keep me your little secret. She showed me all the cuttings of you proudly walking me around Hyde Park in a stroller, just a few weeks after I was born. They made the front pages of most of the tabloids, and they are lovely pictures, too. Probably the only public pictures I've seen of you actually smiling and looking happy; you the proud parent and me in my buggy, a little clone of my mum. All the stories point out how I'm the image of you, that I have your famous pale complexion, your big blue eyes and wisps of brown hair. Only it isn't me in the buggy. The whole photo opportunity was something you and Auntie Pat set up to trick the press. It's cousin Benjamin. He's only a couple of months older than me and has the colourings from your side of the family. But from that day everyone's been looking for the wrong girl. You hid me in plain sight so I could walk home from school, go to the park or even appear in the school play and no one would ever suspect that the little black girl was Pearl Martin's daughter. Auntie Pat also told me about my biological father and explained that your relationship with him was brief. She said he'd never wanted to be a part of my life and that just because a man can be a father it doesn't mean he can be a dad, and I guess that's true of him. But she also said he could have made a small fortune if he'd decided to out himself as my father, and the fact he hadn't showed he was doing his bit to keep me a secret. So I guess that's something.

That night, after that enormous conversation and all of those secrets had been revealed to me, I went home finally knowing the truth. The *Daily Ear* had killed you. And I finally had names for my hitlist: Colin, Valerie, Jason and Twigg. You see, everyone thinks Project Ear is something new, something Uncle Adam dreamed up a few months ago because this government inquiry into newspaper ethics isn't going anywhere. But Project Ear is my baby, my mission. That day, three years ago when I was 15 and lying in my bed with all of this new information swirling around my head, that was the day Project Ear was born. Because what no one seemed to realise is that by hiding me away in perfect anonymity for all those years, I had been given more than just a quiet life. I had been given the perfect opportunity to beat them from the inside. I could teach those bastards a lesson, every single one of them, because none of them would have a clue who I was. I could walk straight up to Jason or Valerie or any of the others and they would have no reason to think I was your daughter. The more I thought about it, the more it seemed obvious what I should do. I would get a job at the *Daily Ear* and I would find out everything about them. I would be helpful and smiling, efficient in my job, reliable and only question them just enough to make it seem like I was a person worth actually talking to. And then I would get them to open up to me, to trust me and then let them brag about their lives and careers or share some secret with me. Perhaps they'd tell me something from their past, or give me access to their emails or calendars. I would expose every slimy, hypocritical, embarrassing, unethical or illegal secret they had stashed away in their past and I would do it all from the inside.

I spent the next three years secretly planning. I researched all the main players, went on work experience at local papers and other companies owed by Harvey News Group and even learnt shorthand and typing at evening class to make me more useful in an office environment. After I'd finished my A-Levels, I picked the one media course that I knew would offer me a 6-month attachment in a genuine national newspaper. No one else wanted the *Daily Ear* (my course is full of broadsheet readers) and so I was selected automatically. I couldn't believe how easy it was. I was in! I spent my first month as the *Ear*'s news desk secretary, and Colin pretty much handed me his secret on a plate. Within days it was obvious he was having an affair. Plenty of people have a mobile phone and a lot of people have two (one for work and one for personal use). But Colin had three and I noticed early on how guarded he was about that third mobile phone and that he never took it home with him. He always left it locked in his desk in the office and the calls he took on it were private and certainly not from his pregnant wife. Part of my job was to make all the hotel bookings for Colin and his team, and I began to notice how often he would tell me exactly where to book him a room even if it was 20 or 30 miles away from where he actually needed to be. It was going to be pretty easy to catch him out, the only problem I had was how to do it.

And this is where Uncle Adam comes into the story. He was visiting London to do some interviews for the new season of *True Blood* and I was meeting him in his hotel room for dinner. Anyway, he was trying out a new 'friend finder' app on his phone and somehow worked out I was at the *Daily Ear* offices. When I arrived at his room, he didn't ask me about it straight away. He let me string out this whole complicated story about my day at the *Guardian* but he knew it was complete rubbish. And once it was clear I was lying through my teeth and had something to hide, he fixed me with this cold stare and said, "Now, why don't you tell me about your day at the *Daily Ear* instead." You really know when there's no point lying anymore, and that was one of those moments. So I slowly told him everything that I've just told you. I explained my great plan, and how I was going to teach them all a lesson. I told him how someone needed to do something, and that it wasn't right that they'd all just walked away from what happened to you like it didn't matter, with no consequences at all. And I told him how I owed it to you, to your memory, to make sure they paid.

And then he gave me the most astonishing telling-off that I've ever had. He didn't raise his voice or use strong language, of course. He just very firmly and clearly told me I was being an idiot, that I was completely out of my depth and that you would be very hurt that I was throwing away my quiet, normal life for a taste of revenge. He talked at me for about 10 minutes straight. He made it clear that I was wrong and that I needed to stop what I was doing immediately. And to be honest, everything he said made absolute sense. I knew that on so many levels he was right. But it's not a case of right and wrong. It's about justice, the sort of justice that Chris Lackie and others denied you. And it's about a little girl who had to grow up without her mum because a greedy, rich family and a group of self-absorbed journalists benefited from ruining an innocent life. So I told Uncle Adam that I loved him but that there was no way I was turning back. I had spent three years planning this and if he really loved me he would walk away and let me carry on. Because there was no way I could stop.

We talked for more than an hour, the same conversation round and round. He told me I was about to ruin my own life, that I was exposing myself to the same media interest as you. "Have you any idea how many years they've been trying to find you?" he asked. "How many journalists, and not just the *Ear*. We've built a brick wall around you, to keep you safe, to keep all the information about you safe. But if you do this, not only will they know who you are but you'll have handed them a 'public interest' argument on a plate. They will tell the world that Pearl Martin's daughter is emotionally unstable and obsessed with revenge. And you will never know a moment's peace or privacy again."

"They won't find me," I replied, innocently. "I know I can upload all of this anonymously. They will never know it was me."

But they would, he said. "Do you really think the British press will walk away from this, not knowing who was behind it? Do you really think the *Daily Ear* team will just accept that it's a mystery they will never solve? Sweetheart, they *will* work out it was you and then they will find out who you are. And everything your mum did to hide you away, to protect you from the sort of life she had, it will all have been for nothing."

He was just desperate to talk me out of it, but he couldn't. My mind was set, my plan was already underway and there was no going back. I was willing to face the consequences no matter how awful because I needed to do this, to hurt them as much as I possibly could. Eventually Uncle Adam had to accept he was fighting a losing battle. And then he did the most amazing thing. He went into his bedroom and made a call in private. I assume it was to his husband. He was gone for about 15 minutes and when he came back he sat down again and said, "Right, change of plan. I'm not going to stop you, I'm going to help you. I will invest in Project Ear. I'm going to give you a budget and people and all the resources you'll need. But on one condition."

And that condition was that I let Uncle Adam take the heat. He would be the public face from the start and take complete responsibility for it. Once his people had gathered all the evidence he would launch Project Ear with a press conference and keep up his public profile throughout the whole thing to make sure no one at the *Ear* or elsewhere in the press would think to look for anyone else. He was going to make sure I stayed a secret. I couldn't ask that of him. I said no. I would never forgive myself. I know you wouldn't forgive me either. But he made it clear it was the only way he would allow me to continue. And so I went home, feeling awful. I was so ready to sacrifice myself that I hadn't ever considered the impact this might have on the people I love. The people who love me. But as I lay in bed that night, my greedy need to have revenge got the better of me. Suddenly I loved the idea that my project was going professional, that I would have people to help me find all those hidden secrets (like who Colin was having an affair with). I'm so sorry, Mum, but I went back to Uncle Adam the next day and I said yes. I said yes I wanted him to help me. And after that, to be honest, the *Daily Ear* really didn't stand a chance.

Within a couple of days Uncle Adam had assembled a small group of ex-journalists to crack the *Daily Ear*. I never met any of the team. Everything I uncovered I fed to Uncle Adam and he passed it on. He really wasn't prepared to trust my identity with anyone. But I insisted that I still do the majority of the grunt work. I didn't want Project Ear to be something that just happened around me. I wanted to do as much as I possibly could. After a few weeks, they had photographic evidence of Colin's affair. It turned out he was seeing his best mate's wife (skanky!) and the reason he kept interfering with my hotel bookings was that she was a businesswoman and travelled around the country quite a bit and he was always looking for opportunities to stay in the same hotel. We'd caught the Kiss-and-Tell King with his pants well and truly down! Once we had one in the bag, the others followed very quickly.

I worked with Valerie as a researcher for her column and soon I was managing her emails and her calendar and listening to all of her stories. Valerie is incredibly indiscreet once you've won her trust, so it was easy to collect all manner of information about her. I fed it all through to Uncle Adam – some of it factual, some anecdotal – and he sent it onto his team. One thing I'd noted was that she had two separate wedding anniversary dates in her diary. I have to be honest – for me, it didn't stand out as a major discrepancy. I fed it through to Uncle Adam all the same along with everything else and our team looked into it and quickly uncovered her secret first marriage to a gay man called Ray. Imagine that – the homophobic columnist had a gay ex-husband. They quickly tracked him down, living an idyllic life with his partner Pete in the middle of the Kent countryside. But Uncle Adam felt a bit torn about involving them. He said they were a couple of innocent by-standers who hadn't done anything wrong. So he made it clear that if we couldn't legitimately get their agreement to take part in the exposé then we'd go with one of the other stories we had about Valerie (we had loads!).

So we sent a couple of ex-journalists from the Project Ear team to meet with them who had plenty of experience negotiating in situations like that. At first they tried to coax Ray and Pete into doing the story by explaining we had a number of far worse revelations up our sleeve, including a hushed-up drink-drive conviction. But that didn't work. After all the revolting homophobic things Valerie has said and done over the years, Ray didn't feel he owed her anything. Next we offered them money, £20,000, which apparently is the current going rate for a standard kiss-and-tell story. But they turned that down too. So after a long discussion we found the clincher was actually something pretty simple. We offered them a five-page colour spread in *Country Homes and Gardens* magazine (which is published by one of the media companies owned by Uncle Adam's husband). We gave them copy and picture approval, even promised a little air-brushing if they wanted it. They nearly snatched our hand off, they were so thrilled. We put them on the front page of the latest edition and it's led to other opportunities for them too. They've just done a couples version of '*Come Dine with Me*' and *OK! Magazine* has offered to pay for their wedding next year. There's even a rumour they're being lined up for the next *Celebrity Big Brother*. They've really caught the 'fame' bug. I hope they know what they're doing, though.

Next up was Derek Toulson. Now, there's a lot of confusion as to why I targeted him because he didn't even join the paper until after you died. We had a very clear remit for Project Ear and just being vile didn't meet our criteria. So, then, why Derek? It all started when I was asked to work in his department for a few weeks as part of my placement. I genuinely didn't think anything would come from it but luckily every new employee goes through a brief honeymoon period with Derek. On my first day I was immediately his new best friend and he gave me access to his email, calendar and planning folders and he asked me to do a piece of work around his Pound-for-Pound scheme. At first it seemed to be pretty straightforward. Derek would offer a local council £50,000 to invest in the local community and all they had to do was match that donation to make the investment up to £100,000. He asked me to pull together a load of stats about the scheme's success for a board report he was writing and what started off as an incredibly arduous task resulted in me having another name for my list.

You see, Derek is a little and spiteful man. It turned out his intentions were far from philanthropic. Whenever he went to a local council to discuss the scheme he would take with him a hitlist of local charities he didn't approve of. He would then explain to the councillors that it was actually very easy to find their half of the £100k by simply cutting funds to whoever was on his list. I cross-referenced his lists with funding decisions across the councils he visited and it became clear that, unfortunately, he was a very persuasive man. One of the charities that lost its funding was a little support group in east London for single parents suffering from depression. It was a charity Auntie Pat set up with the money you left her. It was just a small affair but they did some amazing work over the years and helped a lot of people. Because of that charity and its support and advice, there are dozens of children who were able to stay in their family home rather than being taken into care like me.

I couldn't find any evidence to suggest Derek knew who was running the charity or its link to you. I think he just saw the 'single parent' tag and immediately added it to his hitlist. But that's immaterial because, whatever his motivations, he was still responsible for closing it down, and there was no way I was letting Derek Toulson walk away from that. So I sent the list through to Uncle Adam and I was really excited because I thought I'd uncovered something truly corrupt. I thought we could prove the *Daily Ear* didn't just report negatively about the country's poorest families but actively worked against them, too. However, the Project Ear journalists said it wasn't enough. Apparently we couldn't just expect the public to care. I needed to find something simple they could latch onto, something that would sum up the whole scandal in an easy, bite-size chunk. And that's when

I found Gay's Horse Sanctuary. Thanks to Derek it had been forced to close a few months earlier but I couldn't understand why he would target a horse sanctuary. What did he have against horses? And I couldn't find any links between the charity and his usual targets (the poor, the unemployed, the disabled and anyone who wasn't white, married or straight). Even by Derek's standards, horses seemed a bit of a stretch. But after a few weeks of head-scratching and searching, I finally found an exchange of emails between Derek and Gayesh's son Tharindu which explained it all. Now before I go on, I need to explain to you about Gayesh's children. They are famously stupid (the words 'apple' and 'tree' spring to mind) but their father had somehow stumbled into a very well paid and influential position and he was using every resource and contact at his disposal to shoe-horn his kids into the first top job he could find. There would be no 'entry level' for Gayesh's kids. They would go straight in as management, if he could just find someone to hire them.

So he'd get staff like me to write their CVs for them, and then directors like Derek to offer them work experience to make their CVs seem more impressive. And it was during the two weeks Tharindu worked with Derek that 'Gay's Horse Sanctuary' mistakenly ended up on the Pound-for-Pound hitlist. Tharindu researched the charities in one local authority area ahead of a meeting Derek had with the councillors, but completely misunderstood what Gay's Horse Sanctuary did. He gave Derek a briefing note which included a reference to 'a council-funded sanctuary for gay horses'. Well, that was a red rag to a bull for Derek. He couldn't get the funding pulled quickly enough and handed me my easy bite-size chunk on a plate. The good news is the sanctuary's up and running again now, as are quite a few of the other charities closed by Derek. That's the power of the local press. And of course Uncle Adam's now funding your charity. He told Auntie Pat she should have let him know that she'd run into financial trouble. It's already helping dozens of families and they're looking at expanding across a greater area. I'm so proud to know that it all started with you.

I'm particularly pleased with what happened to Jason Spade. Out of everyone at the *Ear*, he was the one I really wanted to get. He was the one who had caused you the most harm and I thought it would be easy to find some dirt on him. How could it not? The man has no morals whatsoever and so I was expecting to find a trail of clues leading to dozens of revolting, scandalous secrets that would bury his career forever. But that was me being naïve. The moment I set foot at the *Ear* I approached his boss and gave her this whole spiel about how I was really into photography and she agreed to give me a couple of days each week managing their diaries and expenses. And I genuinely thought a couple of days would be all I would need to find my silver bullet. But there was nothing. Or rather, nothing the Project Ear team thought was any use. It's hard to soil the reputation of a man who's spent his entire life in the gutter. Whenever I thought I'd found something that would nail him, the team just sent it back to me and said it wasn't strong enough.

Booking two seats on an airplane because he's so obese - so what? Looking at porn on his work computer - who cares? Claiming twice as much for his meal expenses as he was allowed - big deal! I searched and searched but could not find a single thing that the team thought strong enough. Eventually Uncle Adam had an emergency meeting with the team to talk tactics. It became obvious that out of everyone we were targeting, Jason was the one Adam also wanted to nail the most.

Our break came when I found an exchange of emails between Jason and the *Ear*'s IT department. He was asking for advice about his laptop and obviously needed help to get it working again. The IT team kept emailing him back and telling him they would happily fix it if he would just bring it in. But Jason was adamant that he should fix it himself. I realised there must be some pretty dodgy stuff on his hard drive and that's why he didn't want to drop it into the shop for repair. After all, that's how Gary Glitter was caught.

So I told Uncle Adam and the Project Ear team put Jason's house under surveillance, rummaging through his rubbish at night and following him whenever he left the house with anything even remotely resembling a laptop.

After a couple of days, they followed him from his house to a nearby underground car park where he dumped a package in a bin. After he left, they retrieved the package and found it was a laptop. Our plan had worked. Uncle Adam sent it to his own team of IT experts who quickly unlocked the content and found hundreds of photographs Jason had taken with some hi-tech mini-camera the *Daily Ear* had bought for him. This included shots from inside the female changing rooms during the London Olympics. We finally had the bastard.

You know I did meet Jason before, just the once. He wouldn't remember it though. A few months after I went into foster care he turned up at my new school. To this day, we still don't know how he found out I was there. Social services had been really careful and you always registered me at school under Nan's maiden name, Snow. As far as everyone was concerned, I was just an ordinary little girl whose mummy was a housewife and whose daddy was a security guard. But somehow Jason got a tip that this was the school where Pearl Martin's daughter was a pupil. At the time I didn't really understand what was happening, just that a large man was taking photographs of all the girls as we filed out the school gates to go home. He kept asking each girl in turn, "Is your mummy on the telly?" Some of the parents confronted him and started to threaten him. Eventually the head teacher came out and said he had called the police. But that didn't faze Jason, of course. He just carried on as if he was an ordinary man doing an ordinary job. In my innocence I trotted up to him and pulled on his jacket and said "My mummy's on the telly." But he just laughed at me and then nudged me aside with, "No, you're alright love," while he carried on taking pictures of all the white girls. My foster mum whisked me away in her car and a few days later I started at another new school. I knew I'd been moved again because of the fat man with the camera, so my issues with Jason go back a long way. He's in prison, now. The content of his hard drive got him four years and he's been placed on the sex offenders register too. It has been noted, by many women in the public eye, that none of those hundreds of spy-cam photographs are as explicit or revealing as the pictures he used to take on a daily basis for the *Ear*. It seems a man can get away with a lot if he has a press card. He can lie on the pavement and take photographs up women's dresses as they climb from a car and that's just fine. Or he can travel to a remote island and hide in a bush with a telephoto lens and take pictures of a future queen as she sunbathes topless at a private villa. And that's fine too. But if he takes the same pictures for personal use, suddenly he's a pervert and needs to go to jail and be on a register. I still struggle with the idea that a little bit of plastic with 'Press' printed across the top can protect the likes of Jason Spade from the repercussions of his perverted ways. I hope he rots in prison.

When it comes to Leonard Twigg, I'm going to start by saying I am not sorry he's dead. I'm not happy about it either because it caused poor Uncle Adam a lot of problems. But I'm not going to insult your intelligence by pretending to grieve for that horrible man. The truth is, I didn't need a huge scandal to ruin Twigg. His status and reputation were everything to him. All I needed was something that would really embarrass him and that would make it more difficult for people to take him seriously, to prick that monstrous ego because his self-image was everything to him. I've seen rooms fall silent the moment he walked in. I've seen him reduce a government minister to a babbling wreck without even raising his voice. And Twigg liked that. I could tell how much pleasure he got from seeing the fear and anxiety he caused in others. So whatever I could dig up about Twigg needn't be huge, just humiliating. I had access to his office of course, and on the few occasions when he wasn't around I made myself useful and 'tidied up'. I eventually plucked up the courage to look around his private bathroom and after finding several reels of double-sided sticky tape and special shampoo I realised his flawless, quaffed hair was hiding a very embarrassing secret. It seemed the perfect exposé for such an impeccably private man, the sort of mortifying story he would have printed without a second thought if it was about someone else. Our private detectives quickly located the clinic he went to and it wasn't long before they found an adjoining building that had a direct view into the fitting rooms. I kept an eye on his diary and alerted Uncle Adam when Twigg had his next appointment. We went right up against deadline with that story. If he'd delayed his next fitting by a couple more days it would have really mucked up our schedule. But he didn't. As bad as things were at the *Daily Ear*, he clearly felt the need to keep up his immaculate appearance.

But I have to tell you about something else and this is difficult to admit because it involves a lie I told to Uncle Adam. Perhaps not a lie exactly. A piece of information I withheld from him. Not long after I started at the *Daily Ear* I discovered something in Twigg's desk, an invoice from an undertaker for a funeral and burial. I phoned them to double-check the details and found that Twigg's mother – the centre of his entire world – had died. He hadn't said a thing, to anyone. The impeccably private man, grieving alone in his glass walled office. I struggled with it at first. Not out of sympathy for Twigg, of course. He never let any family mourn in peace or privacy if he could flog a few more papers. This is the man who sent Jason Spade into mortuaries each time a celebrity died to try to get a photograph of the corpse. Why should he be given special treatment? The problem was that Uncle Adam is a better man than Leonard Twigg. I knew if he found out the truth, out of either concern or compassion, he would drop Twigg from our list. And I couldn't let that happen, because Twigg had to pay for what he did to you. And so I didn't tell Uncle Adam what I'd found out. I did regret it, of course. For a day or so it genuinely seemed my silence had cost Uncle Adam everything. There was a moment, the day after Twigg killed himself, when every radio news story, tweet and conversation seemed to accuse Uncle Adam of murder. I was in tears for most of the day, thinking of the terrible harm I'd caused to this wonderful man who had trusted me so completely. Everyone thought I was crying because of Twigg. But I wasn't. I was crying because of what I thought I'd done to Uncle Adam. But then the truth started to come out. Believe it or not, it was Valerie Pierce who turned it all around. She stormed out of the *Daily Ear* and told the world what had really happened, that the Harvey family had as good as pushed Leonard Twigg under that train. She shouted so loudly that no one was able to ignore her. She explained how the Harveys had stripped Twigg of his position and his power, made him feel obsolete and out of touch. Perhaps even a liability. I can't even begin to imagine how many bridges she burnt that day or what that decision cost her. But she showed the world who was really responsible for Leonard Twigg's suicide and, as much as I hate to admit it, for that I owe her some sort of thanks.

Because of Valerie, everyone knows there is no truth in those ridiculous claims that the wig exposé made Leonard Twigg jump under that train. He killed himself because he finally saw his time was at an end. His power was gone, his limitless ability to attack and destroy anything and anyone he pleased. The Harvey family had turned their backs on him, he was facing a demotion at work and even his closest allies had deserted him. Most of all, in his hour of need, Twigg realised he didn't have any friends and in his final seconds, as that train sliced him into a thousand pieces, I hope he knew no one would mourn him.

And then finally there was Audrey. Poor Audrey. Howard Harvey's loyal ex-wife. Always on the side-lines, innocently tending her garden whilst her husband built a fortune by devastating the lives of other people. Year after year she portrayed herself as the benevolent lady from an old-money family who didn't really understand what her down-market husband did for a living. I spent quite a bit of time with Audrey and she showed me how easy it was to pretend not to be involved. But she knew, of course. Audrey always knew exactly what was going on. And it all started with her. Everything you went through, Mum, started with Audrey. All it took was one spiteful comment, a carefully placed criticism during one of her casual 'afternoon tea' appointments with Valerie, and she knew you'd be front page news by the end of the week. And do you know what it was, Mum? What you did that was so terrible it resulted in the *Daily Ear* hounding you until the day you died? Valerie relayed the story to me during one of her self-indulgent afternoon monologues. It all started at one of Audrey's stupid *Amazing People Awards*, where you'd been asked to hand out a trophy. At the end of the evening, as everyone was going home, you careered into Audrey because, she claimed, you were so drunk. You had guzzled as much free champagne as you could (being a trashy soap actress) and were so intoxicated you couldn't even walk in a straight line. The whole spectacle was witnessed by a crowd of horrified mums and kids who could not believe your appalling behaviour.

Only, that's not actually what happened. I know because Auntie Pat was your plus-one that night and the moment I mentioned it to her she clearly remembered the whole thing. You weren't drunk, because you'd just started a new course of medication and you weren't allowed alcohol. You'd spent the whole evening drinking fresh orange juice. And in the hustle and bustle at the end of the evening, you had simply stumbled to one side as a group of mums and kids pushed by to get to their coach. It was just an accident. But that's not the story that Audrey 'mentioned in passing' to Valerie of course. And that's where it all started, the stories about your drinking and then your drug use and then the 'home alone' accusations. None of it true, but it was all started by Audrey. Valerie, of course, thought it was all down to her and actually seemed quite proud of the idea that the *Ear's* whole 'Pearl Martin' obsession stemmed from that first piece in her column. But at last I knew who the real culprit was. Audrey was going to get a phone call from Uncle Adam, I just needed to find her Achilles heel. And it's true, taken individually, she really does appear to have led a good and virtuous life. All that charity work and self-sacrifice; the woman's a virtual martyr. Or at least that's how it seemed.

In the end, it all fell into place very nicely. The Project Ear team had made it clear, from the outset, that the only way we could really justify ourselves in public was to demonstrate we had used the *Ear*'s own tactics and methods. How could Twigg or Colin Merroney or any of the rest complain when all we had done was copy what they did for a living? So as part of this we had replicated the *Ear*'s notorious 'Secret DNA' series. I'd spent months secretly hoarding samples and sending them over to our lab (yes, we have a lab too!). I collected discarded cigarette butts, used paper cups and even saliva swabbed from the mouths of reporters who passed out in front of me at the pub (when no one else was around). It was pretty disgusting at times, to be honest, but in the end we had a DNA database of about 50 employees, trainees and contractors. They were aged 18 to 60, and so we hoped there would be plenty of scope to find some inconsistencies or unexpected connections. You know how incestuous these offices can be. We were somewhat handicapped by Uncle Adam's decision not to pool samples from children. I was more than happy to hang around barber shops or fast-food restaurants and covertly gather hair samples or discarded straws. But Uncle Adam said no, I wasn't allowed to bring children into the mix and so could only collect samples from the *Daily Ear* itself.

To be honest, we were just fishing. We didn't know exactly what we were looking for. And as we started to draw a great big blank, one of the ex-journalists on the team even used an old police contact to have our database run against DNA from unsolved crimes. Surprisingly, that gave us nothing as well. The whole venture seemed to be going nowhere. But that all changed the day Sam Harvey returned to the UK. Uncle Adam was clear he wanted Sam in London. He didn't want him cowering in LA, while the likes of Valerie and

Twigg took all the heat. Because Sam, like his mother, had spent his entire life pretending not to be involved in all the nasty stuff and Uncle Adam wasn't putting up with it. His husband knows a lot of people who have worked with Sam over the years and they all say the same thing: that the Harvey golden boy was actually a weak link, who surrounded himself with talent to hide the fact he had none. Sam had done very well for himself out of Harvey Media International and Uncle Adam thought it was time he learnt a few hard lessons.

But we weren't sure Project Ear would be enough, in itself, for Howard to order Sam back to the UK. We had to create an opening for him. So during one of my days supporting the executive floor I 'accidentally' emailed Gayesh's entire calendar to Howard. I think Howard probably had an idea of how Gayesh spent his time, but seeing his freeloading ways there in black and white proved the final straw. And just like that Gayesh was out and Sam was in. We had our boy! On Sam's first day I turned up at his office ready and willing to help. Uncle Adam had told me I should get in early, as Sam would want to quickly build a new team around him to hide behind (that's his MO). But I also needed to be close enough to get a sample of his DNA too. One of my greatest frustrations was that I'd not been able to get a sample from Howard, because I'd hung all my hopes on finding an illegitimate son or daughter that he'd kept secret all these years. But DNA from Sam would be just as invaluable if it revealed he had unidentified half-siblings wondering around the *Daily Ear*.

So I hired a barber and told Sam it was all part of Gayesh's pampered lifestyle and it would be a terrible shame to waste it. And then I paid the barber an extra £50 to nick Sam's neck. That tiny cut produced little more than a drop of blood but more than enough to blow the roof off this whole project. You see, I'd got it completely wrong. Howard didn't have an illegitimate child. It turned out that his only son wasn't his at all. We matched Sam's DNA to another man at the *Daily Ear* who was already on our database. Who'd have thought Audrey's deep, dark secret was a long forgotten encounter with Colin

Merroney? It was such a find. What a fantastic exclusive for Project Ear! I actually felt quite disappointed that I wouldn't get a by-line for it. I spoke to Uncle Adam and we agreed to save Audrey for last, that we would deliver the final exposé live on TV at the *Amazing People Awards*. After all, that's where all of this started. Just by chance (and it really was simple good fortune) Audrey had inadvertently hired a production company owned by Uncle Adam's husband to produce this year's event. A few phone calls later and key staff were replaced with people from Project Ear. Uncle Adam was going to make a grand appearance at the end of the show and make his final phone call in front of millions of viewers. The Harvey family's great humiliation would be absolute. I even managed to bag myself a ring-side seat and watched it all first-hand. I was sitting right next to them as the whole family fell to pieces. And I loved every shameful, devastating second of it. I destroyed them completely, publicly. And it was wonderful.

I know how this all must sound. You must be wondering what sort of woman your little girl has grown into. To take so much pleasure in the unhappiness of others, to be able to lie to people's faces so convincingly or collect their secrets in such an underhand manner. But I'm not a bad person, Mum, I promise you. Everything I did was for you, the best mum in the world. The mum the *Daily Ear* stole from me.

And I want to tell you that I remember you. I remember everything about you. I remember your big blue eyes, and the warmth of your laugh. I remember cuddles at bedtime and the smell of your perfume. I wear it sometimes. It makes me feel like you're right here with me. I remember eating beans on toast in front of the telly with you on a rainy Saturday afternoon. I remember my eighth birthday, the last one we shared. You gave me a copy of *Harry Potter and the Order of the Phoenix*, and when I opened the first page I saw that you'd had it signed by JK Rowling. I said I wanted you to sign it too and you laughed and said only the author can sign a book. So I got you to kiss the back page instead. I still have it, with JK Rowling's signature at the front and your lipstick mark at the back. Auntie Pat explained to me about your illness and I've read up on it too, and I understand that's why I was taken into foster care. But I don't remember that, Mum. All my memories of you are happy memories. You always made me feel like a special little girl and I wish so much that you were here today. I wish I could have grown up with you, gotten to know you as an adult. It's been great talking to Auntie Pat and Uncle Adam about you. They have so many memories, so many lovely photographs. If only the public had been able to get to know the real you. Perhaps they really would have stopped buying the *Daily Ear*.

So, that's my confession. I hope you can find it in your heart to understand and forgive me. But you'll be pleased to learn that I am still your great secret. To this day, no one knows I'm your daughter. Uncle Adam kept me safe and he still is. As I write this letter, I'm on a plane heading for New York. I'm going to stay with him and his husband for a few months. He's fine, by the way. The public still loves him, despite the best efforts of the *Daily Ear*. He's just launched the new season of clothes for a major high street store and starred in an advert they showed during the commercial break of Monday night's *Coronation Street*. Well, it wasn't during the commercial break so much as it was the commercial break. It was three minutes long and Uncle Adam was singing *'Don't Rain on my Parade'* and doing a fantastic dance routine with hundreds of extras. They reckon about four million extra viewers tuned in just for the advert.

He's asked me to move to America to live with him full time. He thinks I'll be safer over there, because the American press don't know your story and would have no interest looking for your daughter. And I know I'd have so many amazing opportunities if I accepted his offer.

But I'm going to say no. I would miss Mum and Dad too much, and it's nice spending time with Auntie Pat too. And I've so many really good friends in London, many of them from school. There are just too many people I would miss. And it feels like I would be leaving you behind too, and I really couldn't do that. Besides, Uncle Adam is always jetting back and forth so I know I'll get to see him regularly.

It's nice, having a superstar Uncle who takes me out to secret locations for dinner when he visits. It makes me feel special.

And I'm not sure the British press has quite got the message yet. I'm still keeping an eye on the *Daily Ear* and there are quite a few other papers which might need a taste of their own medicine sooner or later too. And, who knows, perhaps Project Ear will be back in business one day.

Maybe one evening at just before 9pm, some unsuspecting journalists or newspaper executive will answer their phone and hear that famous, calm voice saying, "Hello, this is Adam Jaymes. I just called to let you know it's your turn."

Printed in Great Britain
by Amazon